Never Again, No More

Never Again, No More

Untamed

www.urbanbooks.net

Urban Books, LLC
300 Farmingdale Road, NY-Route 109
Farmingdale, NY 11735

Never Again, No More

ISBN 13: 978-1-64556-088-3
ISBN 10: 1-64556-088-0

First Mass Market Printing July 2020
First Trade Paperback Printing September 2019
Printed in the United States of America

10 9 8 7 6 5 4 3 2 1

Distributed by Kensington Publishing Corp.
Submit Orders to:
Customer Service
400 Hahn Road
Westminster, MD 21157-4627
Phone: 1-800-733-3000
Fax: 1-800-659-2436

Dedication

To all the women who struggle daily as single mothers, this book is for you. Your true inner fears and struggles so often either go unnoticed or are misunderstood. This book is your voice, and I am proud to tell your story.

Acknowledgments

My passion for writing comes through my realization that it is a gift. Therefore, I do not take it lightly. I cherish this gift that has been granted to me, and I hope that in all I do, my Father sees that. Every honor, accolade, and accomplishment belongs to Him. I'm simply a vessel.

My angels, Mama, Da'Ja, and Christina, continue your rest, but please continue your watch. You said I could do this, Mama. Years later I understand that you were right. Thank you for planting that seed all those years ago. I promise to continue watering this writing garden.

You're only as strong as the people around you. Chris, Kiana, Christian, and Kameron, you all give me strength every day. I love you always. FOE.

To be a part of the family of Literary Champagne Suite is everything to me. When you have a team that not only reps your work but also understands you, it's an unstoppable combination. And y'all know all we do is win! I could never thank you enough.

As always, my thanks and appreciation go to Carl Weber and Urban Books. Thank you for giving my ink a home to flourish.

Readers, thank you for rocking with me on this untamable journey. This series will take you through the ebb and flow of life. So laugh often, cry hard, and learn from the characters' errors. Instead of simply reading this novel, experience it. Let's grow with Trinity, Charice, Lucinda, and LaMeka. Ready? Let's go! #sountamed

Trinity

Will this shit ever end? I thought while listening to Pooch rant and rave again. It seemed that was all he did lately. I swear, this muthasucka really had begun to piss me the hell off. I loved that nigga, though, and he took care of us. I mean, how many men do you know who would let you live up in their house for free, with two kids that ain't his? Exactly! Slim to damn none. But if this nigga didn't shut the hell up soon, I was gonna slap the piss out of him!

"Trin! Do you hear me? Tri-ni-ty!" Pooch screamed, interrupting my thoughts.

This dude is killing me. "Yes, Pooch . . . baby, I hear you," I said with a sigh as I brought him a roll of toilet paper. "The whole damn neighborhood can hear you, with all that damn fussing and screaming you're doing."

He swung the bathroom door open and snatched the roll of tissue out of my hand. "Well, if you actually listened and hurried your ass up when I fucking called you, then I wouldn't be fussing and screaming. Damn!" he yelled, continuing to take a dump, as if I wasn't standing there. "Hook up with you, bring a bitch in, along with her two snot-faced brats, treat her to the finer fucking things in life, and you treating *me* like shit? You don't treat that nigga Terrence like shit. Oh no, not *that* muthafucka. He gets the royal fucking treatment. I'm your man. I tell you what. Why don't you let that muthafucka take care of you, those kids, and the one me and you had? That would sure as hell free up my damn pockets!"

I wanted to argue, but the stench coming from the bathroom was making my stomach turn. This nigga's scent was so loud, you could smell his shit two doors down, it seemed. "Whatever, Pooch," I mumbled as I turned to walk away.

He reached out and grabbed my arm. "Where the fuck you going? I'm talking to you!"

I held my nose to avoid smelling the odor. "Pooch, it fucking stinks in here!"

"Shit supposed to stink. You think your shit smells like roses? Oh, I bet you didn't say that when that nigga Terrence took a damn dump!" he yelled.

I rolled my eyes, thinking, *Here we go. Terrence this and Terrence that.* "Pooch, please! I need to check on the baby."

"Wait until I get my ass off this toilet. Just wait." With that, he let my arm go and slammed the bathroom door.

"Pooch, I love you," I said faintly before I walked away. I checked in on Princess, and then I headed to our bedroom.

It was true. I really did love Pooch more than anything, and I knew that he loved me. Two and a half years ago, it hadn't been like this between us. The source of our heartache was my first children's daddy, Terrence. Back in the day, I knew Terrence from around our neighborhood in ATL. He used to play football at Frederick Douglass High School, and from what I'd heard, he was working and attending Atlanta Tech. That was just how it was in the hood. Everybody knew everybody, and everybody knew your business. I officially met Terrence at the teen club six years ago. At the time, I was fifteen and he was nineteen, and that dude captured me at first sight. He was so good looking that every woman wanted Terrence. How could they not? He was a tall glass of sexy butterscotch, with muscles for days. I didn't know if it was his light brown eyes, his shoulder-length dreadlocks, or that damn goatee, but everything about him was rugged and sexy.

I still remembered when his six-foot, three-inch frame walked up on me while I was dancing to that new joint by 50 Cent, "In Da Club." While my best friend, Lucinda, and my cousin Charice and I danced, I was damn near ready to rep New York instead of Georgia as *my* home state. Now I was a GA peach through and through, and I'd never turn my back on Hotlanta, but damn, when that song came on back then, like everyone else from the Dirty South to the Bay, I was pumping that shit.

Clad in my tight, dark denim jeans, yellow tunic top, and wedges, I looked hella good, and you couldn't tell me I wasn't one of the flyest chicks in there that night. My long hair was pulled back in a ponytail, and I flipped it as we danced off of the song. My eyes nearly popped out when I saw Terrence checking me out. Not to mention I had some pretty, big brown eyes, so I was sure I looked like damn Bambi in the headlights. As he bit on his lip in a sexy way, it made my body temperature rise instantly. Before I could alert my crew that he was looking at me, he started to walk toward us. All I could remember thinking was, Thank God I didn't eat that Philly cheesesteak sub with extra onions before I came here.

"'Sup yo?" he asked, touching me on my shoulder.

I turned slowly, in a nonchalant way, and threw out, "'Sup?" Then I quickly turned back to my girls and continued to dance.

He laughed. "So you just gon' ignore me like that, huh?"

"What do you mean?" I asked, turning back to face him.

He sucked in air. "Yo, you saw me looking at you."

"Yeah, I did," I said slyly.

He smiled softly, shaking his head. "Check it, li'l mama. This act is real cute, but stop flexin' and holla at yo' boy. On the real, I have to ask you something."

Charice nudged me and giggled. "Go get your talk on, girl."

"Yeah, li'l mami," Lucinda added with a laugh.

"It's mama, you non-English-talkin' heffa." I laughed, rolling my eyes.

Lucinda shot a bird at me. "I bet you got that in the universal language."

After fanning her off, I walked away with Terrence so we could talk. "What do you want?" I asked him once we were off the dance floor.

"A'ight, li'l mama—" he began, but I put my finger up, interrupting him.

"My name is Trinity," I announced.

He followed suit by putting his hands up. "My bad, li'l . . . I mean Trinity. You just so damn little, so I always called you li'l mama."

"Terrence, we ain't ever had no one-on-one conversations, so how you got nicknames for me?" I asked, confused.

"We all know each other from around the block. Come on now, you know that. I give everybody nicknames. It's how I remember people. For instance, to me, you're li'l mama, 'cause you so tiny. And your girl Lucinda is senorita, 'cause she Spanish, and your cousin Charice, she is superstar, 'cause she mess with that pretty muthafucka Ryan, who thinks he's a damn super-duper star."

Even though I hated when people called me tiny or, worse, skinny, I had to laugh. The names were cute, especially the one he had come up with for Charice. That nigga did think he was God's greatest gift to women. That muthasucka was finer than a muthasucka, though, but I would never admit that shit to him. His ego was so high in the sky that he needed a flashlight to see it.

"Okay then. Well, I guess I can call you Dreads, huh?" I laughed.

He shrugged. "It fits. Don't bother me none."

"Okay, Dreads. What you looking at me for? Can't get a girl your age?"

"*You got jokes.*" He laughed. "*You know I can pull 'em, just like I can pull you,*" he joked, giving me a wink.

He wasn't fucking lying. He sure could pull me. "*I ain't no dumb chick, Dreads. I may be young, but you gotta work to pull this.*" I gestured to my body.

"*Well, let's slow down and start by me pulling your art skills first.*"

"*Huh?*" I asked, confused.

"*The reason I came over was that I saw that tattoo design you drew for my homeboy, Chico, and that shit was fresh. I didn't know you were artistic like that. I want you to design one for me,*" he explained.

Talk about crushed. I was glad that word about my art skills was getting around the block, especially since I needed the money, but damn! I had thought he was checking for me, not my abilities.

"*Oh, and to think I thought you were checking out my ass on the dance floor,*" I joked, hoping he wouldn't catch on the fact that I actually wanted him to want me.

"*You think you can hook me up with a tattoo design?*" he asked, continuing on without any acknowledgment of what I'd just said.

Although I was crushed that he didn't want to holla at me, I agreed to do the work. "Yeah. Just stop by tomorrow, around noon, and I'll hook it up for you," I said, hiding my disappointment.

"How much you gon' charge me?"

"Fifty bucks."

"Damn! I still gotta get the tat, li'l mama."

"Yeah, but can't no tattoo place design shit like me. You want the tightest shit? I got it. They don't. You want to pay cheap prices, then go to the tattoo shop and let them show you one of them premade designs." I would've charged him twenty if he was trying to holla.

He shrugged his shoulders. "Ain't no thang. I'll be at your crib at noon tomorrow."

"A'ight," I said, then turned to walk back to my crew.

"Li'l mama!" he called out after I had taken half a dozen steps.

I stopped in my tracks and turned back. "Yeah?"

"Yo' ass did look cute grinding out there on the dance floor. Keep doing that shit. That's your money shot." He winked at me.

I giggled and then walked back to my crew, happy to know that Terrence Marsh, aka Dreads, was checking for me. You know I ended up charging that nigga only twenty dollars.

Terrence and I started dating not long after that, and seeing each other came as a breeze. My mom worked all the time. Since I was the oldest and was left to look after my ten-year-old sister and six-year-old brother, we had plenty of free time to do a bunch of shit we weren't supposed to be doing. Therefore, not only did he become my first love, but he also became my first lover.

Having an older boyfriend who could take me to school and pick me up was so damn cool to me. I was the envy of all the neighborhood heifers who tried to be with Terrence. I had to give it to him, though. He was a one-woman man, and that made me love him even more. I loved him so much that after only two months of dating, I got knocked up. I gave birth to our oldest son, Terry, when I was a sophomore in high school.

Since Terrence never knew his dad, he vowed to be better at fathering, and he was a great dad, and he loved the hell out of me. My mom was pissed with me after I got pregnant, but the fact that Terrence was a good man and a good father pacified her. He could barely take care of himself, but he made sure that Terry and I didn't hurt for anything. We stayed together and were happy as could be. After I got pregnant with Brittany my senior year, my mom had had enough, and she kicked me, Terry, and my unborn baby the hell out. She told me she loved me, but she had two other children to raise, and she couldn't afford to keep us around, since we created more bills for her to pay. Even though I was so pissed, I knew she was right. I had set a horrible example for my little sister, and my mom had struggled with the three of us, so she was hardly in a position to care for five.

After my mom kicked Terry and me out, Terrence did what he had to do and got us a two-bedroom apartment. That move probably helped me finish high school, because I knew that I didn't have my mom to fall back on. There was only Terrence and me to provide for us. But I admit it was rough as shit. Terrence and I began to argue more, because instead of working more hours at the auto shop, like he had promised, Terrence was slinging more dope. I told him to cool it since I was pregnant and wanted to go to art school, and I needed him to be around for the kids and me. He told me to let him be the damn man, and to worry instead about delivering a healthy baby girl and taking care of Terry. I gave up complaining and did what I was told. Surprisingly, everything continued to be smooth on his end, and I delivered a healthy baby girl and enrolled in college.

One month after Brittany's birth, the inevitable happened. Terrence was locked up on drug charges, and my world was flipped upside down. Those damn narc agents not only locked his ass up but also seized all our shit. They froze our accounts, took both of our cars, and evicted me and my kids. The only money I had was what Terrence kept in a safe, and that was only twelve grand. After giving a grand to his attorney as a retainer, I still had to pay an additional fifteen hundred dollars for his attorney to try the case, which he lost. That literally tore me up on the inside.

To further break my damn heart, at his sentencing hearing, Terrence told me some crap about living my life and not waiting for him, then broke up with me. He did, however, make me promise to let him see and care for his kids when he returned home from prison. I would never keep Terrence's kids from him, because I knew he loved them, but damn, didn't he love me too? I guessed that nigga didn't, so I said, "Fuck him too." I wouldn't beg any nigga to stay with me, not even Terrence.

My mom let us stay with her from the day of the raid until the trial was over. After that, the ultimate reality set in: I was back on my own, but now I was alone and had to fend for myself and two kids. I took the ninety-five hundred dollars that was left and got another two-bedroom apartment. After paying the first and last month's rent, I paid cash for an older-model Honda Civic. With only two grand left and no job, I dropped out of school, got on the welfare system, and started working part-time at a men's clothing store. That was where Pooch entered the picture.

Pooch was one of the most well-connected and well-known drug dealers in the city. All his relatives were known hustlers, so he was in the family business, so to speak. Although I knew Pooch from school, he had dropped out. Honestly, the only thing he had tried to learn was how to stay on top of his hustle. Pooch had had a crush on me since elementary school, but I had never given him the time of day, because I knew he and his people were nothing but trouble. Don't get me wrong. Pooch was cool as hell and cute, but everybody thought twice when dealing with him, because once you were affiliated with that circle, you were *in* the circle.

I soon noticed that Pooch was coming into the clothing store at least twice a week and always wanted me to help him. I figured he was pushing up to holla at me, and after six months, he made his move.

"What's good, Trinity?" Pooch asked as he walked over to me.

"Ain't nothing, Pooch."

"Yo, any word on that nigga Terrence getting out yet?"

"Nah, unless you gon' help him."

"Nah. He ain't none of my peoples." He sighed. "I was just checking."

"Why?" I asked as I began folding jeans.

"'Cause I want to get with his woman."

I nearly knocked over the stack of jeans I had folded. Pooch had always been blunt like that. He stood only an inch taller than me, so I tilted my head just a little and looked into his beautiful brown eyes to see if he was for real, and he was. With his brown skin and muscular build, he was cute, but he was no Terrence.

"Quit playing, Pooch," I said, brushing him off. I tried to ignore him and refolded a pair of jeans.

"Word. Trinity, you know I want you. I've been pushing up on you ever since we played in the sandbox. On the real, I already know Terrence broke up with you before he went in. Damn shame that nigga didn't know how to hustle well enough to keep you and your kids set. Hustlin' just ain't for everybody."

"So what are you saying, Pooch?" I asked, getting annoyed with the conversation.

"I'm asking to be your man and to take care of you," he confessed, grabbing my hand. "You too pretty to be busting your ass here and living off the system. Let me be your man and take care of you."

"I don't know, Pooch." I sighed. "I've just gotten myself together. I can't deal with no more of that hustling, and you got one foot in the court and the other in the jail yourself."

He laughed. "Trin, I'd never be caught up."

Raising my brow at him, I asked, "How do you know?"

Pooch leaned over and whispered in my ear, "I know because your man's arresting officer is on my payroll, and his judge is an undercover junkie. And that's just the shit I'm willing to tell you. Trust me, I'd never be caught."

I gasped and put my head down. I was not prepared to hear that Pooch was a certified kingpin. "Let me think about it, Pooch. We are a package deal, me and my two kids. You do remember that, don't you?"

Pooch shrugged. "Yeah, I remember, and I'm trying to make it better for all of you."

"A'ight, but I still need to think this thing through."

Pooch shrugged again. "A'ight, but Ms. Hobbs already gave you a late notice on your rent, and that old bitch doesn't play."

"How do you know I am—"

"Don't nothing go on that I can't find out about if I really wanted to, Trinity. Please believe that. It's not like I'm trying to blackmail you or some shit. I'm offering you the chance to be Mrs. Kingpin. Many have wanted this title, but the chosen one is you. So you let me know," he explained. Then he turned and walked away, leaving me speechless.

I didn't have feelings for Pooch, and although I thought he was cute, I wasn't attracted to him. As I said, he wasn't Terrence. Being late on my rent and being responsible for two kids, with Terrence locked up, I did what I had to do. I agreed and told Pooch that I'd be his lady.

By the time Brittany turned one year old, we were living high on the hog with Pooch. We resided in a six-bedroom, six-and-a-half-bath home and rode around in matching Mercedes-Benzes. And I had fallen in love with him. The downside was that Pooch didn't want me to work. He wanted me to sit around, look cute, and take care of the kids. Better yet, keep them out of his way. Pooch loved my kids, but he didn't like them at all. Not that he had anything against them personally, but Pooch didn't like dealing with kids in general. He took care of them and bought them things, but he didn't spend time with them and was adamant that he wasn't going to do so. He bought them toys so they wouldn't fuck with him.

So ask me why I fucked around and got pregnant a third time. Pooch was mad about the whole pregnancy and told me that I didn't need to ruin my body by having more kids. We had a daughter, whom I named Princess. He kept referring to Princess as *my* baby, instead of *his* or *our* baby. He took care of the necessities for all of us, but in his mind, Princess was all mine, just as Terry and Brittany were.

At least that was how it was until Terrence was released from prison. He began spending time with his children, taking them here and there, and one day he even took Princess along on their outing, and Pooch nearly flipped out. Ever since then, Terrence had been a constant issue in our house. Pooch continued to spaz out more and more, and I was tired of it.

"Did you hear me?" Pooch yelled, spinning me around, interrupting my thoughts. He had joined me in the bedroom, but I hadn't noticed him walk in.

"Huh?"

"Daydreaming about that nigga, huh?" he asked.

I exhaled deeply. "No, Pooch. I daydream only about you."

He smiled. "You better," he said, grabbing his crotch. "I put that shit down, and you know it."

I nodded. "Yep, you do."

"You ain't taking no family photo with Terrence and y'all two kids. You are my woman, not his. His kids are his family, not you."

I didn't feel like arguing, so I conceded. "Fine, Pooch. I'll tell him."

"Now you sound like my girl," he said, softening his tone. He pulled me close to him. "Princess is asleep and Terrence got his kids, so why don't you bend that fat ass over and let me hit that shit right quick? I love the way having Princess blessed you with all that junk in the trunk."

That was the last thing I wanted. I was drained from his damn mood swings. "I don't feel like it, Pooch."

"So you pissed that I won't—" he began, defensive.

"No!" I yelled, interrupting him. "I'm not. I'm just . . ." I sighed, easing my jeans off. "Hurry up." I bent my ass over and used the bed as leverage.

Pooch's pants were on the floor faster than a speeding bullet. Before I could brace myself good, he was ramming his wood up in me.

"This shit good, ain't it?" Pooch asked breathlessly as he banged the hell out of my pussy.

"Yep. Sure is, Pooch," I lied. Not that he wasn't good, but I wasn't in the mood. "Get it, Pooch baby. It's your stuff."

"You damn right! Remember that shit!" he screamed, burying himself deep inside and then releasing with a hard jolt. "Ah yeah, baby. Remember that shit."

Lucinda

"*Ay*, Mama, I just need you to watch Nadia for an hour, maybe two, tops." I had been pleading with my mom for the past ten minutes and was now frustrated.

She'd told me no over the phone, but I had figured that showing up might earn me some sympathy points. But she was adamant that she did not have time to babysit. I knew she was lying, since she didn't have to be at her second job until seven o'clock tonight, and it was only two. I wasn't insensitive to the fact that my mom was tired. She worked two jobs and still cared for my six siblings single-handedly. Normally, I wouldn't ask her at the last minute, but this was for my future, and I didn't just *want* her help. I *needed* her help.

My mom heaved a frustrated sigh as she set the table. "*Ay, Dios mio*! Lucinda! I'm trying to get the table ready for dinner. Lucy and Jose are not here to help, because of their extracurricular activities, and I really want to rest before I have to go into work tonight."

"Then let Anaya watch her. She can do it. She's twelve."

"Anaya is not responsible enough, and you know it," my mom said, giving me the eye. "I really would love to help you out, Lucinda, but I can't."

"You act as if she's a damn burden, Mama. She's your grandchild, your *only* grandchild at that. She may as well be one of your kids. Peter is only two years older than her," I snapped.

My mom spun around, with her arms folded, a move she did when she was about to lay into someone. "You're right, Lucinda. She is my grandchild, my *only* grandchild, as you put it. No one else broke my heart by getting knocked up in school. I had to struggle to help you take care of her for two years, until you were able to do it on your own. She is *your* child, not mine. So don't bring that damn guilt trip over here. She has other grandparents and a father, or did you forget that?"

I rolled my eyes. "Okay. I was wrong for that, but you're *my* mother, and I need you."

She threw her hands up. "Where is her no-good father anyway? Why in the hell can't he do it?"

I looked at the kitchen doorway, to see Nadia looking at me. Her innocent face was so beautiful. "Mom, don't," I said, motioning toward Nadia.

"Nadia, go sit down," my mom commanded. Nadia gasped and hightailed it to the living room. "You need to teach that child that when grown-ups are talking, she waits in another room. I have a right to ask this question about her father. He is the party responsible for her, not me."

"He's at work, Mom," I lied. The truth was I didn't know where the hell Raul was. The reason I was at my mom's house was that Raul had been a no-show when it came time for him to pick up Nadia. That bastard was worse than the scum of the earth.

She looked at me as if she didn't believe me. "Yeah, okay. Well, *if* he's at work, I hope he's on time with his child-support payments, because I can't help you pay the day-care bill this week."

I looked at the clock. It was 2:15 p.m. I really needed to get the hell out of there and to my appointment. "Mom, can you please do it?"

Just then my mom's phone rang. It was my father. I hated that bastard, since he had cheated on my mom and had left her with all these kids. He'd since married the bitch, who was only two years older than me, and I was twenty-one. Now, he had a baby by her and acted as if my siblings and I didn't exist, but get this, he took care of that bitch's four-year-old daughter, who wasn't even his.

"Mom," I said, pressing her, as she was about to answer the call.

Ignoring me, she continued her phone conversation. Irritation danced across her face. With a sigh of frustration, she held out the phone. "It's your good-for-nothing father. Ask him to do it. He's going to be late with my child support and alimony check, so I have no need to talk to him."

As desperate as I was for some assistance, I took that deal. I didn't want to, but what other option did I have at this point? I grabbed the phone and said, "Dad, this is Lucinda."

"*Hola, hija*! Your mother is trippin' . . ."

Now, I knew he didn't think I was going to let him sit on the phone and disrespect my mother. "Um, that's between you two, but I need a favor," I told him. "Can I drop Nadia off for a couple of hours?"

He paused. "I . . . uh . . . well, I'm watching Rosemary right now."

Staring at the phone, I huffed. "Rosemary is four and Nadia is five, so they can play together. She needs to know her *step-aunt* anyway," I said, and my mom burst into laughter.

"I don't have to take this abuse from you. You're the one who needs help, Lucy. Not me. Ask her father to watch her," he snapped.

Why I even bothered, I did not know. He was laughable. "I don't even have time to debate with you, Papa. You can't even get your own children straight from digging up in Maria's ass so much. Wrong kid, *Pops*. Lucy is only seventeen. It is impossible for her to have a five-year-old child."

"I'll tell you what, take care of your own child, *Lucinda*," he barked.

"I tell *you* what, how about you have fun running after that little badass brat *stepchild* all by yourself, and when she gives you a heart attack, don't look for any of us *blood* children to come take care of you at the hospital," I barked back.

He slammed the phone down in my ear, and I handed the phone in my hand back to my mom. Like her, I was feisty and didn't give a damn about talking to him like that. I felt that since he was my father, he should care about my mom, his kids, and his grandchild. No pussy in the world should change that.

My mom noticed the sad yet disgusted look on my face and hugged me. "Don't worry about him. His deeds will come back to haunt him. We'll be fine."

Hugging her back, I kissed her on the cheek. "You encourage me, Mama."

"I just want better for you, Lucinda. That's all I've ever wanted."

"I know."

She patted my cheek, then went and grabbed an extra plate. "You better go to your appointment. You don't want to be late."

A bright smile crossed my face. "So you'll watch Nadia for me?"

"Two hours, Lucinda, no more. I need to rest before work, and I won't be able to with her here. You know, she is my first and *only* grandchild. I can't let anyone else care for her." She smiled.

She didn't need to tell me twice. I kissed her and Nadia, said my good-byes to everyone, then ran out. When I glanced at my watch, it read 2:25 p.m. I still had time to go talk to the admissions counselor at Piedmont Tech. My hope was to enroll at Tech to become a certified medical claims and billing specialist.

Currently, I worked part-time during the day, from nine to one, as a claims verifier for National Cross HealthCare. I also worked part-time three nights a week and every Sunday afternoon at Susie Q Nail Salon, doing manicures, full nail sets, and fill-ins. I preferred to work on people's hands. I wasn't going to mess with anybody's funky feet. Hell naw! The owners, Mr. and Mrs. Choi, were cool; and Mrs. Choi, or Mrs. Susie, as we called her, also served as the manager and head technician. I'd been friends with their daughter, Sue, who had taught me how to do manicures and pedicures, so they had let me work part-time at their shop while I was in high school. I'd been working there ever since.

Initially, Mr. Choi hadn't allowed me to bring Nadia to work with me, but one day her bum-ass daddy had played no-show, and he now allowed me to bring Nadia to work whenever I needed to. Now Mr. Choi loved Nadia, and he was upset when I didn't bring her. Nadia was a good kid, and everyone who met her fell in love with her, except her father. I was just glad that in terms of her personality, she took after me and my mother, and not her father.

The thought of Raul made me cringe. I must have been deaf, dumb, and blind to fool with him, but that was young love for you. Raul and I began dating during my ninth- and his tenth-grade year. It wasn't love at first sight, since I was usually into broader-shaped guys, and Raul was on the slender side. Although he wasn't muscular, I thought he had the cutest face, and he was a straight clown. Too bad his personality didn't match his relationship and fatherhood skills, I thought as I reminisced about how we began dating.

"*Hola, mami!*" Raul yelled at me across the yard.

"*Girl, crazy Raul is yelling at you again,*" Trinity said to me.

"*I ain't got time for Raul Garcia.*" I fanned him off.

"*Oh, it's like that, mami?*" Raul laughed.

Rolling my eyes, I spouted, "*Leave me alone, Raul. You always playing.*"

"*I got something you can play with,*" he said, and then he and his boys began rolling with laughter.

I looked at Trinity. "*See what the fuck I mean? That* hijo de puta *gets on my nerves.*"

"*Don't pay Raul no mind. He just likes you,*" Trinity explained for the millionth time.

With that, I shot a bird at Raul and walked away. He'd been plaguing me for the past month, and I was starting to believe what Trinity had been telling me. I didn't have to wait long to find out that she was right, because he made his move one day soon after, when I was walking home from school.

"*Hey, mami, a muy bonita young lady such as yourself shouldn't be walking home alone,*" Raul said, sneaking up on me.

I jumped. "You scared the shit out of me!" I yelled, turning to hit him.

He laughed. "That's exactly why you shouldn't be walking by yourself. Haven't you ever seen the movie Halloween?"

"Yeah, I have, and you know what? You kind of look like Michael Myers. You're damn sure crazy like his ass." We both laughed.

"That was a good one."

"Why are you bothering me, Raul?" I asked bluntly.

He looked at me as if I'd asked the dumbest question on Earth. "Why does any boy chase after a girl? Come on now."

"For ass," I responded sarcastically. "Ass that you ain't getting," I added.

He shrugged his shoulders. "Damn. You cold, Lucinda, but your ass is fine." He smiled and gave me the once-over.

"Get away from me, Raul," I told him, irritated, and began walking faster.

Raul jogged up to me. "Okay, for real, I'm sorry. Listen, Lucinda, I like you. I really do," he said as I came to a stop.

"Yeah right."

"Seriously. No jokes," he said, turning to face me.

"You're not my type."

"So who's your type? Those playboys like your girls Charice and LaMeka run around with? They ain't about shit."

"And you are about shit?" I asked.

"Yes," he said.

I laughed when I saw that he realized that that analogy didn't sound good.

"Wait, no . . . Damn! You fucked me up with that," he sputtered.

I laughed. "You are kinda cute."

"Come on. Give the skinny dudes a chance. I want you to be my girl. On the real, I really like you, Lucinda. You're smart and pretty. Just give me a chance," he said sincerely.

After little thought, I gave in. "All right, Raul. But don't think I'm giving up the ass."

"I know I gotta work for it," he joked.

I giggled. "You crazy."

"Crazy about you," he said, pulling me to him.

There was something about the way he held me at that moment, like he was claiming me as his forever, that drew my lips toward his. With our lips softly pressed together, we shared our first kiss. It was the first time the expression "sealed with a kiss" made sense to me. At that moment, I knew I was meant to be with Raul . . . or so I thought.

You would've thought that things between us would be straight, but it wasn't like that shit was all roses. As if cheating on me wasn't bad enough, he got a girl named Shanaya pregnant, and I was livid. After I finished slapping the shit out of him, I broke up with him and beat Shanaya's ass for disrespecting me. Good thing no one reported it, or I would've gotten locked up for fighting a pregnant girl. Still, like a lovesick puppy, I took him back and ended up getting pregnant myself.

I tried to stick it out with Raul, but he was a horrible boyfriend and an even worse father. I believed he loved Nadia, but he failed to realize that having a child was a full-time job and not an on-call duty, so I had to let him go. After we broke up, he got someone else, whom I knew only as Boop, pregnant. *What the hell kind of name is Boop*? I wondered. Anyway, all three of us had girls. That was a good thing, because he didn't need any knuckleheaded boys in the world who acted like him.

During my junior year in high school, I gave birth to Nadia. With my mother's help, I cared for Nadia with little to no assistance from Raul. After finishing high school, I continued to work at the nail salon in order to do more of my part for Nadia. And instead of enrolling in college, I opted to find another job, and I had been working for the insurance company ever since. Determined to be independent, I moved out of my mom's house and into a one-bedroom apartment when Nadia was three. My mom used some of her alimony checks and bought me a car. She didn't ask for any money back, but every month I gave her some. I was determined to pay her back completely. My mom played hard, but she was mush when it came to her kids, and we were a mush when it came to her. She was all we had had ever since Papa had walked out on us.

After a couple of years of fighting to pay bills and get by in real life, I decided to breathe easy. There was only one way that was going to happen, and that was taking my ass to school and getting a specialty or a trade. I liked the whole insurance vibe, since I helped people indirectly, and while I was part of a team, I worked solo. I figured that in the medical field, there would never be a recession, and they paid pretty damn well if you had experience and a degree. Now that I had a little experience, I needed the degree. This was the key to putting Nadia and me on the map.

While I circled one of the parking lots at Piedmont Tech, in search of a parking space, my cell phone started ringing. I grabbed it from the passenger seat and answered.

"Hello?" I said.

Raul's voice blared through my receiver. "Bring Nadia over. I'm home."

I sucked my teeth. "Fine time to be home, Raul. You were supposed to pick her up at one thirty. It's two fifty. I told you I had an appointment!"

"Ain't nobody told you to schedule an appointment during the time she wasn't in day care. Shit. I had things to do."

"Like what, Raul? What in God's name did you have to do?"

"Tend to my business, that's what. You don't question me. We ain't together," he said nonchalantly.

I looked at my phone in disbelief as I pulled into a parking space. Then I snapped, "Oh, muthafucka, I know we ain't together, and don't let me remind you that this was *my* choice! But that ain't got shit to do with your daughter. I scheduled the appointment at this time because unlike some of us, I actually show up at my job, and knowing that you may be late or short on your child support, I need every fucking penny I can get!"

"Whatever, *mami*! So are you bringing my baby by or what? If not, I got some shit I can be doing besides listening to your grouchy ass grumble."

"Kiss my ass, Raul."

"Do you mean it?" He laughed.

"Go fuck yourself in the ass," I said angrily before hanging up on him. I took a deep breath to calm my nerves and exited my car.

Murder is still illegal in this country, I reminded myself as I headed to the building on campus that housed the admissions office. Otherwise, I'd buy the biggest gun I could find and go hunt down that muthafucka and any others like him. My father included . . . hell, guaranteed. I stepped through the front door and quickly located the admissions office.

"I'm here to see Francesca Reynolds," I said to the desk clerk after I entered the office.

"Do you have an appointment?" she asked.

"Yes. My name is Lucinda Rojas."

She checked the appointment schedule and told me to have a seat. I sat down in the nearest chair and looked around at all the motivational posters on the walls. From the table next to me, I picked up a flyer about the school, and it contained testimonies by former graduates endorsing the college and a list of all the accolades the school had received. I was beginning to see myself at Piedmont. I *wanted* to see myself at Piedmont. Hell, I *needed* to see myself at Piedmont.

"Lucinda Rojas," the clerk called out. When I looked over at her, she added, "Ms. Reynolds will see you now. Come on back."

I rubbed my hands nervously. I *had* to get into Piedmont.

Charice

"The quarterback faked the throw, and the handoff was made to Westmore. Moore goes in for the tackle, and he misses! Oh, he misses! Westmore cuts back, and he's grabbed by Reese, and oh my God . . . Westmore breaks the tackle, and he is going, and he is *gone*. To the thirty, the twenty, and touchdown, Dallas Cowboys! Now they are up by six. What a run from Ryan Westmore," the announcer yelled excitedly.

"See, this is why he is such a phenomenal player. This is what he does best. He knows how to shuffle, plant his feet, make defenders miss, and find those openings to make big plays. He is a force to be reckoned with and has truly added something special to this Dallas team," the other announcer commented.

"Well, I know what he doesn't do best," my mother said bluntly as we sat in the living room, our eyes glued on the television.

Rolling my eyes, I let out a deep sigh. "Mom, please don't start. I am trying to watch the game with the boys. They want to see their father play."

"And I want to see their father *pay*," she said seriously. "Back pay, current pay, future pay and all."

"Mom," I whined.

"*Mom*, hell," she whined back. "You need to get your head out of the clouds and sue his raggedy, no-good ass for child support. You have three children by his rusty ass, and while he runs up and down the field, making millions, he won't even acknowledge his children. What kind of shit is that? And then you let him get away with it!"

"Ryan, Ray . . . go into the family room with your grandpa and watch the game," I ordered my sons. Once they were out of the room, I turned to my mother and lashed out. "Do not talk about their father like that in front of them. They love him and love to see him play."

"Charice, when are you going to wake up?" my mom replied. "The moment you found out you were pregnant, Ryan, his family, and the coaches shut you down, and it's been like that ever since. All so the kids wouldn't ruin his chances in the NFL. Then they have the nerve to give a grand here and there just to keep you appeased enough not to go after his ass for support. And don't let me remind you that he hasn't seen those kids since they were two years old, when he was drafted. After coming home and telling you his good news, he screwed you, dropped you a hundred dollars for three kids, and left you to get an abortion after he denied being the father of the fourth child he impregnated you with." She took a deep breath. "So forgive me for speaking so *rudely* about their *father*," she added, using those stupid air quotes, which drove me insane.

Well, so much for a peaceful afternoon of Sunday football. I turned off the television and sat back in my armchair. I hated when my mom got into her rants about Ryan. It brought up the pain that I had struggled to hide and was ashamed of. After all these years, I was still in love with Ryan Westmore, a pro football player and the father of our triplets, Ryan Jr., Charity, and Raymond.

When they discussed the consequences of teen pregnancy, they damn sure skipped the chapter about the possibility of having more than one child at one time. I think my mom and I both fainted when we found out that I carried the family gene for multiple births. My great-grandma was the last one to experience multiple births: she delivered two sets of identical twins, first daughters and then sons. One of those daughters was my grandmother Agnes. None of my grandmother's four children had multiple births, but when I got pregnant my junior year of high school, I pulled the golden number. Not one, hell, not even two, but three children.

When Ryan and I began dating when I was a sophomore and he was junior, I thought he was so damn sexy and fine. I think I fell in love with him at first sight. Hell, I'd wanted him since the first day I stepped foot in high school. Our first encounter was when I was a freshman. I dropped my purse, and he picked it up for me.

"Aw shit," I cursed, bending down to grab my fallen purse.

"No worries. I got you," I heard someone say as he bent down, picked up my purse, and extended it to me. "I do believe this is yours."

But I didn't take the purse. Instead, my eyes met his, and instantly I heard "The Star Spangled Banner" playing in my head. Ryan was five feet, eleven inches, with smooth mocha skin. His baby face sported a little chin fuzz, and his shiny brown eyes were adorned with the longest eyelashes that I had ever seen on a man. He had a strong jawline and dimples in both cheeks. Let's not forget his gleaming white teeth and his muscles from head to toe. His hair was cut low, and he kept waves in it. He looked as if he was twenty instead of fifteen, and he was the only sophomore that had played on the varsity football team. He was that good and that good looking.

I bragged on him as if I were the ugly duckling, but don't get it twisted. I was far from it. I had an hourglass figure and long mahogany-colored hair, and almond-colored eyes. So you see, I looked damn good, but when you were Ryan Westmore, you could have your pick of any girl you wanted. So to him, I was just another good-looking girl in the litter. Senior girls were after Ryan. That was how fine he was. Out of the thirty-five hundred students that attended our school, he absolutely was the most attractive.

"Do you want your purse back?" Ryan asked, still holding it out to me.

I shook my head after I realized I had been staring at him like a damn fool. "Yeah . . . um, yes, of course. Thank you so much," I said, taking my purse from him.

He smiled at me, and I could've died. "You're welcome, Miss . . . ?"

"Charice Taylor," I answered quickly.

He shook my hand. "Charice Taylor, pleased to meet you. I'm Ryan Westmore. Let me guess. This is your first year?"

"How'd you know?"

"I'd remember seeing such a pretty face around here," he answered, flirting.

I blushed and then waved him off. "You're just saying that."

"You are pretty," he said, staring me in the face until I looked away. "Don't act shy."

"I'm not. I just . . . I better head to homeroom."

He stepped aside. "Don't let me hold you up. Enjoy your day, Charice, and calm down. It's a fun school."

I laughed. "I'll remember that," I said before walking away.

As I walked down the hallway, I heard one of the football players joke about Ryan trying to catch the fresh meat, but I didn't care. I had already been caught . . . hook, line, and sinker. It didn't take long for me to realize that I wasn't the only one. Even though it appeared Ryan was feeling me, I saw that he was flirtatious with a lot of females. By lunch, I was off his radar, and he no longer noticed me. I had become *just one of the picks of the litter, and what made it even worse was the fact that we had the same lunch period, so I couldn't help but notice him. He sat at the football table, which was the most popular table in the cafeteria. All the star football players sat together, laughing and joking while eating lunch. The only other people allowed at the table were their friends, girlfriends, and the picks of the week. I didn't want to be in the* friend *category, and I sure as hell wasn't looking to be in the* pick of the week *category, or, as I call it, the* ho at the time *category. I wanted to be like Stephanie Galloway and Miranda Hill, in the* girlfriend *category. Stephanie was the quarterback's girlfriend, and Miranda was one of the wide receivers' girlfriend. Those two were the most popular and prettiest females in the school.*

I had it so bad for Ryan that I didn't date anyone my ninth grade year, hoping and praying that he'd step to me. I wanted to be available if and when he asked me to be his girl, but it never happened. I later got an opportunity when Miranda's younger sister, Monique, and I performed in a spring recital together. Afterward, Miranda approached me.

"Hey. Charice, right?" She smiled.

"Yes."

She stuck her hand out. "Hi. My name is Miranda Hill. You probably don't know me, because I'm a junior, but I go to school with you."

I shook her hand and smiled. "I remember you. Your sister, Monique, was in the recital."

"Yeah, she goes to this dance academy. She swears she's going to be the prima donna of her own ballet company," she joked.

"She is good, though," I complimented. Although she was good, she wasn't anyone's prima donna, but I wasn't going to degrade her sister in front of her. I believed that I was better, and her sister confirmed it.

"Yeah, but you're better. You have that it factor."

I smiled. "Thanks."

"Well, I guess I should get to the point of my visit. With skills like that, why didn't you try out for the squad this year?"

"The squad? As in the cheerleading squad?"

"Yes, girl. That split you did onstage was to die for. We need fresh faces and new talent. We came in third at regionals, but if you were on the squad, we could've won first place."

Shrugging it off, I said, "I always thought that the leaders picked their friends, so I didn't think I would have a chance."

She smiled. "We do, but you can consider yourself a friend."

"So you want me to try out for next year?"

With a giggle, she answered me indirectly. "Here is my number. We should hang out this summer. I will be the captain, since Stephanie graduated. It'd be a real good look for you to be on the squad. We always get the flyest guys. I'm sure there is a guy you have your eye on."

Now, I liked Ryan, but I wasn't going to tell her that. "Not really."

"You have a boyfriend or something?"

"No—"

"Please don't tell me you like females?" she interrupted.

I pointed at myself. "Me? Like girls? Hell no. I just don't have a boyfriend. My parents didn't want me to date until tenth grade." That was the truth, but I would've gladly defied that rule for Ryan Westmore.

Smiling with relief, she clapped. "Well, then, I'm right on time. Seriously, call me, so we can hang and get to know each other. Cheering will keep you athletic and do wonders for your reputation all at the same time."

I nodded. "Okay, I'll call you. Thanks again, Miranda."

She hugged me. "If you join, all the thanks will be going to you. You are fire, girlfriend!" she said. Then she walked off.

All summer long I hung out with Miranda. We hung out so much, it pissed off LaMeka and Trinity, and then I was accused of breaking up the crew, because LaMeka couldn't hang with Miranda and me. Why? Simply put, Miranda was an upperclassman, and LaMeka had just got out of eighth grade. I wasn't messing up my opportunity for anybody. Besides, I was trying to put us all in a better position. When LaMeka became a ninth grader, she would have her rite of passage through me. I would be able to get her on the squad, and she would be popular from the jump. Since I was the oldest, it would also pave the way for Trinity and Lucinda. So, there was a method to the madness.

Cheerleading tryouts were at the end of the summer. Of course, I made the squad and quickly became friends with the current squad members, whom I already knew since I'd hung with Miranda over the summer. Your girl had arrived, and I felt so good when I met Miranda at her locker on the first day of school, with LaMeka in tow.

Fresh to death was the look, with my short-sleeved, one-piece jean pantsuit that hugged my curves and a pair of cute platform sandals. With my long hair in a ponytail, I stepped with confidence that day. I'd made sure LaMeka was on point as well. She sported a pair of formfitting jean capris, a batwing top, and a pair of wedges.

"Hello, ladies," I said, then hugged Miranda and a couple of the other squad members.

"Hey, Charice," they sang in unison.

"Who is this?" Miranda asked, pointing to LaMeka.

I turned to LaMeka and winked. "This is my best friend, LaMeka Roberts. She's a freshman, but she's cool as hell."

Miranda gave her the once-over and nodded in approval. This made the other girls smile. "Any friend of Charice's is a friend of ours. Ain't that right, ladies?"

"Yep," they said in unison.

I was relieved that LaMeka had passed the test.

"Thanks for letting me hang with you guys," LaMeka said with gratitude. While she was happy, I was ecstatic on the inside. She didn't understand what this meant for her.

"No problem. Like I said, you're family now," Miranda told her. "You know, we have one freshman slot on the squad left, if you're interested."

LaMeka smiled. "When do I try out?"

Miranda smiled and tapped me on the shoulder. "I like her," she said from behind me while we all walked down the hall.

Luckily, we all had the same lunch period as Ryan, Miranda's boyfriend, and some of the other star players on the football team.

"Okay, ladies. We're headed to the football table. LaMeka, you are probably the only freshman to ever be allowed at the table. I want you two to be cool, and for Christ's sake, don't embarrass me. We are confident, strong, and we are the baddest bitches in this school. Remember that. Now let's go over and grab you two some boyfriends. And, LaMeka . . . Rodney is off limits. He's mine," Miranda said, schooling us, before we reached the football table.

Miranda didn't have to school LaMeka about Rodney, because she already had her sights set on Tony Light, a freshman, who was also at the table. Ryan played recreational football with Tony and liked him. Tony was a starter on the junior varsity team. Like Ryan, there was no doubt that he would be on the varsity squad this year.

As we walked over, I was more nervous than I had been on my first day of school. I prayed to God that Ryan noticed me this time.

"Hey, fellas," Miranda said as she set her tray down beside Rodney's and took a seat.

Rodney wrapped his arm around her and kissed her. "'Sup, babe? Who are your friends?"

She looked at us and smiled. "Have a seat, ladies," she said, and two guys moved to allow us to sit down. "This is Charice Taylor. She's going to be my co-captain on the squad this year. And this is LaMeka Roberts, our only freshman recruit."

"Hello, ladies," Rodney and the fellas said in unison.

"Hey," we sang together.

"We have a freshman recruit too," Rodney said, pointing to Tony. "Mr. Light, but we should call him Muhammad Ali, 'cause he damn sure floats like a butterfly, and those feet sting like a bee!" Rodney joked as everyone laughed. "The boy is tight."

Tony nodded and touched knuckles with Rodney. "'Preciate the love, Rod."

"So, Ryan, are you ready for this year?" Rodney asked.

That was when I noticed that he was staring at me.

Rodney put his hand in Ryan's face. "Earth to Ryan." They all laughed. "Damn, bro. Get your eyes off Charice long enough to answer me, dude."

Ryan laughed. "My bad, bro. What'd you say?"

"I hope this ain't no indication of how you gonna be on the field. When I hand off, your ass better not be in Alice's wonderland," Rodney joked. Everyone laughed again.

"When I'm on the field, the only thing on my mind is scrambling that defense," Ryan joked in return, then high-fived some of the teammates.

"So what is your mind on now?" I asked before thinking about it. My boldness even shocked the hell out of me.

Miranda gave me a wink and a thumbs-up as LaMeka hit my thigh under the table, signaling that she was proud of me.

Rodney smiled at me. "The lady asked you a question, Ryan," he said before stuffing some fries in his mouth. He pulled Miranda farther down the table. "Let's make some room."

Ryan grabbed his tray, got up, and came to sit beside me. "I think you already know," he said, staring me in the eyes.

By the end of the lunch period, I had achieved my goal of becoming one of the most popular girls in school and being the first to land Ryan Westmore and become his true girlfriend. All I remembered from the rest of that day was sitting in my geometry class and doodling "Ryan and Charice forever" on my notebook.

But that was eight years, two pregnancies, three kids, and one abortion ago. Now my *ex-boyfriend* Ryan Westmore was the Dallas Cowboys' Ryan Westmore. He was now the NFL's number two–ranked running back and the league's third highest-paid running back, and he was steadily trying to achieve number one. But he was already number one in two areas: he was the league's number one playboy and the world's number one deadbeat dad.

Ryan took my virginity the summer of my tenth-grade year. Even though I was afraid of losing him, I had gone only as far as kissing and fingering, but nothing more. Ryan begged me for it, and at the end of the school year, he told me that he would've already cheated if I wasn't one of the most popular girls in the school. Since I made him look good, he couldn't risk me leaving him over dumb shit and ending up with another dude. That would have been a hit to his already large ego. Out of fear of losing him, I let him hit it, and surprisingly, he was patient and loving through the entire process. After the first time, we did it every chance we got.

Eventually, that sneaky sex caught up with us. I'd never forget the day I told Ryan that I was pregnant. Nervous and upset, I didn't know how I was going to tell him. He had recently signed with one of the top colleges, the University of Florida. Although he was excited, Ryan had been under a lot of pressure, and this was a pivotal point in his life. Unlike the average teenager, he wasn't just preparing to go to college. He was preparing for his dream. NFL eligibility. He had come so far and could've gone to any one of the top universities. From the University of Tennessee to the University of Georgia, Vanderbilt, and the University of Alabama, they all wanted him. Ryan was well on his way, and now I had to tell him that he was going to be . . . a *daddy*.

As I lay stretched across his bed, flipping through a magazine, I tried my best to keep my mind off the topic. He was set to leave in a couple of weeks and had already questioned why I had turned over the cheerleading captain slot to Tonya Miller.

"Damn, baby. Your ass is getting phat. But I like that shit, though," he said, gliding his hand over my rear end as he sat next to me. "Umm, juicy." He slowly hovered over me as I felt his nature rise.

"Ryan, not now," I said softly.

"Stop playing hard to get. I leave in a couple of weeks. Give your man some loving before he goes. My parents are gone and won't be back *until tonight. We could make this an all-day thing,"* he whispered in my ear as he kissed me. *"You know I love you, right?"*

A wave of relief came over me, and those three little words were the words that did it. Ryan had told me that he loved me his senior year, and I never grew tired of hearing it. However, this time, it meant I could tell him our news and share all my burdens with him. Tears fell from my eyes, and he stopped kissing on me.

"Babe, what's wrong?" he asked with concern.

I bit my lip and gazed at him nervously. "I have to tell you something."

He held my face, with the sincerest look in his eyes. "You can tell me anything. I'm your man, and I love you. What's wrong?"

I sighed, grabbed his hands, and held them tightly. "I love you too, Ryan. I've been in love with you since the day you handed me my purse in the ninth grade," I confessed.

He smiled. "I remember that."

After mustering a slight smile, I took a deep breath. "Ryan, I'm pregnant."

His face went blank, and his body turned rigid. For a moment, I thought he had blacked out.

"Ryan, baby, did you hear me?"

He snatched his hands away from me, stood up, and then rubbed his head from confusion. "Charice, this shit ain't funny now! Don't fucking play like this!"

Appalled, I jumped up. "I'm not playing! I'm telling the truth. I'm pregnant, Ryan," I told him. "That's why Tonya is the captain. I can't be."

"How? We used protection, Charice," he said harshly.

Now I knew he had bumped his head. We used protection, but there were times when we hadn't. We thought that the "pull out" method would suffice, but obviously, it didn't work.

"Ryan, you know damn well we didn't use protection all the time."

He rubbed his head again. "So what are you going to do? You ain't ready to have no kids, and I damn sure ain't. I have a life to live. I'm going to Florida and then to the NFL. I'm not staying in Georgia to be a daddy and play house with you. Hell no!"

Talk about floored. I had not asked him to stay, nor would I ever. All I wanted was for him to comfort me and tell me he loved me. I hoped that he'd be there for me and our child and that we'd always be together.

"How do you think I feel? I love cheering and dancing. I can't do either now. I'm not asking you to give up football. I'm asking you to say, 'Charice, I still love you. We'll be great parents, and when I get drafted into the NFL, I'm going to marry you so we can be a family.'"

"So you think having this kid is going to trap me? Is that what you thought? So you purposely got pregnant so you could have some claim on me once I got into the NFL? You are so low, Charice," he said, fuming.

I shook my head. "Wait a minute! Hold up! I am not trying to trap you, with the hopes that you make it into the NFL, but we've talked about this before. You're the one who told me that you wanted to stay together, since I was the only female that you could trust and that you knew truly loved you. You knew I would be with you even without the NFL money. Now that you got me pregnant, I've turned into a gold digger? Are you crazy?"

"No, but you are if you think you can pin this kid on me."

"I thought you loved me, Ryan. I love you so much," I cried.

"Then prove it," he said, throwing his hands up. "Kill it!"

"What?"

"You heard me. Kill it. Then you can live your life and I can live mine," he said sternly, with his arms crossed.

"How can you say that about our baby?"

His lip twitched, and his expression was cold. "Well, let me put it to you like this. If you have this kid, I'll never forgive you, and we are done. So you've got a choice. Me or your baby."

Rage like I'd never felt before swelled inside of me. The reality of Ryan's feelings fell on my heart, and I felt betrayed and foolish. "Go to hell, Ryan!" I yelled. Then I ran out of his house, with my heart in a million pieces.

The next couple of weeks were pure hell. My parents were hurt and disappointed, and my dad kicked Ryan's ass. His parents told my parents that Ryan's choice was not to have the baby and that if I didn't comply, none of them would have anything to do with it. My mom told his mother that we'd see their sorry asses in court.

If that wasn't enough, later I had to tell his parents that I was pregnant with triplets and had dropped out of high school after being put on strict bed rest for the last trimester of my pregnancy. That information made his mom soften up and want to be around, but Ryan had turned into a guy I'd never known. After refusing to talk to me, he began denying the babies. His coach told me to stay away from him and not to bring him bad press. Despite his denial, he did come to the hospital the day the babies were born. Ryan signed the birth certificates and took pictures with the triplets. Ryan Jr. looked just like him, Charity looked more like me, and Raymond had some of both of us. Once he left, it was like normal—no calls, no visits, and no money. Every once in a while, he'd pop up to visit and bring toys and get some ass from me, and then he was off again.

My parents wanted me to sue him for child support, but I never did. He was in college, so he wasn't making money at the time, and I'd always held on to the thought that once he made it to the NFL, he'd realize his mistake and we'd be a family. So I struggled, with my parents' help, and did as best I could. His mom would sneak over and give us Pampers, outfits, and money every now and then. When I was nineteen, I received my GED and enrolled in college. I wanted to major in dance, but I realized I still had to do more professional training and hope a company would hire me. So I settled on science and became a nutritionist.

During my sophomore year in college, Ryan showed up with his new Cadillac Escalade. He was wearing a sharp Armani outfit. I knew he had made the number one draft pick, but I let him showboat. After taking me out to dinner, he threw down some loving on me. I knew we were going to be a family. I just knew it.

"I'm so glad you've come to your senses," I said, stroking his chest. "The kids adore you, and I can't wait until we're a family."

My outpouring was met with a chuckle. "Charice, I told you that if you chose those kids over me, we were done."

A scowl mixed with confusion etched my face. "So what is all this about? I thought you were coming home so that we could be a family. I didn't interfere with your college education or when you made it into professional football."

He looked at me sheepishly, and I knew the excuses were coming. "I guess I still care about you and that's why I continue to come around when I'm home, but I can't marry you. These are my rookie years, and I need to focus on my game. I have to be known as a force in the NFL. I can't do that and adjust to being married, with kids."

No, this can't be happening, *I thought. He could not be stomping on my heart like this again. Once was bad enough, but this was cruel and unusual punishment. Desperation found its way into my heart, and a downpour of tears found its way to my cheeks. "Ryan, please, I love you. We need you. I need you. Please, baby, don't leave us like this," I begged.*

Ryan sat up, shaking his head. He didn't even take a moment to consider what I had said. He simply blurted out, "This was a mistake. Get dressed. I'm taking you home."

"But, Ryan—"

"No," he said sternly.

Dropping to my knees, I begged for his acceptance and his love. Yes, I loved him that much. "I'll do whatever you want me to do. I promise. I swear to God, we won't interfere. But we need you, baby. Please, Ryan, please," I cried. "I love you so much . . . so damn much," I pleaded as I sat on the floor, at his feet.

The heartless bastard stood up and said, "I shudder to think how low you can really go to keep me. I don't want this shit, Charice. You wanted these fucking kids, so you deal with it. Now I'm taking my ass to the Cowboys, and you're taking your ass home to take care of your kids."

With that, he walked into the hotel bathroom and ran the shower as I sat there crying. After putting on my clothes, I waited for him to finish his shower. When he exited the bathroom, he didn't say two words to me, and the ride home was the same way, completely silent. When we arrived at my house, he stopped me, and I thought for a moment that he'd changed his mind. Wrong again. He peeled off a hundred-dollar bill, handed it to me, said it was for the kids, then told me that it'd be the last time he'd see me, since I was confused about how our situation worked.

Too overcome with hurt to respond, I jumped out of his truck with the hundred dollars he'd given me for the kids and ran into my house, past my mother, engulfed in tears. I cried as I told her what had happened.

One month later, I relived the hell again as I sat on my bathroom floor, puking my guts out, after my mom read the pregnancy test that confirmed that I was again pregnant by Ryan Westmore. I told Ryan, but of course, he denied getting me pregnant and said that I wasn't going to pin another one on him. I wasn't foolish that time. I couldn't risk another multiple-birth pregnancy, so I went to the clinic with LaMeka and my mom and had an abortion. It was the hardest decision of my life, but probably the wisest.

You'd think I would hate him after all this, but I was the ultimate ignorant chick. My crazy ass still loved him. After all this time, all the pain, and two pregnancies, I loved Ryan Westmore. Nothing, not even Ryan, could change that. The sound of my mother sighing brought me out of my reverie.

I turned to her and said, "Mom, I can't deny anything you've said. I can't. But the kids still love him, and I want him to explain to them why he was never around. I'm not going to bad talk their dad in front of them."

"I guess you have a point about that, but I hate the fact that you support him. You're pining away over a boy who couldn't care less about you. Every other day he's dating this celebrity or partying with that celebrity, spending money on cars, trips, and houses, while you're busting your ass to support and raise three children on a forty-five-thousand-dollar-a-year income."

"We're not hurting, Mama."

"But you damn sure ain't living in the lap of luxury like Mr. Westmore," she argued. "Then his mama has the nerve to come and drop off a grand here and there of Ryan's money, like she's doing us a damn favor. Oh, she just kills me, rolling up over here in her SUV and Donna Karan suits, spending all of fifteen minutes with her grandkids."

Rubbing my temples, I exhaled. "I have an SUV, Mama."

"Yes, you have a Tahoe. She has a *Mercedes*. There is a difference. And do you know what that difference is? Ryan Westmore."

"Every Sunday I come over here, and it's the same thing. Can we change the subject for once?" I asked as I stood up from the armchair.

"If you would change the subject to child support, there wouldn't be anything left to discuss." She threw up her hands. "I'm sorry if I want my grandkids' father to actually be a *father*. I mean, he *is* Ryan Westmore, professional football player, *God's gift*," she said.

I knew she was right, but she could be so animated at times. "Okay, Mom." I bent down and kissed her on the cheek. "I love you," I said as I headed to the door.

"I love you too!" she shouted as I walked out the door.

I walked to my Tahoe, climbed inside, and reached for my cell phone to call LaMeka and tell her about my mom's latest rant, but I immediately noticed the message light flashing. I dialed my voice mail, and Ryan's voice came through.

"Charice, something has come up, and I'm not going to be home next weekend to visit you and the kids like I said. I transferred two grand into my mom's account for them. Get them set up for Christmas and buy yourself something too. I have a game this afternoon, so I won't be able to talk. Let the boys watch me play. My mom said they like that. Anyway, I have to go. I'll talk to you sometime. Peace," Ryan's recorded voice said.

Despite the disappointment of not being able to see him next weekend, I was overcome by giddiness. I couldn't help but get excited over the fact that he had thought of doing something special for the kids for Christmas. I was glad he was polite enough to call and explain ahead of time why he would miss seeing them. Maybe he was changing, I thought. I shook my head and called LaMeka.

"'Sup, honey?" LaMeka asked when she answered the phone.

"Nothing. Sitting at my mom's house, listening to her gripe about Ryan."

"As she should be," LaMeka observed.

"Don't start," I warned. "Where the hell is your baby daddy?"

"Out of town with your baby daddy," she answered sarcastically.

I furrowed my brow. "For what?"

"Tony will be gone for nine days. This weekend in LA is some kind of big-time celebrity fashion show, and Ryan invited Tony and some of his teammates. Apparently, Ryan is one of the male models for Ralph Lauren's new collection or some shit," LaMeka informed me.

"Son of a bitch," I said abruptly.

"What?" LaMeka asked.

"Nothing. Let me call you back," I said and quickly hung up.

As I sat in my SUV, I cried over the fact that Ryan had ditched his kids for a fashion show. Why was I constantly falling for this nigga's lies? When would I ever learn that no matter how much I loved him, he couldn't care less about me and, worse yet, our children?

LaMeka

Charice hung up the phone on me so fast that I didn't have a chance to ask if she could take me and Tony Jr. to his therapy session. But I knew why she did. Well, not exactly, but I could speculate. I'd been friends with her long enough to know that her reaction had Ryan Westmore written all over it. I loved her, but I wished she would let go of this fantasy that Ryan was going to one day wake up and come running back to her like Prince fucking Charming, marry her, take her and their kids, and ride the fuck off into the sunset. Oh, but there was a sunset. The *sun set* on their relationship when she first told his no-good ass that she was pregnant. If I could turn back the hands of time, I never would've walked with Miranda and Charice over to that football table back when I was a high school freshman. Hell, I wouldn't have let Charice walk over there. Both of our lives had changed dramatically that day, and that change had come attached to two names: Ryan Westmore and Tony Light.

I wasn't as smart and talented as Charice. She had actually had a chance at finishing school with an actual high school diploma and going to college for dance, except God had thrown one more monkey wrench in her plans and had given her three times the blessing instead of one. I, on the other hand, had dropped out because I hated school in the first place, with the exception of science, and I had got pregnant in high school by Tony, but there was a story behind that.

In high school Tony had been Ryan's protégé, so to speak. Tony had had the potential to be every bit as good as Ryan, if not better, and Ryan had molded him. Tony had played football and had run track and had been one of the school's premier athletes. However, compared to Ryan, he had been a little more subtle in the way he handled things. While Ryan had approached Charice at the lunch table, in front of everyone, that day, Tony had caught up with me in our sixth-period science class. In fact, we'd been science partners. I remembered that conversation like it had happened yesterday.

"You know, your girl and my boy are going to be the new 'it' couple now that Stephanie and Joe have graduated. It's going to be Miranda

and Rodney and then Ryan and Charice," Tony told me.

I smiled. "I guess so," I said, putting some of the contents of the petri dish on the slide.

"So when Miranda and Rodney graduate, who is going to be the next 'it' couple with Ryan and Charice?" Tony asked.

"I'm not sure, but I'm sure you're going to tell me," I said to him, examining the slide under the microscope.

When I looked up, Tony stared back at me. "Me and you," he said.

I had a crush on Tony but played coy. "You think?"

"I know."

"Talk about confidence."

"Tell me you don't like me, then," Tony said, challenging me.

I wanted to say I didn't, but that would've been a bald-faced lie. Just looking at him made chills run down my spine. Tony Light was extremely fair skinned, had a few freckles, and had red hair, which he kept in braids. He was the perfect blend of light. Not albino light and not dirty red. He was a nice clean-cut, handsome, fair-skinned fellow who had long, slender legs and a masculine upper body. Not to mention, his head was in the right place. Oh *yes, I was definitely feeling Mr. Light. But I didn't let on.*

"Cat got your tongue?" he asked, smiling at me.

"Huh?"

He laughed, having realized that my lack of response clearly meant I was feeling him. "You know you're the right woman for Mr. Light. We are royalty in the making. I'm the next Ryan Westmore, and you're the next Charice Taylor. I like you, LaMeka, so let's do this."

You couldn't wipe the blush off my face if you tried. "Tony, do you really want me to be your girlfriend?"

He nodded his head yes. "Girl, ain't that what I've been saying for the past five minutes?"

"Well, as your girlfriend, let me tell you we better finish this assignment before Mr. Hopper gives us both detention for talking." I pointed to the front of the room, where the teacher was standing and glaring at us.

Tony grabbed the microscope and peered inside. "Hurry up and write something before he comes over here," he whispered. I giggled and began writing down my initial findings.

That was how Tony and I began dating. Unlike Ryan, Tony was extremely thoughtful and was a good boyfriend. When I say that, I mean it. He even went so far as to help me with my schoolwork. Most guys wanted nothing but sex during alone time with their girl, but not Tony. He wanted the best for himself, and because of that, he wanted the best for me. For instance, since he was good in all subject areas in school, he helped me, because if it wasn't science, I wasn't interested. I remembered one night of studying in particular.

"Did you hear me, Tony?" I asked him. We were at his house. He was studying as I flipped through a magazine.

"Yeah, I did," he answered, his head still in his book.

"So what did I say?"

"Huh?" he asked, looking up at me.

"You didn't hear me," I said angrily.

He sighed and closed the book. "Babe, we are supposed to be studying. You are so good at science, but when it comes to other subjects, like social studies, algebra, English . . . hell, all of them, you couldn't care less. Why?"

"Because I hate school, and science is the only subject that interests me. Everyone can't be a brainiac like you."

"Yes, you can. You just have to break it down in a format you can understand."

I shrugged. "So show me, genius."

Gazing at me, he accepted the challenge and called my bluff. "Grab your book and sit down."

"What?" I asked, laughing.

"You heard me."

I groaned but did as I was told.

With a serious expression, he said, "Okay, so say we're studying about the law—"

"I know about the law. It ain't for black people," I joked.

He laughed and nodded in agreement. "I can't argue with that, but still, the law would be like a person. The president is like the brain. Congress would be the major organs."

My eyes flashed, as I understood what he was getting at. "I see where you're going."

"Exactly." He kissed my forehead. "By the time we're finished, you'll love every subject in school."

I didn't understand everything that night, but I had a better understanding of social studies, and my baby was the key to that. He helped me, and we encouraged each other. I loved the fact that he took everything in his life seriously, even his athletics. Tony wasn't egotistical like the other ballers, who used sports as a means to gain in popularity and attract females. He actually had goals in life. After making competing at the Olympics one of his goals, Tony discussed his options with his parents, trainer, and track coach. Tony was already ranked third in the region in running. And he'd never admit it, but he was better than his so-called mentor, Ryan. Ryan was fifth, which really burned his ego. With time and a little practice, Tony was on his way to becoming number one.

Our relationship was built for romance novels. We had dated since ninth grade, and we were definitely the "it" couple after surviving four complete years of being together. Don't get me wrong. We had a few rough spells. We both cheated on the other once, but we rekindled our relationship because we realized how much we had taken each other for granted and how much we loved one another.

I later learned that the reason Tony cheated was that his boys had convinced him that he was being soft by staying tied down to one girl. Tony didn't want to admit that he was in love with me, which also prompted him to cheat. I suspected he was cheating because for two weeks, he was really evasive with me, not returning my calls as he had promised and making excuses not to see me. See, besides being a couple, Tony and I were thick as thieves. So I knew that this was not typical. Now, because I had older friends, they schooled me on what that behavior meant.

Either Tony was tired of being in a relationship with me and didn't know how to break up or he was cheating. When we saw each other, he acted as if everything was okay, so I figured it was the latter of the two reasons. And so I did my own investigation into the matter.

This was where boys were dumb. Routines spoke louder than words. If you changed up the routine, your words had better match. I knew that every Friday before a game, the football team met at their favorite McDonald's to chill and grab some food. Usually, the girlfriends would be there as well. It was another place to show you were a "couple" with a popular boy or girl. This fool had the nerve to tell me he wasn't going to go one Friday, and he gave me some lame-ass excuse, one that I no longer remembered. I played it cool, though, and my girl, Trinity, and I rolled up to the Mickey D's to check out the situation. Surprisingly, there was my boyfriend, hugged up with the slut of the year, Monica Simmons. Initially, I thought maybe he was playing, but when she kissed him on the mouth, that was all the proof I needed. I took pictures with my cell phone and left.

No confrontation was needed, because I had my own plan. What boys failed to realize was that girls turned down boys' advances every day. A young boy's hopes of getting ass were enough to make him betray many a friend. Tony didn't know that two of his so-called "boys" had already approached me. So I took Trey Watts up on his offer. Tony had already taken my virginity in the ninth grade, so in our sophomore year, I didn't feel bad about letting Trey hit this good stuff. Knowing that slut Monica, Tony had definitely hit that. Trust me, she wasn't a slut by rumor. She was a slut by admission. She had no problem confirming the guys she'd slept with or stolen from another chick. She had to be the most hated female at school. So I called Trey up, he came to my house, we did it, and the next day we strolled through school together, with his arm around my shoulder.

Talk about an explosion. Tony was laughing it up with his boys, but when Trey and I did the proverbial "walk" down the main hall together with his best friend and my girls, Tony couldn't hide the fact that he was pissed. I thought he'd just be jealous and let it go, but no, he confronted Trey right in the hallway, and one of the biggest fights of the year ensued. In the end, Tony beat Trey like he had stolen something. I confronted Tony about being with Monica by showing him my cellphone pictures and, of course, revealing her admission of having slept with him. Begrudgingly, he admitted it, and we broke up.

After a couple of weeks, Tony came over to talk to me. He told me that he'd slept with Monica because he'd fallen in love with me. That made no sense to me, until he admitted he had got a lot of pressure from his boys to be a player, and this was the only reason he'd cheated. Also, he admitted that seeing me with another guy had made it clear to him that he'd rather be picked on for being in love than lose me. That was when I admitted that I'd been with Trey only out of revenge. We forgave each other. After that fiasco, we decided it was best to stay together and not let people influence how we felt about one another.

When I looked back now, it dawned on me that we were a lot more grown up then than we were now. For a couple of teenagers, we made wise decisions based on love. That was until the end of my junior year, when we decided that we were too horny to use a condom. That sole incident led to the conception of our son, Tony Jr. I was due in March, and with the sickness I endured due to the pregnancy, there was no way I could keep up with my studies. Since school was already a struggle for me, I decided to drop out.

Tony's parents and my mom were extremely pissed that we'd fallen into the same trap as our friends. However, Tony's parents wanted him to succeed, and my mom, the low-budget bitch that she was, just kept telling me that I wasn't shit and that I'd finally proved it. Tony's parents were supportive toward me, too, and told me that they'd help me with the baby, but Tony was still going to do the things he needed to do in his life, such as finish high school, go to college, and go to the Olympics, for which he'd finally qualified. I was fine with that, since he wanted to stay with me and our child. He was adamant that accomplishing his goals was for our future.

Tony graduated from high school with honors. While I was happy for him, I was a little jealous that while I had to care for our son, he got the benefit of graduating. Hell, I'd busted my ass in school too. In addition, he got the chance to celebrate his trip to the Summer Olympics with a banging senior trip. While he was training nonstop, Tony left the brunt of the responsibility for our son on me. His mom helped, but of course, she was just as focused on Tony's career as he and his dad were.

One day, I got a call that would change our lives forever. The week Tony was set to leave to compete for the Summer Olympics, he went out to hang with his boys after we had gotten into an argument about him spending less time with his boys and more with the baby. Apparently, they drank a lot, and Tony swerved as he went around a sharp curve in the road and got into an accident. Although I was distraught, the fact that he was still alive was a great relief. That was, until I got to the hospital.

"Mrs. Light!" I screamed when I saw Tony's mom in the hallway outside Tony's room.

She hugged me and took the baby out of my arms as tears poured down my face. "He's in the room," she cried.

"Is he all right?" I asked through my tears.

"He's alive but . . ." Her voice trailed off as tears flowed down her face.

"But what?"

She shook her head, unable to speak, as she slowly sat down on a bench with the baby. An eerie feeling tapped at the pit of my stomach as I headed toward the room and the unknown. When I walked in the room, I found Tony literally in tears as his dad held his hand while praying and comforting him.

"Tony," I said softly, causing them both to look up. I rushed to his side. "I'm so glad you're all right."

"All right?" he said, his voice filled with disgust. *"All right!"*

"You could've been killed, baby. I was so worried," I wailed, grabbing his hand.

He quickly snatched it away. *"This is your fucking fault!"*

"Wh-what?" I asked in disbelief.

"If I had never gotten into that argument with you, I wouldn't have been drinking, and I wouldn't have done this!" he screamed.

I looked at his dad for answers, and he obliged. *"Tony's leg was crushed in the accident. He's going to have to have surgery to repair the damage."*

"Oh God!" I cried.

"So there goes my fucking future!" Tony yelled.

My heart dropped, but just as quickly, I hoped to offer him some comfort during this time of despair. Rubbing his shoulder, I said softly, *"You'll get better—"*

"You are so damn stupid!" he yelled, interrupting me. *"Who gives a damn about being better? I won't be able to run. Not now, not later, and not ever again!"* he screamed.

"Tony, calm down. It's not her fault. She loves you," his dad said sternly. Seeing the dejected expression on my face, his father continued, *"I'm sorry, LaMeka. Maybe you should leave.*

*You can come and see him when he's a little
calmer and levelheaded."*

*Not up for an argument, I agreed. "I love you,
Tony."*

*He rolled his eyes as I turned and walked out
of the room. I took the baby from his mom and
headed home.*

That moment changed Tony. During the surgery, he had so many pins and screws placed
in his leg. The physical therapy after that was
excruciating, to say the least, and despite all
of that, he still walked with a slight limp. Even
though he didn't want it, he was able to get disability due to his injury. He hated being labeled
as a cripple and felt that being on disability did
just that. Worst of all, Tony refused to go to
college, even after being offered an academic
scholarship, since he could not, for obvious
reasons, accept the track scholarship. After a
year of staying home, drinking, and smoking
weed, his dad kicked him out of the house. That
was when he came to live with Tony Jr. and me
in public housing. We continued to live off the
system, and we used his disability checks as an
additional source of income.

Then I got pregnant again with our second
child, LaMichael. That was also around the
time I noticed something odd with Tony Jr. He

would sit in a room full of kids, such as at his pediatrician's office, and not interact at all. He'd just gaze at everything around him. I knew he wasn't blind or deaf, because he could walk by himself and he responded when I called him. He would mimic sounds and repeatedly say, "Mama." After having him tested by specialists, I found out that he was autistic. When I told Tony, the news seemed to send him into an uncontrollable downward spiral. After finding that out, he became someone no one knew.

"He's what?" he asked, confused, while he drank out of the orange juice carton as we stood in the kitchen.

"Autistic. Tony Jr. has autism," I cried as I sat holding the test results in my hands.

"What the fuck is autism?"

"It's a developmental disorder that affects certain neurological functions of the brain, like the ability to communicate or interact," I explained.

He looked dumbfounded. "So you're saying my son has a disorder, and he can't get his mind right?"

"Why you gotta put it like that?"

"Are you telling me my son is a fucking retard?" Tony yelled at me.

His comment pissed me off, but somebody had to remain calm. Instead of lashing out, as he had done, I decided to attempt to have an adult conversation. "No he's not. Most autistic kids are very intelligent."

"So he's a damn weirdo?"

That was it! "God, Tony! Do you have to be so harsh about this? He's our son, and this is very real. Be serious and stop trying to overanalyze this! And stop disrespecting our son!"

He shot a glare at me. "Oh, and look who just stepped off the short bus themselves. You've been around these doctors so much, you're starting to sound like one. I'm the one who had to help you with your English, or have you forgotten? I'm the one who graduated, so stop treating me like I'm just some illiterate hood nigga!"

My mouth flew open. We'd been arguing more and more, but Tony had never been so disrespectful. Sure, I wasn't a self-proclaimed genius like he was, but I was nowhere near stupid. I just didn't like school, and it wasn't solely my fault that I had never graduated from high school. So to say I was pissed was an understatement.

My anger boiled over inside as I thought of all the sacrifices I'd made for him and our children, and I slapped him on the cheek. "Don't you ever talk to me like that again!"

Tony rubbed his face and glared at me. Then he did something I'd never thought he'd do. He slapped my ass right back. "And you keep your fucking hands off me. He probably got that shit from your ass anyway!"

He hit me so hard, it felt like he'd knocked my eyeballs out of their sockets. I sat there for a second, stunned not only by the impact of his hand but also by the fact that he'd actually hit me and spoken such harsh words.

"I should—" I began angrily, but he interrupted me.

"You should what?" he asked, walking up on me, daring me to test him.

I remained silent, froze in place.

"Say something!"

I coiled up, afraid that he'd beat the hell out of me. "Why are you doing this?" I asked as tears began falling down my cheeks.

Rather than respond, he huffed and walked to the door. "Fix my son, and you better not be telling all your little friends about this shit. The last thing I need is for people to know that my son is mentally challenged," he said sternly. Then he walked out of the kitchen.

I wanted to go kick him in his bad leg. How dare he accuse me of giving this condition to my son! On top of that, he acted like I alone would be responsible for our son's care going forward.

During the year after we found out about Tony Jr., Tony's behavior didn't get any better. It was damn near unbearable to deal with him, Junior's autism, and a small baby all at once, but I loved Tony and figured I'd stay by his side until he got over the funk he was in. And here I was now, still waiting for this funk to end.

As I was preparing dinner, my phone rang. "Finally calling me back, huh?" I asked, thinking it was Charice. She had never called me back last Sunday, even though she had said she would.

"This is my first time calling you," Tony said.

"Oh! I thought you were Charice. How was your flight?"

"Good. I'm at the hotel now. This shit is nice, for real. Ryan and the fellas will be here tomorrow. You know they got that game in Dallas tonight."

"Yeah."

"How are the babies?"

That question brought a smile to my face. It was the first time he'd shown genuine interest in their well-being in a long time. "They are fine. LaMichael is playing, and Junior is watching television."

"You should try to get Junior to play with LaMichael, instead of allowing him to sit and watch television," he said, his tone slightly rude.

I huffed. "I'm trying to cook for them right now, Tony. Not all of us have the luxury of flying out for days on end to chill with our friends and act rich and fancy," I said, smarting off, taking a dig at him.

To my surprise, he came right back at me. "No, not all of us do. Those of us who don't could be a little more responsible, don't you think?"

I looked at the phone. I could've reached through it and slapped him. "You're right. Since it seems I'm the only responsible parent around here, let me get back to cooking and taking care of my babies, while you get back to relaxing in a hotel that your boy is paying for."

He sucked his teeth. "I could've afforded it myself if I still had a career," he mumbled.

"Be safe and stay out of trouble," I said and ignored his comment.

"I'll call you and check up on you in a couple of days," he told me.

A couple of days? So that's the game we're playing now? I thought. "Why a couple?"

"I just said it. I mean, I'll probably call you tomorrow," he said, sounding aggravated.

"*Probably*?" I asked with a smirk. "Humph, okay. I guess I'll *probably* answer."

"I guess you probably *better*," he said sternly.

"Bye, Tony," I said and hung up in his face.

I didn't have time to go back and forth with him, and I'd grown rather tired of his awful attitude problem and mood swings. He had become unpredictable, like Georgia's weather in the winter. You know, you'd wake up in the morning and it would be freezing cold and cloudy, but by noon the sun would be out, and by evening it would feel like summertime. Yeah, he was like that, brand new at any given hour of the day. But what I did know without a shadow of a doubt, was that something was going to have to change.

Trinity

As I sat there, I admired my handiwork. Although I hadn't gone to art school, I had a talent for drawing and designing tattoos, and I missed doing it for extra cash. One word as to why I had stopped: Pooch. He had hated the fact that niggas were around me all the time, asking for a design, so I had stopped. Every now and then, a female would want a design, and I'd happily oblige, but for now, all I could do was admire my previous work.

"Why are you looking at me like that?" Terrence asked, with his signature smooth smirk.

His shirtless body showed off three of my designs. One was on his back, another was on his arm, and the last one was tattooed on his chest. While I was waiting for him to get the kids ready to go, the tattoos had caught my eye.

"I was just looking at my work, the tats," I answered.

"They are still the freshest thing to me. You need to get serious about that and pursue it."

"You know how Pooch is," I said and waved off his comment.

He tensed up and turned to look at me. "Fuck Pooch," he said in a serious tone.

Nope, after an entire weekend with Pooch and his antics, I wouldn't go through the BS again with Terrence. I rolled my eyes and fanned him to continue what he was doing. "Can you hurry up? I need to get home."

He gave me the evil eye before turning his attention back to our son. "All right, little man, you're all set. You like the jacket I bought you?" he said to Terry.

"Yes, Daddy." Terry smiled. "It's the bestest."

Swiping his hand across Terry's freshly cut hair, he smiled. "*Best*, little man. Just *best*," Terrence said, correcting him. "I'll pick you up from school tomorrow."

"Can I stay with you, Daddy, please?" Terry begged, hugging his leg.

Angry, I jumped up. "Don't start that crap, Terry—"

Terrence shot a hard glare at me and put his hands up. "Fall back, Mama. I got this. Dude just wants to be around his daddy," he told me. I did what he said as he turned back to Terry and kneeled down so that they were at the same eye level. "Look, man, you know you live with your mommy. I'm always going to be here for you. That's my word. Now, your mommy misses you, so spend some time with her and your sisters, and tomorrow it's me and you, okay?"

Terry smiled. "Okay, Daddy," he said, hugging him tightly.

"I love you, little man."

"I love you too, Daddy."

Terrence stood, then picked up our daughter, Brittany, and hugged her. "You know I love you too. I would get you tomorrow, but you have to get your hair done. Daddy's princess has to be cute all the time."

She laughed. "You silly, Daddy. I love you too," she replied.

"That's my princess," he said, then placed her down and zipped up her jacket.

Although I fought this battle of the kids not wanting to leave their daddy all the time, I couldn't help but admire the relationship he had with them. Terrence was absolutely wonderful with our kids, and they loved the hell out of him.

Terrence handed me their overnight bags. "Let's go, kids," I said as I turned to go.

"Hold up." He stopped me.

When I turned back around, he slipped money into my hand. Spreading the crisp bills, I counted out five hundred dollars. I gave him the side eye, because I knew that was a stretch for him. He was a brickmason, and with all the recent rain, business was slow.

"You don't have to give me that much. You know they're well taken care of."

Terrence stood back, with a grimace on his face, and slid his thumb across his lips before he spoke. "Yo, kids, go to your bedroom for a second," he ordered. They shuffled off to the bedroom.

Lord knows I didn't have time for this argument. "I gotta go, Terrence. Look, take a couple hundred back. I know business is slow right now."

The heat that radiated off him could've scorched my soul. "Let me tell you something. Those are *my* kids, not *Pooch's*. I will take care of them, and I don't need that nigga to do shit for me. So you taking this money, and I don't want to hear a damn thing about it."

Was it always going to be a battle between those two? Beyond frustrated, I blurted, "Well, who you think was taking care of them when you were locked up?" The moment the comment came out, I regretted it, because I knew I was wrong for saying that.

Terrence looked as if he could spit fire. Instead, he took a deep breath to gather some composure. "That's fucked up, yo! I know I messed up really bad in more ways than one, but you ain't gotta throw that up in my face. You know how I feel about my kids, Trinity."

Feeling remorseful, I grabbed his hands and expressed my regret. "You're right, and I'm sorry. I shouldn't have said that. I'm just tired of dealing with the attitude from you and Pooch toward each other. I want him to respect that you are my kids' father, and I want you to respect that he is my man."

"I do respect that. I just don't like the fact that that nigga thinks he owns you, and I know he really don't like having my kids around," Terrence retorted, fuming.

Hell, I couldn't argue the point, so I didn't try. "He is who he is, Terrence, but he takes care of all of us."

"That's cool. He's supposed to. But I also take care of mine. So take that money and do what you need for my kids. I saved it up." He paused for a moment. "I'm not hurting, and no, I'm not slanging," he assured me.

"All right." I nodded my head in agreement. "Come on, kids," I shouted, and they came out of the bedroom. "See you tomorrow," I told Terrence.

As the kids and I were walking out the door, Terrence reached for my hand, and I came to a stop. "I meant what I said about messing up in more ways than one."

My heart began racing. *I know he doesn't mean what I think he means*, I thought to myself. "Yeah," I said, careful not to stir whatever he was trying to cook.

Sensing my apprehension, he released my hand. "Be easy, li'l mama."

It'd been years since he'd called me that, and it made me blush. "You too, Dreads."

He smirked and rubbed my chin with his thumb. "Damn. You bringing me back."

I quickly jumped back. *What the hell?* Was that a tingle in my coochie that I just felt? Oh, no, I was not going to let Terrence ignite some kind of old-ass flame over here. I had to get away from this nigga . . . *fast*.

"I gotta go," I said, then quickly walked toward the kids, who were way ahead of me now.

"I bet you do," he said sarcastically.

"Good night, Terrence," I threw over my shoulder as I headed down the hallway, toward the main entrance to the building.

After getting the kids in my Mercedes, I sat behind the wheel for a moment to collect myself. I put my hand down my pants. Yep, I was moist. How in the hell did that happen? I wasn't trying to get caught up in any mess between Terrence and Pooch. Besides, I loved Pooch, and I wasn't looking back. I just needed my pussy to remember that.

I jumped at the ringing of my cell phone. "Oh shit!" After I yanked the phone out of my pocket, I took the call. "Hello?" I answered frantically.

"Everything okay with you?" Terrence asked.

"Yeah. Why?"

"You haven't pulled off yet, so I was just checking."

"You don't have to watch us until we leave. We're fine," I replied.

"Looking out for you and my kids will always be my responsibility," he said seriously.

"Well, thank you."

"I don't do it for your thanks."

"I know."

"Trinity—"

Suddenly, my line beeped. I noticed it was a call from Pooch. "Hey, Terrence, I gotta go. Pooch is calling me," I interrupted him.

"Okay. I'll holla at you tomorrow."

"Peace," I said before clicking over. "Hey, babe. What's up?" I said to Pooch as I started my car.

"What the fuck is taking you so long to pick up the kids?" Pooch asked angrily. "You've been gone thirty minutes. He lives only ten minutes away."

"Damn, Pooch. The kids weren't ready, and you know how Terry is about his daddy," I explained in an irritated voice. "I'm leaving now."

"Fine. Pick up some Popeyes on the way home. Get me the usual."

"A'ight. You know I gotta stop at Mickey D's for the kids."

"Yeah. Hurry up, though. Princess is whining, and you know I can't tolerate that shit for long. Besides, I gotta eat. I got some business to handle tonight."

"I thought you said you were spending time with me tonight," I whined.

"Something came up with my dude Tot," he explained. Tot was one of Pooch's connects. Tot was nowhere near his real name. It was a name Pooch had given him in case there were ever wiretaps. I figured Tot was in town to help Pooch re-up.

"A'ight. I'm disappointed, though."

"I'll make it good for you, babe. You know I always do," he said. "But hurry up and get here with the food."

"A'ight. I love you, Pooch."

"Love you too, babe. Remember that shit," he said before he hung up.

Lucinda

My drive home from my visit to Piedmont Tech was a somber one. My meeting had gone well, and I loved everything Piedmont Tech had to offer. The counselor had been nice, and the tour had been more than I could've expected. The only problem standing in my way was my schedule. I had been all set to fill out all the paperwork when the counselor had sat the course book in front of me.

"So you'd have to take English, math, and a science to start. All those classes are scheduled between eight a.m. and three p.m. on Mondays, Wednesdays, and Fridays," she'd said.

My heart had dropped. "Are those all the class times that are available?"

"Yes, I'm afraid so."

"I can't take night classes or late afternoon classes?" I asked, hoping on the off chance that she'd overlooked part of the schedule.

"No, sweetie. These are daytime classes only," she informed me. "Is there some kind of conflict?"

"It's just that I work from nine to one."

"I see. Does your company offer more than one shift?"

"Yes, they do."

"Well, perhaps you can get your work schedule changed to accommodate your school schedule. Why don't you speak with your supervisor at work first and then let me know?"

I couldn't help but feel disappointed that I wasn't able to enroll at that moment. "Okay."

Noticing my expression, she patted my hand sympathetically. "Lucinda, it's not the end of the world. You will be at Piedmont. Just you wait and see."

Even though I put my best face on in front of the counselor, I was still disappointed, since I had thought I'd be walking out of that office as a college student. On my way home, I had to pick up Nadia, who was with my mom, so I called ahead and explained the college situation to my mom. She encouraged me but couldn't offer a solution. However, she did resolve one issue for me; my mom made sure Nadia was good and full before I got there, so I didn't have to worry about feeding her. That was a blessing since I had only thirty-five dollars in my bank account, and I still needed gas, milk, bread, and some juice for Nadia until I got paid on Friday. That was two days away, which was a hell of a long time to wait when you were living paycheck to paycheck.

"We have to stop by the store first before we go home, okay?" I explained to Nadia once I got her settled in the backseat.

"Okay, *mami*. Can I have some Starburst?" she asked happily.

"I'll see, okay? No promises."

"Okay," she replied. "*Mami*? Why didn't Daddy pick me up like he said?"

I gazed in the rearview mirror questioningly. I knew I had heard her right, but I was puzzled that she had asked this, so I didn't have a quick response.

And so she continued, "You told me Daddy was going to pick me up. Why didn't he?"

"I think he had to work," I answered, trying to mask my anger.

I hated to lie to Nadia, and that fucking Raul always put me in that position. Sometimes I wanted to tell her the truth and come right out and say, "Because your father is a deadbeat, and he can't take care of himself, let alone you." But I was not going to give Raul the satisfaction of knowing that I was the one who had upset Nadia.

That selfish bastard was going to have to ruin his own relationship with his daughter without my help, and it seemed he was well on his way.

"So is he going to pick me up when he gets off work?" Nadia asked, pulling me out of my thoughts.

"I don't think so," I replied as I pulled into the grocery store parking lot.

"But why?"

"Because he already missed his time frame."

"But why?"

"Because I think he had to work. Remember I told you that."

"But why'd he have to work if he was supposed to pick me up?"

Damn, she was worse than the police. "You know what, little missy? You ask too many questions."

"You said there's no such thing as a stupid question, *mami*."

"I didn't say it was stupid. I said you ask too many questions," I replied as I got her out of the car.

"You also said I could ask you whatever I wanted. Now you say it's too many. So is it too many because I'm asking stupid questions, or too many because . . . why, *mami*?"

Exhaling deeply, I knew I had to end this quickly. "*Ay, Dios. Por favor. No tantas preguntas!*" I told her. "It's just that *mami* needs to think about what it is she needs to get at the store, okay?" Nadia was a bright child who could drive you completely insane, in a good way.

"Okay, Mommy. I promise not to ask any more questions *if* I can get some Starburst," she said, trying to hustle me.

"Okay. Deal," I agreed, just to change the subject.

"Yes!" she exclaimed, then took my hand. We ran across the parking lot and into the store.

After getting my odds and ends, and Nadia's Starburst, and putting gas in my car, we headed home. To my surprise, her raggedy father was sitting on my stoop when we got there.

"Daddy!" Nadia exclaimed as she ran full force ahead to Raul.

"Nadia! Wait!" I yelled, to no avail. She was already in Raul's arms.

"'Sup, *hija!*" Raul exclaimed, hugging her.

"*Nada, papi.* I thought you were at work."

Raul looked at me, and I gave him a look that said, "Go along with it." He looked back at Nadia with a nervous smile. "I was." He hesitated. "But I got off early just to come and see you. I'm sorry I couldn't pick you up earlier."

She smiled brightly. "It's okay. I thought you didn't want to see me."

Raul kissed her cheek. "Never that. You're my baby doll."

"I love you, *papi*," she said, hugging him tighter.

"I love you too," he said to her.

That was when I got pissed. Wasn't this the same man who, a few hours ago, had told me he couldn't pick up his child, because he had other things to do with his time? Yep, this was the same man, Raul Deadbeat-Ass Garcia. Now he had the nerve to sit here and act as if he had so much love for her. I could've slapped the hot piss out of his ass. Instead, I planned on giving him a piece of my damn mind.

"Nadia, here is your Starburst. Go inside the house and then go to the bedroom and read a book, okay?"

"Yes, *mami*," she replied before taking the candy and trotting inside.

As soon as she was out of earshot, I turned and laid into Raul. "I'm not covering your ass anymore with her," I said sternly to Raul while pointing my finger in his face. "She deserves better from you."

He dismissively fanned my finger away. "I didn't come to argue." He reached into his pocket. "I got my child support."

Shocked, I calmed down. And I eased up. Usually, child support was something I had to track his ass down for, as if I was a damn bounty hunter. This time he had actually shown up at *my* house with it. Wow!

"Ahead of schedule?" I asked in amazement. That was, until I saw how much he had brought. I should have known it was too good to be true. He just would *not* do right. "Um, Raul, you're about a hundred and fifty dollars short."

He gave me that usual dumb look he plastered on his face when he was about to fib, so I waited for the lie to come. "I know, but this is all I could spare. I'll try to get—"

I put my hand up to interrupt him. "How do you need money when you live at home with your mom?"

"I have expenses too, Lucinda," he said with an attitude.

With my neck drawn back, I leaned my head to the side and placed my hand on my hip. "Yeah, you do, and the number one expense is your child," I said angrily. "And you can take the bass out of your voice when you're talking to me."

Ignoring my attitude, he continued with his own. "Like I was saying . . . I'm *trying* to get up the rest," he said in the same dismissive-ass way as he again fanned my finger out of his face.

The one who wanted to go ham on his ass was me! I felt the heat rise from the bottom of my feet to the crown of my head, but instead of activating ghetto mode, I tried to reason with him. My hope was that if he understood the dilemma, he'd follow through on the promise he'd made to me earlier this week. Times were hard, and I needed him to do his part.

"Okay, listen," I said calmly, and surprisingly, he gave me his undivided attention. "Her day-care payment is due on Friday, and I do not have the extra money to pay for it. I have some other bills to pay. You promised to have my back this week. You *promised*."

"And I'm going to . . . I just don't have it all right *now*," he lied.

"Well, if not now, *when*?"

He shrugged. "Soon."

This sum-ma-ma bitch! Fuck it! I was too tired and frustrated to stand there and argue with his ig'nit—yes, ig'nit—ass any further. He had bypassed regular ignorance years ago.

"If they ask me about the day-care bill, I'm going to point them in your direction," I said sarcastically.

"Whatever, man! Let me just go in here and say good-bye to my baby. Can I do that without you bitching and moaning about it?" he said. Then

he went inside without waiting on my response.
I rolled my eyes and followed him inside.

"I have to go, Nadia," he said when he found
her in the living room.

"But I wanted you to play with me," Nadia
whined.

"I know, and we'll have another day to do all
that. I promise you that. But for now, just be
good and get ready for bed. You have school
tomorrow."

"Okay, *papi*. Can you read me a bedtime story
before you leave?"

He smiled hesitantly. "Sure," he responded,
looking as if he didn't want to.

She produced a book from behind her back as
he sat down on the sofa with her.

While he read, I took my items into the kitch-
en and looked at my checking account register,
which read $9.60, the entire balance of my
account. As I looked back and forth between the
bank account register and my shorted child-support payment, I tried to figure out how in the hell
I was going to make a dollar out of fifteen cents.
The longer I looked at this grim picture, the
more pissed off I became. I wanted to run into
the living room and whip Raul's ass, and only
one thing stopped me: Nadia's laughter. Were
it not for the fact that I knew just how much

Nadia loved him, he would be residing in Grady Hospital tonight. That little girl was my *life*, and I would *never* do anything to upset her. Even if it meant that I had to swallow my anger to allow her the few moments of joy she got to experience with her so-called father. My love for her far exceeded my hatred for him, and since she wanted to spend time with Raul, I did not interfere.

I just didn't know how I was going to do this by myself anymore. Raul could run up in here like he was the best daddy in the world, and I had to deal with paying my cell phone, electric, and car insurance bills this Friday. Not to mention that I was probably going to be stuck with coming up with the rest of the day-care money. All I asked was that he took care of that one bill—I had the rest—and he couldn't even do that. Tears of hurt and anguish filled my eyes as I listened to Nadia giggle at his silly-ass sound effects as he read the story.

As I opened my empty refrigerator and stared at its contents, the sound of Raul's voice surrounded me. The sight of my week-old milk, wilted lettuce, two slices of bread, and half a pitcher of Kool-Aid infuriated me even more. This was no way to live. While he sat down to a home-cooked meal at his mom's house every night, I had bread and no meat, old milk and no cereal. Kool-Aid with no *food*. I needed the extra money from my paycheck to put groceries in the house. If Raul had given me my full child-support payment, I could pay the day-care bill. I could not turn to my parents for help. My father, or lack thereof, was going broke to care for Rosemary, a child that wasn't his, while my mom couldn't afford to spare any money, since she was the sole provider for my sisters and brothers.

How could Raul treat Nadia like this? Did he not know the pain it caused me when she asked for simple things like Starburst and it was a stretch for me to give her such things since he refused to do his part? Did he even care? My shorted child-support payment told me the answer. Hell to the no! If there was one thing Raul had been completely consistent about, it was that he didn't give a damn about anybody except Raul.

I wiped my tears and filled my refrigerator with the few items I was able to purchase today and wondered how I was going to put more food in the refrigerator this week. After paying all the bills, I would have no money left. Something had to give.

It looked like I was going to have to ask Trinity for help again. I hated to ask her for money. Although she didn't mind, I hated being indebted to anyone. I didn't like borrowing drug money especially. She was my girl, but she was playing with fucking fire by dealing with Pooch. You'd have thought she had learned her lesson after Terrence, but some people never learned. Oh well. In the interim, her relationship with Pooch was now going to benefit me too. No shade intended. I wasn't trying to use my friend. I was trying to survive for my daughter.

When I glanced at the time and saw how late it was, I pulled myself together long enough to go and break up the father-daughter meeting so that Nadia could get ready for bed. After Raul's lying ass left, I bathed Nadia and put her into bed. Then I showered and lay down to ponder the counselor's words. *You will be at Piedmont. Just you wait and see.*

I hoped so.

Waiting was all it felt like I was doing. I had requested a meeting with my supervisor at work, but for the past three days, he'd been tied up in meetings and traveling, and so now I was frustrated. However, this morning, when I walked into work and booted up my computer, I had an email waiting for me from my supervisor, asking me to meet with him at ten o'clock in his office. I couldn't wait for ten o'clock to roll around. I needed to get my work schedule changed so that I could take the next step toward my future by enrolling at Piedmont Tech.

"So, Lucinda, you wanted to see me?" my supervisor asked after I walked into his office and shut the door behind me.

"Yes, I did, Mr. Sharper," I said, sitting down in the seat across from his at his desk.

"I'm all ears. What's on your mind?" he replied.

"Well, I was wondering if there was another shift that I could work. Perhaps a night shift or an early morning shift," I said, getting right to the point.

He furrowed his eyebrows. "Why? Is something wrong with the shift you're currently working?"

"No. I love it. It's just that I was accepted into college and am eligible for financial aid and grants, but all the classes I need to take meet during my work hours. In other words, my work schedule would conflict with my college schedule," I explained, crossing my fingers that this meeting would go over smoothly with my supervisor.

"Well, congratulations, Lucinda. I love to see young adults excel, so let's see what shifts we have available," he said as he opened the employee schedule. As he examined the schedule up and down, he scratched his head and frowned. I knew I was in for some bad news. "Lucinda, it seems that all my early morning part-time positions are filled, and I don't have any night shifts available."

"Well, what about the afternoon?" I asked.

"I do have one five-to-eleven evening shift available, but that would include Saturdays," he responded.

This couldn't be happening. There was no way I could work from 5:00 to 11:00 p.m. I didn't have anyone who could keep Nadia that late, especially with my mom working a second shift. I might be able to arrange for my siblings to watch her for a couple of hours if I got off at nine o'clock, but they definitely couldn't watch her until eleven o'clock. And since I already worked at Susie Q on the weekends, I couldn't take a shift at the insurance company that included Saturdays. I wouldn't have time to do any coursework, and it would take more time away from Nadia on the weekend. Without a babysitter or her father's support, I had no one to watch her.

"Please don't say that," I whispered.

"I'm sorry. I mean, I have full-time slots, but they would probably still conflict with your school schedule. The only times I have available are seven to four, ten to seven, and two to eleven," he explained.

He was right. Those work schedules would conflict with the college schedule.

"What about another department? Surely, someone has something available."

He sighed and looked as if he was in deep contemplation. "Robin would request that you do a formal transfer, which takes three weeks, and Joe is at maximum staff right now. If they're hiring in any other departments, you would have to see if a position is available, apply, and then interview for it. The only other thing I can do is put in a word for you with Robin to see what she has available."

"Could you please do that? This is extremely important to me," I pleaded.

"Sure, Ms. Rojas. I can do that for you," he said happily. "I'm sorry I couldn't be of more assistance to you," he added, apologizing with sincerity. He reached his hand across the desk to shake mine.

Putting my best face forward, I shook his hand. "It's no problem. I understand."

"Okay, good. I will put in a word with Robin and get back with you."

"Thank you," I said as I stood. As I walked out of his office, I had only one small glimmer of hope, and I prayed that Robin would pull a rabbit out of a hat for me.

Just then, my cell phone buzzed. It was Trinity. "Hey," I said when I answered.

"You called me?" she asked as I hurried into the break room.

"Yes, hon, I did. I need a favor."

"Day care?" she asked quickly.

"Yeah. Raul didn't come up with his full portion—"

"No need to explain," she interrupted. "Stop by after work. I got you."

"I really appreciate this, Trinity."

"Aren't you my best friend?"

"Yes, but—"

"But that's what friends are for," she interrupted again. "I said I got you. Now stop stressing."

"I love you, girl."

"Back at you," she said before disconnecting the call.

As I headed back to my desk, I thought, *Okay, God . . . That is one favor down and one more to go.*

Charice

Ever since Ryan had canceled his plans to visit this weekend, I had been a blubbering mass of emotion. I didn't know why I was so shocked that he had canceled on us. I guessed a part of me still held on to the little bit of goodness I knew was in him. Ryan had been arrogant, conceited, and selfish even back then, but there was good in him. There was a side only I saw . . . and perhaps his parents did too.

I remembered when I had the flu during high school, Ryan had skipped school and had come to my house, armed with cans of Campbell's soup and a box of Theraflu. He had missed a chemistry test, which he'd been unable to make up, and during this time it had been crucial for him to keep his grades up if he was to get a scholarship. Yet he had stayed with me all day, had held me, made my food, and made sure I got plenty of liquids and medicine.

He'd always make sure to give me a kiss after every game, and he had constantly shared his dreams and aspirations with me. After singing me to sleep every night, Ryan had made sure I received a wake-up call every morning. That was the Ryan I knew and loved. That was the Ryan that I couldn't let go of, and I refused to believe that he could never go back to being the Ryan of then. I had it bad.

It was sad to say, but I even kept a picture of him on my desk at work, which was where I was at the present moment. Somehow that photo just kept me close to him.

"Is this Roderick Bell?" I asked as a man walked into my office, holding a six-month-old baby and a baby bag.

"Yes, it is," he responded as he sat down across from me and settled the baby on his lap.

"And you are?" I asked, flipping through the baby's chart.

"I'm his dad, Derron Bell. His mom is sick, so I told her I'd take him for his checkup and to pick up his WIC," he answered.

I looked at them closely, and they looked damn near identical. I was impressed that he had brought his son to his appointment. In my line of work, dads were few and far between. Hell, in my own life story too. It was refreshing to see a young man stepping up to the plate and doing what he had to do for his child.

"Well, I am Charice Taylor, his nutritionist. It is very sweet of you to bring him in," I said, introducing myself, as I played with baby Roderick.

He shrugged. "Ain't no thang to me. He's my little man. The way I see it, it's also my responsibility."

My mouth nearly hit the floor. "How old are you?"

"I'm nineteen," he answered. "Check it. I never had no pops. My moms was all we had, so I promised myself that when I had kids, I'd never be like that. I feel like I owe it to my son's mom to be there. I didn't like the way my dad did my moms and me, so I wasn't going to do my son's mom and my son like that."

"Raynelle is a very lucky young woman to have a man like you," I said, suddenly remembering the mother's name.

He shook his head. "Nah, you got me twisted. I'm not with Raynelle no more. I mean, she is psycho crazy. I mean not, like, for real, but she be buggin' on a brother, so I had to bounce. Regardless of that, this is my man, and Raynelle knows she can count on me. We may not have gotten along in a relationship, but we ain't got no problems concerning little man."

Before I knew it, tears were at the base of my lids. I quickly grabbed some tissues to keep from balling right then and there.

"Damn. You all right, Miss Lady?" he asked.

"I am so sorry. It's just . . . That was so touching."

He laughed. "Are you pregnant or something? You are mighty emotional."

"No, I am not." I laughed.

"Yo! Shit! Is that Ryan Westmore?" he asked excitedly as he pointed to the picture on my desk.

"Yep. The one and only."

"Man, I heard he was from here, but I never believed it." He stared at the photo. "You know him?" he asked.

"Yes. We dated," I revealed.

"And you still have his picture up? He must've been one hell of a boyfriend. Raynelle has a picture of me and little man, but she keeps it in his room, so it ain't blocking her from getting a man," he said with a chuckle.

With a shrug, I commented, "Hey, you can't blame her for that." After releasing a sigh, I answered his question. "Yeah, he was a good boyfriend back then."

"What happened? You seem to really care about him. I'm sure a brother in his position needs that kind of woman around him, especially with so many groupies waiting to get that money."

"Life happened," I said as I flipped through Roderick's chart again. "Sometimes men just don't know when they have a good thing."

"Sometimes women don't know either," he noted.

I understood where he was coming from. "I guess not, Derron. I guess not. Let's get started so you can get out of here and spend some real quality time with your son."

Once we had finished, I told him where to pick up the WIC vouchers. "It was a pleasure meeting you, Derron. And, little man, I will see you when you are one." I rubbed Roderick's head, and he smiled at me.

"Thanks, Ms. Taylor," Derron said, grabbing the baby bag. He stood and headed to the door, then walked back over to me and said, "For the record, Ryan Westmore may be a genius on the field, but he was dumb as hell for leaving you behind."

I laughed. "Honey, you are preaching to the choir!" I exclaimed, and then we gave each other daps.

It was a long Friday, and I kept thinking about Derron and how mature he was for a nineteen-year-old. Ryan was twenty-four and still a damn idiot. I couldn't blame it all on him, though. I was also to blame. I had not dropped these damn feelings I had for him, and I had not forced him to take care of his responsibilities, so I couldn't complain. It was just that I didn't want to fight him in court, where I would look like the desperate baby mama. I wanted him to *want* to take care of his children and, if I was being completely honest, be with me. If he was forced to do it, I still wouldn't be happy. My kids would be financially sound, but every mother wanted her kids to have a loving father, not a court-ordered one.

By the end of the day, I had made up my mind that it was time to put my personal feelings aside and make Ryan put up or shut up. Ultimately, it boiled down to a choice between my kids or my feelings. I chose my kids. That meant either he was going to take care of our kids or the media was going to get the story of the year at his expense. As I drove to my mom's house to pick up the kids after work, I felt buoyed by the decision I had made.

"Mommy!" the kids screamed as all three of them came running full speed to me when I stepped through my mom's kitchen door.

"I love you, Charity," I said, kissing my daughter. "And you, Ray, and you, Ryan." I kissed each of them. "Were you guys good for Grandma?"

"Yes," they said in unison.

I looked at my mom for confirmation—as if she would ever say they weren't. She loved my kids so much that I thought she loved them more than me at times.

"Of course they were good. These are Grandma's babies," she said, hugging them. "Do you all have your book bags and the treats that I gave you?"

"Mom, I told you to cool it with the sweets," I huffed.

"And I told you that these are my grandkids, and I will do no such thing. When you have grandkids, you'll understand," she said as the kids ran around gathering their things.

"Well, I guess someone has to spoil them, since their daddy won't," I said aloud without thinking.

My mom's mouth dropped. "Did you just shade the great Ryan Westmore? I'm in utter disbelief!" she joked.

I rolled my eyes and peered over her shoulder to see if the kids were within earshot. After reassuring myself that they weren't, I leaned over to her. "I'm going to do it, Mom. I'm suing him for child support if he doesn't willingly comply," I whispered.

My mom dropped her spatula on the kitchen counter and hugged me. "Thank God! What happened? What changed your mind?"

"I was slapped with a little dose of reality today. I had a nineteen-year-old come to my office with his son. He was no longer with the baby's mother, but he was so adamant about being a father to his son. I just couldn't see a man so young having that much maturity and depending on the system, while Ryan runs around making millions and acting like he doesn't even know his kids exist."

"Well, I don't know who this young man is, but I'll be damned, I love him!" she said excitedly.

"I'm sure you do."

She put her hand on my shoulder. "I know you love him, sweetie, but this is what's best. We can't help who we love, but you owe it to yourself and your kids to do the best thing, even if that means making the tough decisions. Prayerfully, through this, he will come around. Sometimes the best love we can give a person is tough love."

It was the first time my mother had shown that she truly grasped my feelings for Ryan and had empathy for me because I felt that way about him. For once, it made me feel as if she truly understood, and it brought tears to my eyes. It felt good to know that she didn't think I was crazy for loving him.

"You're right," I said, wiping my eyes, as she hugged me again.

I left my mom's house with a renewed sense of confidence and strength to carry out my plan to make Ryan be responsible for his actions. As I pulled up at my house, I noticed someone standing on my front steps. His back was turned, and I couldn't see his face. I was on the phone with my mom, and I told her a stranger was on the stoop. From her voice, I could tell she was as alarmed as I was. I brought the car to a stop, then decided that was a bad idea, but before I could drive away from the danger, Ryan Jr. jumped out of the car.

"Ryan!" I screamed as I pulled into the driveway. I jumped out of the car and ran after him.

"Daddy!" he screamed.

Ryan turned and faced us. "What's up, little man?" he asked as he picked up Ryan Jr. and hugged him.

"Oh, dear God! I was so scared! I didn't know who was on our steps," I said. "Ryan Jr., don't you ever do that again!"

"But I saw it was Daddy from the car, Mommy. Oh, please don't be mad," Ryan Jr. said.

Before I could answer, Charity and Raymond ran up to their dad. "Daddy!" they yelled in unison as they hugged him.

"Hey, Ray. What's up, dude?" he asked, putting Ryan down and hugging Ray.

"Nothing, Daddy. I missed you," Ray replied.

"I missed you too," he said.

"What about me?" Charity asked.

He put down Ray and picked up Charity. "I could never forget my princess! How are you, baby?"

She blushed. "Good, Daddy! I missed you too."

Ryan looked at me and smiled. "Hey, Charice."

I rolled my eyes. "What are you doing here?" I asked nonchalantly.

"I wanted to surprise my family," he replied as he put Charity down. The three kids gathered around his legs and clung to him.

"Oh, well, you have the wrong house. Your mom and dad live in a gated community across town," I told him.

His look turned serious. "I'm at the right house." He leaned in toward me and said in a low voice, "Don't do this right now."

"It's never a good time, according to you," I said, getting angry.

"Please, Charice," he begged, his tone apologetic.

I relented, letting out a sigh. That was when I remembered my mom was still on the phone. I put my cell to my ear. "Oh God! Mom, are you still there?"

"As if I would hang up after all that commotion."

"I'm sorry. It's Ryan," I told her.

"Uh-huh. I heard. Tell him we're suing him for child support," she said bluntly.

I rubbed my forehead. "I can't do this right now, Mom."

"Well, you're going to have to tell him."

"Charice, tell your mother I said hello," Ryan interjected. "I really need to speak with you, if you don't mind."

"Ryan said hello," I told her.

"Tell him I said, 'Go to hell,'" she responded angrily.

"Mom, I have to go. We're standing out here looking crazy, my truck is still running, and Ryan needs to talk to me."

"Hold your ground, baby."

"Uh-huh," I said before hanging up. I let Ryan and the kids into the house, turned my truck off, then brought our things inside.

"You should've told me you had stuff in the car. I would've gotten it," Ryan said, grabbing the kids' book bags from me at the front door.

I shot a hard glare at him. Enough was enough with this "Daddy's home" routine. "What the hell are you doing here?"

He sat the book bags down and faced me. "We'll talk. Just let me spend some time with the kids first, please. Can I do that? Then, when they're asleep, we can talk."

As much as I wanted to force him to have this discussion right now, the kids were excited and chomping at the bit to spend time with him. For them, I let it go . . . for the moment. "Fine."

Ryan took off to play with the kids, and that was exactly what he did. He played with them under my watchful eye as I made myself busy tending to the house to give them alone time. As dinnertime neared, Ryan ordered pizza, and we had a good time eating and watching a movie with the kids. After that, he played tea with Charity and then *Madden* on the PlayStation with the boys while I finished up the laundry and cleaned the kitchen. I needed to do something to keep myself from blowing up on his ass. These might be good moments or whatever, but I hadn't forgotten that this was an exception and not the norm. All of a sudden, he was here and playing Daddy? Oh no. He would not pop in and out of our kids' lives, and I planned to tell him so as soon as I could.

Once I was done with the kitchen, he helped me bathe the kids, read bedtime stories, and put them to bed. In minutes, all three of them were asleep, like the angels they were. Ryan and I went into the living room and sat down. The tension was so thick, you could cut it with a knife.

I plowed into him before he could speak. "So are you going to answer my question? What are you doing here?"

He pulled up his sleeves and moved closer to me on the sofa. Giving me that slick-ass, sly smile, he said, "It's like that?"

"Ryan, things have changed. I've changed."

"So have I," he claimed.

"Well, we can agree on that," I said sarcastically.

With his head bowed, he threw up his hands. "Okay, I deserved that."

"Oh, you don't want me to get started on the list of things you deserve or the list of things you don't deserve and never did," I said angrily.

He nodded. "I deserved that too."

Frustrated with just his presence, I pressed him again. "Why are you here?"

With his fingers intertwined, he leaned forward and looked over at me. "Charice, I've been thinking. Maybe I have been missing out on a wonderful life with you and the kids. They love me so much, and spending time with them like this just felt . . . I don't know . . . right. You know what I mean? I've really been thinking about this, and I think maybe we should see where this family thing could take us."

Did he say what I thought he said? *Bullshit. There's no way.* I had to paraphrase it aloud to be sure it wasn't my imagination playing tricks on me. "So you mean to tell me that after all this time, you want us to be a family? As in you want *me* and *you* to be together, as a *couple*, with *our* children?"

He gave a shrug and nodded. "Yes, that's what I'm saying."

My bottom lip was probably dragging on the floor. After all these years, and right after I'd finally decided to pursue child support, he was offering me my heart's desire. Was he for real? Nope. He couldn't be, I thought.

I frowned. "I don't believe that shit for one minute."

He moved even closer to me. "It's true, Ricey."

Aw, hell naw. He did not hit me with "Ricey." Now, that was a nickname I hadn't heard in a long time. He had called me Ricey on the day he told me for the first time that he loved me.

"Don't call me that. You lost your privilege to call me that."

"Maybe I did, but can't I at least have the opportunity to try to earn it back?"

"And what the hell do you think I've given you all these years? Opportunity got to the point that it stopped knocking and just sat down on your doorstep and took a damn nap!"

He laughed. "I can't argue with that," he said. His laughter ceased when he saw the expression on my face. I wasn't amused by or enthused about his revelation. His expression turned serious. "However, that was then. This is now. All I'm asking for is a chance to get it right," he pleaded, running his fingers through my hair.

Ooh, he knew my weak spots. Hands in my hair, his fresh breath as he whispered in my ear, tickling my senses, and the heat radiating off him were my kryptonite. I refused to look at him. If I did, I'd be a goner. Something about his mocha-brown skin and those sexy-ass dimples paired with those bedroom eyes melted my heart and my box every time. Even still, I felt my emotions sparking like firecrackers, and I felt myself giving way.

His other hand touched my thigh, and this heifer between my legs took over. She shut down my brain after scrambling its signals. I hated myself for succumbing to this. My hot box was moist just from his touch, and my resilience was completely gone. Still, I found the strength to try to fight him off.

"Stop, Ryan."

He got up and kneeled in front of me, which forced me to look at him. "I'm sorry, Charice. Please forgive me and take me back."

I forced my brain to reactivate and jumped up from the sofa. "You leave me with these kids for five years, and now I'm supposed to forgive and forget? I killed my baby or babies because I couldn't afford to support anymore children on my own, and that's supposed to be cool? Now I'm supposed to run into your arms, as if you'd been on some extended business trip and nothing had changed? Well, a lot has changed, Ryan, including my love for you!" I said sternly and turned to walk away.

Following behind me, Ryan grabbed my arm before I could get across the room. He pulled me close and kissed me passionately. Lord knows I tried to resist him. I promise I did.

"Stop," I mumbled as he continued kissing me.

"Is that what you really want?" he asked before he slipped his tongue in and out of my mouth. "I'm sorry, so sorry," he whispered in my ear, then kissed my lobe. Tears were in his eyes, and I couldn't help it. I gave in.

"Oh, Ryan," I moaned.

That did it. These fucked-up love feelings of mine were pouring out as his pheromones intoxicated me. All the anger and toughness I'd built up over the years fell down faster than the walls of Jericho. One touch from this man and it was as if we'd never broken up. How was it possible to still love this man this much? To still want him this bad? As we kissed with wild abandon, I couldn't stop this if I wanted to, and that was the thing . . . I didn't want to. The next thing I knew, we were in my bedroom, where Ryan undressed me from head to toe.

"God, you are still so fucking beautiful," he said in a raspy voice, admiring my naked body.

Shit. I wasn't the only one. All those training-camp workouts had him finer than I remembered him being. Trust me, I didn't think Ryan could get any finer.

"Aw, baby," I said, lifting my legs so he could enter me. Suddenly, it hit me. I wouldn't go through this again. *No glove, no love.* "Baby, do you have a condom?"

Ryan looked at me strangely. "No. Come on, baby. We don't need one. This is me and you."

I gave him a crazy look. "This was us three years ago—"

He bent down and kissed me, interrupting me. "I'm here now."

I wanted this, so I wouldn't stop it, but the fear of pregnancy forced me to pause. I sat up and looked in my nightstand. I found a condom and grabbed it. Since I worked at the clinic, I had brought some protection home, in case I got lucky enough to ever get "some" from someone. I hated to admit it, but the last man to fuck me was the one trying to fuck me now, the one who had fucked me in some form or fashion for eight years. Yep, Ryan was my first and only lover.

"Here," I said, offering him the condom.

"This shit is going to be tight. Damn, baby. I just want to feel you—"

Now I was on a hard pause. As bad as I wanted this, it would not go down if he didn't wear protection. I needed to feel as though what I needed mattered before we could move forward. If he refused to put my feelings first, then he would have to hit the door. Mentally, I prepared myself to be let down again.

"For years I've done what you wanted me to do. Do something for me for once. I need to know that you're serious about this thing, and I need to rebuild trust. I love you, Ryan. I always have and always will, but I have to start looking out for Charice," I told him.

He looked downcast, but then he kissed me, sat back, took the condom from my hand, and ripped open the wrapper. "If it will make you happy, then I will do it. I'll do anything for you, Ricey."

My heart sang. He was serious this time. Serious about me . . . about us. I fell back and gave him complete access to me. I felt just how

Bella felt toward Edward in the movie *Twilight*. At that moment, I felt that I was unconditionally and irrevocably in love with this man. I spread my legs with ease.

"Welcome home, Daddy," I sang to him.

"That's right, baby. Daddy's home."

The sound of my cell phone woke me up out of my slumber. I turned to see Ryan sleeping peacefully beside me in my bed, and I smiled. It hadn't been a dream. He'd returned, claimed me as his woman, and made passionate love to me for two hours. I had thrown everything I had into that lovemaking session. I had learned some great moves from a pole-dancing class I took to keep my body in shape, and the class damn sure paid off. For the first time, I had had Ryan screaming like a bitch! He was normally good for one climax, but I had successfully brought him to four in one night! He was so in shock that he tried to cuddle me all night like a damn baby, but his muscles were even heavier when he slept. Although I wanted to spoon with him, I needed to breathe, which was why I chose to get up to answer my phone now.

As I watched him rest, my feelings continued to bubble forth. I loved this man, and his earlier interaction with the kids and our lovemaking had made all the ill shit we'd gone through seem like water under the bridge.

I threw on my robe and went into the living room to answer my cell, to avoid waking up Ryan or the kids. "Hello," I said into the phone when I answered the call.

"He got to you," my mom said.

"Mom, it's not like that. He's back and wants to be a family," I protested.

"Oh really? A family, huh?"

I rolled my eyes. "Yes, he does," I said confidently. "You know what? I'm not going to sit here and let you dog my man. He has his faults, but we're a family, and we're going to work through them."

My mom gasped. "Wow! Your man, huh? You're a family now? And you're working through it? Humph, okay. I sure hope he put on a condom this time."

"You are certifiable."

"And I ain't the only one. Before you go riding off into the sunset with your *man*, please turn on the television, to channel six."

I picked up the remote, turned on the TV, and went to channel six. *Extra* was on.

"Now we bring you the story that everyone has been buzzing about. Caught on camera yesterday afternoon was the horrific breakup of supermodel Iris and her on-again, off-again beau, Dallas Cowboys star running back Ryan Westmore," the correspondent said. "In the footage, Ryan runs into Iris when she is on a date with actor Tobias Tate. The two had been suspected of fooling around in recent months. Westmore confronts Iris, and spectators say that Iris admits her affair with Tate and her love for him. After breaking up with Westmore, she leaves with Tate, with Westmore looking like he's just lost the game of his life."

"Actually, the *love of his life* sounds more like it," the other correspondent said jokingly. "It is rumored that Westmore was ring shopping for Iris, and he has publicly stated on more than one occasion that he is in love with her." Both correspondents nodded in agreement. "This has to be a big blow to him."

"Yep, and no one has heard from or seen the Dallas Cowboys star athlete since," said the first correspondent. "His publicist released a statement saying, and I quote, 'Ryan wishes nothing but the best for Iris. While he wished that they could've parted in a more amicable fashion, it was for the best. He asks that you please respect his privacy as he takes a few days to relax and take time for himself.'"

"Poor thing," the second correspondent said. "He's been known to be a bit of the bad boy type, but you have to feel sorry for him. He seemed to be quite smitten with Iris. Don't worry about it, Ryan. There are plenty more fish in the big sea."

"Yes, I'm sure he will not have any trouble finding takers. In other entertainment news . . ." The correspondent continued until I hit the POWER button on the remote.

"Looks like your boy came home to have you lick his wounds and sow his royal oats," my mom said. "Oh, but I forgot. You're a family now. It's mighty strange that he wants to be a family after he was publicly humiliated yesterday by his supermodel ex-girlfriend."

I couldn't find any words to say. It was eleven o'clock at night, and I had just confessed all my love for Ryan and damn near blown my back out giving him pussy when just yesterday this fool had been ready to marry another woman! Well, that is, until she had broken up with him.

I hadn't been following Ryan's life, because I couldn't bear to hear the stories about him being with other women. I had only watched his games, and if I heard his name on any type of news, entertainment, or gossip show, I changed the channel. I refused to read blogs about him unless they dealt strictly with his career. I was so disappointed, hurt, and so fucking livid!

"I knew he was lurking around for a reason, so I searched until I read about this story, which they said would play on *Extra*. Sweetie, he's played you again," my mom said regretfully.

I stifled my tears. "I gotta go, Mom."

"Sweetheart—"

"Bye, Mom," I said and hung up. I turned off the lights in the living room and sat in the bay window and gazed out. I wondered why I continued to let Ryan do this to me.

"Baby, what are you doing up?" Ryan asked as he came into the living room an hour later. "Come back to bed. I need to feel you next to me."

I turned and faced him, with my face drenched with tears. "Leave, Ryan."

He rushed over to me. "Baby, what's wrong?" he asked, attempting to wipe my tears. "What happened?"

I swatted his hand away. "Just make this easy for me and the kids and just leave now. I don't have the energy to argue, and I'm done wondering and hoping for the best when I know the worst is inevitable. Just leave and don't come back."

Ryan stood firm and crossed his arms. "No. Not until you tell me what happened. We were all good, I thought. I'm here and we're working on us and—"

"Do you love me, Ryan?"

"Huh?"

"You heard me. I've told you all night long, so I want to hear you say it to me. In order for you to come back to me, either you must love me or it's due to some other reason."

He shifted nervously. "I do, Charice."

"You do *what*, Ryan?"

"I have love for you. You know this."

"No. I asked you if you love me. I have a love *for* ice cream, Ryan. I love people," I said sarcastically.

"Where the hell is this coming from, Charice?" he asked in exasperation.

I shook my head. My mom was right. I was his fall back chick. "Maybe you loved Iris and were going to marry her before you caught her with that fine ass Tobias Tate yesterday."

It was as if I'd knocked the wind out of him. He stumbled back and then sat on the arm of my sofa. "That wasn't serious. She was just a girl."

"A girl who broke up with you in public yesterday. A girl who humiliated you so much that you had to release a press statement and come home to get yourself together."

"Charice," Ryan began sadly.

"Just admit it, Ryan. For Christ's sake, for once, tell me something real! I was your fall back chick. You knew I loved you, and you needed me to cater to your ego, didn't you? You had no intention of staying with me. Just tell me. Maybe if I hear you say it, I'll finally get it. I'll get that all we had and all we ever were and are going to be is a teenage love affair," I cried.

He shook his head. "Charice . . . I . . ." He sighed and nodded. "At first, yes. I came here to visit my kids, and yes, I needed my ego stroked. I knew that you loved me, and yes, I needed that. My breakup with Iris was hard on me, and I just needed to know that someone loved me. I knew you were the one woman who always would, but after spending time with the kids and after the incredible time we had, I honestly want to try, Ricey. I want to fall in love with you again."

He'd said it and actually admitted it. I'd never felt so liberated and heartbroken at the same time. As much as I wanted Ryan—wanted to love him and wanted what he was offering—I realized that he was no good for me. I was nothing to him but a holla-back chick. But I refused to let him holla anymore. Since my heart couldn't let him go, my mind did. I was drawing my line in the sand. I was done.

I stood up and walked over to Ryan. "Thank you."

He hugged me. "You're welcome. I plan on making up—"

I put my finger to his lips. "No, you're not. I want you to be a father to your kids. I want your support for them financially, emotionally, and physically. You owe them, but as for me and you, we're done. I can't be with you, Ryan."

"Charice, come on, baby. I admitted it, but I want—"

"This is not about you, Ryan," I said, cutting him off again. "It's about *me* and what I *need*. In a lot of ways, it's also about what I don't need. I love you and guess I always will, but I can't do this with you. Please leave."

"But, baby—"

"Go!" I hollered, interrupting him once more, as tears began to fall from my eyes.

He turned slowly and went into the bedroom, and when he returned, he was fully dressed. He sat down and wrote out a check.

"Here is a check for ten grand. I'll send six thousand dollars every month for the kids. Is that fair?" he said.

I nodded. "Yeah," I said, tightening my robe.

"We'll work out visitation when our heads are a little clearer," he told me as I walked him to the door. "Can I pick them up tomorrow?"

"Yes. From my mother's house at noon," I told him. "Do not stand them up."

"Charice, it doesn't have to be this way," he pleaded as I opened the front door.

"Yes, it does."

"I'm sorry, Charice. I truly, truly am."

"Me too, Ryan. Me too," I said and then shut the door in his face.

I lay on my sofa and balled my eyes out. Despite everything he had put me through, I loved him. It was the second time in one night that I felt just like Bella in *Twilight*. I was unconditionally and irrevocably in love with him. Nothing could change that . . . not even him.

LaMeka

I could barely stand the thought of having to go over to my mom's house; however, my sister, Misha, needed me. My mother and her live-in boyfriend were in a drunken rage, so Charice had let me borrow her Tahoe to go and pick up Misha. She had a couple of tests to study for and couldn't get any work done at home.

I loved my mother, but for no other reason than she was my mother. I looked at it like this: We couldn't help who God gave us as parents. We just have to love them in spite of it, because at the end of the day, we had only one mom and one dad. Now, it was hard to say that I loved my father, since I had never known him, so I gave my mom props for at least keeping us. She could have abandoned us, although sometimes I thought I would've been better off if she had.

My mom's problem was men. She loved to love them, and when she had a new man, my sister and I would fall to the bottom of her list, no matter how long she had known them. The worst incident had happened when I was thirteen. I was at the grocery store with my mom when she met Charles. One date and three days later, Charles was living with us as her new man. Only a week after he'd moved in, she had the nerve to tell me that they were getting married and that he would be my new daddy, so I had to respect him. *Respect* him? Hell, I didn't even *know* him, and neither did she. Oh, but she found out plenty about him when his actual wife showed up at our place three weeks later and dragged his cheating ass back home with her and their seven children.

Apparently, he was known to wander every time they had a huge fight, and it wasn't uncommon for him to shack up with a female until his wife hunted him down. It was a sad sight to see my mother clowning about how much they loved each other. She looked like a damn fool, and Charles's wife told her so. Charles confirmed it when he told my mom that she was too clingy and that he wasn't ever leaving his wife. He had just needed a space to clear his head. Wow! Yeah, right. After they left, my mom took out all her frustrations on me. She beat my ass for every little thing for the next week, but that was how it was growing up with her as Mommy dearest.

I hated that my sister had to be mixed up in our mother's mess. When I'd lived at home, I'd taken the brunt of the abuse and protected my sister. Ever since I left, she'd been all on my sister. If I could afford to take care of my sister myself, I would. Since I couldn't afford that, I did the best I could by picking her up or paying for her to take a cab over to my place so she could get away as much as possible, like today.

When I pulled up to my mom's house, I heard plenty of commotion and ran full speed up the front steps to find out what in the hell was going on. I burst through the door to see my mom's boyfriend, Joe, holding her back from my sister, who was curled up in the fetal position on the sofa, crying.

"What the fuck is going on in here?" I screamed.

"Get your slutty bitch sister out of my house!" my mom yelled.

"Don't you talk about Misha that way!" I shouted as I ran over to Misha and grabbed her. "Honey, what happened? What's wrong?"

She shook her head and buried it in my chest and held on to me. "Take me away, Meka, please!"

"That's right! Take her ass away. Both of you get the fuck outta my house!" my mom yelled.

"Joe! What's going on?" I shouted at him.

He put his shirt back on and zipped his pants. "Hell if I know."

My mom hit him in the back of his head. "Hell if you know? You muthafucka!"

Before I knew it, Joe grabbed my mom and shook her like she was a rag doll. "Hit me one more time and I'm gonna knock you the fuck out!"

"You won't do a thing to her!" I hollered at him.

Facing me, with malice in his eyes, he shouted, "I'll fuck you up too, LaMeka. Don't try me!" He pointed at me.

"Space and opportunity, Joe!" I said, daring him, with my arms outstretched.

Misha jumped up between Joe and me and grabbed me. "No! Let's just go!"

"Not until somebody tells me what happened," I said, looking from Misha to Joe and our mother.

My mom put her hands on her hips. "You wanna know what happened? Ask your slutty little sister. Oh, I forgot. She ain't gonna tell you." Her anger increased as she ran up toward Misha in a fight mode, and I stepped between them, blocking her from laying hands on my sister. "She's been fucking my man! Why you gotta fuck my man? I know your little slutty ass is fucking your little schoolhouse boyfriend, Vince! What?

He told you to get some experience or some shit?"

My mouth fell to the floor. I didn't believe it. I turned to Misha. "Did Joe rape you?"

Joe had taken a seat, but he jumped up after I posed that question. "Wait a minute now! I did no such thing. I can't help it if your sister is a freak like her mama."

My mom's hand connected with his face before the words could fully come out of his mouth, and he slapped her right back. Misha and I both yelled out in fear, because we both knew that this situation had escalated beyond our control. It had happened so fast that before we could really react, Joe was already clutching my mom by her neck and squeezing.

"Barbara, I told you to keep your hands off me! Didn't I?" he yelled, in a rage, as he gripped her neck.

Despite the fact that my mother fought back, Joe had a death grip on her. We knew that if we didn't come to her rescue soon, it would get a lot worse. The only thing we could do was take him on ourselves and try to stop him from killing our mother. Misha and I jumped on Joe, and with all our might, we tried to pull him off her.

"Let her go, Joe! I'll call the police on your ass! Let her go!" I hollered.

We managed to pry his hand off her neck, but then he knocked me and Misha onto the floor. My mom stood there, massaging her throat, gagging, and choking, as she tried to get herself together. Misha and I got up off the floor and ran to her aid. Luckily, Joe left her alone.

"Is this what you want, Mama?" I asked her. "A man who beats on you and molests your daughter?"

My mom looked at me, still huffing from the assault. "This ain't none of your business. Take your ass back over there with Tony, and take your slutty sister with you."

"Mom, please! Don't kick me out. It's not my fault," Misha pleaded.

Pissed wasn't even the word to describe my feelings. Here, we had stopped this man from choking her ass to death, and my mom was still being harsh to her own daughter. Nah. Something had to be said.

I pointed at Misha. "This is your child, Mother. Do you see her hurting over here?" I said sternly as Misha cried. "You need to do what's right."

After a few moments, my mom looked at me hard. "I am," she said as she walked over and wrapped her arm around Joe's waist. "Now, you take your sister. I can't deal with her anymore. I will not have her here sleeping with my man."

"Mom!" Misha cried, and I consoled her.

"Mom, hell! Leave my house," my mother yelled. Then she grabbed Joe by the hand and walked into the kitchen.

"Sorry, Misha," Joe threw over his shoulder.

"Meka!" Misha screamed as she held on to me for dear life.

All I could do was hold her in my arms tightly to let her know that I was there for her. In between her sobs, I offered her some comfort. "Sweetie, calm down. Go upstairs and get some clothes and your school stuff. I got you. I'm gonna take care of you," I said and hugged her before she went to get her stuff.

Neither of us said a word to my mom before we left. It was for the best. Besides, she'd made her decision, and I hoped to God she was happy with it. Lord knows, she was going to face it again. I prayed that I wouldn't turn out to be that kind of mother to Tony and LaMichael. I couldn't bear it if they grew up hating me.

The mood in the car was somber. I had to figure out what the hell I was going to do. Misha had to get to school every day, and I didn't live in her school district. Taking her in also meant an additional mouth to feed. Misha worked in the mall part-time and rode the bus back and forth from Mom's house, but the bus line wasn't available from my house. I definitely had to come up with a game plan.

"Why are you so quiet?" Misha finally asked.

"I have a lot of shit on my mind."

"You think I did what Mama said?"

"I don't even care about that. It doesn't matter what I think anyway. It matters what happened."

"What do you think happened?" Misha asked, exasperated.

I didn't want to answer. If I pursued this discussion, then I'd have to be prepared for her answer, and I really didn't want to have to deal with that, considering all the issues I was already pondering.

I swallowed, reached over, and patted her knee. "Joe is an asshole, and I knew sooner or later some man she brought home was going to look to the younger version of her for satisfaction. She never knows any of these lowlifes she brings home. I just prayed it never happened to you."

She squeezed my hand. "I love you, Meka."

"I love you too, Misha," I said. "What happened to you and Vince?" I asked out of curiosity.

She turned and looked out the window. "We broke up," she said plainly.

Sensing that she was bitter about it, I didn't pry. "Okay. You'll be all right."

She shook her head and changed the subject. "So how the hell am I going to do this . . . living with you and all?"

I drummed my fingers on the steering wheel as I pulled up to Charice's house. "I don't know, sweetie, but I'll think of something. Just leave it to me."

Did I even know what "leave it to me" meant for me and my family? How the hell was I gonna take care of two children and my sister? Tony would flip the fuck out when he found out Misha was going to be living with us. I just knew it. Could my life get any more complicated? *News flash to self. LaMeka, it already has.*

Now what the hell was I really going to do about it?

Trinity

Ever taken a step back, looked at your life, and wondered, *How in the hell did I get to this place*? That was how I felt. I loved my life. For all intents and purposes, I had nothing to worry about. Pooch took care of me and my kids, and Terrence was a good father to his two. I was blessed to have two men in my life that looked out for me and mine the way they did.

Yet it was beginning to be not enough. I was tired of sitting around the house and playing housewife, for two reasons. One, no matter how well Pooch took care of me, we weren't married, and I was aware of the fact that at any time he could get tired of me and cut me off. At that point, I would be in the same damn boat I was in when Terrence was locked up. Don't get me wrong. Pooch and I were straight, and he was crazy jealous, so I didn't expect that to happen, at least not anytime soon. Even so, I still didn't like the feeling of being trapped. I liked having my own.

Secondly, I wanted to get back to my own dreams of going to school and majoring in art design. I wanted to do something with my God-given talent. The only thing I'd done with it while I'd been with Pooch was draw murals, which I put in the kids' rooms. That had been fulfilling at the time, but that was done, and that feeling had long since worn off. In short, I needed to feel like I was doing something with my life.

"I am beat!" Pooch hollered, startling me out of my thoughts, as we pulled out of the parking lot at the mall.

I sighed. "Yeah, me too."

"You should be. Girl, you know how to shop a brotha into the ground! I gotta make sure I hustle double time to make up for the tab I spent on you today." He laughed as he reached over and rubbed my leg. "You wanna go to the Chop House for lunch?"

"Huh?" I asked. I hadn't heard a word he'd said.

"You been real low key today. What's going on, babe?" Pooch said.

"Just thinking."

He shrugged. "Just thinking about what?"

"Just thinking about art design and stuff. You know, thinking about going back to school and finishing."

He huffed. "You back on that again? Listen, you are fine. We damn sure ain't hurting for no money and shit. The only thing you need to do is shop 'til you drop, raise them babies, and be Pooch's girl. That's it."

"But what about what I want for myself, Pooch?"

He laughed. "You want me to buy you some coloring books or some stencils and shit? Damn, girl. It's a hobby. If it makes you feel better, you can draw on all the walls in the house."

Did this Negro really just say that? Wow. I rolled my eyes and sucked my teeth. "I'm just a joke to you."

Pooch picked up on my attitude and rubbed my leg again. "Don't act like that. I'm just play-ing. Look, you wanna draw and shit, then do it. Just don't be talking about no school and shit. I like you being around the crib, so go get you one of them recreational classes for 'bout an hour or some shit, so you can get out of the house. That's what you need. A little break will keep you fresh, and then you can be back at the house, waiting for Big Daddy. How's that?"

No, he was not looking at me with that Cheshire cat smile on his face, like he'd just solved my dilemma. I could've smacked his ass. He had no clue about what I wanted out of life, and I was starting to think he didn't care.

"Yeah, whatever." I shook my head at his ignorance. "You can grab you something to eat. I need to go to the nail shop."

He flailed his hand in frustration. "Come on. Princess is with my sister, and Terrence got his two. I can take you to eat, and then I'll take you to get your nails done." Luckily, his cell phone rang at that exact moment. "Talk to me," he answered after picking up his cell from the holder. "Yeah. Uh-huh. Yo, for real? A'ight. Yeah, I'll get up with Unc and tell him that Auntie is hungry. She gonna get fed, though."

Whenever he mentioned someone was hungry and was going to get fed, it meant that one of his boys was short on his money, and one way or the other, he was going to get his money. I already knew the lunch and the nail trip would be canceled, and I didn't mind one bit, either.

"You need to go, huh?" I asked after he hung up his phone.

He sighed and stroked my chin. "You know Daddy gotta handle his business. If I let one of these muthafuckas slide, then all of 'em think they can slide. I ain't having that shit. I gotta put one of my sons in place, and then I'll be free for you."

As if I was disappointed. Hell, I was glad I would be rid of his draining ass for a little while. "It's cool. I'll go get my nails done."

"A'ight," he said as we arrived at the house.

When we pulled up, I jumped out, grabbed my shopping bags, and carried them into the house. While I went into the house, Pooch stayed in his truck to make a few more calls. When I came back out ten minutes later and headed to my car, Pooch called me over to his truck.

"'Sup, baby?" I asked as I walked up to his window.

"You just gon' leave without a good-bye kiss?"

I leaned in and planted a nice soft kiss on his lips. "My bad, baby."

He shook his head. "Damn girl. Them lips so fucking soft. I'm gon' make sure I dick your ass down real good tonight. You've been holding out on me and shit. But I ain't having that shit tonight, babe. You feel me?"

"A'ight, Pooch. I feel you," I answered. It was true. Lately, I hadn't been in the mood to have sex with Pooch. "I love you."

He winked at me. "I love you too. Remember that shit," he said. Then he backed out of the driveway in his GMC Sierra Denali pickup truck.

After Pooch pulled away, I jumped into my car, happy as hell to be away from him for a little while. I loved Pooch, but he was damn sure a dream crusher. I hated what he did for a living, but I supported him nonetheless. Now, I didn't help out in his business, because I wasn't getting locked up for no one, but I listened when he let out his frustrations, and I encouraged him to handle things in a way that kept him off the police radar. Did I get that support in return? Hell no. That muthasucka offered to buy me . . . *a coloring book*. If I wasn't so pissed, I probably would've laughed at the stupidity of it.

Once I arrived at the nail salon, I couldn't help but be grateful. There was nothing like a little rest and relaxation to get my mind off Pooch and his foolishness. While I was waiting for my pedicure to dry, my cell phone rang. It was Terrence.

"Hey, Terrence. The kids all right?" I asked before he could say a word.

He laughed. "Damn. Hello to you too."

I giggled. "Oh hey. When it's your weekend with the kids, you usually don't call me. I figured if you were calling, then something was wrong."

"Naw, li'l mama, ain't nothing wrong, so you can calm down."

"So what do you want, Dreads?"

"Um . . . you gotta minute to stop by? I have to show you something. I promise it won't take long."

"Yeah, I'm almost done getting my nails done. I can be there in, like, twenty minutes, if that's cool."

"Yeah, that's cool."

"A'ight. See you then."

Within twenty minutes, I pulled up to Terrence's apartment. *I wonder what he wants to show me*, I thought as I got out of my car. I smoothed out my khaki mid-thigh shorts and slipped out of my pedicure flip flops and into my wedges. It was still pretty warm for mid-September, and I could be out enjoying the last bit of the summer weather right now, so I hoped this trip was worth it.

"What's up?" I asked Terrence as I walked into his apartment after he'd opened the door.

After he closed the door behind me and turned around, he joked, "Girl, it must be jelly, because jam don't shake like that!"

I laughed and gave him a playful nudge. "And that line is about as old and tired as you are. Where are my babies?"

"Taking a nap," he answered.

"Wow! You get them to do the things I can't, at least not all at once," I said, plopping down on his sofa.

He sat down beside me. "That's because I'm stern and you're not."

"Shit, as much as I fuss at them damn kids, I'm stern." I rolled my eyes.

"No, you fuss so your bark is loud, but you ain't got no bite. Daddy got bite to match his bark."

Feigning shock, I said, "Well, excuse me."

Giving me his classic smirk, he shrugged. "I'm just saying you are a pushover."

"Did I come here for you to talk about me?" I asked, copping a fake attitude.

He put his hands up. "My bad. I got side-tracked," he said, then picked up a piece of paper that was on the coffee table and handed it to me.

"What the hell is this?" I asked, looking over the paper. "God, family, wealth, forgiveness, and everlasting love," I read aloud.

"It's all the things I want to be symbolized in my new tattoo. These are the things that are important for me to have in my life, and I want you to design something that embodies all these concepts, please," he told me.

I nodded happily. "That's a good idea. I'll have to think about it, though. I need to research some symbols for each of these and see what I can come up with, but I got you."

"How much are you gonna charge me?"

I laughed. "We are so past that, aren't we?"

"You didn't charge me when we were a couple. We're not a couple anymore, and this is gonna require your time. So how much?"

I shrugged. "I don't know."

He reached into his pocket and pulled out a one-hundred-dollar bill. "This should cover it," he said as he handed me the money. Then he picked up his Coke from the end table and took a swig.

"You know this is too much money. You probably need this—"

He put his hand up, interrupting me. "What I need is for you to stop assuming that because I don't live out in McMansionville, USA, with you and Pooch, I can't afford to do the things I want to do or take care of my kids," he remarked. "And I still ain't slanging no dope, if that's what's on your mind."

I followed suit and put both my hands up. "You know what? You're right. My bad. I stand corrected, and I apologize. You don't have to worry about me doing that to you anymore. Besides, if you want to pay me for my hard work, who am I to refuse?" I said. I lowered my hands and put the money in my pocket.

"You damn straight! Make people pay you for your work, even me and Pooch. God gave you that gift. We didn't."

On that, we could agree. His viewpoint was a much- needed breath of fresh air. However, Terrence had always been philosophical like that. And I couldn't knock how he felt. He made sense a lot of the time and was usually right, just as he was now.

"How soon do you want it?" I asked him.

"Whenever."

"Give me about a week."

"Cool." He shrugged. "You know I trust you," he said, looking down at my feet. "Nice pedicure. I've always loved the color of jasmine on you."

My jaw literally dropped. "You remember that? It's been years since I've gotten my toes done in this color."

"How could I forget? It was the first color you picked out the first time I took you to get a pedicure. I loved it then."

"Damn. Thanks, Dreads. I can't believe you remembered that." I smiled and blushed slightly.

"I'm paying attention even when you think I'm not. That leads me to my next thing."

"What's that?"

He took a brochure from the coffee table and handed it to me. "I had to pick up one of my homeboys at his job around the way, and I thought I'd help you out a bit."

It was a brochure for the Art Institute of Atlanta, and it included an application. "Oh, my freaking God! I have been so busy that I didn't have time to stop there. Are you serious? You picked this up for me?"

"Yep, and I asked some questions. Classes aren't that bad. You can take morning, afternoon, or night classes, and tuition isn't bad, either. Plus, I'll work with you on the schedule and stuff. That's if you decide to go. I'll help you with the kids. I got your back," he said, encouraging me.

Screaming with excitement, I leaned in and hugged him tightly. "Dreads! Thank you so much! You don't know what this means to me."

He hugged me back. "You're welcome, li'l mama. I fucked up your dreams once, so I want to make it right."

"Aww, Terrence."

I went to pull away from him, but he held me in place and caressed me in his arms. It was as if something came over us. Staring into his eyes as he held me closely suddenly felt familiar to me. It almost felt natural. Then it happened. We kissed.

I pulled back quickly afterward. "I'm so sorry," I said nervously.

He pulled me back toward him, held me tightly, and began kissing me deeply. We kissed so deeply that we both began to moan. I pulled back again, and this time I jumped up from the sofa.

"I b-better go," I stammered and turned to walk away.

He stood up quickly and grabbed my hand. "You don't have to go." He pulled me into an embrace. "Damn. I've missed you, Trinity."

This was the second time he'd tried me. I'd always have love for Terrence. He was my first. We had history. He was my children's father. But we were done, and that was on him. I had moved on, so I was going to have to put a stop to this yo-yo routine.

I pushed him back. "Don't do this to me now. You know I'm with Pooch," I said forcefully.

Terrence shook his head as he continued to look at me the way he used to, seductively. He bit his lip. "I know that, but on the real, Trinity, fuck Pooch."

Shock and anger coursed through my veins. "*You* can say that. *I* can't. I love him. He's my man." I folded my arms across my chest defiantly.

Terrence rolled his eyes. "So what was that just now?"

"A mistake!"

"Somebody is in denial, but it's okay." He sniffed and gave a cocky laugh.

"I'm not even going to argue with you," I said, grabbing the brochure and the paper about the tattoo. "We have children together, and that's all we have."

"Why does it have to be just that?"

Had he lost his mind? Facing him, I went completely off. "First of all, didn't I just tell you Pooch is my man? And secondly, didn't you dump me before you did your bid?"

Terrence moved closer to me, gently lifted my hand, and caressed it. Pinching the bridge of his nose, he tilted his head downward as he shook it and let out a deep sigh. "I regret that, but I did that for you, not me, Trinity." When he looked up, he gazed into my eyes with such sincerity. "Damn it. Don't you know the hardest thing in the world that I've ever had to do was let you go? I only did that because I felt it was unfair to tie you down while I was locked up. I knew you'd need help with the kids, and I wanted you to live your life and fulfill your dreams. I felt like I owed it to you to let you go. But trust me, not a single, solitary day goes by that I don't regret that decision," he confessed, cupping my face in his hands.

Literally, I was mesmerized. All this time, I had thought he broke up with me before he went to prison because he didn't love me anymore. I had never understood that he made that decision not because he *didn't* love me, but rather because he *did*. But what was I going to do with this information now? Our relationship was a thing of the past, and I was in love with Pooch. I was his woman. He couldn't fuck with Pooch. Pooch was not someone to mess with, for real. He didn't give a shit that Terrence was my kids' father; he would kill him.

His confession caused my eyes to spring a leak, and he wiped the tears that fell down my cheeks. "I'm sorry that you never told me this before, but I am not going to betray Pooch. I'm sorry, Terrence."

He kissed my forehead. "It's cool. I understand. One of the things I have always loved about you is that you're loyal. I've tried to date some females, and no one is as loyal as you."

Tilting my head down, I blushed demurely. "I gotta go."

After he walked me to the door, I turned to face him. "Terrence, I'm sorry, for real. You know I have mad love for you."

As he stared into my eyes, his usual smirk turned into a gentle smile. "It's my own fault. I handed you over to Pooch in a sense," he said, holding my waist and pulling me toward him. His erection was evident, and truth be told, so was my wetness, but I couldn't let him know it. "But trust me, let that nigga slip one time, and I'ma turn into an Indian giver."

I pulled away. "Stop, Dreads. I really better go now," I said uneasily.

"Yeah, you better," he said, holding on to his crotch. "I have some stress to relieve, and it comes in the form of lotion and an old picture of you."

"OMG!" I gasped, then turned around to leave. "Bye, Terrence." I took a few steps and threw back my hand.

He reached for my hand before I was a safe distance away, and turned me around to face him. Leaning in close, he whispered in my ear, "When you fucking that nigga, I want you to think about how I used to put it down. Say what you want, but I know your scent, and I can smell it. It's like rose petals to my nose. I crave it, and if you let me, I'll remind you of the reason why we made Terry and Brittany. Go on back to my substitute for some snacks, but if you ever have the need for a home-cooked meal, you can come home anytime, whether it's temporary or permanent. It's your decision. You feel me?"

I gave him a nod. It was all I could do. His words had set me on fire, and I was too engrossed in trying not to drop my drawers right there and fuck him in the hallway to say anything. "I gotta go," I repeated, pulling away. Then I walked out of his apartment.

Lord knows I needed strength in a major way. Terrence was right. I loved Pooch through and

through, but when it came to throwing down in
the bed, Terrence beat Pooch hands down. Pooch
was great, especially when he was actually making love to me, instead of trying to get a quick nut.
I was not dogging Pooch's skills, but there was
great, and then there was amazing, and Terrence
was amazing. He made love like he was the artist
and I was his canvas. He took his time and paid
attention to detail. He was slow when I needed
it and fast when I wanted it. In the end, he didn't
just create art; he orchestrated a masterpiece.
Terrence was like *that*.

Shit, five minutes later I was riding with all
the windows down and the AC on, trying to
cool my ass and pussy down. At the light, I took
out my perfume and sprayed myself all over.
I didn't need to arrive home and have Pooch
smell my scent too. I was convinced men were
like bloodhounds. When their woman's scent
was in the air, they could smell that shit a mile
away. That was the reason I had had to get away
from Terrence. My essence had been about to
start running down my damn legs. I swore that
muthasucka could bring me to a climax just with
his words.

When I walked into the house, Pooch was
sitting on the sofa. "Hey baby," I said, then
kissed him on the lips.

He threw down the remote. "Where you been?"

"I told you I went to the nail salon," I said. I walked into the kitchen to get some water, and he followed behind me.

"I stopped there before I came home, and they said you'd already left. I came right home from the nail salon. It's only a five-minute drive from the salon to the house, and that was over an hour ago. So how the hell I beat you home?"

Was he serious? I gave him a crazy look as I swallowed my water. "Damn, Pooch. Since when do I have to go straight to one place and come right back home? You got me on some kind of schedule or some shit?"

He posted in his no-nonsense pose. "Don't fuck with me right now, Trinity. Stop avoiding my question. Where the fuck you been?"

"If you must know, I stopped by Terrence's to check on the kids, and because he wants me to come up with this tattoo design for him."

"That shit couldn't wait until you picked the kids up tomorrow?"

"Well, Pooch, you have me on such a tight schedule, if I spend more than five extra minutes, then you will go berserk," I countered. "Damn. And where is all this shit coming from? You know I could've been out eating, or did you forget we didn't grab anything?"

He laughed and pulled me to him. "Then I would've known you were lying," he said. "I told you before you became my woman, nothing goes on that I can't find out about if I want to know. I knew you were at Terrence's house, so it wouldn't have been a good look if you'd lied to me."

I was shocked. My mouth nearly fell to the floor. "You tracking me or some shit?"

"Nah. One of my runners saw your car at his apartment complex and called me to make sure I knew. Everybody looks out for Daddy. Now, you sure he called you over about a tattoo?"

I was nervous, but I held my ground. "Yes," I said, then I showed him the paper Terrence had given me. "He wants me to think of a design to symbolize these words. He even paid me for it." I showed him the money.

Begrudgingly, he relented. "Fine. Do the tattoo, but tell that nigga to wait next time. I don't like you over there unless you have to be. And tell him you don't need his fucking money unless it's going to his kids. I got you, not him."

"He just wanted to pay me for my work," I said in Terrence's defense. Then I turned to put my glass in the dishwasher.

"As long as that shit is paid only in green," he threw out.

I looked over my shoulder. "How else is it going to be paid, Pooch?" I asked, playing dumb about his remark.

He laughed. "Humph," was his response. He walked up behind me and began kissing me on my neck. "You ready for some of my loving?"

Feeling his breath against the nape of my neck turned me on, and I moaned as I caressed his face. "Yes," I replied, and I was. Terrence had worked me the fuck up.

Without another word, he spun me around, lifted me into his arms, and kissed my neck as he carried me upstairs to our bedroom. He took his time undressing me as he kissed me from head to toe. By the time he was inside me, a thought entered my head that I had never thought would. I pictured Terrence on top of me. I ain't gonna lie. That shit heightened my arousal, and I started throwing everything into it. When we climaxed, we were both spent, and even Pooch was amazed.

"Damn, baby. I haven't seen that side of you in a while," he said, holding me from behind. "That shit was fucking awesome."

I laughed, although I was feeling guilty at the same time. "Yeah, it was," I agreed. "I love you, Pooch."

He turned me to face him and held my face in his hands as I looked into his eyes. "Like I said earlier, the only payments given to you are in green. Now, you *feel* me on that, and you feel me *real* good. I love you, Trinity. I love *only* you. I'm a good nigga to you and for you, and I want to remain good. Remember that shit, and remember that shit *real* good."

Pooch's words sent chills up and down my body. "Okay, Pooch. I remember."

He kissed my forehead. "Good. Now let's get some sleep. You've drained me," he replied, and within seconds he was snoring, but I wasn't.

Pooch's sixth sense had told him that Terrence was lurking, and I had to convince Terrence to stop before Pooch or one of his boys found out. I didn't want anything bad to happen to Terrence. I would die if it did. I realized at that moment, that no matter how I felt about Pooch, a part of me would always love Terrence. For both of our sakes, I had to tame that side.

LaMeka

"Oh hell no!" Tony said, pacing back and forth in our bedroom. "What the fuck were you thinking when you decided to move your sister in here?"

Heaven help me. The moment we walked in the door, he had begun his third degree and a temper tantrum. He was worse than our boys. Why couldn't he just let this go? She was my sister, for goodness' sake. At the end of the day, she was my sister, and I was going to have her back, no matter what.

"What the hell am I supposed to do, Tony? Our so-called mother kicked her out, and she's only seventeen. Where the hell is she supposed to go?"

"Check it. We have a two-bedroom apartment. Where is she going to sleep? Our kids are in one bedroom, and we're in the other. We have only a kitchen, two bathrooms, and the living room outside of that. Where the hell is she going to stay? In the bottom bunk, with LaMichael, or in their bathtub?"

"Then why don't you try to get us a three-bed-room?"

He pointed to himself. "Me? Shit. I didn't create this little situation—"

"Well, neither did I," I interrupted him. "She's my sister. I am all she has left. We're just going to have to make the best of it."

Tony threw his hands up. "Whatever, man. What the fuck ever." With that, he stormed out of the bedroom.

That went lovely, I thought as I sat on my bed. Even though Tony wasn't happy with my decision, I was glad he had relented. I'd had enough drama at my mom's house. I didn't need any extra at my own.

My bedroom door opened just then, and I looked up to find Misha standing there. "I'm sorry to cause problems, Meka, really I am," Misha said, apologizing, as she entered the room.

I stood up, walked over to her, and hugged her. "You don't have nothing to apologize for. Tony is being an ass right now, but he will come around."

"Thanks, Meka."

"You're my baby sister, and this is what we do. We look out for each other."

I left Misha alone in the bedroom to study for her tests while I played with Tony Jr. and LaMichael. Tony sat in the living room, watching television, although I could tell that he was pissed as hell. I knew the conversation was far from over, but he could talk until his bum leg was healed, because my sister wasn't going anywhere unless my mom let her move back in. With the way I felt, even that was questionable.

After thirty minutes, Misha emerged from my bedroom and helped me make dinner, and of course, Tony then went back into the bedroom, claiming we were all making too much noise. I swear, I didn't know what had crawled up in his ass lately, but he was beginning to get on my last nerve. At any rate, I enjoyed chopping it up with Misha and cooking. It actually felt like a relief to have her there and to have someone to talk to and make me laugh. The arguments between Tony and me had increased lately, and if we weren't arguing, we were plain ass ignoring one another. That shit couldn't be healthy, but I loved him no matter what.

Surprisingly, we all made it through dinner together. We had a civilized conversation and shared a few laughs among ourselves. I had to admit it, we felt like a family. Maybe my sister being here was the extra life we needed to bring us back together again. Sometimes we thought that we were helping others, when in actuality, God had turned evil into good to help us.

After dinner, we got ready to call it a night. I told Misha that Charice would be by to pick her up for school the next morning. Then I got some blankets and a pillow for her to sleep on the living-room sofa before I bathed the boys and took my shower. After I climbed into bed with Tony, he pulled me close to him.

"It's been a minute," he whispered in my ear as he kissed me on my neck.

"Yeah, I know." I giggled.

"Let me put this thang on you, LaMeka," he urged, pressing his nature against my thighs.

"Sure, but I need to talk to you first."

Rolling onto his back, he huffed. "What *now*? Come on, baby. Okay, look, I get your sister had nowhere to go. I'm not even going to stress that shit. It'll work itself out."

"Good, but that's not what I was going to say."

"Can we please discuss our issues later or, better yet, work them out?" He laughed and began grinding on me.

"Yes, we can, but that's not what I was going to say, either."

"I give. What's up?" he asked, propping himself up on one elbow.

"Well, it looks like my sister might be here for a while. We both know how my mom is, but she never kicked me out. I think she's pretty serious about this, and Joe—that lowlife—is going to ride my mom's gravy train until the wheels fall off. Having said that, I have a lot more responsibility on me with her in the house, and I'm going to need a vehicle," I explained.

He gave me a confused look. "How the hell you gonna get a car when you don't have a job and neither do I?"

Taking a deep breath, I grabbed his hand. "I was hoping that maybe you could ask Ryan to buy us one, and we could pay him back in payments with your disability checks, like maybe three hundred dollars a month."

He snatched his hand away from me so fast, he almost bent my fingers. "Man, I ain't doing that shit!" he exclaimed.

"Why not?"

"What man do you know asks another man to buy him a car? What kind of shit is that?"

"Ask for me. If he feels like I'm asking—"

"So now you want me to look like an even bigger ass," he interrupted. "How do I look asking him to buy you a car because I can't?"

"Well, then, why can't we buy a car for ourselves? We have twelve thousand dollars saved up between what's left of your lump sum money and what you've saved from your checks. We could use half of that and get a used midsize car," I explained.

"That money is for the kids, man!"

"This *is* for the kids! I still need to get Junior back and forth to appointments, and it would really help me out when I go grocery shopping. Plus, I have to get my sister back and forth. I can't keep depending on Charice, Lucinda, Trinity, or one of your boys to come through," I argued.

"A'ight, so we need a vehicle. How much have you saved up from Junior's disability checks?"

"Only, like, five hundred dollars, Tony. I use his money to take care of the bills for the house, since you've been slacking off lately with helping with that," I said with an attitude. I was tired of doing everything my damn self.

"Well, how about you get a damn job, then?" Tony said sarcastically.

Now I was fired up, and I lit up on his ass. "How about you get me a damn car so I can get one? Or, better yet, how about pulling your load in the house you live in as well?"

Tony's eyes grew wide. Normally, I didn't take digs at him. "See, this is why I don't like dealing wit' yo' ass. A brotha is always being underappreciated. I ain't never got no credit for the shit I do for you," he said, lying on his back.

I wasn't trying to attack Tony, but he had a way of turning everything into an epic debate, so I tried a different approach now to make him reconsider. I rubbed his shoulder. "Look, baby, I wasn't trying to piss you off, but we really need a car. I understand that it may be difficult for you to ask Ryan for something like that, and maybe we shouldn't. I don't want to demean you as a man. So maybe I could ask Trinity if she would buy me one, and then we could pay her and Pooch back."

Tony laughed. "Either I get my manhood ripped by asking my boy or I risk getting my shit confiscated by the narcotics agents once Pooch's ass gets busted. Ain't that a hell of a choice," he said, giving voice to exactly what he was thinking.

"But it's a choice we have to make," I asserted, rubbing his arm.

"Well, get to asking Trinity, then."

My mouth nearly hit the floor. There was no way I wanted to be indebted to Pooch. Was he out of his mind? "Are you serious?"

"We need a car, right? 'Cause I'm not asking Ryan to do that. That shit is gay," he said, pulling me on top of him. "Now, where were we?"

"You seriously want me to ask Trinity?" I asked, now appalled.

He nodded. "Yes. It was your idea."

"And what if she says no?" I asked, pushing back.

"She won't say no. You know how Trinity is. She is generous like that."

"But what if she does?"

"Then I guess we better stay current on them bus passes," he joked, but I knew he was serious. "Now, let's move on to what the hell we started before this discussion."

I knew it wasn't worth discussing it anymore because it would only lead to another fight. I was tired of fighting and arguing and damn sure tired of him. It was becoming apparent that he was hiding from his responsibilities. I simply couldn't fathom that he'd rather me get the car from a known drug dealer than to make a way on his own.

Disgusted, I no longer wanted to have sex. I tried to get comfortable and stay in the moment because it had been a while for both of us. Between the fussing, fighting, hooting, hollering and arguing there had been no makeup or attempts at it. So when I say both of us were in need, I meant that. But how do you get in the mood with your man when he's acting like anything but your man?

"What the fuck is wrong?" Tony asked angrily as my thoughts came back to the present moment.

"Nothing," I mumbled.

He smacked me on my ass as he attempted to hit it from the back. As I said, my mood was shot. "The hell you say ain't nothing wrong. I've been back here pushing and trying for like five minutes. Help a brother out or something before my shit go down."

"I'm ready," I said frustratingly.

He sucked his teeth as he continued trying. "Bullshit Meka, no you ain't. I need that shit flowing like the water in a waterfall. I ain't trying to stick my shit between the rocks in the waterfall. Come on now."

"Well, why don't you try a little harder to get me in the mood?"

He stopped and walked around the front of the bed with his shit hanging in my face. He grabbed it and began bouncing it up and down in my face. "This shit don't get you ready no more or something? You looking for something new?" he asked angrily.

I didn't have the energy to argue. I got up, put on one of his wife beaters, and climbed back into bed. "Go to bed, Tony."

"What the fuck?"

I rolled my eyes and looked over at him. "I said go to bed. This shit ain't happening tonight."

His eyes danced with anger. "Hell no! I want some. Now get your ass up and handle your business."

Before I knew it, I replied, "I'll handle mine when you handle yours!"

"What's that supposed to mean?" he asked, standing and looking like a superhero with his arms crossed in front of his chest.

I sat up and looked him dead in the eyes. "Be a man, Tony!" I yelled. "Stop sitting around here all day, every day, like you're a fucking king and acting like anything but one. Help with the kids, cook, help with the bills or, better yet, go get a damn job! Stop sitting around here as if the whole world owes you something because your leg is fucked up!"

The moment the last statement came out of my mouth, I shut up, instantly regretting it. Tony's leg was a taboo subject for him. The mention of it would either set him off or send him into depression mode. He had never gotten over it, and to say it was a sore subject for him was an understatement. It was like picking up his heart and smashing it with your bare hands.

"No the fuck you didn't," he growled angrily in a voice I'd never heard before. His anger was so obvious you could've barbecued ribs on his ass.

I put my hands up apologetically. "I'm so sorry, baby. I didn't mean it that way. All I'm saying is that just because those dreams didn't come true doesn't mean you can't have new dreams," I explained, empathetically trying to cover up what I'd said.

Suddenly, Tony was on my side of the bed and I was met with a fist to the side of my face. That muthafucka knocked me clean across the bed! I was seeing birds, stars, *and* stripes. He hit me so hard I couldn't even scream because it felt as if my voice was lodged in my throat.

"You fucking bitch!" he yelled, pulling my feet toward him. He reached and grabbed me by my neck and began strangling me.

"To . . . Tony!" I gagged and coughed. "You . . . Cho . . . king . . . me." I managed to get out.

"I should kill your bitch ass for that shit!" he yelled, releasing me as I coughed and gagged for air. "Be clear, don't you ever come at me like that again! I don't talk about the fact that your ass has gained weight since LaMichael, or that the reason you don't have a job and can't get one is that you couldn't even finish high school or get a GED with your ignorant ass! That's what I get for dating a ghetto bird with a big ass instead of finding a bitch on my fucking level," he said harshly.

Now I was hurt by his comments. We'd been together for eight years, and this was how he was treating me and talking to me? The only other man I'd ever been with was Trey Watts, and that was once in high school out of revenge when Tony cheated on me. He was my first love in *every* way. I am the mother of his children and the only female to have his back. I'd been taking care of his ass since his parents refused to have anything to do with him. I thought we were a family. Everything I'd done, I did for the benefit of him, Tony Jr., and LaMichael.

"How can you say that and do this to me? I love you," I cried, holding my burning face and my throbbing neck.

I tried to remain calm for fear my sister would hear. I was surprised she hadn't come in. Then I remembered she slept like the dead. A freight train could've rolled through and she would've kept on sleeping. It was something she learned to do because of our mother's drunken fights and rages.

"Shut the fuck up before I pop your ass again!" he said as I balled up in fear. "Now you may not want none and that's cool. I'm getting tired of your '*has been*' pussy anyway. Learn some tricks or some shit. Still fucking like we in high school and shit."

"Tony!" I shouted in tears. He'd never disrespected me this way.

"But I'm gon' get my shit off, and you're going to help me," he said, pulling me by my hair with one hand and grabbing his shit with the other. "Open your mouth."

"No," I said defiantly.

Tony released my hair and slapped me across my mouth so hard spit flew out. He grabbed my hair again. "How long you want me to do this? I can go all night. Now open your muthafucking mouth like an obedient bitch."

I was officially horrified! Shaking and trembling, I couldn't believe this was *my* Tony. I didn't have time to contemplate this shit, so I did what I had to do. I parted my swollen lips and opened my mouth like an obedient bitch.

Tony's head flew back in delight as he gripped my hair with both hands and easily slid his shit in and out of my mouth. With my face burning and lips stinging, slobber easily poured out.

"That's right," he moaned. "Get that shit nice and wet. Yeah, baby, suck that shit just like that. You gon' take it all in tonight. Swallow that shit whole," he said as he pushed it so far back that I began to gag. "Don't throw up on my shit. I'll beat your ass. Open that throat up."

I did as he said and relaxed my throat. If this lesson had happened during a time of actual lovemaking, I might have enjoyed it, but right now, all I wanted to do was bite his shit off. My teeth grazed him as I thought about it.

He gripped my hair and looked down at me. "Bitch, I dare you. I'll rip that used-up coochie right out of its socket if you do it."

That stopped me cold, and he resumed his stroke. I wanted it to end quickly, so I let more wetness pour out of my mouth and put a nice, soft but tight suction on him.

He pumped faster. "Just like that . . . Oh shit! Just like that. I'm 'bout to blow in this muthafucka!" he hollered. I tried to lift up. "Hell no, you gon' swallow this shit tonight," he commanded as he held my head down on him. He released, and all of it went pouring into my mouth and down my throat as he held me tight. "Shit! That's it . . . Shit!" he yelled in ecstasy as another load shot off. It was so much that it began pouring down the corners of my mouth. He finally released me as I quickly spit the rest out into the trash.

Tony grabbed my face. "You're such a good bitch when you act right. That shit felt so fucking good, Meka, baby. Who says you can't teach an old bitch new tricks, huh?" He laughed, climbing into bed next to me. All I could do was wipe the remnants of his massive explosions on his wifebeater.

I tried to get up, but he pulled me back. "You ain't going nowhere. Lay your ass down and let me hold you. I'll put some ice packs and shit on your face tomorrow. You'll look brand new. I love you, Meka," he said as he held me closely and fell asleep.

However, I couldn't sleep. My ass was beat up and sore. My feelings were now permanently hurt, and my self-esteem was beyond low. I had watched my mom get the shit beat out of her this afternoon and many more nights prior to that, and now I was going through the same thing with the one man who I had thought would never betray me.

I guess the old adage was right. *The apple doesn't fall far from the tree.* Like mother, just like fucking daughter.

Lucinda

Working both jobs every day for the past two weeks had exhausted me. At this point, I was running on fumes, and to top it off, my frustration was building, because my manager, Mr. Sharper, still hadn't found out anything about getting my shift changed. I really needed to get the show on the road. I knew good things came to those who waited, but I felt like I had spent my entire life in a waiting period. I had waited to finish high school, had waited for Nadia to get older, and I was still waiting for Raul to be a better man and father, and was still waiting for my own father to be a better man . . . just waiting. I was ready for action, but at this very moment, I'd settle on a nice hot bath.

It was Saturday night, and I was glad to have a Sunday off. My schedule had finally leveled off, and I hadn't had to go into Susie Q for three days straight, and I welcomed the break. I knew that Nadia was tired of sitting at the shop with me with little to nothing to do, so surprisingly, Raul had agreed to keep her the past two days. The night before, he'd dropped her off to my apartment for me after I got home from work, which was an added bonus.

Tonight I stopped by to pick her up after work, and when I pulled up at his house, I nearly fucking lost my mind. It was nine o'clock at night, and my daughter and her half sister, Raulina, were outside playing in the front yard. Raulina was the ghetto-ass name Shanaya had given her daughter to piss me the fuck off after I had beaten her ass in high school for fucking Raul. But fuck all that. Why in the hell was my child outside with no adult supervision at this time of night?

Angry, I jumped out of the car. "Nadia! Come here!" I yelled.

She ran up to me. "Hey, Mommy!"

"Why in the hell are you outside at this time of night?" I asked quickly. I normally wouldn't curse in front of my child, but I couldn't help it this time.

"Ooh, Mommy. You said a bad word." She laughed.

"Ay, Nadia, not now! Answer me!" I yelled.

Nadia's facial expression turned serious once she realized that I was truly upset.

Raulina ran up to me. "Hey, Lucinda. Our daddy is in the house."

"It's *Ms. Lucinda* to you, and why is y'all's daddy in the house and you two are out here?" I said, looking back and forth between the two of them.

Raulina shrugged her shoulders. "I don't know. He told us to go outside and don't come back in until he told us to." She paused. "Didn't he, Nadia?" she asked, looking at Nadia for confirmation.

Nadia nodded her head in agreement. "Yes, ma'am. We did what Daddy told us to do."

Pissed, I put my hands on my hips. "Oh, okay. Well, you two sit on the porch and do not move," I ordered sternly.

"Why? I don't know what the big deal is. I mean, my mama lets me stay home by myself sometimes. She told me that I know how to dial nine-one-one," Raulina said defiantly.

I shot her a hard glare. "Why? Because I damn said so! And since you know how to dial nine-one-one, then you get ready to dial that damn number."

"I think we should sit here, because my mommy is really mad," Nadia whispered to Raulina as they quickly sat down on the porch steps.

"Damn straight. Now sit, and don't either one of you move," I demanded angrily.

I barged through the front door and expected to see Raul sitting in the living room, watching television, but he wasn't there, nor was he in the kitchen.

"Raul!" I yelled angrily as I tromped through the house and then stormed up the stairs. It didn't make a lick of sense that neither his mom nor his siblings were there. Talk about pissed off. Whew, if this muthafucka wasn't here, either, I would murder his ass. If he had left my child at this house by herself, he would regret the day he ever got me pregnant!

I swung open his bedroom door. "Raul!" I yelled, but I was stopped in my tracks. The scene in front of me caused me to choke and nearly vomit.

"Whose is it, Naya?" Raul yelled, holding Shanaya's legs up in the air as he pounded inside of her.

"Yours, Daddy! All yours! Oh, shit, Raul!" she hollered.

"Fuck Daddy! Call me *papi*, bitch!" he screamed, banging her.

Disgusted and pissed as hell, I yelled out, "The only muthafucking *papi* or daddy your ass is supposed to be right now is Nadia's!" I threw my keys at him and struck him in the middle of his head.

As Shanaya's legs dropped, he rubbed his head. Stunned, he spun around with his shit swinging and yelled, "Oh damn! Girl, what the fuck is wrong with you? Shit!"

Shanaya jumped up and pulled down her skirt. "Stop being a fucking hater, Lucinda!" Shanaya yelled angrily. "Raul is mine now, and we will do what the fuck we please!"

"I don't give a muthafuck what the hell you and Raul do, but when my child's life is at stake, I draw the fucking line!" I said, pushing Raul in the chest as he tried to walk up on me.

"Don't bring that shit over here! Me and my girl were getting our loving on," Raul said angrily.

"Bitch, please!" I sucked my teeth. "You better be glad you still have a dick to please her with, you nasty, 'fuck anything moving' son of a bitch! I don't give a damn who your girl is or what you do, but I will cut your fucking balls off for messing over my child . . . guaranteed, Raul!" I yelled, getting up into his face. "Don't you ever leave my child unsupervised or tell her to go outside this time of the night so you can get some crab-infested pussy!"

"Crab-infested pussy? Bitch, who the hell do you think you are?" Shanaya said as she headed toward me. Raul quickly stepped in between us.

"No, let her come this way. Apparently, this bitch needs a reminder, and I am all about refresher courses!" I screamed.

"Y'all ain't tearing up shit in my mom's house, so both of y'all bitches can cancel that right now!" Raul yelled.

Remembering this was his mom's house, I eased back. "You're the one to talk! You're up in here disrespecting her house and both of your kids. You are unbelievable!" I yelled, still in his face. "Check it. I don't care how you and this ghetto bird are raising Raulina, but Nadia is going to have respect and values. That means that you are going to respect her! Get ass on your own time and not during my child's time. You should have more respect for yourself than to show your daughters some shit like this! Anything could've happened to them, Raul! They are five- and six-year-old little girls! What the fuck are you thinking about?"

Suddenly, his mom appeared in the doorway. "What the hell is going on in here?" she questioned.

"*Mami*!" Raul exclaimed.

She put her hands on her hips and stared at Raul and then looked back at me. "Lucinda, what is going on, and why are you screaming?"

I looked her dead in the eyes. "Where are Nadia and Raulina?"

"I found them sitting on the front porch steps, so I told Benita to bring them inside. Do you want to tell me what is going on? Why the hell were they outside by themselves at this time of night? Why are you three in here yelling?" she said angrily.

"Well, I just came to pick up Nadia and found the kids playing outside, unsupervised. According to Raulina, their *father* ordered them to stay outside until he told them to come inside. So, I busted into the house, to find him and his little ghetto bird baby mama jump-off screwing while my child was outside! Your son is certifiable! Risking his children's lives for some booty, and this dumb ass who calls herself a mother is right up here with him," I yelled, pointing at Shanaya.

Raul's mom turned and looked at him. Her expression was priceless. "Raul!" she yelled. "I know you're not fucking in my house!"

"Ma! It wasn't like that. I mean, I can explain," Raul replied, stumbling over his words.

"And you had my grandbabies outside at night?" she asked angrily.

"Ms. Ana, they were fine," Shanaya interjected, trying to explain.

"Shut up!" Raul's mom hollered. "I have never liked your disrespectful ass. You have been a thorn in my side ever since you coaxed my son into fucking you and tried to break up him and Lucinda back in high school! Take Raulina and get the hell out of my house!" she screamed at Shanaya.

Shanaya rolled her eyes and kissed Raul on the lips. After grabbing her purse, she walked up to me and pointed to the hickey on her neck. "He likes this now," she said, trying to get a rise out of me.

"I don't give a fuck," I replied, shrugging my shoulders, as she walked out, yelling for Raulina.

Raul's mother turned to me. "Lucinda, I'm so sorry, sweetie. I know you're trying to get yourself together. On my son's behalf, I apologize for what happened. I assure you it will never happen again."

"Oh, Mama—" Raul said in a nonchalant tone.

"Shut the hell up!" she interrupted. "You are two seconds from being homeless." She turned back to me. "I will personally make sure that Nadia is taken care of when she is over here."

The only thing I could do was hug her. Ms. Ana and I had always been cool, and our bond was so tight, you'd have thought I was her child instead of Raul. She was like a second mother to me, and I valued her place in my life, though I stayed away out of respect for the fact that Raul and I were no longer together. She never looked at it like that, but the drama with Raul wasn't worth it. We knew what it was between us, and that was good enough for me.

"Ms. Ana, that's not your job or your place. Your son needs to grow up and learn how to be a man. I appreciate everything that you do, but Nadia is our responsibility, not yours. He should be the one apologizing, not you."

He shrugged his shoulders. "Well, I ain't apologizing for shit—" he began, but Ms. Ana hauled off and slapped the hell out of him.

"You will not disrespect Lucinda in front of me! It's bad enough you disrespected your daughters tonight. *Ay, Dios mio*! I don't know where I went wrong with you, Raul. I didn't raise you like this!" She glared at him. "Can't you see that Lucinda is a good woman? Why couldn't you get it together and marry Lucinda and raise Nadia together?" she asked, pleading with him. It looked like her heart was literally breaking.

He pointed at me. "That was her fault. She broke up with me," he huffed, rubbing his stinging face.

"Because you weren't a man!" I yelled at him.

"Fuck you, Lucinda!" he yelled back.

Ms. Ana slapped him again. "I told you not to disrespect her. Dating her was the only wise decision you've ever made, and you still couldn't get that right."

"Ma! You can't keep slapping me! I'm a man. Damn it!"

She looked at him cross-eyed. I knew in my spirit something epic was about to happen. Raul was Ms. Ana's firstborn. She had had him while she was in high school, and so she had been in the same situation that I was in. I guessed that was why she'd spoiled him so much, but that was also why we got along so well. She wanted desperately for me and Raul to be together as a family. However, her son was a boy, and I needed a man. By the expression on her face, she was also fed up with him acting like a boy.

"Oh, you're a man, now? Real men have stable jobs and provide for their families on a consistent basis. Real men know the value of a good woman and make her his wife. Real men love and care for their children and don't put them in harm's way. Real men don't live with their mothers and screw their baby's mama or anyone else in their mother's house! Lucinda is right! You are certifiable! I swear to God, I have tried my best with you, Raul, but you are just like your father!" she yelled at him.

The moment the words left her lips, Raul looked up. Anger danced in his eyes. "What did you just say to me?"

She looked at him with tears and anger in her eyes. "You heard me. I said you are just like your father. Rotten to the core."

Those were fighting words. Raul hated the ground his father walked on. He'd never forgiven his dad for leaving them, and any mention of that man set him off. The saddest thing in the world was that even though he hated him, he *was* just like him. I knew at that point I should've left earlier, before Ms. Ana got home, but I had felt obligated to stay. For the first time in my life, Raul looked as if he would kill his mother. Trust me, Raul may do many things wrong but lash out physically at his mama was never one of them. Somehow, however, I felt the tide had changed.

"Mama, you're going to take that back right now," he said in a soft but angry tone of voice.

"I will do no such thing!"

I peeked out the bedroom doorway, and Raul's sister, Benita, and Nadia were standing there, looking scared shitless. I'd almost forgotten they were in the house. Raul and his mama looked like they were in a Mexican standoff. Fearful, I quickly ran out of the room.

"Is Ms. Ella home?" I asked Benita, suddenly remembering the old lady next door.

"Yes. What's going on, Lucinda? They sound really mad," Benita remarked.

"I don't have time to explain. Take Nadia over to Ms. Ella's house and stay there until I tell you to come home. Go now," I ordered. She and Nadia hurried down the stairs and out the front door.

I ran back into the bedroom, and it was as if Raul snapped when he saw me. "You fucking bitch! Don't you ever tell me that I'm like that muthafucka!" he screamed as he ran toward his mother. He rammed into her, and she fell up against the wall.

Ready to spit fire, Ms. Ana slapped Raul so quickly that I thought Muhammad Ali had run through there. "Who do you think you are running up on me? I'm *your* mother, damn it!" she screamed.

Raul shoved her, and I quickly stepped in and blocked him from attacking his mom any further. He was on some other shit right now.

"Raul! Please! Don't hit your mother," I begged, protecting her.

"You're going to hit me?" Ms. Ana asked, pointing to herself. "You get out of my house! Get out and don't come back. You are no longer my son! Get out!"

Raul stepped back, with his eyes narrowed to slits. "Fine. Because you damn sure ain't my mother," he declared, then turned and left.

I embraced Ms. Ana as she cried heavily. I didn't know what to say, so I just let her hold on to me and cry until she couldn't anymore. Raul was wrong, dead wrong. I couldn't imagine Nadia fighting me or me having to kick her out. I knew how much Ms. Ana loved Raul, because I was a mother myself, and I loved Nadia just as much. The pain I felt oozing from her as she cried let me know that even though he was a grown man, cutting him off hurt her to her core. However, I couldn't blame her. A line had to be drawn at some point, and unfortunately, she'd reached her breaking point tonight.

"I'm sorry you had to see that. I'm sorry for everything, Lucinda," she said, drying her eyes. "I wish Raul could've been a better man for you. You deserve so much more than what he can offer. It's hard when you raise a child and they turn out to be nothing."

I continued patting her on the back. "Don't fault yourself. You did your job, and Raul has to find his own way. Hopefully, he will. I want Nadia to have a relationship with him, but I can't put her or myself through these changes for it. I'll let you continue to see Nadia, but until Raul gets his stuff together, he won't see her."

She agreed. "I understand. I really do."

"Ms. Ana, I might as well tell you. I'm taking Raul to court for child support, and I'm asking the judge not to grant him visitation, because of tonight's events. I can't put my daughter through this. Raul has got to learn to be a man."

She grabbed my hands. "And I'm behind you. I support your decision, and I'm glad that you finally see that this is what you have to do. I will testify in court about tonight on your behalf. I will do anything for you and Nadia."

I hugged her again. "Thank you."

"No, thank *you* for being a mother to my grandchild. At least she has one parent who loves her. I wish I could say the same for Raulina and Doodlebug," she said, referring to Raul's other two children. We walked out of the bedroom and down the stairs, then went to Ms. Ella's house.

As Nadia and Benita walked out Ms. Ella's front door, we thanked Ms. Ella and explained what had happened, so she could keep a look out for Raul in case he came back. Benita had already called her other two brothers, so they were already hunting down Raul for disrespecting their mama. I'd had enough for the night, so I grabbed Nadia and headed home.

"*Mami*, is *papi* in a lot of trouble?" Nadia asked as I drove.

"Yes, honey, he is. He has to get himself together."

"I want to help him," she said, causing tears to fall from my eyes instantly.

"I know you do, sweetie, but the road to manhood is a path he has to travel on his own. No one can help him with that," I said, choking up.

"I'm going to pray that he has a safe trip, then," she said with such care.

I chuckled. "You do that, then, baby."

"I'm sleepy, *mami*."

"Go to sleep, then, *hija*," I coaxed, and within seconds she was out like a light in the backseat.

I was thankful for the peaceful ride home. As exhausted as I was, I couldn't wait to get Nadia into bed and soak in my bathtub. As I pulled up to the house, I noticed that my voice-mail light was flashing on my cell phone. After I parked the car, I dialed to listen to the message.

"Lucinda, it's Mr. Sharper," his recorded voice blared through the phone. "I checked on the positions for you, and unfortunately, no one has anything available right now. I hate to bring you such disheartening news, but we just don't have anything to accommodate your school schedule at this time. I'm sorry, and I hope you have a good night."

My heart dropped, and tears streamed down my face. "Fuck!" I yelled, throwing my cell phone to the floor.

I put my face in my hands and cried. As I cried, it began to sink in that my dreams had once again been snatched away from me. A wail escaped from the depths of my soul, as if my heart had been ripped from my chest. My heart and soul felt on fire, and the pain and burning in my chest caused me to clutch myself and hold tight. When would this hell ever end? Could God really be punishing me this bad for having a child out of wedlock? I thought all children were a gift from God. I went to church. I was told the sin was in the sex. Hadn't I repented and suffered enough for that? And where was Raul's punishment in all this? *Huh? Tell me. Please, God . . . somebody, tell me . . . why me?* I cried until my face and shirt were drenched and my soul was drowned in tears. After several minutes, I had no tears left. I did what I always did: I picked myself up and went inside to suffer alone.

After putting Nadia in my bed, I got into the tub and cried some more as the warm water relaxed my aching muscles. It was times like this that I'd wish I had a man to come home to and make love to, someone who could ease my pain and heartache and find a way to make everything that was wrong in my world right. But all I had was my child and a dream, a dream that was still deferred. I got into bed and held on to Nadia for dear life.

"I swear to God, I'm going to make it better for us, if it's the last thing I do," I whispered in her ear. I kissed her as she snuggled up against me.

Finally, sleep found its way into my eyes. I drifted off, hoping and praying for a break-through.

Trinity

The day after our momentary rekindling incident, I called ahead to let Terrence know when I would be on my way to pick the kids up, so he could make sure they were ready when I arrived. I wanted no mess out of Pooch and couldn't afford to be around Terrence longer than necessary. He obliged. Surprisingly, he made no mention of the day before and didn't attempt to come on to me again. The only thing Terrence said after getting the kids strapped in the car was that the ball was in my court. I knew what he meant, but it wasn't going to happen. I was with Pooch, and I loved him. Even if I didn't love Pooch, it damn sure wasn't going to happen after Pooch's threat, even if a part of me might've thought I wanted it to.

I should've told him about Pooch's threat then, but I couldn't bring myself to do it. Pooch had never threatened me before, and I knew the only problem between Pooch and me was

Terrence. Pooch didn't give a damn what I did any other day of the week, but whenever I had to deal with Terrence, that nigga bugged out. I knew that with Pooch acting crazy, I had to tell Terrence to fall back.

While I was working on Terrence's tattoo design back at home, the doorbell rang. I knew it had to be LaMeka, since she'd called earlier in the week and said it was important that she meet with me and Pooch. I just hoped that shit didn't involve any illegal shit. Pooch's hood ass would be down for some shit like that, but not me. I believed that LaMeka had better sense than to try to involve us in any mess, so rather than getting overly concerned, I had decided a few days ago to wait and see what was really up.

I went to the front door and opened it. "Hey, girl," I said as she walked into the house.

"Hey, Trinity," she replied as we hugged. "Thanks for meeting with me. I really appreciate it."

"Ain't no thang, girl. We're practically family. You know we been down, like, four flats on a broke-down Cadillac with a diamond in the back ever since my cousin Charice introduced us on the playground," I said and laughed as we walked into the family room.

"You're as silly as ever. I miss when we used to be able to hang out." She sighed, remembering the good times.

"I know. Remember Saturday nights at the Rooftop and Sunday nights at Skateland?"

"Oh snap! You brought me back. Hell yeah! We used to pretend we were drinking by getting those virgin daiquiris at the Rooftop. And remember we always showed out during the couples' skate?"

"'Cause we were always the ones with boyfriends," we said in unison and laughed.

"Damn. Those were the times, boy. I miss that shit for real," I said. "Hold up. Why in the hell you got on your shades up in here? I mean, you fresh to death in that outfit, but ain't no sunshine in here, cool mama."

As she pulled off her shades, I stopped dead in my tracks. "This is why," she replied sadly.

"Who the fuck ass we got to beat?" I asked, getting pumped up instantly. "Who was it? Was it that muthasucka who lives with your mama? Girl, his ass is as good as got," I huffed. I knew I had said I wasn't going to get involved with no shit, but that was pre–black eye.

She put her hand on my arm and shook her head. "It was Tony."

My eyes bugged out of my head. Out of all the niggas in the world, I never would've suspected Tony. Tony was the most levelheaded of all the knuckleheads we had dated. Back in the day, Terrence had had his vice with drug dealing, and while the others had been deadbeat dads or dope dealers, Tony had been there for LaMeka as her man. He had wanted a clean future for himself, his woman, and his child, so to say that I was shocked was an understatement. I was flabbergasted.

"*Tony*?" I asked.

She nodded as tears formed at the base of her eyelids. "I told myself not to do this," she admitted as tears poured down her cheeks.

I rushed her to the hall bathroom and gave her some tissue. "Spill it," I said after she'd gathered her composure.

She sat down on the toilet lid, and I sat on the clothes hamper. After she collected herself, she began to tell me about Tony's mounting arrogance and disrespect over the past year. First, he had stopped helping her, then there had been nothing but arguing between them, and then he had started beating her ass and raping her for oral sex.

"And you still got that nigga staying with you?" I asked, amazed at what she'd just told me.

She nodded sadly. "I'm scared of him, Trinity. I don't know what he's capable of, and the fucked up part is that I still love that nigga."

I shook my head in disgust, but I understood. Tony was the only guy LaMeka had ever dated, he was her kids' father, and for all intents and purposes, they had been a family for nearly ten years.

"I can't say I don't feel you, Mama, but damn!" I told her. "So is that why you wanted to speak to me and Pooch? You want Pooch to handle that shit for you? You know . . . send him a message."

"No. I'll handle Tony on my own."

"You sure about that?" I asked, looking at her skeptically.

After she nodded, I knew she wasn't going to do shit but sit around and get her ass beat by Tony some more. She loved that muthasucka, and I prayed that she'd come to her senses or that Tony would come to his.

I relented. "A'ight. So what's up?"

"Can I speak to both you and Pooch?" she asked.

"Yeah," I said. "Come with me."

I led her back into the family room. LaMeka sat down on the sofa.

"Let me go get Pooch out of his king suite," I told her.

Pooch had a room in the house that he called the "king suite," and since he had a safe hidden in a wall in that room, it was off limits to everyone except me, and that was only when he *allowed* me in. You'd never know there was a safe in that room. It looked like an entertainment room, with a flat-screen television, every gaming system imaginable, a pool table, a card table, a bar, a sofa, and a stripper pole. Yeah, guess whose ass stayed on the pole? You're right. Mine.

I walked to the king suite and knocked on the door. "Pooch?"

"Yeah, babe?" he called out.

"Open up. LaMeka is here to see us," I said through the door.

A few seconds later, he came out, with a cigar in his hand. "She told you what she wanted?"

"No. She said she wanted to talk to both of us. She's in the family room. Put that cigar back in the room. Princess is also in the family room, playing in the playpen."

He took a pull from his cigar and blew a puff of smoke in my face and laughed. "You so damn protective. Let me put it up before you swear I gave you and the baby lung cancer," he said, then walked back inside his lair and killed the embers in his ashtray.

I stood just inside the doorsill. "Thank you."

He walked up to me and pulled me to him and kissed me on my mouth. "Anything for my boo. You know that, babe."

I smiled. "I know," I said, looking him up and down. Something about seeing him in a wife-beater, jeans, and a pair of Timbs just turned me on.

He grabbed his crotch. "Keep looking at me like that and I'm gonna take you in this room and dick you down. Fuck Meka. She can wait," he said, then kissed me on my neck.

"The baby is up, Pooch," I informed him, pushing him away.

"That fucking baby is always up," he said, rolling his eyes. "Do she ever fucking sleep?"

"Yes, Pooch, she does," I said, ignoring his comment.

"Well, let me know when the fuck that is, so I can get some pussy around this muthafucka. Damn! Kids always cock blocking like a muthafucka around here. It's always one of they asses doing some shit. Terry wants to play football, Brittany wants to play beauty salon, Princess is awake, homework, cooking, one of them sick, and shit. It just goes on and fucking on! God damn! When is it Pooch's turn for some attention around this muthafucka? Don't have any more of them damn cockblockers, for real man," he fussed irritatingly.

I gave him a kiss to calm him down. "I'm sorry, baby, but let's deal with that later. Meka is over here now."

He relented with a sigh. "A'ight." Then he smiled as he shut the door behind him. "Hey, babe. I got an idea," he said as we walked toward the family room. "You want to draw and design and shit, right?"

I nodded my head yes, hopeful that he'd mention the Art Institute. "Yeah," I replied, smiling at him.

"Then why don't you draw a picture of your pussy on the wall in the king suite, and that way when Princess isn't sleeping, I can still jack off," he joked.

I rolled my eyes as he laughed. I wasn't going to dignify that with a response.

"Damn! Where do I get that shit from? Babe, I kill myself," he went on, clowning. "But on the real, that ain't a bad idea." He took my hand in his.

Oh, he must've bumped his damn head, I thought as I looked at him as if he were retarded. "If you think I'm going to draw my pussy, or anybody else's pussy, on a damn wall, you have lost your ever-loving mind," I fumed, snatching my hand away from him.

He reached for my hand again. "I'm sorry, babe," he said, realizing he'd pissed me off.

"Whatever, Pooch." I rushed ahead of him.

Pooch grabbed my arm and snatched me back to face him. "Hey, hey now. Calm that shit down. You made your point. I crossed the line, and I apologized. Drop that tantrum shit with me. For real, yo."

"Okay. A'ight." I shrugged away from him and stood there.

"Give a nigga a kiss and forget that shit," he ordered. I leaned in and kissed him. "Good. Now, let's go see what the hell your girl wants." He pointed for me to lead the way, and I did, with no further argument.

When we entered the family room, I took a seat next to LaMeka on the sofa.

"What's up, Meka?" Pooch greeted as he sat down across from me and LaMeka.

"Ain't nothing, Pooch. How you been?" she said.

"I'm straight. Business is good. The kids are spoiled, and so is my girl." He paused for effect. "Now, if I can get your girl to give up them drawers a little more often, I'd be all good," he joked, and I rolled my eyes. "And you?"

"I've been better," she answered.

"I can see that." He pointed to her eye. "Who fucked you up?"

"Pooch!" I hollered.

"What?" He shrugged.

"You can be so insensitive," I said shaking my head in disgust. "I'm sorry, Meka."

"Hell, I'm trying to find out if she needs me to handle that for her," Pooch told me.

LaMeka put her hand up. "No, it's nothing. I have that situation under control. This is about something else."

"A'ight, but if you need me to handle that shit, you come and see me."

She let out a nervous laugh. "I know you will, Pooch."

"So what's up?" he asked, leaning forward.

"Okay, here's the deal. My mom kicked Misha out, and she is living with me and Tony. That means I have an extra mouth to feed, and I have to get her back and forth to school and work. You guys, along with Charice, Lucinda, and some of Tony's boys, have been really good about helping us with rides and stuff, and I appreciate that."

"You're welcome," he said.

"Thanks. But now I need a real favor. With all this going on, I need a ride of my own. You know I don't have a job, and neither does Tony, so we can't get financed—"

"So what are you asking me?" Pooch interrupted.

She took a deep breath. "If you could . . . you know . . . like . . . let me borrow some money to get a car, and we could pay y'all back in installments? I promise to make monthly payments to you guys. I just really need the help, y'all, for real."

Pooch sat back, contemplating. "So how much you talking?"

"Well, Charice took me down to Hennessy Auto Sales, and they have a used Envoy that is still under warranty. It's only thirteen grand, and it has only forty-eight thousand miles on it," she explained.

Pooch looked at me. "It's on Trinity. I don't mind."

LaMeka smiled. "You don't?"

"Nah. I trust you. Besides, you know the deal if you cross me, so having said that, it's on Trinity. If she says to do it, I'm all good. You just pay us whatever you can afford until the debt is settled. I'll call my dude Rick. He's the finance manager at Hennessy. I'll get it for eleven grand, cash," Pooch said.

LaMeka looked at me. "So can you help me?"

This was her decision, but I knew that she really didn't want to ask Pooch and me. "If you are comfortable with it, I don't have a problem with it."

Without a second thought, she smiled and hugged me tightly. "Thanks so much, Trinity. I really appreciate this."

"Ain't no problem," I said.

Pooch got up and called Rick. Just like he'd said, Rick told him he'd have the car ready for her in a couple of hours, and he would take the eleven grand.

"So everything is set up. You need us to take you down there?" Pooch said.

"Nah, I got Charice's truck. I'm going to pick her up, and we'll head on down."

"Cool," Pooch replied, then walked to the back of the house. When he returned, he brought the money in eleven stacks of ten one-hundred-dollar bills in a brown envelope. "You fuck me, I'll fuck you. Remember that shit," he warned, offering the envelope to LaMeka.

LaMeka took it. "I won't, I promise." She stood up and hugged Pooch. "I appreciate you, Pooch."

"Let's just say I'm giving back to my community." He laughed. "I'll let you and Trinity chop it up among yourselves for a minute, but listen, you enjoy that ride."

"I will, Pooch. Thanks again," she said.

"It's all good. If Tony needs a job, tell him to stop by. I got some work he can do," Pooch advised.

"I think he's straight."

He laughed. "A'ight. The offer is on the table," he said and then turned to me. "I'm going to my suite." He kissed me and left the room.

"So do I need to get the title and bring it over here?" she asked me.

"No, you keep your title, honey. Just handle your business, because Pooch don't play about his money," I warned.

"Okay. How's three hundred dollars a month?" she asked me.

"Make it two hundred, because I know that's a stretch for you."

She let out a sigh of relief. "Thank you, girl. With everything going on, I'ma have to get a job, and when I do, I'm gonna give you a good chunk when I get my income tax money too."

"However you want to handle it is cool with me. Just make them monthly payments."

"Thanks, Trinity. I owe you big-time. Every tenth of the month, I got you," she said, hugging me.

"You don't owe me shit," I replied. We walked to the front door, and as I opened it, we said our good-byes.

Though I was worried about LaMeka owing Pooch that type of money, I was happy that Pooch had let LaMeka get the car. She needed it for those babies, and I knew how her mom could trip out. I just prayed shit would get on track for her and Tony.

After LaMeka left, I went back into the room and finished up the design for Terrence's tattoo. The tattoo was fresh. The main part of it was a cross with praying hands inside. Then there were two rings, one on each side, with a crown on top of the cross. There were streaks indicating a light shining off the cross, as if it were standing in the reflection of the sea. The cross, of course, represented the place where you bore all your sins and cares; the crown represented keeping God at the head of your life; the two rings represented family and wealth; the praying hands represented everlasting love; and the waves in the sea subtly had the word *forgiveness* in them and thus represented sins being washed away. By the time I finished the design, it was time to go and pick up the kids. I was putting on my tennis shoes when Pooch walked in the room.

"You about to go get the kids?" he asked.

"Yeah. Can you watch Princess for me?"

"Oh, you don't have to worry about that."

"Thank you, babe," I said, smiling at him. Pooch hated watching the kids, so the fact that he would so graciously do it now, without a battle, made me happy.

"'Cause I'm coming with you," he said boldly.

I looked up at him. "Why? For what?" I asked, confused.

"Is there a reason I can't go?" he asked, eyeing me strangely.

I put my hands up. "No reason. I just know that you don't care for Terrence, and I'm just going to pick up the kids. You've never wanted to go before."

He smiled as he grabbed his jacket. "I ain't got no problems with Terrence. We are all good. Why wouldn't we be?"

"No reason," I responded.

"Well, in that case, I'm going. I just want to roll with my babe. I can do that, can't I?" he said, grabbing Princess's diaper bag.

"Yeah," I said solemnly.

"Good. Get the baby and let's go," he ordered.

When I picked up Princess, we headed out. I didn't have a good feeling about this, but I couldn't argue. That made me look guilty, so I went along with Pooch's demands. Once I strapped in Princess, I got in the driver's side, and Pooch popped in a CD once we had pulled off. When the first song began to play, I knew what the CD was. Whenever he was going into a confrontation of some sort, he played this CD. The first song was "Tear the Club Up," by Three 6 Mafia. Pooch had his head leaned back, with his eyes closed, and he was bopping his head to the beat of the music. He really got into his zone when the next song, "Whoop That Trick," played. As it played, I couldn't take it.

"Can we please listen to something else?" I asked.

He looked at me. "Fine."

I turned on the radio, and Mary J. Blige's song "I Am" was on.

He laughed. "That's a good selection too. Sing it, Mary! *Ain't nobody gonna love you better, boy, than I am. Than I am,*" he hollered at the radio.

I loved Mary, but not tonight. I just settled back and let the music play. Pooch was happy as hell listening to Mary for the remainder of the ride to Terrence's house. Once we got out of the car, Pooch stepped in front of me and knocked on the door. I fell back. I wasn't gonna argue with this fool.

"What's up, Trinity?" Terrence said, smiling, as he opened the door. But when he saw Pooch standing in front of me, his smile quickly faded.

"What? You ain't happy to see me?" Pooch asked sarcastically.

Terrence smirked. "You just caught me off guard. Usually, Trinity comes solo."

"Yeah, well, not tonight," Pooch replied.

"Come in," Terrence said through clenched teeth.

Pooch and I walked through the door.

"Y'all want something to drink?" Terrence asked.

"Nah, we straight," Pooch answered.

Terrence turned to me. "And you, Trinity? Do you want anything?"

"I just said *we* were straight," Pooch said before I could answer.

Terrence reared back on his legs and swiped his hand over his chin, then cuffed his beard. "I know what you said, Pooch, but I thought you were referring to yourself, since Trinity didn't say anything," Terrence said. Then he walked into the kitchen and grabbed a beer from the refrigerator.

"No, I was referring to both of us. *We* straight. I know my girl. She ain't thirsty, and she don't need nothing from you," Pooch said sternly when Terrence reappeared.

"Is that right?" Terrence asked, turning to face Pooch.

"Yep, that's right," Pooch replied angrily.

Suddenly the kids ran into the room and hugged me. Their timing couldn't have been more perfect if it had been planned.

"Hey, babies. Let's get ready to go quickly," I instructed them.

"Okay, Mama," they said in unison and then went to collect their things.

I put Princess down, walked over to Terrence, and handed him the tattoo design. "Here you go."

He took the paper and smiled. "Hey, yo, this is so tight. Man! You are so creative. Let me see if I can figure it out. The crown is God. The sea is forgiveness . . . That was hot. The rings are love and family. So what's wealth?"

I smiled. "You're welcome. But actually, one of the rings is wealth and the other is family. The praying hands represent everlasting love," I said. Then I turned to see if the kids were getting their things together. "Kids, hurry up, please."

Terrence nodded. "I get it. I almost got it completely correct. I swear, you should own your own shop or some shit. Tattoos by Trin. That sounds hot right there."

Pooch walked up behind me and wrapped his arms around my neck, then pulled me into a backward embrace and kissed me on the cheek. "My baby don't have to work, Terrence. That shit there is just a hobby, a pastime. It's just shit she does for niggas who want to give up their money to her."

Terrence laughed. "Well, she's got a true talent and deserves to be paid for it." He placed the paper on a nearby table.

Pooch let me go and smirked, rubbing his hands together. "She's got plenty of talents, and trust me, she gets paid like a muthafucka for *all* of them."

"Kids!" I yelled, sensing this shit was about to escalate. I was too afraid to go and check on them and even more afraid to leave those two in the room together.

"Damn, Trinity! With a man like Pooch, who needs dreams and aspirations? Your man has your whole life planned out for you. Just sit around and be eye candy." Terrence looked me directly in the eyes and continued, "I mean, that's cool too, if that's what you really want." He sat down on a barstool and drank his beer. "This beer is good and cold, Trinity. You sure you don't want one? I remember Michelob being your favorite. You could never turn one down . . . when *we* were together."

The situation had officially escalated! The entire time I had been looking at Terrence, but as soon as he made that last comment, I nearly blacked out! Suddenly, the air in the room felt thick, like the smoke from a California wildfire. I could barely breathe or move, because I was afraid of what was going down. I couldn't force myself to look at Pooch. My insides began to tremble, and my heart was racing a mile a minute. Terrence looked as if he was on ready, set, go, and his expression was stone cold. As he looked past me, or rather through me, he was daring Pooch to make a move. He took a slow, deliberate sip of his Michelob and hissed the rough aftertaste away . . . waiting.

If there was one thing Pooch could *not* stand, it was the thought or mere mention of my old relationship with Terrence. The kids were reminder enough. Pooch had wanted me since *forever*, and while I had had little puppy love crushes—you know, "check the yes or no box" type relationships, Terrence had been my first true boyfriend. Pooch had *always* . . . *always* . . . been jealous of that fact, even before we'd hooked up. For the most part, he had kept it under wraps, until Terrence was locked up. Once I'd given him a chance, he'd felt like he'd beaten Terrence in a sense. Although Pooch would never admit it, I knew in the back of his mind he'd always been fearful of any feelings that Terrence and I had for each other.

So to have *Terrence* bring up our old relationship was like opening a lifetime wound. Pooch would *definitely* remember *that* shit.

If there was one thing I knew at this moment, it was that it was most definitely time to go. Hell, it was *half past* time to get the hell out of Dodge. For my kids' sake, I had to make a move. Sweat beads began to form on my forehead as I stood in silence. I slowly turned to look at Pooch, who had a scowl so big on his face, he looked like he could chew Terrence for breakfast. His stare at Terrence was hard enough to burn a hole through him. His jaw was clenched so tightly that I thought it'd break from the pressure. Mostly, it was that stare—that cold, hard, serious, emotionless, damn near evil stare— that kept fucking with me. Pooch's reaction was downright frightening. Pooch was the type of nigga who reacted and did it *quickly*. The mere fact that he was standing there and staring at Terrence as if he could kill him, instead of trying to fight him, spoke more volumes than anything. When Pooch was contemplating his actions, it meant he was considering serious consequences for that person. Two words: *toe tag*.

Terrence's actions were no better. He did not scare easily, *especially* if the perceived threat was Pooch. Pooch had something he wanted . . .

me. He didn't give a damn what he said to piss
Pooch off, nor did he respect my relationship
with Pooch. I wasn't afraid for Terrence when
it came to Pooch, because I believed Terrence
could match Pooch toe-to-toe and pound for
pound. What made me afraid for Terrence was
Pooch's entourage. He had niggas *everywhere*
who were willing to do *anything* for him to get
that right-hand-man seat, and for every nigga *in*
his crew who would go to battle for Pooch, there
were ten more niggas trying to *get in* his crew
who would do it just to have the opportunity to
be down.

Terrence sat there, cool and collected, with
a smirk on his face, *knowing* he was taunting
Pooch. I didn't know what was going to happen, so I tried to intervene before Pooch set
off Terrence or vice versa. The fact of the matter was Pooch could stare at Terrence like he
was crazy, could talk crazy and, hell, could even
act crazy all day, because Terrence did . . .
not . . . give . . . a . . . fuck. Terrence wasn't afraid
of Pooch or any of his family, friends, or "employees." He was a man through and through,
but I was afraid enough for both of us.

I stepped up to Pooch. "Baby, why don't you
just wait in the car? I'm going to the room to
get the kids right now, and we'll be coming out

the door before you even get settled in the car. Wouldn't that be better?" I said as I held his face between my hands and forced him to look at me.

Pooch stared at me for a moment. As his nose flared, he bit his bottom lip. Those were the things he did when he was ready to tear up on some ass. Suddenly, he smiled and kissed me on the mouth.

"Damn. I love those lips. I can't wait to get home with them too," he said, then looked up at Terrence as he gripped my ass. "And with that too, because it's all mine. I'm so glad that everything about you is *all* mine, from your ass to your aspirations."

Terrence's nose flared as he glanced away.

Pooch began walking toward the door. "See, Terrence, I can afford to pay for her dreams. Every last one of them. And she don't hurt for shit. That shit is for people who need to come up. She's arrived. She's already got a six-bedroom, six-bathroom home, a *Hercedes*-Benz, designer clothes and shoes, spa treatments to keep my body . . . my bad . . . *her* body tight, and anything else she wants. I can afford to make her my eye candy, because I made her a five-star chick." He put his index finger up to his temple, as if he'd remembered something, then snapped his fingers. "Matter fact, I made *your* kids five-star children. So you don't have to worry about nothing concerning her anymore. Just concentrate on coming up for yourself. I know you still trying to come up after that bid, bruh. It's cool, because everybody got to have a dream," Pooch said disrespectfully.

With my hand covering my mouth, I had absolutely no idea what was going to happen, especially with Pooch bringing the kids into this shit. Terrence didn't play that shit about his kids, but Pooch wasn't finished.

"Damn, bruh, that beer does look mighty good, but I'ma let you hold on to it so you can have your *memories*. But check it, if you need work, come holla at me. I can help you out. Oh, and, um, if you ever need a place to stay," he said, looking around the apartment as if it were beneath him, "I can help you with that too. Give you a room or something. Maybe we could put a bunk bed in your son's room for you." He walked over to the front door and yanked it open. "I'ma be in the car, Trinity. Five minutes. You be easy, Terrence."

Unlike Pooch, Terrence wasn't the type to do a lot of talking, so he had sat there idle as Pooch had gone off on his rant. The more Pooch had talked, the more Terrence's eyes had narrowed. I knew . . . absolutely *knew* . . . that the *only* reason Terrence didn't have it cracking and popping up in here yet was that the kids were there. Thank God for small favors.

Terrence took a long swig and laughed. "You too, Pooch. We'll have to chop it up again one day, you know, man-to-man. That's how I roll. You know, away from the lady and my children. You understand, right?"

Pooch chuckled sinisterly. "I see you."

"I need you to *feel* me on that one."

Pooch's jaw twitched. "I *feel* you, bruh."

"Good," Terrence replied. "I hope you have a good night, bruh. I'm going to grab me something to eat after this. What are you having, man? Leftovers?"

"Oh Lord," I said, throwing my hands up. "Kids!" I yelled as they ran into the room.

Pooch laughed. "I'ma be in the car. Enjoy your dinner, Terrence, and nah, bruh, I don't do leftovers. I eat five stars every night," he said before shutting the door.

"Say good-bye to your daddy right now," I said hurriedly to the kids.

Terrence grabbed me by my elbow and pulled me into the kitchen. "Put your jackets on," he shouted to the kids. "Is that what you want? A muthafucka who degrades you and acts like you're only there for his pleasure and enjoyment?"

I rolled my eyes. "Pooch said that only because he can sense that you want to be with me, Terrence," I whispered. "You have to end this shit. Don't be trying to meet up one-on-one with Pooch. He's dirty."

"I'm not afraid of Pooch and nobody he is affiliated with. You *know* that. Besides, that muthafucka is gonna pay for that comment about my kids. Nah, who I'm afraid for is you. You're losing yourself in this relationship. You are a five-star chick, but you were five stars before you got with him, and you are also an independent dime. Don't let him do this to you. He's turning you into a high-paid mistress," Terrence pleaded.

His care and concern for me were noble, but his nobleness would get him bodied. I couldn't have fatherless kids, nor could I handle it if something happened to him. I touched the side of his face with care. "I know you care about me, Dreads, but let it go. Please. I don't want nothing ugly to happen. I'll be fine."

Terrence threw up his hands. "A'ight, li'l mama."

After he hugged the kids and said his goodbyes to them, he whispered in my ear, "You know that I love you, Trinity, and I only want what's best for you. Pooch ain't what's best.

He never has been and never will be. Men pay
for hookers, but they love their woman. Don't
let money turn you from the latter to the first.
You're a *woman*, Trinity, and a damn good one."

Nodding, I swallowed the lump in my throat.
"Good night, Terrence."

With that, the kids and I walked out of the
apartment, down the corridor, and to my await-
ing car, where Pooch sat brooding and staring
out the window.

"What that nigga say to you?" Pooch asked
when we got in the car.

"I just told him not to say nothing and not to
fuck with you," I answered, telling the partial
truth. "So he was playing with the kids and
telling them good-bye."

"Damn straight," Pooch said, feeling like he'd
won. "That's what's up. Let him know, baby."

"You know I got your back, Pooch," I lied,
hoping this was the end of it.

He gripped my thigh. "I know. I just have to
make sure that any nigga knows that you are
Pooch's woman, because I already know you
damn sure remember that. Ain't that right?"

I nodded in agreement. "Yes, baby."

He leaned over and kissed me on the cheek.
"Good. Now he can feel me on that shit," he said,
leaning back in the passenger seat, as I turned

up the radio. "Feenin'," by Jodeci, was on the smooth sounds station, and Pooch began to laugh. "When we get home, you put all the kids to bed, because I want to eat five stars tonight. Matter of fact, I'm upgrading that shit to six stars, 'cause we hitting the pole."

"All right, Pooch."

I was ready to get my freak on with Pooch, but for all the wrong reasons. The way Terrence showed concern for me and defended me had aroused me in a way I hadn't been aroused in a long time. I was definitely going to be thinking about Terrence's ass tonight, especially since it was the only way I'd ever get to be with him again. I loved Pooch, but I missed Terrence. I missed him a lot.

Charice

Giving up Ryan was the toughest thing for me to do. Surprisingly, as promised, he'd arrived at my mother's house at noon that next day to pick up the kids. My mom had agreed to pick them up from me and take them back to her house and then to drop them back off after the visit just to prevent any "Ryan sightings." I was truly grateful for that. He had kept the kids for about six hours that day. After taking them over his parents' house for a barbecue, he'd taken them to the park and to the toy store. By the time they'd got home, they were loaded with toys and clothes that Ryan and his mother had given them.

I should say *grandmother*, as funny as it sounds. Once Ryan had decided he wanted to play Daddy, she had suddenly wanted to jump in as a full-fledged grandma. For a full month, she'd been calling three times a week just to check on the kids, and she'd even kept them all day one Saturday a couple of weeks ago.

An even bigger surprise was Ryan had been calling to check on the kids at least twice a week, each time making sure he spoke with all three of them. He'd even tried to converse with me on more than one occasion about giving our relationship another try. I should've been happy that everything I'd always wanted was coming to fruition, and for the kids, I was. However, this last incident with Ryan had done something to me. Although I loved him, I couldn't let myself be with him. Believe me, as much as I loved him, being with him would be the easiest thing to do, but every time I felt myself giving in, a voice in the back of my head kept saying, *He only has love for you, Charice. He doesn't actually love you.* Then, without hesitation, I'd hold my ground. I was finally facing the fact that Ryan did not love me anymore. Deep down I'd always thought that he did but that he wasn't mature enough to handle it. Now that I felt he didn't, it was easier not to dream about being with him, you know? So here I was, with everything I had thought I wanted at my fingertips, and I refused to grasp it. My, how the tide had turned.

It'd been a long day at work today, and I was thankful that the kids were spending the night at my mom's house. There was nothing like a little downtime for myself. I planned on spending my time wisely too. I stopped by my mom's house to kiss my babies and then went to Boston Market to grab some food. While I sat in the restaurant and ate, I decided I was going straight home to soak in my whirlpool tub, with my Twilight Woods bubble bath, while I listened to soft music. Afterward, I was going to cuddle up with a book entitled *Something on the Side*, by one of my favorite authors, Mr. Carl Weber. One of my coworkers had told me that he had put his toenail in this one, and I was anxious to get to it. The three women at work who had read it before me kept telling me to get to the part about Coco getting revenge on the skinny chick from the gym. I didn't know what she did, but I wasn't going to stop reading until I got to that part or passed out from exhaustion for trying.

Once home, I grabbed my mail and headed into the house. I prepped my whirlpool bath and got into the tub. Soft music serenaded me as the warm water soothed me. As I rested my head against the back of the tub, I let out a deep sigh.

"This is the life," I said aloud to myself. "Oh, shoot! Let me open my mail."

I dried my hands and grabbed the stack that I'd placed on the side of the bathtub. The first two pieces of mail were my water and light bills.

I hurriedly put them to the side so that they wouldn't spoil my high. The next piece was a Frederick's of Hollywood catalog.

"Ha!" I laughed. "And just who the hell am I supposed to buy this stuff for? I have no one to enjoy it with besides the Lord, and I'm positive he ain't looking for that." I giggled to myself as I put down the catalog.

The last item was an envelope addressed to me. It was handwritten, with only a P.O. box as the return address.

"Who the hell is this from?" I asked aloud as I opened the envelope.

Low and behold, there was a letter inside from Ryan and a check for seven thousand dollars. This mofo had actually kept his promise and had sent the child support, with an extra grand. I nearly pooped in the tub. Hell, I'd expected the check from him for ten grand to have a stop payment, but it had gone through, so I had used some of that money to pay off my credit card bill and the kids' day care bill for two months and had put the rest in their savings account. Even still, I had never figured I'd get more from Ryan. I had just thought he was doing that at the time out of guilt. He must be really serious about taking care of the kids, I thought to myself as I opened the letter. It read:

Dear Ricey,

I know I lost my privilege to call you that, but to me, you'll always be just that, my Ricey. By now, I was hoping that you'd be calm enough to talk directly to me, but I see every time I call, you cut me off at the pass. I can't say I blame you, though. I hurt you for so long and so many times that I know you don't know what to trust from me at this point. Hell, I barely trust myself to get it right after so many years of getting it wrong.

I will admit that I loved Iris. I really did, and I hope that doesn't hurt you. I'm not telling you to hurt you. I'm telling you that because I want you to know that I was served with a dose of my own medicine. I know how it feels to give your whole heart to someone and have them rip it from you like it wasn't shit. That's what Iris did to me, and that's what I did to you. For that, I am truly sorry and I wholeheartedly apologize.

The incident with her forced me to look at my life. You know, really evaluate it. When I came home a month ago, I came to get my ego stroked and to prove that I still had it. To prove that there was a woman in this world who still wanted and loved me. The problem was that I was trying to prove that to Iris instead of realizing it for myself.

When we made love—and I do mean made love—that night, about five minutes into that, I knew it was far beyond sex. There was a moment when you were on top of me and you looked me in my eyes and you said to me, "Ryan, you have my heart forever." That changed me. Here I was, heartbroken over a woman who could care less about me and on a mission to prove some shit that she could care less about. When you said that, and I looked into your eyes, it was as if for the first time, I saw your soul. You were so pure and real. You were a diamond in the rough.

Our entire relationship flashed before my eyes, and I remembered the way you looked at me the first time we met in high school. I remembered that sexy yet devilish smile you gave me when you first sat at the football table. I remembered how you came to every game and cheered for me. I remembered how you'd talk to me, encourage me, support me, and how you loved me. I remembered how you made love to me. You did anything I wanted and gave me everything I needed, and when you needed me most, I abandoned you. Except for this time, I also abandoned my children.

So many people preached to me about it. As you know, I lied to everyone I knew about having children. Only one person saw through that, and that was my boy Lincoln. He's, like, one of your favorite ballplayers. He's like my big brother, and he says he could tell by the way I kept my family life a secret and how I avoided the topic of marriage and children as if it was the plague. He says he was in my predicament, and he denied his seed as well, but he regrets every moment of it. His words of wisdom have been healing me and hurting me at the same time. I want to learn to fix my mess before it's too late.

You may not believe this, but my mom and dad preached to me all the time about turning my back on the kids. I know they seemed to have supported me in front of you and your family, but trust me, it was only a front. I am their child, so they would never betray me to someone else, but my mom has been angry at me for

*years for abandoning them. She stayed
away because she was scared to get attached to them out of fear that you would
snatch them away from her because of
me. So she did the minimum she could not
to piss you off and still keep tabs on her
grandchildren. So I beg of you to please
let my mom be involved in their lives. She
would be so happy to finally be able to be a
real grandmother to them.*

*As for me, I'm learning about myself
every day. I look at my teammates, with
their spouses and kids, and I get a pain
in my chest, because for the first time, I
realize that could have been me if I hadn't
been so damn stupid. Don't get me wrong,
Charice. I loved you back then. I did. It's
just that I was young, and for my entire
life, all I could ever see was the NFL and
then a family further down the road. I
never intended to get the family first, so
I didn't know how to handle it. I'm not
making excuses, because I realize that
you didn't know how to handle it, either.
It's just that for the first time, I finally
get it. And now that I got it, I can't have
it. And that shit tears me up a little more
every day.*

I know I can build a relationship with my children, and I fully intend to, but what I want also is the woman who was meant to be my wife, and that is you. I told you at your house that I wanted to fall in love with you again. But, Charice, I already have. Now that I have quit lying to myself, I realize that I always have been in love with you. I just forced myself to look in another direction after the last time I got you pregnant, because I was afraid. No one has ever compared to you, and no one ever will. I understand that your heart won't allow me inside, and I can't help but face the fact that it's my own fault. So like a man, for the first time, I accept that. But if you ever change your mind, I'm here and ready to love you forever. ☺

I hope you read this letter and see that everything I've said is true to form. Maybe you will, and perhaps you won't, but I had to let you know exactly how I felt about you and about the new me. Having said that, I'm keeping my promise. I've included my monthly child-support payment and an extra grip just for you. Before you reject it, I included it because I want you to bring the kids to Dallas to see me play. I have a home game in two weeks, and I wanted you to get some nice things for yourself. If you agree to come down, give me a call and I will get the tickets together. You are welcome to stay at my house, and if not, I will pay for the hotel expenses. However, I do ask that the kids stay with me. Please. It would mean the world to me. Hopefully, while you're here, we can come to a visitation agreement.

Again, I apologize for everything I've ever done to you, not done for you and the kids, and most importantly, I apologize for not realizing that I could search the world over and still end up at you.

I pray this letter finds you in good spirits, and may you find the peace that surpasses all understanding.

Love you always and forever,
Ryan

By the time I finished that letter, I had cried more tears than there was water in the tub. He had actually handwritten the letter himself. I knew his writing just like I knew everything else about him. Talk about shocked. My heart was running through a gamut of emotions. While I believed him and, for the most part, loved him in return, I wasn't ready to go down that road with him and didn't know if I ever would again. Regardless of what we had gone through, we had children. Therefore, I was going to agree to this trip to get away for a while and enjoy spending the hell out of this grip he'd sent. The kids deserved it, and I loved football. Besides the Falcons, Dallas was my favorite team, and no, it was not because he was on it. I was a Cowgirl who watched all the famous Cowboys play, including Ryan and his friend Mr. Lincoln Harper, long before I was a Dirty Bird. Believe that.

As I leaned back in the hot water and bubbles, I picked up my cell phone and dialed Ryan's number. He answered on the second ring.

"Hey, Charice," he answered, excitedly.

I laughed. "Hello, Ryan. I didn't catch you at a bad time, did I?"

"No. I was just sitting here watching ESPN," he replied.

"All work all the time, huh?"

"Most times." He laughed.

"I feel you on that note."

"I take it you're calling me about the letter."

"That's correct," I answered.

"Before you reject my offer about the trip, just hear me out—"

"I wasn't going to reject it. I was going to accept it," I interrupted him.

He gasped. "You were?"

"Yes, I was . . . am. And you don't have to worry about the hotel stay. The kids and I will stay at your home that weekend."

He yelled out in excitement. "Ricey, I know that I've done some messed up things to you in the past—"

"Ryan, I'm not getting back with you," I said sadly, interrupting him.

"Huh?" he asked, confused. "But I thought you said that you were staying—"

"Staying, yes. I want to grant your wish about the kids staying at your house, but I'm not letting them stay in a strange house overnight by themselves. I will be there, but it will be for the kids."

He let out an exasperated sigh. "That's fair enough. I will get the tickets together, as promised. Would you prefer me to schedule a morning or afternoon flight?"

"What day are you scheduling the flight?"

"On that Friday. I wanted to spend time together, if you don't mind."

"Then make it for in the morning. I'll keep the kids out of school that day, and we can get on the plane early, so you all can spend time together."

"You sure it's okay for them to miss school? I don't want to interfere with their schedule," he said.

"It's no problem. It's only one day."

"Okay," he replied. "I'll call you later in the week with the details."

"Okay."

"So where are the kids? I don't hear them."

"At my mom's, spending the night."

"Oh okay. Well, good. You get a little break."

"Yep."

"So what are you doing? It sounds noisy."

I laughed. "I'm in my whirlpool tub."

He coughed, nearly choking on something. "Oh, okay. Real talk?"

"Yeah, real talk."

He paused for a moment. "I wish I was a bubble in the tub," he mumbled.

I laughed. "Well, you could've been."

"I know, Ricey, I know. Will I ever be again?"

"As far as I know now, the answer is no," I said sternly.

He cleared his throat. "Well, I'd love to chat, but honestly, I can't sit here in good faith and have a discussion, knowing you are naked in the tub on the other end."

I giggled. "All right, then. Just call me with the details."

"All right. Good night, Ricey. Enjoy your bubble bath," he said seductively, as if he was picturing me in the tub.

"Oh, I will. I have my glass of wine, my soft music, my scented candles, and the water is good and wet . . . I mean hot. Good night, Ryan," I said, fucking with him. I laughed because before I hung up, I could hear him cursing himself for being stupid.

My, oh, my! How the tide is turning! I thought to myself.

Charice

The kids were completely stoked about going to spend the weekend with their daddy. I hated to admit it, but I was a little excited as well. Not because I wanted to see Ryan but, damn it, this would be my first vacation since the triplets were born. I'd been working, going to school, and tending to children for so long, and I had never taken a break. Although the kids were coming with me, this was "Daddy time" for Ryan, so I was going to soak up as much alone time as I could. We'd have time to do family things together, but best believe that Daddy was going to get his fair share of alone time with the kids.

My mother was livid that I had agreed to go. She didn't think I was strong enough to withstand Ryan's wooing. I hadn't told her about the letter and how it had affected me. If I had the strength to tell him no after that, then Ms. Charice had come a long way. You don't understand how much power Ryan had over me. If that nigga wanted me to drop my drawers and screw him buck naked in the middle of the freeway during lunch-hour traffic, with a police roadblock set up, I would do it. Ass, titties, and pussy would be swinging and getting it all to please him. Maybe that was a little extreme, but my feelings for him had been just that, extreme. Back then, I had loved him more than I had loved myself, but the difference now was I had learned to love myself more. Although the letter, the trip, the money, and the opportunity to get down with Ryan were enticing, I wasn't going to make myself available, period.

However, I did spend the hell out of the grand he gave me. Knee-high designer boots; designer jeans; pants; tops; stilettos, a clubbing outfit, spa treatment complete with a facial, hairdo, manicure and pedicure; and I was set. I used some of the money he'd sent for the kids and got them all new outfits as well. My babies couldn't half step now. Damn, representing Ryan Westmore. They were representing Charice Taylor. My little dudes were GQ with their jeans, button-down shirts, sweater vests, and Polo boots. They were Sean Johned and Ralph Laurened down. Oh, and my little mama was designer galore. Looking at our duds, you'd think we were a part of the rich and famous. Well, technically, the kids were.

The first-class flight was amazing. The kids ate burgers and fries, while I ate lobster and drank champagne. After eating, I covered my-self up with my warm blanket to sleep, while the kids enjoyed a movie. A sister could get used to this real quick, especially now that Ryan was financially supporting the kids. No lie, it was a happy feeling to be at work, knowing there was no financial need to be there. It felt good to collect my paycheck and not have one single, solitary bill to pay with it. My bank account had grown tremendously with the hefty child-support checks, and I was spending wise-ly. I had an interest-bearing savings account and a life insurance policy for the kids. I had also invested a little in the stock market, which was doing well. Your girl ain't no slow leak, and this shit could end tomorrow if anything hap-pened to Ryan, so I wanted to be sure that what we had multiplied.

It was two in the afternoon when we arrived in Dallas. To avoid the fans that would try to flock to him, Ryan had sent over his car service to pick us up from the airport. I didn't feel like being bothered with the public and preferred not to be on Media Takeout before I even set foot within the city limits.

A man wearing a black suit approached us as we headed in the direction of the baggage claim. "Ms. Taylor?" he asked.

"Yes?"

"I am your limo driver. Can I assist with your baggage?" he said.

"Yes. It's at the baggage claim."

He walked with us to pick up our luggage, and we carried the suitcases to the car. Once we were in the car and settled in, the driver told us that we'd be at the house within twenty minutes. The kids were so full of excitement that they babbled one hundred miles an hour. On the other hand, I paid close attention to the route the driver took, in case I needed to get back to the airport on my own.

Exactly twenty-two minutes later, we pulled up to the entrance to a gated community. The guard requested the name of the person we were visiting, asked for our limo driver's license, and wrote down his name and tag number, along with the time we arrived. After calling Ryan to confirm, the guard opened the gates. As we pulled into the neighborhood, I took in some of the most exquisite houses I'd seen in my life. The kids were all oohs and aahs. Hell, I would be too if I wasn't busy paying attention to the turns the driver made. It was a right, left, straight, and then left again. I plugged the route into my mind. By the time we pulled into Ryan's driveway, he was standing in the yard, with a big smile on his face.

"Daddy!" the kids yelled as they jumped out of the car and ran to him.

He ran and met them, and they all jumped on him with excitement and fell to the ground. "What's up, kiddos? Miss me?" he asked, wrestling and tickling them.

"Yes!" they said in unison, laughing.

The driver and I laughed at the scene as he grabbed the bags out of the trunk.

"Ryan, this man probably has other work to do," I said, bringing his focus to the driver.

Ryan jumped up. "Oh man, my bad," he said, rushing toward us. He hugged me and held me tightly. "How you been, Ricey?"

"Just fine."

"I can see that, but I asked how you been," he said jokingly.

I laughed. "Whatever. You're lame," I said, pulling back from his embrace.

He reached into his pocket and pulled out a gwop of money. After peeling off two hundred dollars in bills, he tipped the driver. "Thank you. You have a good one, my man."

The limo driver nodded his approval. "Thanks, Mr. Westmore. You do the same. Good day to you, ma'am."

Once Ryan and I got the bags into the house, he took us on the grand tour of his estate. I called it an estate because I didn't think I'd ever stop walking around it.

"This is your room, boys," he said when we entered a huge bedroom with double-sized bunk beds. It was decorated with Dallas Cowboys paraphernalia and a huge Fathead of Ryan in his uniform on the wall. The room also came equipped with a PS3, an Xbox 360, PSPs, and a forty-two-inch flat-screen television with a DVD player, and the furnishings looked like something out of the Ashley Furniture catalog.

"Cool! Way cool!" Ray exclaimed, running around the room.

"Double way cool!" Ryan Jr. laughed. "Top bunk!" he yelled out.

"I wanted the top!" Ray said.

"I said it first!" Ryan yelled.

"No fair! You didn't ask first!" Ray replied.

"Mom!" they yelled in unison.

I looked at Ryan. "The joy of having boys that are the same age," I said, shaking my head.

"I got this." He smiled.

I shrugged. "Go ahead, *Dad*." Actually, I wanted to see how he handled his first dispute.

"Hey, guys, listen," he said, and they turned to face him. "You two are brothers, and as brothers, you have to look out for each other. You always have to have each other's back."

"But—" Ryan Jr. began.

"I know, dude," Ryan interrupted. "You called it first, but don't you think the best thing to do is to ask your brother if you can have the top bunk?" Ryan asked his miniature-sized twin.

Ryan Jr. exhaled and rolled his eyes. "Can I please have the top bunk, Ray?"

"So I guess I'm supposed to be nice and say yes, huh?" Ray asked, looking at his dad. I had to stifle a smile. Ray was so like me. I guessed that was why he and Ryan Jr. fought all the time. It was like watching Ryan and me go at it.

"You do what you feel is right, my man," Ryan said.

Ray rolled his eyes. "Fine, Ryan. You can have the top."

I knew it. Just like me. He is so willing to give in to Ryan Jr., just like I gave in to Ryan Sr., I thought.

"Yes!" Ryan Jr. exclaimed as Ray gave him a sad look.

And Ryan Jr. is just like his daddy, so willing to accept his good fortune, despite others feelings, I thought.

Suddenly, Ryan Jr. noticed Ray's expression and instantly felt bad. "Okay, well, like Daddy said, we have to have each other's back. What if you sleep up at the top tomorrow?"

Well, I'll be damned. Maybe he's got a little of me in him too, or perhaps he's changing, like his father.

Ray smiled. "Yeah! Thanks, Ryan," he said, and they gave each other a high five. Like that, the problem was solved.

I was impressed. Ryan's little talk about looking out for one another had gotten somewhere with them. I guess it was true. Boys did need their fathers.

I couldn't help but clap. "Good job!"

Ryan bowed. "Thank you."

"They won't all be that easy, you know," I informed him.

"They can't argue *that* much," Ryan said, then looked at me, expecting me to agree.

Charity and I looked at one another and laughed. "Oh, grasshopper, you wait and see," I said to him.

After leaving Ryan Jr. and Ray to enjoy their room, Ryan walked Charity to hers. "And this, my little princess, is for you," he said, opening the door. The Cinderella carriage–style bed was accompanied by a vanity, a dollhouse, and every doll, book, and accessory you could imagine. Hanging on the wall was another forty-two-inch flat panel with a DVD player, and Charity's room also came stocked with Disney movies.

"Oh, Daddy!" she squealed, hugging him tightly. "I love you."

Ryan picked her up and held her close. Tears formed in his eyes. He had to clear his throat.

"I love you too, Charity. I will spend the rest of my life showing you and your brothers just how much."

I had to turn away. That statement touched me. Suddenly, Charity was out of Ryan's arms and shooing us out of her room so she could set up her tea party.

"Wow. She kicked us out fast." Ryan laughed.

"Oh yeah, love lasts only a moment with these kids, and then it's like, 'Okay. Go away,'" I joked. "Kind of like their father," I added, taking a dig at him. I couldn't help it.

He looked at me sadly. "Charice, I know I've been an ass, but I am sorry. I'm changing."

"I was just joking," I said regretfully. "Seriously, I was."

"I guess a hit dog will holler."

"Basically." I giggled.

After playfully pushing me, he opened a door down the hall. "This is your room, jokester."

"It better not be in your room," I joked as I entered. "Wow. This *is* beautiful."

The high-top bed showcased the best plush linens, a fireplace took up part of one wall, and the room was outfitted with top-notch wood furniture, including a chaise lounge, and an en suite full bath. The bedroom was complete with a sitting area, and there another forty-two-inch flat-panel TV and DVD player hung from the wall.

"I'm glad you like it."

I sat down on the chaise lounge, lay back, and stroked my long mane. "A girl could get used to this!" I joked.

When I opened my eyes, Ryan was standing over me. "You can have this," he said, looking down at me. His voice was sincere, and the look in his eyes told me that he hoped I felt the same way.

When I stood up, we were face-to-face. This was why I had my reservations about staying at his house. I knew he would find a way to try to open the doorway to my heart. A part of me would always love and care for Ryan. Hell, up until a few months ago, this was everything that I wanted and felt that I needed. However, after all the drama behind the Iris situation, there was no way I could look back. I still felt a pain in my heart for what could've been. That was what made this so damn hard.

"It's not for me," I told him.

"It's *all* for you," he said, pulling me close to him. "I want it to be."

Damn my body and my emotions. Despite what my mind was saying, my pussy had a mind of its own and was two seconds from being wet when Charity burst into the room. Thank God.

"Daddy, come have tea!" she shouted, running toward him.

Ryan deflated. "Baby, can Daddy do tea later? I was really in the middle of something," he pleaded.

Stepping out of his embrace, I waved my hands back and forth. "No, don't let me interfere. This is all about the kids, remember?" I reminded him.

"Charice," he pleaded.

I smiled and shook my head. "No, Daddy, you have to do tea."

Begrudgingly, he relented. "Okay, so who wants tea?"

Charity jumped up and down. "I do! I do! Come on, Daddy," she said, pulling him by his hand out of the room.

"We have unfinished business," he shouted to me as I shut the door behind them.

Okay, Charice. Pull yourself together. This ain't what you want, I pleaded with myself. This was what I was afraid of. I didn't want Ryan to feel like I was here to give us a second chance. I was strictly here for the kids, but of course, who wouldn't want the man they'd always loved to love them back and offer this lavish lifestyle? However, opting for it was making the choice to open a door that I had vowed to keep closed.

Ryan had hurt me over and over again without any regard for my feelings, and this last time had nearly ripped my soul in half. It had taken a lot of prayers, meditation, and self-reflection to realize that I didn't need Ryan to be complete. So I didn't care how vulnerable I was emotionally or physically; I kept everything in perspective. Ryan and I were done.

After unpacking, I took a shower, a quick nap, and got dressed again. I loved the alone time. It was so rejuvenating. Luckily, the kids had Ryan so tied up that by the time he had a breather, it was close to dinnertime. Ryan wanted to take us to this "well-to-do" restaurant, and although I tried to explain that the kids hadn't acquired a taste for fine dining yet, he insisted. Ryan quickly found that out for himself. Dinner was absolutely hilarious. Once we were seated, Ray and Ryan Jr. kept trying to pop one another with the linen dinner napkins, and once Charity found out they served duck, she screamed and cried and told the waiter that they killed the ducks on Old Macdonald's Farm. While the others patrons laughed at the innocence of the moment, Ryan decided it was time to leave and tipped the waiter for the inconvenience. We settled on the ever-famous Pizza Hut.

Once we got home, I gave Charity a bath and let Ryan handle the boys. After getting Charity ready for bed, I walked her to her bedroom and then searched for Ryan to tell him to tuck her in. When I found him, he had fallen asleep beside the bottom bunk in the boys' room. It was so cute that I had to take a picture of it, but the flash woke him up.

"How long have I been out?" he asked, jumping up.

"Not long, I'm sure, but I had to take a picture. Looks like the boys are knocked out as well. They had a long and exciting day. I was actually coming to get you to say good night to Charity."

"I'm right behind you," he said as he pulled the blankets up on Ray and Ryan Jr.

Once we got to Charity's room, she was already asleep. "Looks like she couldn't hold out," I said, moving to tuck her in.

"Allow me, please," he said before he pulled the blanket over her and kissed her forehead. "She is so gorgeous, just like her mom."

"I know," I joked as we walked out of the room. "Ryan, I really appreciate this. The kids needed this, and I'm so proud that this moment has finally come," I said to him as we walked toward my bedroom.

"So why don't you make the moment complete?" he asked, walking up on me.

"It already is. You have a relationship and a bond with your children, and that's the most important thing in the world."

"You know what I mean."

"And you heard what I said," I replied with a slight sternness. "Look, Ryan, I care about you and even love you, but our time has come and gone. I need for you to understand that."

"I understand it, but I can't accept it," he said, holding my face between his hands. "Please, Charice. I'll do anything you want, anything you say, and whatever you need. I'll do it all for you."

His request was so sincere. Even the old Ryan wasn't as thoughtful and genuine. He was in rare form, and for the first time, I truly believed I saw his heart in action. Yet it wasn't enough. My love for him was blind, so I had to be sure that I could see the forest for the trees when it came to him. It all seemed wonderful, but I'd been stuck on the grandeur of his wonderfulness in the past, and it had left me brokenhearted and knocked up. This time I would stick to my head and let my gut and heart take a back seat.

After taking Ryan's hands into my own, I held them, then looked into his eyes and kissed him softly on the lips. "Thank you, Ryan. I've waited for so long to hear those words come out of your mouth, but it's too late for us. I don't want to hurt you. I know we've been through a lot together, but we just cannot be together."

As Ryan nodded slowly, I could tell his feelings were hurt. "Hopefully, I'll be able to change your mind about us one day," he said.

"Good night, Ryan," I said, and then I went into my bedroom and locked the door.

When I arose this morning, I felt completely rested. Admittedly, it'd been the best night's sleep that I'd had in a long time, if ever. Whew. I could fully understand why there were certain things that the rich became accustomed to having. Once you'd had a taste of the luxuries that came along with having money, it was hard to break back down to less. Struggling was never easy, but the struggle knew only the struggle. The problems arose when you came up from the struggle. Even simple things, like two hundred thread count versus two thousand thread count, felt like a nuisance. No doubt I felt like a brand-new woman when I went to the kitchen that morning to make some coffee. Surprisingly, I found that Ryan's chef had prepared pancakes, waffles, eggs, bacon, sausage, French toast, grits, and fresh fruits, and the coffee was already brewing. Lord, a sister could most definitely get used to this. Between Ryan and this lifestyle, it was hard not to give in to Ryan's vision of us being together.

"Good morning, Ms. Charice," the chef said respectfully.

"Good morning," I replied, smiling. "It sure smells good in here."

"That may be the food or the beautiful-smelling lady in the kitchen," Ryan said as he entered the kitchen.

"Good morning, Ryan." I smiled, turning to face him.

"Good morning, Charice," he said. "I woke up the kids, and they are washing up to come down and eat. Did you have a good night's sleep?"

"Did I? I barely wanted to get up."

He laughed. "Good."

"So what's on the agenda for today?" I asked, making the kids' plates.

"Actually . . . ," he said nervously. He walked up to me at the kitchen counter. "I have a little surprise for you and the kids today."

Suspicious, I asked, "What kind of *surprise*?"

He inhaled deeply. "Remember the letter I sent to you?"

"Yes," I replied, putting the plate down and drumming my fingers. I wanted him to get to the point.

"Well, I, um . . . I called a meeting with my coaches and teammates, and I explained to them about you and the kids. I wanted them to hear things from me first, and not the lopsided version from the media. They all support me and are happy that I am becoming a better man and father. They want to meet you and the kids, and I kinda told them that I would bring you all down there to introduce you," he confessed.

Hold up. Wait a minute. The kids' feet were just getting wet with establishing a relationship with Ryan. Hell, this was uncharted water for all of us. To me, it wasn't the best time to go about adding the layers of Ryan's life to the mix. There was a certain preparedness that should come with that, and neither the kids nor I was ready for it.

I shook my head and waved my hands no. "I'm not sure about this, Ryan. The kids are just getting used to *you* being in their lives. I'm not positive I want them exposed to your celebrity lifestyle all in one swoop."

He grabbed my hands and sat me down on one of the barstools that surrounded the island. He then asked the chef to give us a moment alone. "Charice, I realize it seems like a lot at one time, but this is something that should've been done a long time ago. I know you have your reservations about my lifestyle, but it's who I am. I will shelter my kids from anything that I think will hurt them, but the fact still remains that I am not only Ryan Westmore, their father, but also Ryan Westmore, the pro NFL player. Besides, when you show up at the game, it's going to be a media frenzy. There are highs and lows to having me as their dad. I really want to take you all to visit the stadium and introduce you to my teammates, especially Lincoln. He's been my backbone, my brother, and my friend throughout my career, and I want you guys to meet him. I can bet that a reporter has snapped a picture of us somewhere anyway, so you may as well be prepared for that."

I pondered this for a moment and realized that he was right. I couldn't hide the fact that the triplets' father was famous, and the kids were bound to be exposed to that lifestyle now that Ryan had stepped up. Besides, we were just meeting the team and the coaches. He did make a good point about the media firestorm that was sure to ensue when we went to his game. So, I agreed.

"You're right. We can't hide this forever," I said.

He stood up from the barstool and hugged me. "Thank you so much. This means a lot to me. The team is like my second family, and I think it's high time that my extended family meets my immediate family."

I was proud of him. He'd come a long way, and it felt good to see him finally grow up. "You're welcome."

After eating, showering, and dressing, we headed over to Cowboys Stadium. During the ride, Ryan explained that he'd set up a casual meet and greet for us with his coaches and teammates. I was a little nervous about the get-together and could tell Ryan was nervous as well. Meeting his teammates made it real for him. Football was his life, and he'd longed for that life since he was a boy. The personal life he'd kept under wraps for five years was about to collide with his professional life. He would go from being a new football playboy to a father of triplets.

The closer we got to the Cowboys Stadium, the more intense his nervousness became. "We don't have to do this if you don't want to," I said, giving him an opportunity to renege.

He shook his head. "It's time to do this, even though I'm going to look like an idiot in more ways than one."

"Why is that?"

"They know that we are not together, and now I have to bring you in here looking all kinds of fine. You are killing those jeans and thigh-high stiletto boots. On the real, you looking mighty damn hot."

I blushed as we pulled into the office parking lot.

After we got out of the car and entered the stadium, Ryan led us into a room where his teammates had assembled.

"Westmore!" they yelled as Ryan and I stood at the front of the room, the kids on both sides of us.

"Hello, everyone," Ryan replied as his teammates took their seats.

After everyone was seated, Ryan turned to face me and bowed his head. I grabbed his hand for encouragement and urged him to continue. Then he held his head up, turned around, and addressed his team.

"A couple of weeks ago, I called a meeting to tell you all about my kids. I want to thank all of you—each and every one of you—for your support. You guys are my fam, my home away from home, and I just wanted to be straight up with you all. None of you have judged me after my announcement, and that has meant the world to me," Ryan said. The vibrato in his voice hinted at the emotion that was welling up inside him.

Lincoln and the head coach walked over and patted his shoulders for encouragement as the entire room clapped for him. After the whole Iris incident, I might have had little empathy for Ryan at this moment, but given Ryan's new leaf, I understood. There was no telling what emotions he was dealing with after the lies he had told and the façade he had kept up for all those years. Pain, embarrassment, and probably joy filled him now, and as he raised his hand to his face, the tears slid down his cheeks as the reality of the situation hit him.

"Ryan, we're behind you. You're a good kid, and I'll stand on my mother's grave and admit that to anyone who asks. You made a mistake. All of us in this room have, and some of us continue to, but that's okay. We're a team and a family, and we stand by one another," the head coach said to uplift Ryan.

Ryan hugged him and shook his head as his teammates and the other coaches clapped in agreement. "I really appreciate that, Coach, but honestly, I wasn't good about this, far from it. But I appreciate the love and support," he said. Then he pulled me forward. "With that said, I promised that you all would meet my kids and their mother, and they are here with me today. This young lady here is Charice Taylor. She's a good woman and has loved me ever since I was a kid playing varsity ball at fifteen. She'll never know how truly sorry I am, but I will make amends for some things, even if I can't for everything," Ryan said, looking at me sorrowfully.

I swallowed the lump in my throat. I couldn't believe he had said that about me in front of his teammates.

He went on. "And my three beautiful kids are Charity, Ray, and Ryan Jr. These are my kids, whom I had my freshman year in college."

One of his teammates cheered, and then slowly, everyone joined in. Ryan smiled as he picked up Charity, tossed her in the air, and caught her.

"Way to man up, baby bro! We're proud of you, Ryan," Lincoln said between the thunderous applause and cheering.

"Hey, I learned from the best," Ryan told Lincoln.

Everyone took their turn meeting me and the triplets. They made sure we felt welcomed, and of course, my sons loved every ounce of the attention they received. To them, it was like they had backstage passes at a concert. They were so young, they didn't understand that they would now be the center of attention, probably a lot more than they hoped to be. I prayed Ryan could keep his word and shield them from the ugly side of this life. Lord knows, I would.

After we were introduced to most of Ryan's team members and the coaching staff, we finally made our way over to Lincoln.

"Fam!" Lincoln yelled as he put his arm around Ryan's neck and faced me and the kids.

"My man!" Ryan greeted. "Let me personally introduce you to Charice," he said as I shook Lincoln's hand. "She's a fan."

Lincoln cocked his eyebrow to one side. "Oh really? Well, I'm honored. I'm pleased to meet you, Charice," Lincoln said happily.

"Likewise," I replied, smiling at him.

"I'm proud of him. Finally, some of my yappings are paying off," Lincoln joked, giving Ryan a playful nudge.

"I'm a knucklehead. What can I say?" Ryan shrugged.

"We all are at one point in our lives, but it's about redemption and moving forward. You have done good, son," Lincoln replied, patting him on the chest.

Ryan shrugged and shook his head. "I'm trying."

"And that's what matters most," I added, and they both agreed.

"Speaking of moving forward, what about your relationship?" Lincoln asked. "Y'all gonna work that out?" He motioned back and forth between Ryan and me.

Ryan shook his head. "No, my bed has been made on that subject, and I'm lying in it," he replied, then turned and faced me. "Even though not a day goes by that I don't regret it," he added, and I looked away. "My focus is to be a father to my kids. It's time to man up, and that's my primary concern."

"That's both of our primary concern, Lincoln. I just want him to build a good relationship with the kids," I said, facing Ryan. "That is what's *most* important."

More of Ryan's teammates walked up just then, and rather than impose, I made my way around the room, making small talk. Everyone had been extremely hospitable and cordial. I wasn't sure what I had expected, but I didn't think this meet and greet would be this warm and inviting. That in itself made me feel good about agreeing to allow the kids to have this soft introduction to Ryan's life.

While Ryan and the kids played and he chopped it up with some of the other teammates, I walked out of the room to find a vending machine and get a bottle of water. I searched a little but didn't find a snack room.

"What are you looking for?" a man's voice said behind me.

I turned and saw that it was Lincoln who had addressed me. "The vending machine. I'd love some water," I told him.

"It's down this way," he said pointing in the other direction.

Lawd. The entire time I'd been in the meeting room, I'd tried to hide my wandering eyes. Lincoln Harper was fine on television and even finer in person. He was a sight to be seen, and it was hard not to be captivated by his aura.

"Oh, thanks," I said. "I couldn't remember where I saw it."

"I'm going to get one too," he said, walking beside me. "I think what you did, despite Ryan's actions, was truly admirable. It takes a hell of a woman to do that."

"Yeah, I guess."

He gently touched my elbow, which caused us both to pause. "I *know.* I don't know if Ryan told you about me, but three years ago, I was just like Ryan. My daughter is nine, and her mom refuses to let her see me. I send the child support, but I miss my daughter. I knew Ryan had kids. I could sense it. I kept talking to him about manning up, because I didn't want to see another man act like I used to, especially a black man. We have to stand up and be accountable," he explained.

His renewed outlook on life and fatherhood touched me. I loved the fact that not only did he make the decision to stand up, but he forced others around him to step up to the plate as well.

"That's commendable. I'm sorry about your daughter. I think it's sad that her mother is using your daughter as a pawn. Regardless of what happened between Ryan and me, it's his choice to remain a good father. I'd never take that right from him. I just want what's best for our children."

"That should always be the main focus. He doesn't realize how good he has it." Lincoln shook his head. By now we had reached the vending machine, and he bought two bottles of water.

"Oh, he doesn't have anything good in *me*, but he's got a true blessing in our children." I laughed as he handed me my bottled water.

"Oh, he's got a good baby mama in you, even if it's not a good woman." He laughed. "I can tell he truly fucked up on the latter, though. You're a down-ass chick."

I laughed. "Yeah, I am . . . or I was."

"You still are." He smiled.

Suddenly, our eyes connected, and I couldn't help but blush. Did I just feel a tingle in my twat? Yep, I did, I thought to myself. Lincoln's honey-kissed skin had a beautiful glow to it. It was probably from the many hours he'd spent on the practice field. It didn't help that the practice jersey he wore clung to his hardened chest. His beautiful eyes, set off by long lashes, gave him a boyish look. Yet his chiseled jawline and defined neck muscles were undeniably manly features. When he smiled, his pearly whites were gorgeous but not as gorgeous as his masculine and muscular thighs. He was the embodiment of sheer and utter perfection. Our gaze was broken when Lincoln spoke.

"I better head back. We're supposed to begin workouts in a little while," he said nervously. He turned to walk back to the room where the team was gathered.

Surprisingly, I did something that I never thought I'd do and, more importantly, that I never planned to do. "So do you think we can go out to dinner or something? Or are you scared of a down-ass chick like me?" I asked, then laughed nervously.

What the hell? Did I really just come out and say that? I asked myself. Yep, my crazy ass did just say that. I could not believe it. I had no idea where that had come from. The last time my emotions took over my mouth like that was

when I made the first move on Ryan at the lunch
table my sophomore year. I'd admit, I was attracted to him, but I couldn't believe I was bold
enough to say that to *Lincoln Harper*, Ryan's
best friend.

He smiled and shook his head no, seemingly
against his will. "I see you, Ma." He laughed.
"But you know that's too dangerous."

I shrugged. "Then I guess you're gonna miss
out too," I said to play it down as I breezed past
him. I walked back to the room, trying to play it
cool, but on the inside, I was a nervous wreck.

Of all the people in the world, I had to be
attracted to Lincoln Harper! I swear I was going
certifiably insane. I prayed to God that Lincoln
didn't tell Ryan what had happened.

But on the flip side, it may have been bad,
and it sure as hell was wrong, but it had felt so
damn good. For the first time, I was attracted to
another man, Lincoln Harper. When I looked
over my shoulder, I saw him looking at my ass.
That let me know that he was attracted to me
as well. Even with the twinge of guilt that I felt,
I wondered, Would Lincoln and I ever get an
opportunity? Probably not.

LaMeka

Lately, life had been hard. It felt as if I walked around on eggshells to prevent anything that would set off Tony. It was to the point that I didn't ask Tony for shit, in an attempt to avoid a repeat of that fateful night. So to keep the peace around the house, I did what I had to do. I took Tony Jr. and Misha to school every day and drove Misha to work. Then I'd come home, clean up, and cook to keep my mind off Tony. Whenever I didn't have anything to do, I'd take LaMichael and go over to Trinity's to pass the time away. I did anything to avoid being around Tony.

To avoid arguments, I found myself catering to his needs as if he were a child. Literally, anything he asked, I did. If he needed a beer, I would go to the kitchen to grab a cold one and be back in a nanosecond. I cooked whatever he wanted, let him watch as much television as he wanted, left him alone when he wanted, and even fucked him when he wanted. Now that I'd mastered the art of sucking dick, Tony wanted to get his rocks off every morning and night, and I did it, sore jaw and all. I gave him everything and required nothing of him. He seemed happy that I'd turned into this doting housewife, and he eased up with the attitude.

Still, I kept my guard up and continued my routine. There was no need to rock the boat, because shit seemed kosher on the outside. The fact of the matter was that I felt used, unwanted, underappreciated, and overworked. It hurt to know that the man I'd loved all these years had become someone unrecognizable. I'd devoted what seemed to be a lifetime to him, and this was what I got in return? I knew I should've kicked him out or left myself, but deep down, I felt there was still the "old" Tony in there somewhere, if only we could find him.

For a month, everything was cool. The time I spent at Trinity's gave me something to do and someone to talk to. While LaMichael and Princess played, that gave me a break. I was sure it gave Trinity a break as well, since I knew damn well Pooch didn't take care of the kids, not even his own.

As usual, I headed over to Trinity's today, but this time it was different. LaMichael and

I wound up right back at the house because Trinity wasn't at home as usual. As I walked into the house, I heard Tony in the bedroom. My stomach did a somersault at the thought of his presence. I quickly dismissed that when I heard what sounded like other voices in the house. As the music blared, I could hear giggles and laughter coming from the bedroom. I didn't know what in the hell was going on, but I was going to find out. Quickly, I took LaMichael to Jena, my next-door neighbor, and then I walked back into my house and headed to my bedroom. When I walked in the room, I heard Tony before I could focus on the view in front of me.

"This shit is fiya, baby!" he hollered while some half-naked bitch lay on my bed. Before he noticed me, this muthafucka had the nerve to snort up a line of coke with a rolled-up dollar bill!

"I told you, baby, that's that good-good," the bitch said and laughed.

"Tony!" I yelled.

He jumped up off the bed and turned to face me with coke under his nose, and the naked bitch jumped out of the bed too.

"I thought you said she was going to be gone for a while, babe," the bitch said, confused, with her hands on her hips. She had the *nerve* to have an attitude, as if she were paying the bills up in this bitch. *The nerve of this ho.*

Rage built up in my chest as I took in the scene. Not only was the bitch half naked, but he also had his shirt off and his pants unzipped. I knew this bastard hadn't fucked this bitch in our bed and snorted cocaine with her ass.

"What the fuck is you doing home? You supposed to be at Trinity's house!" he yelled.

"And you supposed to be *my man*!" I yelled back. "Who the fuck is this bitch?" I screamed, pointing at the girl.

"*Bitch*? I got your bitch!" she hollered. She attempted to come at me, but Tony pushed her back down on the bed.

Tony gave the bitch a seething glare. "Cool that shit, girl," he demanded. After turning to me, he raised his hands in surrender. "Okay, so you caught me. I admit it. I'm guilty as a muthafucka, baby. I've been screwing this ho on the side and snorting, but that's only because your ass is so inexperienced, and plus, I know you won't hit this good shit," he said, picking up a a vial of cocaine and holding it in his hand.

Tears formed in my eyes. There were so many things wrong with this picture. And what the hell did he just say to me? Did he really say he knew I wouldn't snort coke with him? Did he degrade me in front of his cracked-out whore? My body felt as if it had gone into shock. Aside from the vile words that had spewed from his mouth, the worst thing of all was that he had violated me in the worst way.

"You've been fucking this dopehead bitch and then fucking me too? We got kids! I'm the mother of your children, Tony! What if this bitch catches something and gives it to you and you give it to me? Did you even think about that?"

"This bitch knows better, but on the real yo, I strap up every time," he said uncaringly.

"Every time, ho!" the bitch yelled. "He 'bout to be mine anyway. You can't feel a nigga like Tony. He needs a bottom bitch like me to hold him down."

"You ghetto-slut ho!" I shouted and charged at her, then punched her in the mouth. Once my hands landed on her, I didn't let up. I whipped her ass so hard that I accidentally punched Tony as he tried to separate us.

"Fucking bitch!" Tony yelled, and then he backhanded me so hard that I flew off the bed and hit the floor. "My lip is fucking bleeding."

As I stood up and held my swollen face, the reality of the situation settled inside me. Here I was, in love with a man who was on drugs, who beat me, and who cheated on me while I took care of all the household responsibilities and our kids. *Oh, hell naw.* This couldn't be life. I refused to let this be life. I couldn't take it anymore. I had reached my breaking point.

"Get out of my house! Take your bitch and get the fuck out, Tony! I hate your ass! I hate everything about you! I even hate that I had kids by you! Fuck you! I don't need this shit in my life! Go on, nigga! Take your bottom bitch and be out!" I yelled as I tried to rub away the sting of his slap on my cheek.

Tony had a sinister look in his eyes when we made eye contact. It felt like I was looking into the eyes of the devil himself. For the first time since I'd known Tony, I looked at him and didn't know who he was. The Tony I'd loved and given children to no longer existed. He had become a stranger in my house.

"You think you gon' kick me out and tear me away from my kids?" he seethed, pointing to himself.

"You don't give a fuck about them anyway. Just leave," I cried, praying that he would just go.

Biting on his bottom lip, he reared back on his legs and made the cut sign across his neck with his hand. "No, bitch, I ain't going nowhere," he said sternly as he shook his head.

Before I knew it, he was on top of me. I put my arms up to shield my face, but he gut punched me twice. I yelled out in pain and grabbed my stomach. Suddenly, he popped me across my face with his fist, splitting my lip. It felt like I had gotten hit by a truck as blood poured out of my mouth. As I sat there, dazed, he took off his belt and beat me with the buckle.

"I'm gon' teach your ass a lesson about frontin' on me! You are *my bitch*, and I ain't going nowhere, and neither are you!" he yelled.

"Please!" I cried as he repeatedly hit me on my back and thighs with the buckle. Each hit felt as if a brick had landed hard on me. I could feel my skin burning and swelling wherever the buckle landed.

"I'm *Daddy*! I'm *king* in this bitch, and you gonna respect me!" he hollered as spit flew from his lips and landed in my face. His coke-induced high caused his nose to run, and he kept wiping it in between hits.

I noticed the bottom bitch standing next to the bed, giggling with her high ass. "Get her, baby. Teach her who the boss is! You the boss, baby!"

He laughed. "Yep, I am. Ain't I, Kwanzie?"

She danced in a circle tauntingly. "Yep, shol' is! Go, Tony. Go, Tony."

At this point, I could only take the abuse, but my mind was fixed on murder. I swore I was going to kill him and Kwanzie's ass as soon as I healed. When I got my hands on them, it would be over for them.

He grabbed me by my hair and yanked me up off the floor. "Now, who is your daddy?" he asked, looking at me.

I spat blood in his face. I knew it was a stupid move, but I was pissed. He kicked me in my stomach, I fell down, and he pulled me back up by my hair, but this time, he reached in his waistband, pulled out a nickel-plated 9 mm pistol, and pointed it in my face. "Wrong answer, bitch!"

I'd never understood the statement about your life flashing before your eyes until that moment. I saw my life flash before my eyes as they grew wide from fear. Any rage I had subsided in an instant. My survival was all that mattered now. I had my kids to think about.

He took off the safety on the pistol and pointed it at me again. "*Now*, who is your daddy?"

Warm tears rolled down my cheeks and mixed with the blood in my mouth. "You are, Tony," I replied in between sobs.

He slowly lowered the gun from my face. "Good answer. That's a good bitch," he said, releasing his grip and rubbing my hair.

I walked away slowly, holding my stomach, and prayed that I made it out of the house. I hadn't made it to the bedroom door yet before he yelled at me.

"Where are you going?" he asked as he pushed Kwanzie back down onto the bed.

I turned and faced him. "My stomach . . . my face," I said, barely able to speak.

"This shit turns me on. Come over here," he ordered, motioning to me with the gun.

Afraid of the consequences of disobeying him, I slowly walked over to him. He turned and held me so that my back was against him.

"Kwanzie, pull them panties off," he ordered.

"What are you doing?" I asked fearfully as she lay back on the bed and removed her underwear.

"I'm gonna fuck you from the back while you eat that good pussy." He laughed.

Instantly, I became nauseated and covered my mouth. "No, please no!"

"Bitch, come on! My pussy is wet just thinking about this shit. I love when females eat me out," Kwanzie said with a sinister laugh.

Desperation and panic filled me as I begged relentlessly for them to stop this. "Tony, please don't make me do this. I'm not gay. I don't like pussy, please."

With no mercy shown to me, he grabbed me by my neck and held tightly. He pulled me close to him so that his lips grazed my ear. "Eat that shit, and eat it proper, or I will pull this trigger," he said, his voice low and stern. The pistol's round muzzle pressed into the back of my neck, and I was scared speechless.

He pushed me down on the bed doggy-style, snatched my pants down, and penetrated me raw and rough. He pumped and yelled, "Eat that bitch now! Open wide, Kwanzie. Mama gotta eat you."

I forced the bile that threatened to escape my lips back down my throat, put my face in her pussy, and began to lick and eat that shit while Tony fucked me from behind. He gripped my ass, and I felt the weight of the gun lying on my back.

"Ohhh, yes!" Kwanzie yelled. "Tony, this bitch is a natural. She's eating my shit proper!"

Tony became more turned on and immediately nutted all over my ass. "Ooh! Shit. That was hot!"

"Let me taste!" Kwanzie said as Tony flipped me over.

She went down in between my legs and ate me while he grabbed the Vaseline. This sick nigga masturbated with one hand while pointing the gun at me and Kwanzie with the other. This sick shit must've really turned him on, because he came in his hand as he watched her violate my pussy. Kwanzie then turned and sucked all that cum off his dick right in front of my face.

"That shit was the bomb!" he yelled. "Bitch, get out and go home. My baby gotta get herself together so she can take care of my son. Now go!" he ordered Kwanzie, barely giving her time to finish swallowing the cum off his dick.

This crackhead ho stood up and wiped her mouth with the back of her hand and then dressed quickly. She kissed Tony on the cheek. "See you later, baby."

He popped her on the ass before she left. Then he looked at me. "Get up and clean yourself. Where is LaMichael?"

"Next door," I replied weakly.

"Cool. I'm 'bout to take a dump. Clean up and get him," he said, then placed the gun on the dresser before he walked out into the hall bathroom.

I ran into our master bathroom and hurled into the toilet repeatedly. When I reached the point that I couldn't vomit anymore, I got up and poured a load of mouthwash into my mouth. After spitting repeatedly, I brushed my teeth three times, until my mouth was minty fresh and clean. I stood in front of the sink and, using a fresh cloth, washed the blood off my face. My swollen lip couldn't be hidden, and my body ached from the bruises left by the belt buckle. I couldn't focus on that, because I had to get my son. Rather than try to cover the many welts and bruises, I put on my shades and walked next door to pick up LaMichael. Despite Jena's protests, I gathered my son and left, because I needed LaMichael to make it.

When I returned, Tony emerged from the bathroom and grabbed LaMichael out of my arms. "'Sup, little man?" Tony asked.

Fearful of what he might do, I attempted to take the baby back. "I got him."

Tony pushed my hands away as he continued to grip LaMichael in his arm. "No, I got my man. You go get some ice and get that lip better, and them bruises too. We gon' sit here and watch the game together, Daddy and son. Then I want you to join us. It's family time," he said, as if he hadn't beaten me into sexual submission with another woman and raped me just ten minutes ago.

Protesting against him had proven almost lethal, so I walked in the bedroom and locked the door. That was when I noticed Tony's gun lying on the dresser. In his coke-induced high, he'd forgotten about his piece. I grabbed it and hid it where I knew he'd never look. He was so high, I knew he'd probably forget where he'd even put it. The thought made me laugh as I went into the bathroom and ran the water in the bathtub.

"Who got the rock now, ma'fucka?" I said aloud to myself as I immersed myself in the tub of hot water.

Lucinda

After the incident with Raul and Shanaya, I was all set for battle in court. I didn't waste any time setting my plan in motion. Trinity loaned me a couple of grand to hire an attorney to help get child support for Nadia, so I hired the best attorney in town, Ira Cheatham, to handle my case. Everybody knew that if Cheatham was on your case, you'd get what you wanted and more.

I had never wanted to go this far with Raul, but I couldn't stand the half-ass payments and the disrespect of our child. I needed him to be in Nadia's life as a full-time parent sharing full-time responsibilities. While I tried to figure out a way to go back to school, I wouldn't continue to work myself to death to make sure Nadia was taken care of. She was Raul's responsibility too, and he was going to do his fair share. I meant that shit with every fiber of my soul.

It had been an uphill battle since the incident. I had tried to talk to Raul once, after I located

him over at his dad's house. The sight had been
nothing short of pathetic. The two of them
looked like twins with a twenty-year age difference. As they'd sat on the porch and drunk beer
as they shot the breeze, they had acted as if they
had no cares in the world. When I'd tried to talk
to Raul, he'd told me to go check on his mother
and that he didn't have shit to say to me. You
would've thought his dad would've intervened
and told him to grow up and not disrespect me
or his mother, but that ignorant bastard had
continued to drink his beer and had snickered
at Raul's comments. I'd wanted to take the beer
bottle and bash both of them upside their heads,
but instead, I had left with my pride and had
decided that this was going to court.

Rumor had it, he lived with Shanaya and
Raulina, but I wasn't sure. Above all, I didn't
give a damn. Shanaya could have him. I wouldn't
settle for any old *thing*, especially a boy in a
man's body. However, I would give a real man
my hand in marriage. If she wanted to accept
his shit, she was more than welcome, but I was
allergic to bullshit.

Fifteen minutes ahead of schedule, I arrived at
the courthouse, just as my attorney had instructed me. When I walked in, I saw my attorney
conversing with Raul's mom in the hallway.

I approached them. "Hi, Ms. Ana," I said, and we hugged each other.

"Hello, Lucinda. I wanted to see if Attorney Cheatham needed my testimony," she informed me.

"As I was explaining to Ms. Ana, I want to hold her as my wild card. I'm not sure who's representing Mr. Garcia, and I like to surprise, not be surprised," Attorney Cheatham explained. He turned to Ms. Ana. "For now, you can wait in the waiting area, until we know if you are needed."

After she hugged me again for encouragement, she walked to the chambers. I sat outside the courtroom with Attorney Cheatham, and he discussed particulars with his assistant. What I saw next made me want to submit a television pilot for a new sitcom. Raul walked into the courthouse, dressed in a purple three-piece suit and matching gators, looking like he had shopped at Pimps 'R' Us. Shanaya was with him, her arm linked with his, and she was looking casket ready. This silly ho had on a knee-length black dress, a black Sunday hat with a veil attached, and white gloves, and she was carrying a Bible. Raulina followed behind, wearing a flowered dress that was so long, she looked like Celie from *The Color Purple*. If she stepped in the wrong direction, it seemed as if she would trip over her

dress. She could've been best friends with Laura
Ingalls from *Little House on the Prairie*. Shanaya and Raulina looked straight ridiculous.

Attorney Cheatham, his assistant, and I looked
at them and immediately burst into laughter.

"What in the hell is so funny?" Raul shouted
at us.

"Calm down, sir. Do not use that language in
the courthouse," a guard ordered.

Attorney Cheatham and I walked over to Raul.
"I'm sorry, Mr. Garcia. I am representing Ms. Rojas. I'm Attorney Cheatham, and whom do you
have with you today?"

Shanaya stepped forward and shook my attorney's hand. "God bless you, Mr. Cheatham. I am
Raul's wife, Shanaya, and this is our daughter,
Raulina. We are just here for moral support
today. I'm not sure why Lucinda wants to put
my husband through these changes, but you
know we are just leaving it in God's hands. Jesus
will prevail," she said, using a phony Southern
accent and sounding as if she'd just stepped out
of revival service.

Oh, now they wanted to lean on the Lord. I
rolled my eyes. "Oh, Lord, have mercy."

"Yes!" Shanaya blurted, as if she'd caught the
Holy Spirit. "Lord, have mercy on your soul,
Lucinda Rojas. I rebuke your evil spirit in the
name of Jesus! Hallelujah!"

"Yeah, well, I hope you brought some tithes and offerings too," I shot back.

Attorney Cheatham snickered as he put his hand on my arm to calm me down. "Okay. Pleased to meet you. Mr. Garcia, are you being represented by someone today?"

"No," he answered.

"No, the Lord is all the representation we need. He's a doctor in the sickroom and a lawyer in the courtroom! Hallelujah," Shanaya interjected.

Literally, it took everything in me, and in everyone else who was witnessing this spectacle, to hold in the laughter. This girl was really on one today. I was sure King Jesus got a thrill out of this.

Attorney Cheatham couldn't help but get his dig in also. "Okay, then, since I'm going up against Jesus today, will you all excuse me so that I can go have a little talk and tell Him all about our troubles?" he joked as I giggled.

"Do not be deceived, Attorney Cheatham, Jesus is not mocked!" Shanaya shouted. "It says so in the Twenty-third Psalms."

"Mama, it's pronounced *psalm*, no *s*. And the Twenty-third Psalm is the psalm of David. Grandma Ana showed that to us," Raulina said, correcting Shanaya.

"So! Hush, Raulina. You don't know what verse in the psalm I was referring to. Don't interrupt grown-ups when they're talking," Shanaya scolded as Raulina rolled her eyes.

"I'd really love to chat with you all some more, but we need to be heading into the courtroom. Are you ready, Ms. Rojas?" Attorney Cheatham said.

"Yes, I am." I took a step closer. "Do I need a church program before I sit down?" I whispered to him.

"I don't think so, but they may need a church fan to revive them once I'm finished doing my praise dance on them around the courtroom, though," he said as we walked inside the courtroom. He laughed.

We all took a seat and waited. When the judge walked into the courtroom, we all had to rise. After he took one look at Raul and his family, the judge shook his head. Even he knew that Raul and Shanaya were on some bullshit. It didn't take a genius to see that. I could only imagine the amount of foolery that came through his courtroom on a daily basis. By the look on his face, it was a lot, which further told me that Raul had better have his A game and the entire host of angels in Heaven to make it through this day. Once the judge finished the review of the court papers, he addressed Raul.

"Mr. Garcia, you do not have counsel with you today?" the judge asked.

"No, we don't, Judge. Jesus—" Shanaya began, but the judge interrupted her.

"I'm sorry. Who are you?" he said.

"I am Raul's wife and—"

"Are you an attorney, Ms. Raul's wife?" the judge asked sternly, once again interrupting her.

"No. I'm here for moral support."

"Well, in my courtroom, moral support is given in silence, unless you're a representing attorney or unless I address you. In this case, I was speaking to Mr. Garcia. Please be quiet." The judge turned his gaze on Raul. "Now, Mr. Garcia, answer my question."

"Um, no, sir—"

"You can say Judge or Your Honor," the judge said, cutting him off.

"No, Your Honor. I am representing myself. Jesus will guide me," Raul replied, stealing a page out of Shanaya's book.

The judge laughed. "Okay. Attorney Cheatham, are you ready to begin?"

"Yes, sir. I'd love to get this over with before Jesus returns." He laughed, as did the judge and I.

My attorney tore Raul to pieces. Raul didn't know that I had kept a log of all his payments, and the twenty thousand dollars in support that he claimed he had given me amounted only to two thousand over the past five years. After Raul indicated that he worked part-time at an auto parts store, the judge told him he needed to work full-time, since he wasn't a student and he had no other legitimate reason not to work full-time. He was ordered to pay $350.00 per month in child support going forward and $2,100.00 in back child support for the past six months. To catch up with his arrearage, Raul was ordered to pay $450.00 a month until the entire sum was paid off.

When we addressed the supervised visitation, Raul argued that he kept Nadia often and that she was familiar with him. When Shanaya was called as a witness for Raul, she made it seem as if he was the best father on this side of Atlanta. However, my ace in the hole proved otherwise. When Attorney Cheatham called Raul's mom as a character witness to testify about the occasion when Raul left Raulina and Nadia outside unsupervised while he and Shanaya had sex, it was a wrap. Shanaya's and Raul's mouths dropped when the judge asked Raulina if her grandmother and I were telling the truth. Once she admitted that we were, Ms. Ana acknowledged the fact that after she kicked Raul out, Raul and

Shanaya did not marry but were living together. Raul begrudgingly admitted that was also true.

"Okay, I've heard just about enough of this foolishness in my courtroom today. Along with the ruling on the child-support payments, it is also so ordered that Mr. Garcia will have supervised visitation rights one weekend a month at his mother's house, with Ana Ruiz present. After one year, if Mr. Garcia has proven to become a viable part of said minor child's life, this issue may be brought back before the court for review," the judge announced. Then he signed the order.

"What?" Shanaya yelled. "This is some—"

"Well, I guess Jesus prevailed, ma'am," the judge said. "Now sit down, before I have you thrown out of my courtroom. I'm just about ready to do that anyway, with you pretending to be a child of God and acting like a seed of Satan. So you can stop your antics right now. On a personal note, Mr. Garcia, if you miss one payment or violate one visitation, I will hold you in contempt of court and will throw your butt in jail so fast that only God will know where you're at. I suggest that you go find Jesus and change your life so that He can convince you to pay this support every month, before you get convicted by me. Do I make myself clear?"

"Yes, Your Honor," Raul said in a low voice and swallowed hard. "Perfectly."

"Good. Now, all of you go and have a blessed day. In the name of Jesus, this case is adjourned," the judge said, then banged his gavel as we stood.

As happy as I was that this was over and that Raul now had to take responsibility for Nadia, it felt like a betrayal to place another man in the system. Regardless of what Raul thought of me, I had a heart. It was the reason I had never put him on child-support enforcement before, but at some point, you had to make a decision to put your child first. If he couldn't choose Nadia on his own, I had to make him choose her. I should've been dancing out of the courtroom, but I accepted my small victory with class and simply attempted to leave without further comment or conversation.

That was until Shanaya opened her mouth.

"This is not over, Lucinda!" Shanaya said just before walking out of the courtroom.

I walked right behind her into the hallway. "Why don't you go and talk to Jesus about it?" I shot at her.

"You gon' have a talk with my fist!" she shouted as Raul pulled her back.

"And if you come near me, you gonna wake up walking around Heaven all day!" I shouted right back.

"Don't feed into her foolishness," Attorney Cheatham said after he and Ms. Ana caught up to us in the hallway.

"He's right, Lucinda. She's not worth it," Ms. Ana interjected.

As they calmed me down, Raul walked up to his mom, with a mixture of pain and anger in his eyes. "How could you? You're *my* mother."

"And Nadia is *my* grandchild. She can't fend for herself, so it is my responsibility to make sure you do whatever you have to, to be there for her," Ms. Ana retorted.

"You have a responsibility to me too! I'm your son!"

"You are my son, but you are grown, and as a grown man, you need to get your grown self together. Nadia is my main concern, as she should be for you too," Ms. Ana stated sternly.

"Well, I hope you know you just traded your son for Lucinda. Live with that, because from this point on, you're not my mother, Ana."

"Careful what you wish for, Raul. Be careful," Ms. Ana replied, and then she walked out of the courthouse.

Now, I was all for Raul having to take care of Nadia, but I had never wanted to come between him and his mom. In some way, I felt responsible for their tattered relationship. At the end of the day, Ms. Ana was still his mama, and I knew how I'd feel if my mom were ever to betray my trust. All children, grown or not, needed their parents in their lives, if for nothing else but support. I knew that would be on my conscience, and I didn't know if I could live with that.

"Ms. Ana, maybe you should go and talk to Raul. I mean, he *is* your son," I pleaded when I caught up with her outside the courthouse.

"He's a man now, Lucinda. Sometimes the best thing you can do for your children is to let them go. That's what I'm doing to Raul. I'm letting him go. I love him just as much as I did the day he was born. He'll always be my son. However, I have an obligation to my grandchild, and until my son can see that, I have to let him be to himself. I pray that he'll find his way," she said. I only hoped that this was the right thing to do.

Trinity

The secret that I was hiding from Pooch made my life rough, but with Terrence's help, I had enrolled in art design classes finally. My classes were three hours long and during the day, so I didn't have to worry about anyone but Princess. Thankfully, Terrence paid his sister, Tomika, to babysit Princess for me at her house. His sister was cool as hell and had always wanted Terrence and me to be together. Since she wasn't a close friend of mine, Pooch would never suspect a thing.

I'd rush to do my work before Pooch got home and hide my books in the trunk of my car. The good thing about being with the head kingpin was that he moved during the daylight hours, right under the Feds' noses. He stayed on the grind for much of the day, but he was a family man at night. He had a few front businesses that did well, and he hung out there during the day mostly. I loved his "hours" now more than ever, since they freed up my time to pursue my dream. And this way Pooch didn't suspect a thing. I also had my own bank account and could move money so that I could pay my tuition without him knowing. He trusted me but would check me when he felt there was a reason, so I had to be careful. Doing something that Pooch didn't approve of was like testing the will of God, and I wasn't trying to get caught in that wrath.

"Terrence, I don't know how I'm going to repay you for helping me," I said as we walked from the front door of his sister's house to my car. I'd just picked up Princess, and Terrence had paid Princess's "day care" bill and given Tomika a big tip.

"You don't have to repay me. You know what I want."

I looked down. "You know I can't."

"If you could, would you?"

"Dreads, please."

In his frustration, Terrence threw caution to the wind and let me know how he really felt about me. "Trinity, I love you," he said, forcing me to look at him. "I love you like my life depends on it to survive. Please don't close our chapter yet. Just look back and remember how good we were together, and you'll know that this shit is worth fighting for."

My teary eyes reflected my sorrowful soul. Terrence had put his feelings out there for me, and there were so many reasons to listen to him and restore our relationship. However, there was one reason that prevented any thoughts of that. Pooch. I swear, I had to remind myself that I still loved Pooch. Lord knows I was *feeling* Terrence, and it was hard having some-one in your corner who supported your dreams and wanted to tend to the kids. Especially when I was in love with a man who refused to do the things I needed him to do, because he was so consumed by what *he* wanted for me. Don't get me wrong. Pooch was a good man, despite what he did for a living. He had some fucked up ways that he did things, but at the end of the day, I knew he loved me and wanted to give me only the best. The only problem was he wanted to give me what he *felt* was best, instead of what I actually needed.

"Terrence, I know you care, and I appreciate that you are there for me. I really do—"

"But . . ."

I sighed. "Yes, *but* there is Pooch. I love him, and he loves me, and I have to be devoted to that relationship. Pooch has given me so much . . ."

He rolled his eyes and fanned off my words. "Pooch has given you only stability. That fool can't see past his money and drugs to give you shit else! I can give you stability, Trinity. I mean *real* stability this time. No matter how untouchable Pooch thinks he is, he can be touched. Believe that."

I looked at him as if he was crazy. "What the hell is that supposed to mean?"

"It means just what I said."

After raising my index finger, I pointed at him angrily. "That's some ole informant talk you on right now, and I don't like it, Dreads."

He frowned at me for even having the thought. "I'm no damn informant," he scoffed. "All I'm saying is that life will bring you down someday in some way. Pooch better have an exit plan, because it can end only in jail or death."

His words made a shiver run through me. "Don't talk like that please."

"I'm not trying to scare you up. All I'm saying is I put you through changes before. Don't let Pooch put you through the same changes now."

"I hear you, but I gotta go."

He kissed me on the cheek. "See you later, li'l mama."

I blushed. "Bye, Dreads."

"Bye, Princess," he said, then kissed her forehead as she smiled at him.

Although I agreed with Terrence, Pooch and his family had had the game on lock for as long as I'd known them. Half of the city was on their payroll, and the other half either was family or friends or was scared of them. Then the small percentage of people who hated them weren't bold or crazy enough to take it to them, except Terrence, but he kept his temper at bay for me.

When I pulled up to the house, Pooch's truck was in the driveway. I didn't know what the hell was going on, since he was never home this early. I prayed he hadn't found out that I let Terrence's sister keep Princess or that I was taking classes.

"Where the fuck have you been?" he asked as soon as I stepped foot in the living room.

I knew something had gone down, since a couple of his lieutenants were in the house. Pooch rarely had his people over, unless it was a party or something had happened. He said the fewer people that were there and the less traffic there was, the less suspicion that was drawn.

"Princess and I stepped out for a minute. Why?" I said nonchalantly, hoping he didn't know anything.

"You been gone at least an hour. That's how long we've been here."

"So what? Was y'all waiting for me or something?"

"No. I just wanted to make sure you were all right, since you haven't returned any of my fucking phone calls," he said through clenched teeth.

What the hell was he talking about? I hadn't heard my cell phone ring, so this was news to me. I put Princess down and dug into my Birkin bag. When I retrieved my iPhone, it was dead.

"See? It's dead. I didn't realize it," I said, throwing it at Pooch.

He caught it and looked at it for verification. "Well, keep your shit charged. Damn. We have car chargers, Trinity," he said, fussing.

"Um, excuse me." I looked around the room. "Hey, everybody," I said, waving to the fellas.

"What's up, Trinity?" they said in unison.

"Pooch, can I see you in private for a second?" I asked. I walked into the kitchen, with Pooch following behind. "Okay, what the hell is all this about?"

"One of my spots got robbed today," he said angrily. "I just wanted to make sure nothing happened to you." He grabbed me and hugged me close. "If one of them muthafuckas had hurt you or, hell, even Princess, I'd be in jail right now, for real yo."

I wrapped my arms around his neck and kissed him to reassure him that everything was all right. "Well, nothing is wrong with me, baby. I'm fine, and so is Princess. So how much did they hit you up for?"

"Them muthafuckas got me for at least two hundred," he said, hitting the countertop.

"I hope you mean two hundred dollars."

"Hell naw! I mean two hundred large," he replied angrily. "See, muthafuckas always got to try you. Heads 'bout to roll in this bitch. It's time to send a message that I ain't the one to be fucked with. See, the streets been too quiet lately, and so have I, but trust me, these niggas are about to feel Pooch for real. I swear, them muthafuckas don't want it with me, baby. I'm murking them muthafuckas, for real yo."

I couldn't believe someone had got away with hitting Pooch up for that much money. "So what are you going to do, babe? Do you know who it was?"

"Hell naw, I don't know *exactly* who it was, or else I wouldn't be here. But trust me, the streets are live now, so I got people on location. Somebody gon' get loose lipped for real, and when they do, it's gon' be they last conversation," he said, his anger mounting even more.

At that moment, I thought about Terrence's comment. I shook my head and dismissed the thought. He wouldn't. Still, his words rang loudly in my mind, because it seemed like what he had said had come to fruition. And real talk, that shit scared my ass a bit.

I pulled him close to me. "Don't do nothing crazy. I don't want you to get locked up or worse."

Pooch looked down at me and smiled. It was the first time in a very long time that I could remember him being so gentle and attentive to me. "Damn, babe. Ain't nothing gon' happen to me. I'm Pooch. Don't worry about shit. I'm gon' always be around for you. You hear me?"

I nodded. "Yeah, I hear you."

"Come on," he said. After a peck to my lips, he took my hand and led me to his king suite.

"What are you doing, Pooch?"

"All this fucking pent-up frustration has got to come out. Let me hit it right quick, baby. I need to feel my shit all up in you right now."

"You've got company, and the baby is in the playpen in the living room with them niggas."

"So? Shit. They can't hear shit in the king suite, and them niggas ain't gon' fuck with Princess," he pleaded. "Don't make me beg for my own fucking pussy. Damn."

I didn't want to argue, so I followed Pooch into the king suite. He locked the door behind us, pulled my pants down, and told me to lie doggy-style on the sofa. Within a few seconds flat, his pants were around his ankles and his dick was ready, set, go. He spat on the tip of his dick, smeared the saliva around, and then stuck it inside me.

"Ooh, shit. I need this," he moaned, getting into a rhythm.

Angry or frustrated sex with Pooch was so damn good. I didn't love the timing of this, but I would be lying if I said it didn't feel great. Hell, in his attempt to fuck his stress away, he also fucked mine away. I moaned deeply as he settled into a groove, and the jiggle of my ass from his deep pounding rocked my core. After only a few solid pumps, there was a knock at the door.

"Yo, Pooch? You in there?" Big Cal asked.

"What, muthafucka? What do you want?" Pooch yelled in frustration. "I'm handling some shit right now."

"Sorry, man, but yo, Princess is crying, and it smells like she dropped a load of shit in her diaper. Plus, um, I got a call from li'l Juice, and he said some niggas over at his location talking grimy about you."

I looked over my shoulder and saw that Pooch's expression had turned to rage. "Pull your pants up," he commanded, disengaging himself, and I hurriedly pulled up my pants.

Pooch opened the door while trying to buckle his pants. Big Cal looked on in amazement as he realized what business Pooch had been tending to. "You just get the call?" Pooch asked.

"Huh?" Big Cal asked, looking back and forth between Pooch and me.

"Nigga, what are you? Deaf and mute? I said, How long ago did you get the call?" Pooch barked.

"Excuse me, baby. I need to get Princess," I said, walking up behind Pooch.

He pulled me to him and kissed me deeply as he gripped my ass and whispered, "Fuck! Keep that shit wet for me. I'm gon' finish my business when I get home. You hear me?"

"Yes, baby. I need to get the baby."

"I love you, Trinity."

"I love you too, Pooch."

Pooch smiled at me. "A'ight. Remember that shit," he said, smacking me on my ass. When I walked past Big Cal, he licked his lips at me.

"Nigga, I suggest if you want your lips and eyes, you keep your focus on me," Pooch said. "Let's saddle up, nigga. And be clear, homie, if you even *think* about stepping to my lady, I will toe tag your ass."

"A'ight, Pooch. Damn," Big Cal said as they walked down the hallway. "I'm just saying, she *is* fine, though. All I was doing was admiring the—"

Suddenly, I heard a loud noise at the other end of the hallway and spun around to see what in the hell had happened. I gasped when I saw that Pooch had chin checked his ace and number one henchman.

He grabbed Big Cal by his collar. "Keep your muthafuckin' eyes focused. I better not ever catch you looking at Trinity again, and if you speak about my lady's fineness or anything else, I'll cut your fucking balls off and feed them to you, muthafucka. Do you hear me?"

"A'ight, muthafucka! Now let me go!" Big Cal yelled. Pooch released him, causing him to trip backward and fall. "Crazy-ass muthafucka," Big Cal muttered, shaking his head. Big Cal grabbed a Kleenex from the small table nearby and wiped the blood that trickled from his mouth.

"Yeah, a'ight, then. Remember that shit. You damn right I'm crazy. Crazy about my woman," Pooch said, helping Big Cal up. "Now let's go handle this business. You still my number one dude."

Pooch continued to walk down the hallway, and Big Cal followed behind, still wiping his mouth. Hurriedly, I grabbed Princess from the living room and left them so that they could discuss the information that li'l Juice had provided.

After they all had left the house, I sat in the living room and prayed a silent prayer that Pooch would be fine and that he would be able to retrieve his product. I wanted to call Terrence and tell him what had happened, but I couldn't give him the satisfaction of knowing that his words were coming to fruition. But if they were, what would that mean for me and my kids? I tried not to worry, but now I had to. I loved Pooch, but I loved my kids more.

Charice

My vacation in Dallas was just what the doctor had ordered. After I returned, I found that I was more productive and stress free. Honestly, I was ecstatic about the memories that had been created while we were there. For instance, Ryan had kept his promise and had spent much-needed time with the kids. So I had had a break, which had been long overdue for me. The Cowboys had won the game we attended by a score of 27–14. There was no greater rush than watching that team in action. Even Charity had loved the game, and she was an extremely girly girl, so sports had never been her thing. Before we left Dallas, Ryan had laced my pockets with three grand just for me. Of course, I hadn't wanted to accept it, but then he'd told me to consider it back child-support payment and to spend it on myself. Now, that had been the clincher. That Dallas trip had wound up being a lot more beneficial than I'd bargained for.

Since the trip, Ryan had called every day to check on the kids, and his mom had been really involved in their lives. The media, of course, had gotten wind of the fact that Ryan had kids and had broken the story about Ryan and his three children. He had released a press statement confirming it and stating that his focus was on his career and his kids. I could admire that and now vouched for it. He'd been true to his word thus far.

My mom was impressed with Ryan's efforts of late. Trust me, for Ryan to do that, it took an act of God, especially since she was upset with some of the consequences of him taking responsibility for his kids. Which ones? Well, being that she was no longer the kids' only "acting" grandmother, she was no longer getting all the "Grandma" shine. She didn't care that the media constantly tried to film Ryan's mom with the triplets or interviewed her about her role as a grandma, but she was upset about the fact that she had to split her grandchildren time with Ryan's mom now. Believe me, I'd much rather have my children be with my own mom, but the kids requested to be around Ryan's mom just as much as she requested to see them. I believed that was what had given my mom the streak of envy, and I could understand that.

You'd think after the five years I had cared for them, the triplets' devotion would be to their mama, but if Ryan was mentioned, it was all about Daddy to the kids. It was like being introduced to your first taste of chocolate candy. Their relationship with Ryan was new, fun, and sweet, and it came with plenty of perks.

Hell, even their mama benefited from the perks. One of which was spending part of my Christmas vacation back in Dallas. This time I let the kiddos stay with their daddy solo. I trusted Ryan to do right by them. With his feelings for me still open, I didn't want to test the waters. Ryan was a charmer and could be very persuasive and persistent. I didn't want to fall victim to any of his antics, especially since I still hadn't gotten any loving since the last time we were together. It had been hard enough to resist the first time, but since I longed for a taste, it wasn't a good idea to tempt fate again. You didn't take a wolf into a butcher shop, and I was hungry like a wolf. So, I made sure I handled my business via four AA batteries and stayed at the Westin Hotel. Ryan let me drive his Benz, which came complete with a navigation system, in case I wanted to get out and explore on my own, which I did.

The second day in Dallas, I shopped until I dropped and took in the beautiful sights in the city. After my long day, I relaxed in my whirlpool tub and sipped on champagne in my hotel suite, while the kids stayed at the house with Ryan. After I emerged from the tub, I glanced at the bedside clock and saw that it was only ten. I didn't want to stay in, so I decided to go to the hotel bar and lounge and have a couple of drinks and listen to some music. I put on a nice backless black cocktail dress that fit the contours of my *assets* and a pair of stilettos.

As I sat at the bar, I noticed the men watching me, but I wasn't interested in any of that. I was a girl with morals and standards and was not into one-night stands. Since these men were in Dallas and not back home in Atlanta, that was all it would be, a one-night stand, so I focused on the music and enjoyed myself.

"Fancy seeing you here," a male voice said behind me.

Quickly, I turned around to see who it was. Then I smiled demurely. "Lincoln. How are you?"

After walking up to me, he bent down and hugged me. "I'm well. And you?"

"I'm good. I brought the kids to visit their daddy before Christmas."

"Ryan told me you all were coming. I'm just surprised that you're not with them," he stated, puzzled.

I waved my finger. "Nope. It's Daddy's time, and this is Mama's time." I laughed, pointing to myself.

He held his hands up apologetically; at the same time his lips curled into a playful grin. "I can feel that. Mama needs a break too."

"Linc, what are you drinking?" the bartender asked, interrupting us.

"Disaronno on the rocks." He turned to me. "And you?" he asked.

"I'll have an apple martini," I told the bartender. Then I focused on Lincoln again. "So what brings you to this hotel? Don't you have a home with a full bar here in the big city?"

With a chuckle, he took the empty seat beside me and said, "Yes, I do, but I like to get out too. I like the Westin and often visit the bar and lounge."

"I can tell. You're on a first-name basis with the bartender."

He shrugged. "I tip well."

"I'm sure," I said as the bartender handed us our drinks.

"Let's toast," he said, and we raised our glasses. "To beautiful women and great drinks."

"Also, I'd like to toast to good times and new friends," I said.

We both blushed and smiled as we tapped glasses. "Hear, hear," we chorused.

For the next hour, Lincoln and I laughed and talked as if we'd known one another for years. The conversation flowed like water, and so did the drinks. He had three Disaronnos, and I had about three apple martinis and a cosmopolitan. We found that we had a lot in common, and like me, he was a great debater.

"Well, *Linc*," I said, calling him by his nickname, which he'd given me permission to use, "it's been real, but I'm going to dance for a bit. The deejay is playing some real songs up in here now."

"Say it ain't so, Ms. Lady! You don't dance."

"Please. You don't know me, Linc. Before I settled on being a nutritionist, my dream was to be a dancer and own my own dance company. I was good. Ryan loved my splits," I joked.

He swiped his hand over his chin beard and chuckled. "Show me what you got."

Now, who did he think he had challenged? I felt loose after the alcohol, so my inhibitions were as low to the ground as I was about to drop it. "You ain't said nothing but a word," I said and grabbed his hand and led him onto the dance floor.

I was fluid and sexy as I showed off the latest dance moves with the grace of Beyoncé in my stilettos. Lincoln cheered me on and nodded his head in approval.

"I must admit, you are really good," he complimented me.

"Told you."

"Moving like that, Ma, it wasn't just your splits that got Ryan, either," he joked.

The dance floor was my sanctuary. Between being a full-time employee and a full-time single parent, I hadn't had time to enjoy my other first love. It came like second nature to me to set the dance floor ablaze. For the first time since I could remember, I felt carefree. Almost like the old Charice. I hadn't realized she'd gone missing, but I found her on the dance floor, and I loved the fact that Lincoln provided the space and the judgment-free zone for me to do so. After about another fifteen minutes, I decided to take a rest, so Lincoln and I made our exit from our small center stage.

As I headed back to the bar, Lincoln touched my arm. "I know it's late, but would you like to take a walk with me?"

"Sure," I replied.

He settled our tabs with the bartender, grabbed his coat, and rejoined me. Then we walked out into the night air.

"It's cold. I forgot that it's wintertime," I said.

Lincoln put his overcoat around my shoulders. "Feel better?"

"Yes. Thanks," I said as we continued our stroll. "This city is so gorgeous. I guess I feel that way after being stuck in ATL for so long and having to tend to my babies."

"Dallas is a beautiful city, Ma."

"You must be from up north, with that slight accent and 'Ma' talk."

Lincoln flashed a proud smile. "Yep. I'm from New Yitty."

"What part?"

"Queens."

"What do you city boys know about the dirty South?" I joked.

"It's different. I'll say that. But I like it down here. Hell, why wouldn't I? I play for the greatest team in the league."

"True, and your secret is safe with me. I won't tell the city boys that you like country living," I joked.

"Thanks, Ma. I appreciate that."

We strolled for a few moments in silence as we took in the night sights. The glow of the city, with its mesmerizing beauty, cast a spell over me. It was then that I realized no matter where you traveled and for what reason, you always had to take time out to enjoy the beauty of a place.

"So tell me, you really fell in love with Ryan during ninth grade?" Lincoln asked, catching me off guard with such a candid question.

I didn't necessarily want to stroll down memory lane, but conversing with Lincoln felt easy and therapeutic. Still, reliving that period of heartbreak was not something that I readily dived into. After all, I'd just purged Ryan out of my system. So to avoid the risk of reopening my heart, I gave him the CliffsNotes version.

"Ryan was the king of our high school, literally. Not that I was attracted to that. I didn't know who he was, but he captured me the first time we spoke. When we eventually linked up, I fell hook, line, and sinker. I loved him with everything I had until about four months ago."

What I meant suddenly dawned on him, and he nodded. "Hmm, the whole situation with Iris. You felt used." Silently, I agreed, and Lincoln continued. "Listen, Ryan is my boy and all, but I understand. I try to help him because I see a lot of my old self in him. I want him to understand that this NFL shit is temporary, and so is everything that comes with it—the lifestyle, the fame, the women, and the money—especially if you get injured. Everyone loves you when you're flying up and down the field on Sunday afternoons, but no one is checking for you when you're forty and a sports announcer. In the end, he's going to want to a firm foundation beneath him, with someone who is solid."

Lincoln took me to church with that. Whew! His words spoke to my soul and made an otherwise difficult conversation so simple to have. "Exactly! And not that Ryan hasn't used me before, but at some point, you have to say enough is enough. I had to let go for myself. I'd devoted too much time to loving him and not to looking out for Charice. My heart, my head, my body, and my soul needed a release from him. I'm elated that he's stepped up to the plate and taken your advice into account, but I'm not going back. I know how he feels, but I can't open myself up to him like that again. I refuse to."

"I know. You have to do what's best for you, for your own sanity," he agreed. "I feel you on that, because I've been there. My daughter's mother is finally letting me see my baby, and I'm glad, but I can barely tolerate seeing my daughter's mother. She tries to fight every time she sees me, partially because she's bitter over our outcome, but I can't let that stop me. I'm better than that. I just want to take care of my seed. Fuck the rest."

We took in each other's words and briefly allowed them to sink in. I noticed the distant, bothered expression on Lincoln's face and chose to make light of the situation. "Being an adult is not easy for everyone," I said, placing my hand on his shoulder, which caused him to look over at me. "You don't think I could kick Ryan's ass every time I see him? I mean, I think about all the shit he's done to me. I haven't forgotten that. So yes, I could feel like kicking his ass every time I see him, but I'm not here to fight or argue. I'm here to let him be a father, plain and simple."

When I finished my speech, I glanced over at Lincoln, who was staring at me in wonderment. "You are amazing," he said. "Ryan fucked up. He so fucked up."

I laughed. "You don't have to say that. You know that's your boy." I playfully nudged him.

Suddenly, he stopped, turned me to face him, and gently pulled me close. "Check it, Ma. I don't say shit I don't mean. My boy or not, he fucked up. A woman like you comes along only once in a lifetime," he said seriously.

As we stood there looking into each other's eyes, surges of electricity passed through us. Though we knew we should break the connection, it was if we were stuck in a trance, neither one of us able to move away. As I stood there, mesmerized by his eyes, I unconsciously wrapped my arms around his neck, leaned in, and kissed him. We had been lost for minutes in our sensual kiss when suddenly, he pushed me back.

"I'm sorry," I said, turning away quickly out of embarrassment.

Lincoln gently and swiftly grabbed my hand, which caused me to slowly face him. He gazed solemnly at me for a brief moment and then chuckled. "I'm sorry for liking it."

We both laughed nervously.

"We'd better head back to the hotel," I said shyly.

"Yeah, we'd better," he replied.

The walk back was as quiet as it had begun. I thought we refrained from talking or breathing for fear of what might happen next. Rather than cross those blurring lines, we settled for silence, because silence was safe. Once we arrived back at the hotel, Lincoln, being the gentleman he was, escorted me to my room.

"Thanks for the great evening." I glanced down at my watch. "Well, morning . . . I didn't realize that it was after one o'clock," I said.

"Time flies when you're having fun," he joked nervously.

Both of us danced on the awkwardness of the moment. As I shifted my weight from foot to foot, he fidgeted with his keys. Since I didn't want to cause any undue stress, I decided to end the evening.

"Good night, Linc," I said softly, then kissed him on his cheek. After stepping inside my room, I stood at the door and said, "For the record, your baby's mama fucked up too."

He smiled devilishly. "Seems like I'm always finding myself in fucked up situations."

I smiled knowingly. "Good night."

"Good night, Ma," he replied sweetly, and I closed the door.

Immediately, I kicked off my heels and was determined to grab my bedroom toy, because Lincoln had my pussy hot as fire. Yes, forget the bullshit. My kitty had stopped purring an hour ago, and this heifer was now screaming at me to give her some attention. And attention she was going to get. In mid-stride for my bullet, I heard a knock on the door. After racing back, I looked through the peephole and saw that it was Lincoln.

Fuck. I need to handle this, I thought. "Did you forget something?" I asked after opening the door.

I couldn't read his expression clearly, but he looked confused. "No, but I hope to God this is the right decision."

Now it was my turn to be confused. "What?"

He stepped inside the door and swept me into his arms. "Tell me that you want me as much as I want you. Tell me that this will not just be a one-night stand. If I pursue this with you and betray my boy, I have to know that this isn't a casual thing for you."

Without a pause, I exhaled and said breathlessly, "I want you, and this isn't just a casual thing for me."

As soon as I said that, he kissed me and kicked the door closed. We both knew what was going to happen and accepted it. Lincoln wasted no time as he carried me into the bedroom and laid me down on the bed. I was nervous but didn't want to appear to be, so I lay there and watched as he slipped off his Ralph Lauren button-down, wifebeater, and slacks. As he stood there, wearing only his boxers, he slowly pulled me off the bed and helped me to my feet.

"You are so beautiful," he whispered in my ear.

I gasped from the surge of sexual energy that shot through my body. I reached for my zipper, but Lincoln stopped me.

"Allow me, please. I want to unwrap you like a Christmas gift under my tree."

I nodded, silent, and he slowly unzipped my cocktail dress, removed the straps from my shoulders, and slid the dress down my body. He took his time and kissed my neck . . . shoulders . . . . stomach . . . hips and thighs. I kicked out of my dress, and he lay me back down on the bed and massaged my feet.

"Mmm, Lincoln," I moaned.

"That feels good, doesn't it?" he asked in a raspy voice.

My moans were the answer he needed. Lincoln continued his seductive path and removed my thong and bra. Once I was completely naked, he used his hands to knead out all the nervous tension in my body, from head to toe, then replaced his hands with kisses along the way. This felt so good, too good. Lincoln awakened senses I never knew I could feel.

Suddenly, I felt a draft and tilted my head forward to see that he reached into the ice bucket and placed a piece of ice in his mouth. When I lay back, I felt the coolness slide down the center of my chest, around my breasts, and then into my navel. The mixture of cold from the ice and hot from our body temperatures sent my skin blazing as the ice melted on my body. His foreplay was off the chain. No foreplay Ryan and I had ever engaged in could compare to what Lincoln was doing to me. Once he pushed my legs apart, he blew softly on my throbbing bud.

"Mmm, Lincoln!" I hollered, gripping the bed.

"Yes, Ma," he moaned as he teased my clit with the tip of his tongue.

"I can't . . . fucking . . . take it . . . anymore! I need you!" I wailed, literally delirious with anticipation. "Do you have protection?" *Fine time to ask*, I thought, *but better late than never*.

He nodded as he bent down and retrieved a condom from his slacks, then waved it. "I never leave home without one."

I took no offense, and giggling, I leaned forward, opened the nightstand drawer, and pointed inside. "I never leave home without a box. Just in case," I said, and we shared a brief laugh.

Though I was still a small ball of nerves, I waited with high anticipation as he slipped the condom over his massive erection. He hovered over my body and held me close. Tenderly, he pushed against me.

"You are so tight, baby," he said, gliding in and out of me. "Damn. It feels so good."

This was heaven. I was sure of it. I was thankful that Lincoln was taking his time. It felt good as hell, like nothing I'd ever experienced, but the pressure hurt a bit from his girth due to my long bout of abstinence. But did it ever hurt so good!

He was giving it to me so good that I wanted to give him some pleasure in return. I attempted to roll over on top of him, but he stopped me.

"No, Ma. Tonight is about you. I want you to enjoy this. You deserve this. I want you to feel and receive all the pleasure. I'll give you as much as you want, just how you want it. Let me please you," he whispered in my ear, continuing his erotic lovemaking.

With a smile on my face, I decided not to argue that point at all. For once, I felt like the receiver of special attention instead of the giver. Armed with plenty of condoms, we made love all night, until sleep consumed us.

The next morning I woke up with a huge Kool-Aid smile on my face. I looked over, and Lincoln was still sleeping peacefully. He was still nude, so I admired his fine self. Last night was the most incredible night of passion I'd ever experienced in my life. He had taken his time and adored my body. For him, it wasn't about getting off. It was about my pleasure and ultimate satisfaction. And, boy, was I pleasured, and did I ever get off, again and again and again!

After I got up and showered, I threw on a T-shirt and boy shorts. Then I pulled out the guest toiletries for Lincoln and made some coffee. Ten minutes later, he stirred and awoke when I reentered the bedroom.

"Good morning," he said, rubbing his eyes.

"Good morning. I didn't mean to disturb you. You were sleeping so peacefully."

He sat up and flashed that award-winning smile at me. "You didn't bother me. I only wish you'd stayed beside me. I would've loved to wake up with you in my arms."

The blush that washed over my face could not be stopped. Geesh, he had a way with words. Avoidance was the key, so I tap-danced all the way around that comment. "I made some coffee, and there are some toiletries in the bathroom, if you need them."

"Thanks, Charice," he said as he stood up. He walked into the bathroom. After several minutes, he came out and found me sitting on the bed, watching the television. "The shower felt good, and I'm all minty." He bent down to kiss me.

I wrapped my arms around his neck. "You sure know how to make a girl feel special."

He furrowed his brow. I was positive it was because of what I'd said and the way I'd said it. "You *are* special," he told me.

I couldn't help but let out a groan of uncertainty. My insecurities had begun to set in. I know what we said the night before, but now that a much clearer head prevailed, I realized that this was Lincoln Harper, a six-year veteran of the NFL. He played and lived in Texas, and more importantly, he was Ryan's best friend. "You don't have to say that."

Lincoln lifted my chin. "Where is this coming from?"

I sat up and turned to the side of the bed, and Lincoln sat down in the chair beside the bed and faced me. I clicked off the TV and took a deep breath. "Let's be serious, Linc. We know some things about one another, but we don't really know each other. In two days I'll be back in Atlanta, and we won't see each other again until I return to Dallas or if you all come to Atlanta to play the Falcons. We both know that last night was a one-time deal."

"No, *we* both don't," he argued, fanning his hand between us. "So, what? We don't have the time? Then we'll make time. Last night was amazing, Charice. Not just the sex, but the entire night. I've never experienced such realness or had a genuinely good time with a wonderful woman. And let's just stop pretending that we haven't been feeling each other and wanting each other since the moment we met." He leaned forward and grasped my hands while gazing into my eyes. "I told you I didn't want it to end there, and I wasn't lying," Lincoln asserted.

No lies were told there, but this was new for me. There was so much against us. We barely knew each other, we would be long distance, and we faced the obvious, which I wouldn't even think about out of fear of the repercussions. Yet it felt so right. Like for no rhyme or reason, this, whatever it was brewing between us, felt good and felt right. Still, I didn't want to get my hopes up. I'd done that with Ryan. A sister ain't about to be the same fool twice.

I sighed, looking away. "Okay, but just promise me you'll be truthful with me. Let me know where I stand, and I'm cool with that."

He gave me a confused look. "What do you mean?"

I rolled my eyes and huffed. "Come on, Linc. I understand that our distance is going to be a factor, so let's just put it out there. It's okay with me if you have a woman on the side. Just be honest and tell me, and I won't interfere. I just would like to know up front."

Lincoln's mouth formed an O shape and he sat back, as if I'd knocked the wind out of him. He stood and cupped my face, forcing me to look at him. "Charice, what do you want from me? Tell me. Do you want me to be faithful to you and treat you with the respect by your being the only woman for me?"

I nodded. "Yes, but—"

"Then say that," he said, interrupting me. "Don't give me permission to go out there and hurt you. Haven't you been hurt enough? If you don't want me to play the field, then don't put the ball in my hands. Tell me what you want and need. Put your requirements out there, because a real man like me will respect that. We know how to handle that. If I'm not ready for that, then I'll tell you. I want you to be my lady. I don't want to be out there playing the field. I'm twenty-seven years old, Charice. I'm not with the games. I've been there and done that."

He went on. "Just because Ryan didn't know how to be a man to you, don't expect or accept anything less from another one. So when I tell you that I want to be with you, that shouldn't come with exceptions and stipulations. We'll make it work. Me and you. It's hard enough knowing that I am breaking every rule in the book by doing this, but for you, I'm willing to take that chance at what we could be. This is our inner circle, and we are the ones who dictate our circle. When I made love to you last night, I didn't make it as your jump off. I made love to you with an offer to be your man." He paused. "So, you tell me right now. Which one do you want me to be?" Lincoln asked sternly.

I'm sure my face reflected the shock coursing through my body. I was absolutely floored. I'd never had any of this in Ryan. It was a welcome change, and I was ready to welcome new beginnings with this man. "I want you to be my man."

He stood up, and pulling me up into his arms, he said, "Then, baby, that's what I am, because that's what I want to be." With that, he planted a kiss on me.

Talk about a whirlwind. Was this what grown folks' relationships were really like? I'd wasted so much time on Ryan, and who knew that there was a man out there who was ready to find someone he thought he could be with, without the games? Men like that existed. The thought brought tears to my eyes.

"I'm sorry, Lincoln. It's just that I've never been with another man other than Ryan. You're the first man that I've let into my head and into my bedroom outside of him. And this opens me up to allow you in my heart. I guess I don't want to experience the same fate. I don't want to give all of myself to you and end up with nothing again," I said softly as tears fell from my eyes.

Lincoln walked me over to the chair, sat down, sat me in his lap, and hugged me. "I hate it when a woman is so afraid that she thinks every man is out to get her. I'm not Ryan. We won't always get along or see things eye to eye, but I will never intentionally hurt you. If this relationship is not what we want, then we will part amicably. If you ever have questions, doubts, or concerns, allow me the opportunity to ease your mind. Can you promise me that?"

I gave a nod. "Yes, I can."

"Good. Now, I do have a question."

"What's that?" I asked.

"Are you serious that you've never been with another man other than Ryan?" he asked with disbelief.

I laughed. "Yes, that's true. I'm very loyal."

Lincoln laughed and shook his head. "Well, damn, I must really have done something right. I told you he fucked up. The type of women who are attracted to men like me and Ryan are loyal until they walk out the front door," he joked.

"Not me," I said confidently.

"That's why you're Lincoln Harper's lady," he said, then kissed me on my forehead.

"I like that. No, scratch that. I *love* that."

"That's what I'm talking about, Ma."

"Next question," I said, then paused a moment. "When are we going to tell Ryan?"

Lincoln sighed from exasperation as he leaned his head back.

"Obviously, he has to know," I said. "He's my children's father, your teammate, and your best friend. It's not going to go over well either way. I just don't know how to tell him. I mean, *I* don't owe him anything, but *you're* his best friend. For that reason alone, I feel . . . I don't know . . . bad."

Lincoln looked away, and I could see the turmoil on his face. Lincoln truly valued Ryan's friendship, just as Ryan valued Lincoln's. They were as close as brothers, and that was a fact that everyone knew. Lincoln was sacrificing a lot by pursuing a relationship with me.

"I can't lie," he said. "I do dread the conversation, but we don't have to tell him anything until we're ready. Let's just see where our relationship will go. Then if we need to tell him, we will."

"We can do that, but I'm telling you, you might as well tell him now, because you will not be able to let me go, Linc." I stood up and struck a sexy pose.

"The student is the teacher now?" He rubbed his hands together and licked his lips.

"Oh yes. In more ways than one," I said, lifting my T-shirt over my head and revealing my nude breasts. "Last night was about me, and this morning is all about you."

Lincoln's eyes danced with anticipation. "Show me what you got."

"Oh, I will, especially for my man," I said seductively as I did a striptease dance.

"And I am only *your* man too," he said, breathing heavily.

LaMeka

After the last incident with Tony, I knew I had to change my routine. I couldn't stand to be in the apartment with him any longer than necessary. I wasn't prepared to kick him out, nor was I prepared to leave, so I resorted to the next best thing, complete avoidance. I accepted a day care job at an in-home day-care center. This way LaMichael received free day care, and I was able to be away from Tony. It was rewarding, and I made my own money. True, I provided a service to the parents; however, they didn't know that they also provided something for me— survival.

More and more, I hated entering that apartment. It was like poison, waiting to suck the life out of any and everyone inside it. Moreover, I hated Tony and the ground he walked on. I wanted to tell somebody about the hell I was going through, but I didn't know whom to talk to. If I told Trinity, she'd tell Pooch, and then I'd have to be worried about Tony kicking my ass.

If I told his parents and they didn't believe me, he'd kick my ass, and if I did tell them and they did believe me, he'd still kick my ass. All roads led to my beaten ass, and I couldn't see myself going through it again.

There was one person I could tell who could possibly help me out, my best friend Charice. We hadn't hung out lately, because of Tony's violent mood swings and Charice's frequent trips back and forth to Dallas. We needed to catch up in a major way, and I needed to see if she could get Ryan to talk some sense into his former best friend on my behalf. I gave her a call, and luckily, she was in town and had time to meet up later that day.

"Hey, hon! Sorry I am running late," Charice said as she entered the playland area of McDonald's. In her hands was a tray with a red box of French fries and a large drink.

I hugged her. "That's okay. It's been only about ten minutes." I turned to the triplets. "Hey, babies!" I said, hugging them.

"Hey, Auntie Meka!" they all said in unison, their voices laced with excitement.

"Okay. You guys go and play," Charice ordered as she sat down at the table across from me. "I swear, these kids get bigger every day," she said, giving LaMichael a French fry from the box on her tray. "Soon he'll be out there with them."

"Yes, he will." I laughed. "So, Miss Lady, look at you looking like new money. Are those designer jeans and shoes you're wearing?"

She giggled. "Yes, they are. Having a baby daddy who's rich has its perks."

"I see, I see," I said. "And might one of those perks be getting back with said baby daddy?"

She rolled her eyes. "Girl, no. He wants me to, but it's definitely a wrap for that."

Talk about being shocked. I'd never met a woman who loved a man as much as Charice loved Ryan. Although he had hurt her with the whole Iris thing, I knew that he had changed and had put in work to get her back. So I was extremely surprised at the amount of conviction in her voice when she stated that she wasn't going back to him. Besides, this was what she had wanted for years, so to know she could have it and didn't want it totally blew my mind.

"Damn. He really must've pissed you off."

"I'm over that. I just can't be with Ryan anymore," she said before taking a sip of her drink.

I'd known this girl all my life. Who in the hell did she think she was fooling? I had the "Really, bitch?" expression on my face when I said, "Something else must've happened. It can't be just about what Ryan did. I know you, Charice. You could eat his day-old shit. What's going on?"

With a scoff, she cocked her head to the side. "I've grown up and moved on with my life," she stated confidently.

Just then, her cell phone rang. What got me was the ring tone . . . "If It's Love," by Kem and Chrisette Michele. *What the hell*? I thought. The song spoke about two people who had gone through relationship failures and were ready to be with each other. But if the song shocked me, then what happened next damn near took me out.

"Excuse me a second," Charice said, then turned away from me and answered her cell. "Hey, you. I'm just hanging with my girl, LaMeka. I haven't been able to hang out much lately because of someone I know." She giggled. "You know I'm not complaining. I would never do that. Um, how about next weekend? I don't have a sitter this weekend. Green Bay? Damn. During the week? I'd love it! Tuesday, Wednesday, and Thursday? Damn! I'm definitely going to love it. Listen, let me call you back in a bit. Okay? Me too, bye."

My mouth dropped open as she turned and faced me. "And what man is that?" I asked, smiling devilishly.

"Why does it have to be a man?"

So now I was Boo Boo the Fool. I rolled my eyes. "Last I checked, you weren't grinning from ear to ear on the phone with me, and you certainly never answered any of my calls with 'Hey, you.' The only time I've ever heard that little schoolhouse voice is when Ryan called you. Spill it."

She bit her lip and sighed. "Okay, there is someone in my life—"

"I knew you and Ryan—" I interrupted her.

She quickly threw up her hand, which stopped my rant. "It's not Ryan. I meant what I said about him. I'm done, Meka. However, there is someone who is becoming a very special person in my life, and I'm taking it slow and seeing where it could go."

"So I guess this explains the weird behavior lately. Okay, I get that you have this new dude in your life, but why can't you tell your BFF who he is?"

"For now, it's better this way. I wish I could tell you, Meka, but right now, it's just not a good time."

"Is he in prison? An illegal alien or some shit?" I asked, prying.

She rolled with laughter. "Girl, he ain't neither, and there is nothing wrong with him. We're just keeping it to ourselves for now. Is that fair enough?"

"I guess so. Although, I am highly pissed that I am not privy to your secret."

Suddenly her laughter paused, and I looked up at her, thinking something had caught her attention. But I found her staring back at me with a serious expression on her face. "Just like you were forthcoming in telling me Tony was whipping your ass?"

"I could kill Trinity," I mumbled.

"Don't blame Trinity. She just wanted to look out for you. How come you didn't tell me what was going on?" Charice said, plowing into me.

"I didn't want anyone to worry about me. I'm fine, really," I lied.

"Trinity said you had a black eye, and the other day Misha told me that Tony beat you so bad on another occasion that you had black and blue bruises all over your body. She told me she saw cocaine in your bedroom one day as well." She looked me in the eye. "So how is all this I'm hearing make you fine, *really*?" she asked sarcastically.

No words fell from my lips. There was no way to explain what she'd questioned me about. How could I? The only thing that could explain it was shame. Tears fell, despite my will to contain them. Looking at her face, which showed just how upset she felt, I couldn't hide the truth, and a wave of sorrow fell over me.

Reluctantly, I admitted my truth. With a shrug of my shoulders, I looked at my bestie and confessed. "It's all true," I admitted as she supportively gripped my hands, her expression filled with sadness. "Girl, you don't know the half of it. He's slapped me a couple of times over the past year, but within the past few months, he's beat the shit out of me. The first time he gave me the black eye, he forced me to suck his dick, and this last time, I walked in on him cheating on me with some crackhead bitch named Kwanzie. I tried to kick him out, but he beat me and made me have oral sex with her while he raped me from behind at gunpoint. I felt so low and cheap. I feel used and abused, and I don't know what to do."

Charice stood, came around to my side of the table, and hugged me. "I had no idea. Why didn't you tell me? Is it true that he's snorting?"

I nodded. "He's a monster. I'm scared to leave and scared to stay. I'm scared to speak my mind and far too scared to pray. I feel trapped."

"Is there anything I can do to help you?" she asked with concern.

"Actually, I was wondering if maybe you could talk to Ryan. Maybe tell him what's going on and see if he can talk to Tony about his behavior," I suggested.

Charice rubbed my back but glanced at me skeptically. "I could, but do you honestly think it would help?" She put her hand up before I could respond. "Look, Meka, hear me, hon. Tony is on drugs. There is nothing Ryan or anyone else can say that would convince Tony to kick his habit. Even so, who's to say that Tony won't attack you for telling Ryan? What you really need to do is *leave*. You need to take the kids and Misha and find a new place away from Tony."

I leaned my head on her shoulder and cried for a few moments. She allowed me to get it out. I knew she was right. I hated being around Tony, but I needed time to get things together so that I could get away from him without him knowing it, especially since his ass was always at the house.

After drying my face, I looked up at her. "If I do this, you have to tell me who this mystery man is," I said jokingly, trying to lighten the conversation.

She laughed softly. "Nice try. If you do this, you'll be safe, and so will my godbabies. That's the most important thing."

"I love you, girl."

"I love you too. I am proud of you for getting a car and a job. You can still have a life, despite having children at a young age. You just have to fight for it, Meka. I want you to pursue your dreams. You used to love science and wanted to be a nurse. Why don't you get your GED and then apply to a tech school? You'd have access to medical doctors, and it could benefit you, especially with Tony Jr.'s autism. I think it's high time you stopped taking care of Tony. You've been his slave since the accident, and you didn't tell him to drink that night, but you act as if you owe him your life because of it. It is not your fault."

I couldn't argue with her. She was right about everything she said. I had never tried to pursue my dreams, because I had always felt responsible for Tony being unable to fulfill his. I had figured if I stayed by his side and let my dreams go, it would in some way compensate for the loss of his. Now, look at the predicament I was in. I was in love with a man that I hated.

"I thought I was doing the right thing. I thought I was putting my family first, you know?" I told Charice.

"Yeah, I know, sweetie. And you know I understand, but there comes a time when you have to put *you* first. You have to say, 'Never again. No more will I deal with this,' and stick to it. For you, it's about more than independence. It's about survival."

"I feel you," I said as I took in the words she had spoken.

"Good, and if you need some money, let me know."

"Damn!" I eyed her with surprise. "Ryan got you balling like that?" I asked, in shock.

"Like I said, having him as a baby daddy has its perks, but so does having my new man."

We high-fived each other and hooted.

"Mr. Man is balling out of control too?" I said.

She winked at me. "See, I gave you a little crumb, and before you get too excited, that's all the info I plan on delving out today."

"Well, at least tell me how long you've been dating him," I said, prying some more.

She shrugged. "A month. Give or take a week or two."

"You are really keeping this one in the pocket."

"He's the first guy I've dated since Ryan, and I need to know for myself if this can work before I go announcing it to the world."

"I feel you. Well, I do have one more question."

"What's that?" she asked before drinking some of her soda.

"Does your new man have any friends or a brother?" I laughed.

My humor caught her off guard, and she coughed, almost choking on her soda. She wiped her lip. "You ain't right!" She laughed. "Well, his older brother is married, and his best friend is in love with his baby mama."

"Dang. The good ones are always taken."

"You just concentrate on getting rid of Tony," she advised me.

"Trust me. I am."

Just then her cell phone buzzed with a text message. She read it, laughed, and texted back. "This is my boo right now." She got another text a second later and read that one.

"Lovebirds," I joked.

"I texted him what you asked me, and he is laughing his ass off about it." She giggled.

"I will be glad when I get to meet this man," I said as she continued texting.

I was happy to see my girl finally enjoying life. With every laugh and giggle, she made me realize that there were men out there who could make you feel just as my girl felt. I didn't want to spend the rest of my life being beaten up until I got beat to death. If I did that, what would my tombstone read? HERE LIES LAMEKA ROBERTS. SHE

TOOK A BEATING AND KEPT ON TICKING. Damn that. I wanted my life to mean something, and more importantly, I wanted to live a long and abundant life.

Charice

After my trip to Dallas for part of Christmas vacation, Lincoln and I battled our schedules in a way that would keep our relationship under wraps, which left us with only three times to link up in January. We were able to get together during the New Year's holiday; the week after New Year's, which was during the NFL playoffs; and during my one-day stay in Dallas, when he invited me to his immaculate home, which was in the neighborhood across from Ryan's. Each time, he was nothing short of amazing.

In early February, I did get to go to the Super Bowl, where the Cowboys played the Ravens and won. However, Ryan insisted we make it a family affair with the kids and our parents. Ever since Ryan's newfound attitude had proved to be more than just smoke and mirrors, my mom and Ryan had begun anew, and now they were nearly the best of friends. In fact, she, along with Ryan's parents, pressured me to go to the Super Bowl VIP after-party with Ryan.

Since I was his woman, I knew it hurt Lincoln
to see Ryan fawn all over me that weekend.
He tried to understand since we were keeping
our relationship quiet, as he had requested.
However, his hurt and disappointment were
never more evident than when I showed up at
the after-party on Ryan's arm.

"Westmore!" one of the offensive linemen
yelled when we arrived at the party.

Ryan high-fived him. "What's up, champ?"

"Nothing but them salary caps!" another player yelled. "Good to see you again, Ms. Charice."
He nodded toward me. At that moment, Lincoln
and a few others looked up.

"Hello, fellas," I said with a smile, but that
smile faded when I saw the confused look on
Lincoln's face.

"Ryan, let's go speak to Lincoln," I urged, and
we walked through the crowd toward him.

"My man!" Ryan hollered as he one-arm
hugged Lincoln. "You did your thing out there,
playboy!"

"You too, bro!" Lincoln said. "Good evening,
Charice. Glad you could make it down for the
game, but it is a surprise seeing you here," he
said, then hugged me.

"Ryan insisted on making it a family affair.
Our moms persuaded me to come out to the
party," I explained with a timid smile.

Ryan turned to me. "You don't have to act like I dragged you out by your hair, Charice. I want us to have a good time tonight. Perhaps I can finally show you how much you mean to me," he said softly, holding my hand. Then he hugged me close.

"I'm sorry," I mouthed to Lincoln behind Ryan's back. I could tell Lincoln was bursting with anger.

"Well, I guess I better mingle. I don't want to be the third wheel," Lincoln said, trying not to sound upset.

Ryan fanned off Lincoln's comment. "You could never impose on us, but if you don't mind, I would like a little time with my Ricey."

Lincoln chuckled and patted Ryan on the shoulder. "Your Ricey, huh?" He looked at me. "Far be it for me to intrude. Ricey, you look absolutely amazing tonight. Have fun."

"Yeah, bro, she really does. Lord, have mercy she does." Ryan laughed and twirled me around as Lincoln cleared his throat, swallowed his anger, and walked away.

I spent the whole night feeling uncomfortable, because Lincoln had a permanent scowl on his face and Ryan tried his best to woo me when I would've rather been with Lincoln. I got a harsh dose of my own medicine when I saw Lincoln with some skank on the dance floor. The sight of them together made me rush out onto the balcony for fresh air.

"Doesn't feel so good, huh?" I heard Lincoln say behind me.

Not bothering to turn around, I spewed, "Don't blame me. You're choosing to keep it a secret, not me."

"So is that why you came here with him?"

"Is that why you danced with her?"

Pausing for a moment, he exhaled. Then he said, "Turn around, baby."

Though I was upset, I slowly turned and faced him. "What?"

"Please understand. It's really hard for me when you're saying you want to be with me, and then I have to witness you two together, especially knowing how you once felt for him. I don't even know that girl, and I'm not trying to. I just needed to know that you truly mean what you say."

"Then let's just tell Ryan, so we don't have to go through this!"

"Tell him . . . now? How do you think that's going to go down?"

In my frustration, I wanted to clear the air. Watching Lincoln pretend to flirt with some random chick and lying to Ryan was not how I was built. It was not who I was. But I also knew that this admission required a level of finesse and was inappropriate in the middle of a major party with close friends, family, and teammates, a party where alcohol was involved. That in itself was a recipe for disaster. Mostly, I knew we weren't ready for the fallout of telling Ryan, though I was confident that we both wanted to be out in the open.

"You're right." I sighed. "I'm sorry for making you second-guess my feelings. I know my past with Ryan is hard to cope with at times, and it won't get easier, because we have children, but I assure you that you are the only one I want to be with."

He winked at me. "As are you, baby, and I'm sorry for my actions tonight as well. You deserve better, and I promise to give you that." Just as he walked up to me, Ryan surfaced, causing Lincoln to step back.

"There you are! I've been looking all over for you, Charice," Ryan said after bursting through the balcony doors.

"I just needed some fresh air," I explained as he wrapped his arm around my waist.

"What are you doing out here, man?" Ryan asked Lincoln. "I saw that honey you were danc-ing with. She's been looking for you. I know you want a relationship and all, but in the meantime, you can have some fun, bro. You need to get with that."

I pulled away from Ryan and patted Lincoln on the arm. "Don't listen to him. You need a real woman." I chuckled.

"Don't worry. She doesn't fit the bill," Lincoln affirmed, returning my sarcasm. "I was just getting some fresh air and chatting with Charice. I'm going to head back inside. You two enjoy the rest of the night, and don't get in any trouble."

"I promise, I won't," I said to him.

"Don't make promises you may not keep," Ryan said, flirting with me.

"I don't," I threw back sassily, and then I sashayed past him and Lincoln into the room.

"She's feisty," I heard Lincoln say behind me.

"I know. This is harder than I thought," Ryan replied.

"I bet it is," Lincoln said.

Before I left town, I was able to see Lincoln, under the guise of shopping, which smoothed our rough spot. After that trip, we continued having fun and getting to know each other in our relationship.

Now I was in Dallas again, at my man's house, on the first day of a weeklong stay. I enjoyed the fact that we could finally spend some quality time together. Sitting by the family-room fireplace, I felt like I was in heaven as I indulged in the view and the warmth. A few minutes later Lincoln appeared with two plates of food.

"Breakfast is served."

"I want something, but it's not on those plates," I said sexily.

He sat the plates down on the bricks in front of the fireplace and scooped me into his arms. "You almost made me drop those plates," he said as I wrapped my legs around his waist and kissed him. "Damn, Ma. I've missed you."

"I know, babe." I sighed, unwrapped my legs, and placed my feet on the floor, keeping my arms wrapped around his neck. "This is so hard for me. When I'm with you, I don't want to leave, and when I'm away, I want to hurry back."

"That's exactly how I feel. Now that the season is over, you don't have to worry about that. We'll have plenty of time to grow our relationship the way we need to. I'm going to make sure of that." He took my hand and led me to the huge pillows in front of the fireplace. We took a seat there. "And my first duty as your man is to feed you," he informed me, reaching over to one of the plates and picking up an orange slice.

I shook my head. "I'm not going to be able to leave this time. I feel it," I joked.

"That's the plan," he admitted with a snicker.

"Lincoln Harper, are you trying to woo me into moving here?"

"Is it working?"

He held the orange slice near my lips, and I took a bite, swallowed it, and nearly choked. "You are a trip," I said and giggled after my coughing fit subsided. He popped the rest of the orange slice in his mouth, wiped his lips, then sat back and stared at me, as if in deep contemplation. "What?" I asked nervously. I picked up the croissant on the plate closest to me and took a bite.

"Did you think that I was joking when I asked if it was working?" he questioned with a serious tone.

Chewing my food slowly, I sat back and looked at him. "Lincoln, you can't possibly be serious."

"Why can't I?" he asked, moving closer to me. "All I can do is think about you. You have to be the first person I talk to every morning and the absolute last voice I hear at night. If we're not talking on the phone, we're texting, emailing, or on the webcam every day. With every visit, I dread seeing you walk out the door, and the truth is, I don't want to go through that anymore. We've been together for only three months, but I feel like I've known you a lifetime. I'm not asking for marriage or even for you to live with me, but I wish you would at least consider moving to Dallas."

His plea was so sincere, so I wanted to respond as softly as I knew how without damaging his ego. I held his face in my hands. "Linc, I love the time we spend together. I really do, and you're right. Not a day goes by that we don't communicate in some form or fashion, and I would love to see you every day. However, I'm not prepared to uproot my children and myself to move to Dallas yet. I'm sorry."

Disappointment danced in his eyes, and he swallowed deeply, then asked, "Okay. Well, why?"

I could hear the heartbreak in his question. I didn't want to tell him the reason, because I didn't want him to feel like I was rushing him when, in actuality, I didn't want to rush myself. The truth was that I wasn't moving to Dallas until or unless he put a ring on my finger, and he had said he didn't want a marriage. That was fine, because neither one of us was ready for that right now, and the absolute last thing I wanted was for him to feel obligated to commit to me.

Gently, I pulled his hand into mine and intertwined my fingers with his. "Linc, let's just take this slow. Let's work on us first. Our families don't even know we're dating. On top of that, we still have to tell Lauren and Ryan," I explained to him.

"You have a point, but my baby's mother doesn't care who I date. She hates me anyway. And my mom, dad, and older brother do know about you."

"Lauren might not care who you date, but if I am a constant in your life, she will care who is around London," I said, trying to reason with him. "Wait a minute. You told your family about me?"

He chuckled. After eating a strip of bacon, he said, "I love how you switched gears when that hit you."

Oh, now he wants to hehe. He found it comical; however, I was both shocked and slightly fearful. "Seriously, did you tell your family about me?"

He must've realized how alarmed I sounded, because he wiped his hands with a napkin, turned his gaze on me, and looked me in the eyes. "Yes, I did," he said, pulling me close. "They want to meet you."

"What did you say about me?" I asked nervously.

He chuckled and kissed the top of my head. "Don't be nervous. I told them that I met a woman who makes me smile from the inside out. A woman who is independent, strong, and virtuous. A woman who cares about me, the *me* on the inside, not Lincoln Harper, the Cowboy."

"That's sweet, but did you tell them everything, like that I'm Ryan's baby mama and that I have three children?" I inquired.

Lincoln nodded without hesitation. "Yes, I did. My father's and brother's concern was that you made me happy and that you weren't a gold digger. I was able to ease their minds about that when I told them how you didn't sue Ryan for support all those years. My brother was a little taken aback by the three children, until I explained they were triplets. Then he thought it was somewhat cool. He's a weird one." He laughed, toying with my fingers.

"And your mother?" I asked nervously, pressing onward.

He inhaled deeply. "I won't lie. She's concerned. She feels it's wrong for me to betray Ryan, as his friend. She also has her reservations about your love for Ryan and, of course, the difficulties that I will face with Ryan and your children once the truth surfaces."

Great! More odds stacked against me. I hadn't even met her, and I already felt it would be an uphill battle. Shaking my head, I threw my hand up. "She hates me. She doesn't even know me, and she hates me."

He turned my face toward his. "She doesn't hate you. She just doesn't know you. She doesn't know the wonderful woman that I've come to know. She doesn't know the big heart that you have, or how much you truly care for me. Once she meets you, she'll see it, and she'll be convinced that what we have is special."

As his words soaked in, oddly, I felt a sense of relief. And it was sweet to know that he thought enough of me to tell his family, so that was a positive. I smiled and kissed him. "I can't blame her. You're her baby. She just doesn't want you caught in the middle of any foolishness, and if you are, she wants the woman to be worth it. I get it. I have sons."

"This is why you'll be able to win her over when the time is right," he reassured me.

"Flattery will get you everywhere, Mr. Harper." I laughed.

He moved to his knees and leaned toward me, hovering over me. "Great. So let me start at your lips and work my way down to your feet," he whispered before we kissed deeply.

"I can't believe I get a full week of this," I whispered between kisses as we lay back on the pillows.

Lincoln rose up and removed his shirt. "Me either. I guess I better double strap up, because if not, you'll have to move to Dallas for real, because you'll be having my baby," he joked, referring to the Jodeci song.

"Well, then, you better, Mr. Harper, because I plan on giving as much as I receive, and when I leave here, boy, you gon' think, you gon' think I invented sex," I joked right back, quoting Trey Songz.

"That's right, baby. Make sure the neighbors know my name."

"Oh, they are going to know mine too before it's all over with."

Lincoln and I may not have been ready for a lifetime commitment, but I knew that I cared deeply for him already. I'd never felt anything like this in my entire life. Even though Ryan may have been ready to give it to me, I no longer wanted it from him. Without me even realizing it, everything I felt for Ryan all those years had faded and was slowly but surely being replaced by none other than Mr. Lincoln Harper. Oh, how I was so going to enjoy this week.

Trinity

There had been so much drama since Pooch's trap house got robbed. It seemed Pooch was hunting down any and everybody who looked at him cross-eyed. I talked to Pooch and told him to keep a level head, because people wanted to see him off his game. If there was one thing I'd learned, it was that when you were off your game, you slipped, and all anyone needed was to catch you slippin' one time.

Pooch finally found out that it was actually one of the new lieutenants that had robbed him. The dude had tried to make a name for himself and had thought he could shut down Pooch's operations. He had managed to get some boys to set it up and had actually thought Pooch wasn't going to track them down. I didn't ask one question the night Pooch left the house after explaining that he'd found out who'd done it. I will tell you this, though. Pooch didn't come home for three days, and when he did call, it was from some phone in the Florida Everglades, and he simply said, "I'll be there in six hours," and hung up. The next day, while Pooch and I sat up in our bed and ate breakfast, he switched on the news, and all five of those dudes that had robbed him were on there as missing persons. Pooch wiped his mouth and hands, turned the television off, and lay on his back, with his hands behind his head and with a smile on his face, as he stared at the ceiling. See why I didn't fuck with this nigga?

On the flip side, I was actually upset that the drama had died down, because Pooch's focus had been on that and not on me. I'd done very well in school, so well that I had made the dean's list my first semester and had achieved a 3.8 GPA. It would've felt good to share that joy with Pooch, but Terrence had celebrated with me. He'd brought a bottle of bubbly to his sister's house, and we'd drunk to my accomplishment.

Lord, Terrence. My spirit was so torn. The fact that I could share my life with Terrence slowly tugged at my heartstrings. Terrence provided the emotional support and love that I needed and wanted, which made it hard as hell not to catch feelings for him. And I would be lying if I said that I wasn't feeling him. I loved Pooch, I did, but now my feelings for Terrence had resurfaced.

"What you thinking about?" Pooch asked me as the daylight shone into our bedroom one morning soon after the trap-house drama had died down.

"How'd you know I was awake?" I responded with my back to him.

"I could feel you . . . thinking."

Sometimes his senses were uncanny. I swore this nigga had eight senses instead of five. "Nothing much really. Just thinking about my day."

"What's going on today?"

"Nothing special. I was just pondering," I lied.

He huffed. "So you don't want to tell me."

"Pooch, I swear it's nothing—"

"Don't swear when you're lying, babe," he interrupted.

I turned to face him as he lay on his back, hands behind his head, looking up at the ceiling. "Can't I just think? Is there something wrong with that?" I snapped.

Pooch sucked his teeth and sniffed. "Naw, you can think, but as Kathy Bates says in the movie *The Family that Preys*, 'It's your private thoughts that give me pause.'" He turned his head and glared at me.

I furrowed my brow. "Why is that?"

"Do I make you happy, Trinity?"

That caught me off guard. "Yes. Why would you ask that?"

"You snap off on me lately for no reason. I mean for real yo, you've been real short and impatient with me. That's not you. That's me, but I'm just like that. When a woman acts in a way that's not hers, usually there is a problem. When a woman is unhappy, she usually acts just like you been acting, because she don't have the courage to walk away," Pooch said, dropping that philosophical shit on me. And you thought Pooch was only a thug. This was how he stayed on his game. He was a mind reader and an attitude analyst. This nigga knew people.

"Pooch, I don't want to walk away from you. It's just that I hate when you try to get all in my psyche," I said, my irritation becoming evident. "You smother me sometimes." I let that slip before I knew it.

"Smother you?" he asked, surprised. "I'm barely here."

Since I'd already let the cat out of the bag, and he was in the mood for discussing shit, maybe we could discuss some things and clear the air between us. "Smother me with what you want for me, Pooch. I feel like a kid or one of your niggas half of the time, instead of your better half. I want to feel like I'm your equal," I confessed to him. It was the first time in all these years I felt that I could be completely honest with him.

"You wanna get in the business with me?" Pooch asked excitedly. "You wanna be on some Bonnie and Clyde shit? Why didn't you say so?" He laughed, totally misreading what I had said to him.

I shook my head in frustration. "Hell no! We have children, Pooch. I would never. I meant to feel like an equal as a person in this relationship! I want to feel like I matter more to you than tits, ass, and eye candy!" I yelled before I could stop myself.

"*Eye candy*? You on that nigga Terrence shit now. You been fuckin wit' that nigga, Trinity, huh?" he asked, becoming defensive.

"No, Pooch—"

"Don't lie to me!" he yelled. "Don't you ever fuckin' lie to me! Now, you tell me if you been fuckin' wit' that nigga. I ain't fuckin' playin' wit' you, Trin!"

This nigga had made me mad as hell, and I was tired of being accused of something and yelled at. All he ever did these days was question me, bark orders, and accuse me of bullshit. I was a grown ass woman. It ain't like he didn't know that I could be gone and linked up with my ex-baby father, but I chose to stay with him.

Damn. A bitch couldn't get any credit for that? It was high time to check his ass on the way he treated me, and today was the day I checkmated his ass.

Jumping up from the bed, I screamed, "No! This is not about Terrence! This is about you and me! That's it! This is why I don't talk to you, Pooch. You're impossible. I'm trying to come at you with some real shit, and you chalkin' it up to me being unfaithful. Do you even really know me at all? I'm one of the most loyal bitches in this fuckin' city! I always put your ass and our kids first. Always! Terrence is my children's father. Yes, we had a relationship, and yes, I used to fuck him, but that is my past! You knew all of this when you approached me. If you couldn't handle that, then why did you even bother me? I may have been struggling, but I didn't ask you for shit! Nothing. The only thing I'm asking for is space and respect. That's it! Damn. Or would you rather me go out there and fuck every dope boy I see, so you can be right?"

Pooch jumped up. His muscles bulged, and his eyes were red with anger. His steps were fluid as he rushed around the bed toward me. I had never before seen him so angry with me. Before my mind could process what was happening, he was on me. He grabbed me by my arms as if I were a rag doll and pushed me full speed into the wall. My back hit the wall so hard, the force knocked the wind out of me. As he pressed me against the wall, he pushed his forehead against mine.

"I don't know what the fuck has gotten into you, talking to me like that," he said angrily, his voice low. "But if you ever in your muthafuckin' life think about giving my pussy to another man, I will hurt you, Trinity. Do you fuckin' feel me?" he growled, looking deranged.

I nodded in fear. "Yes, I hear you."

"No, don't just hear me, Trinity. *Feel* me," he warned, gripping me harder. His head was pressed so hard against mine, it felt as if he was about to shatter my skull. "I fuckin' love you so fuckin' much. The thought of you and another nigga . . . Just don't ever say that shit to me again! Do you fuckin' hear me?"

"You're hurting me, Pooch!" I cried out.

It was as if he snapped out of a trance or something. Gone were the deranged eyes and the tight expression. Suddenly, his muscles relaxed, and he pulled his head back and gazed at me with the most apologetic look in his eyes. He loosened his grip a bit, then took one hand and rubbed the side of my face.

"I'm sorry. I'm so sorry," he said and pulled my face close to his. "Don't say that again. I'll give you space and shit. I know you're mine. It's just that Terrence makes me fuckin' insane, because I know you loved him. And I . . . I just get crazy thinking about that shit. I'm sorry. Forgive me."

I pushed against him as tears rolled down my face. "Get off me! Get away from me," I cried harshly. He moved back, and I slid past him slowly.

He reached for me, and I jumped. "Trinity," he said softly.

"Don't touch me!" I cried. "I can't believe you put your hands on me."

"Baby," he said, speaking in a low voice, his jaw twitching. "I didn't mean that shit. You know it. Don't do this. Let that shit go. Let it go now."

Fear had struck me, but I relaxed, because I didn't want to piss him off again. I nodded without saying another word. He pulled me close and hugged me. The pain in my back made me wince.

"I'm sorry, baby. I love you, and I want you to remember that shit. Don't ever fuckin' forget it. I don't want to hurt you, Trinity."

I stood stiff as he kissed me from my lips to my shoulders, then circled around me to kiss my sore back, easing down my nightgown as he went. "I love you, Trinity," was all he repeated, his tone full of sexual energy. As he slid my gown over my ass, he bit my cheek and then kissed it. I was stuck, as if in a trance, with a gamut of emotions running through my veins. I felt angry, hurt, abused, and trapped, and I didn't know if I loved or hated Pooch. He dropped to his knees in front of me and pushed my legs open.

"Let me taste it. Let me taste my pussy," he moaned. He pushed one of my legs outward and teased my clit with his tongue. "Fuck! It tastes so fucking good!"

Just then Princess's crying came through the baby monitor. "I have to get the baby," I said nervously.

"Fuck!" he roared. "Can't one of the kids grab her?"

"Pooch, she's a baby."

"She's a fuckin' year old," he complained.

"She's still a little baby girl. Come on, please. We'll have time for this," I pleaded, loathing his touch.

Pooch stood up and sat on the bed. "Go get the baby. Damn."

I pulled up my gown and threw on my robe quickly. I had never loved Princess's interruptions more than I did right then. I swore she knew just when her mommy needed her. I hurriedly left the room to go and tend to her, and I was going to make every second count. I knew that soon Pooch would get up to leave the house and head to his businesses, and I couldn't be happier. One thing was for damn sure. This was the first time in three years that I'd questioned my love for Pooch. I loved Pooch, but I didn't love him enough to let him beat me. Of that, I was positive.

LaMeka

Life at home had gotten worse in all aspects. Tony Jr. had violent spells at home. It had even started to affect him in school, when he had done so well in his class. That upset me, because I'd welcomed the break from the task of homeschooling him. The doctors seemed to think it had something to do with him not being able to recognize Misha as someone that lived in his home. I could agree with that theory. With Junior, life changes had to be slowly introduced to allow him time to adapt. Back when LaMichael was born, we had planned for months to get Junior used to the baby. While other parents took joy in their children's milestone accomplishments, like their first steps, my joys had been more simplistic. For instance, it had been such a wonderful accomplishment when Tony Jr. accepted his baby brother when he was a month old.

At any rate, in my haste to help Misha, I hadn't considered the effects on my son. However, I

thought his change in behavior was more at-
tributable to his dad's anger and abusive behavior. Tony Jr. had reached too many milestones
to have setbacks, and I felt like less than a mother because I was allowing this to happen, but I
wasn't sure how to stop it my damn self. I mean,
I couldn't change Tony, and even though I had an
opportunity to relieve some pressure at home by
allowing Misha to go back home with our mom, I
refused. Misha didn't want to go, and although
our mom claimed to be rid of Joe, I wouldn't
abandon my sister and throw her back to the
wolf. Add to that, I had another little one to tend
to, and I was damn near close to having a stroke
from stress. I was so confused and emotional
these days that I could barely see past my own issues to deal with Tony Jr.'s.

Today I didn't have any other choice but to
deal with Tony Jr.'s issues. He'd had a violent
episode at school, so I had had to leave work and
bring him home. I had to get this under control,
otherwise I would have to quit my job and stay
at home with him again. And I couldn't put him,
LaMichael, and myself through endless days
of abuse from Tony. Our nights were already
horrific enough.

"Here you go. Roll the car," I said sweetly to
Tony Jr. as I tried to interact with him while we

sat on the living room floor. LaMichael was still at the day care center, and Misha was in school, so it was the perfect opportunity for some therapy time with him.

Keys rattled at the door about twenty minutes later, and I knew Tony had come in from wherever the hell he'd been. Worry plunged to the pit of my stomach, because I never knew what to expect, and I absolutely dreaded having to deal with him. When he staggered in with bloodshot eyes, I knew he was both drunk and high. He hadn't been home since yesterday, and he looked and smelled like day-old funk. For all I knew, he had hung out with that Kwanzie bitch.

"Fuck is you doing home?" he slurred.

"Tony Jr. is having some problems at school—"

Before I knew it, Tony was up on me and yanked me off the floor by my hair. "What in the fuck is you doing to my son, huh? You are already done fucked him up enough! Now, what the fuck wrong with him?" he screamed at me. The stench of the alcohol on his breath nearly knocked me out.

I tried to pry his fingers out of my hair. "Ouch! Tony, please let me go! You're hurting me! I didn't do nothing! Please!" I begged with my eyes shut, anticipating the blow that was sure to come.

This time he let me go instead. "Sorry, bitch! You're right. You didn't do nothing. You don't ever do nothing! Nothing right anyway! Stupid bitch!" he hollered.

I rubbed my head fiercely to calm the ache as Tony Jr. sat there. He held his truck and stared at me. I sat down on the sofa so that I could keep my eye on Tony, just in case he wanted to issue an ass whupping. He staggered into the kitchen.

"Ain't no food in here!" he bellowed after he snatched the refrigerator open and drank the kids' orange juice straight from the carton. He leaned into the fridge and continued his quest for something to eat. "What you cooked?"

"My food stamps haven't been loaded yet, and I haven't had time to cook. I've been helping little man," I explained.

Tony slowly stood up straight and looked over at me, with orange juice running down his chin. "You ain't what?" he snarled, slamming the refrigerator door shut.

I stood up and sat Tony Jr. on the love seat. I knew his dad was about to go on a rampage, and I didn't want him to get hurt. "Tony, please. I'll cook. Just give me a moment to finish up little man's therapy," I begged him.

He looked at me half crazy as he slammed the carton on the counter. "Bitch, I'm hungry now!"

"Tony, please," I pleaded, feeling both sadness and fear. My skin was clammy, and my stomach did flip-flops. I swallowed the lump in my throat and prayed that he'd let it go.

His nose flared, and his jaw twitched. "So you mean to tell me that I have to wait for some food? Is that what you're saying?"

"You want me to go buy you something? I can do that." I was so nervous, I had begun to tremble.

Tony hissed and charged straight for me.

"Tony, wait! Wait. No!" I screamed as I backed up and put my hands up to protect myself. He backhanded me so hard, I fell on the sofa, bounced off, and hit the floor.

He kicked and spat on me, then seethed, "You worthless piece of shit! I swear, I hate you. A man can't even get a home-cooked meal. You are just a worthless, triflin', ghetto slut bitch!"

I held my stomach and cried. I looked up, and the next thing I saw was Tony Jr. take his toy and bash Tony in the back with it. "Ugh! Ugh! Ugh!" Tony Jr. grunted with each blow. Tony yelped in pain.

"You little bastard!" he yelled. He was about to strike my little man, so I jumped up off the floor and leaned, face forward, over my son to cover him up and take his licks.

"You ain't gon' hit him, Tony! Beat me! But you ain't touching my son!" I yelled, protecting Tony Jr. I waited to feel the blow from Tony's fist, but there was nothing.

I looked up to see Tony laughing. He backed up. "Fuck both y'all. I'm going to Burger King," he muttered, fanning us off, as he staggered to my purse, stole twenty dollars, and left the house.

I held Tony Jr. with my arms over his to keep him from swinging the toy at me. He rocked forcefully back and forth, so I rocked with him. "It's okay. I got you. It's okay," I whispered.

"Mean daddy. Daddy mean," he repeated softly until he calmed down and drifted to sleep in my arms.

I sat there holding him for a few moments and broke down in tears once he was completely asleep. "God, if you're real, please help me. Help me," I whimpered as pools of tears ran down my face. I didn't know how much longer I could take this. It was one thing to beat on me, but I'd rather die than let him touch my kids. I'd rather die.

Lucinda

My picture had to be beside the word *drama* in the dictionary, I swore. It seemed that regardless of the fact that I was a peaceful person, drama surrounded me like a black cloud. Ever since the court ruled in my favor, Shanaya had been off the fucking chain. She called my house and hung up frequently, until I finally cussed her out. Raul was no better. He showed up a couple of times at his mom's house and ranted so much about when his mom had stuck up for me that his younger brothers whipped his ass in the front yard. *Dios mio!* All I wanted was for Nadia to be taken care of, but the stress and foolishness behind that were damn near unbearable.

It pissed me off so bad that I actually decided to go to the one person I had vowed never to fuck with again . . . my dad. My mom couldn't help me control Raul, and I had gotten Ms. Ana involved entirely too much as it was. I needed a man to step in and put the fear of God in

Raul before one or both of us ended up in prison
and left Nadia to be raised by one of her grand-
mothers. Raul's dad surely wasn't going to do
it, because he was an even bigger deadbeat than
Raul, and there was no way in hell Raul would
listen to the threats of my younger brothers, or
even his brothers, even though they whipped his
ass. He needed someone who could forcefully
get him to see that either he would stop harassing me and help raise our daughter, or he would
suffer major consequences, and I felt the only
man who could deliver this type of message was
my dad.

As I sat in my dad's driveway, I contemplated
leaving. The last person I wanted to depend on
was his ass. I sat there for a few minutes longer
and took in their lifestyle. They had a classy
three-bedroom, three-bathroom ranch-style
home in a nice middle-class neighborhood.
Maria's trifling ass drove in a brand-new Chevy
Suburban, and he had a West Coast Chopper
and a Dodge Ram extended cab truck. Their
impeccably manicured lawn had an automatic
sprinkler system, and the swing and the well in
the front yard gave their house such a warm and
loving family feeling.

However, I was cold and bitter. They were
the perfect little fucking family, and we, his first

set of kids, were the outsiders. We could only work and pray for a life like this. It was like being denied access to your own birthday party. For the life of me, I just couldn't figure out why we weren't worthy of the same life he provided Maria and their children. I hated the fact that my little half-sister Eva had everything that my siblings and I didn't. I hated even more the fact that Rosemary and Maria had all that too. It wasn't just about the lifestyle, though. It was about the relationship they had with my dad.

As this weighed on me, I had made up my mind to leave when my dad opened the front door and walked out onto the porch. He motioned for me to get out of the car. "Come on in, Lucinda. What are you doing sitting in the car?"

I took a deep breath. After I'd told him on the phone that I needed to talk to him, he had invited me over for dinner, and begrudgingly, I had accepted. It would take the grace of God to help me through this dinner.

"Coming," I sighed as I put up my window and got out of the car. *All right, Lucinda, just be cool and ride this whole dinner thing out*, I thought.

As soon as I stepped foot on the porch, my dad embraced me. "*Hola, hija!* I'm so glad to see you," he said, seeming happy to see me.

I gave him a half hug. "Hey, Dad," I responded plainly. I was never one to fake emotion.

"Come inside. Come," he urged, then ushered me inside the house.

"Wow. You've redone some things in here," I said, looking around. "Brand new hardwood floors, new furniture—"

"And just wait until you see my kitchen," Maria whispered behind me and then ran around me and hugged me. "Hey, Lucinda! It's so good to see you," she cooed in a motherly voice.

This irritated the fuck out of me. Can I please mention again that this heifer was only two years older than me? Why did she act like June Cleaver and treat me like I was Rosemary's age? She was basically my sister. *Child, please.* Just as I was about to say, "Fuck it," and finally go off on his little airheaded wife, Rosemary came in the room, holding the hand of Eva, who toddled along. She was so cute. I loved Eva, but I had to admit that I was envious of her.

"Oh look. She's walking!" I shouted with glee, covering my mouth. "The last I saw her—"

"She was still in a blanket," my dad interrupted. "We must change that. Eva needs to know her siblings."

I wanted to say that her siblings needed to know their dad first, but I bit my lip to squelch the remark. I really just wanted to get this over with. I hugged Eva and said hello to Rosemary.

"Aunt Lucinda, why didn't you bring Nadia?" Rosemary asked.

"Honey, she's not your auntie," Maria said, correcting her.

"Then what is she?" Rosemary asked.

"Um, sweetheart, she's your sister. She's my daughter too, remember?" my dad explained to her.

"But she's old," Rosemary said with her little smart-mouthed ass.

"So is your stepdad," I countered before I knew it.

"Lucinda," my dad scolded, with a glance of disapproval.

"Sorry, but it is the truth," I mumbled and shrugged my shoulders.

"Honey, your daddy and I will explain it to you later. We have to get ready for dinner. Take Eva in the kitchen, and I will be in there in just a moment to wash your hands," Maria directed Rosemary.

"They've really grown up," I said in an attempt to keep it light.

Maria faced me. "Yes, they have. I just want to say that I'm glad you're here, but I ask that you not refer to Emilio as Rosemary's stepdad. To her, he is her daddy."

"And by law, he is her stepdad," I shot back, pissed at her attempt to correct me.

Maria threw her hands up. "Emilio, I can't. I can't deal with this. I try and I try," she said, pretending like she was all frustrated. My dad played knight in fucking shining armor and rushed to hug and comfort her. Oh, I was just damn sick.

"Go and get the girls washed up," he said to Maria.

My dad turned to me. "Lucinda, let me speak to you in private in the living room for a second." I followed him into the living room, and we sat on the sofa. He faced me. "Lucinda, I know that my divorce from your mother was hardest on you. You are the oldest, so you saw a lot of things you shouldn't have, and for that, I apologize. I know that I may not be the best father in the world, but God has granted me a new start with Maria and the girls. I just ask you to accept that, even if you can't be happy about it. Now, Rosemary has never known her real dad, and I'm the only man she's ever known. So please don't take that away from her. She's a little girl. You're old enough to understand that and know better. As for Maria, she's my wife. I love you, but I can't let you run over her."

There was a rage that grew inside of me the size of the heavens. Here he had just made a case for Rosemary and Maria, but he had offered no apologies for leaving my mom or us kids! A new start with a new family? Had he really just said that without any consideration or any attempt to make amends for the family he had left behind? Now, I was supposed to respect that he wanted to be a father to Rosemary and Eva, when he couldn't be a father to us. I was supposed to respect his marriage to Maria when he had disrespected my mama. Oh! I had to get the fuck out of here before I exploded.

"You've made your point," I said and stood up. "On that note, I think I will be leaving," I told him.

"Lucinda, please don't run away. Stay and have dinner with us," he begged.

I shook my head. "I think I need to go, so you and your *family* can enjoy your time together."

"You're my family too," my dad insisted. "At least tell me why you came over."

"Yes, please tell us," Maria chimed in as she walked into the living room with the girls.

I really wanted to leave, but more than cursing out my dad, I wanted to get Raul off my back. I shrugged. "Look, I took Raul to court for child-support payments and supervised visitation. Long story short, I caught him and Shanaya doing the nasty up in his mama's house while Raulina and Nadia played outside, unsupervised, at nine at night." I took a deep breath.

I continued. "Anyway, ever since I took him to court, he's been off the chain. He's harassing his mom, since she was a character witness for me, and filling Nadia's head with lies, making it seem like me and her grandma are the bad people. Every time I see him, he threatens me, and we end up in shouting matches. I just want it to stop. I feel that if he knew I had a man who stood behind me and Nadia, he would understand that he can't treat me like this. Basically, I need you to put the fear of God in him so that he will do what he has to do by Nadia but will leave me alone."

"Lucinda, I feel sorry for you and Nadia, I really do, but that seems kind of dangerous. I don't want my husband caught up in any mess," Maria protested.

"*Caught up in any mess?* He's my dad." I couldn't believe she had said that.

"I understand he's your dad, but he has two little girls who need him. You're grown, Lucinda, and we will help you out if we can, but you can't expect Emilio to go to battle for you," Maria countered.

On that note, I went off. I put my hands on my hips and glared at them. "So are you going to help me or not?" I asked him.

"I'd love to, Lucinda, but Maria has a point—"

"You know what . . . ? Fuck you, and fuck you too!" I screamed at my dad and Maria, cutting him off.

"Lucinda!" my dad hollered.

"Emilio!" I shouted back. "You've said your piece, and now I'm going to say mine." I turned my attention toward his bitch wife. "How dare you stand here, all high and mighty, and tell me that my father—who is just as much my father as he is Eva's, and more my father than he is Rosemary's—can't help his daughter out? Who the fuck died and gave you the right to decide that?" I screamed at Maria, who stood there, blinking her eyes, in shock.

I went on, glaring at her. "You make me sick! You are nothing but a home-wrecking slut who's trying to pass my dad off as Rosemary's biological father. You are two years my senior and are sleeping with a man old enough to be your daddy and Eva and Rosemary's granddaddy! How fucking nasty is that? So don't sit up here and act like you have a lick of morals and home training when the only way you can stand up here in your fancy-ass home with new floors, a new kitchen, and a brand-new Suburban is by lying on your back and spreading your fucking legs!"

I turned to my dad and pointed my finger at him. "And you, Mr. Brand-New Start, are less than a fucking man to sit up here and let this child that you married tell you not to be a father to your children. You're less than a man for not wanting to be a father to me! A real man wouldn't let no *bastardo* disrespect his daughter, no matter how fucking old she is! And then you have the nerve to want me to respect your role as her husband and Rosemary's father when you can't even be a father to me and my siblings! You left my mother destitute to fend for seven children while you ran to less responsibility with this whore! You're late on child support and alimony payments so you can provide wood floors and brand-new cooktops to this bitch that can't even cook."

I continued. "You speak as if the children you left are in the past, when we are all well and very much alive. My siblings are crammed into rooms, they sleep on mattresses with springs sticking out, and they eat peanut butter and jelly sandwiches at night for dinner because that's all Mom can afford, while Eva sleeps in her own room, with her own bed, and she is only a year old! You disgust me, and I swear to God I wish I'd never known you and never loved you. At least that way I wouldn't miss what I never had.

So both of you can kiss my entire ass! I hope with every fiber in my soul that all your kids rise above this and look back on you two and laugh, because the same people you stepped on to get to the top, Father, will be the same ones you see falling down. And trust me . . . you : . . will . . . fall, you bastard!"

My dad swallowed the lump in his throat. "Is that all? Are you done?" he asked calmly, even though he was trembling from anger.

"Yes, I am," I said nonchalantly. "You don't have to say anything. I'll gladly leave. I've had enough pretending for one night anyway. You don't ever have to worry about me coming around again."

"Good! Because you're no longer welcome," Maria blurted out.

I laughed. "As if I care! But just so you know, I already knew you would say that I wasn't welcome here anymore, and my so-called father is far too little of a man to correct you." I turned, stomped over to the front door, and snatched it open.

"Lucinda, I had really hoped that we could begin working through our differences—" my dad began as I stood at the threshold, but I interrupted him.

"Work through this." I shot a bird at him. Then I caught Rosemary's eye. "Oh! And, Rosemary, the reason I seem so old is that your mom and I are about the same age. Your stepdaddy here is the old one. When you get older, you'll understand," I said to her and then stomped out onto the porch.

Behind me, Maria gasped in disbelief. Why the hell should I be concerned about Rosemary's feelings when my own father wasn't concerned about me or his granddaughter? Yeah, I was wrong, but so were they, and I simply didn't give a fuck.

So much for recruiting help with Raul. I was going to have to face this battle with him as I had everything else in my life . . . alone. I didn't understand men like Raul and my father. What made them think that they could continue to hurt people and never had to suffer for it? I guessed it was because it seemed that they never did. There was no way my father could be suffering from anything, I thought, as I looked around his beautiful yard. I climbed behind the wheel and backed out of his driveway. I couldn't believe that after all he'd done to my mom, my siblings, and me, he got to live high on the hog. I loathed everything about him, and I vowed yet again never to have a thing to do with that man.

Charice

I never knew love could be so wonderful. I had to admit that I had absolutely fallen hard for one Mr. Lincoln Harper. Every time I thought about that man, my heart sang. I'd loved Ryan, but to have my love returned at the same magnitude at which I gave it was beyond words. My relationship with Lincoln was reaching unimaginable heights, and I didn't want it to ever come down.

We had truly jumped into one another's lives, despite the fact we hadn't told everyone about us. He had asked me to help him manage his personal, business, and nonprofit accounts; therefore, I had access to all his financial accounts. And I had my own credit card and debit card courtesy of my new beau. Lincoln paid all my bills and made sure I was a very well-kept woman, so my job was nothing more than daytime busy work. He'd even purchased a brand new Range Rover for me.

Wait . . . before I continue, let me be clear. I had told everyone that I was making payments on the vehicle and that I had used some of Ryan's money to put a down payment on it. There was no way in the world I could tell them or Ryan, for that matter, that I had paid cash for it. I was not naïve. Ryan was fair and generous with child support, but I was sure he'd flip his wig if he even remotely suspected, wrongly, that all his money had gone into a luxury SUV. And if he thought really hard about it, he'd realize he hadn't given me that much money to pay cash for an eighty-thousand-dollar vehicle, and then he would wonder who had.

Now, that I've clarified that, back to my baby. Lincoln and I were connected in more than the obvious ways of lovers. For instance, he would call just when I needed him to, and I could finish his sentences. He was my air, and I was his rib. Without him, I couldn't breathe, and without me, he couldn't live. Jokingly, we called each other Adam and Eve, because that was how strong our relationship had grown. I was convinced that there was no other man for me. Now it was time to convince his mom that I was perfect for him.

I had my reservations about meeting Lincoln's parents, but I would make the most of it. His mom had been insisting for some time that she meet the woman who'd virtually stolen her baby son's heart. I preferred to meet her after everyone knew about us, but Lincoln convinced me that there was no better time than the present. I guessed he was right. When the truth did surface, there was no telling what Ryan might say or do, so perhaps it was better to meet Lincoln's parents before the shit hit the fan. At least if his mom hated me, her feelings about me would be based on her own experience and not on some bullshit she had heard off TMZ. Understanding the sensitivity of the situation and my utter and complete nervousness, Lincoln chartered a private jet to fly us to New York, where his parents lived. This way I could be comfortable and the news of our relationship wouldn't be back in Dallas before we were.

We sat in large leather seats on the jet and the service was top-notch, but I couldn't get comfortable. Eyes closed, I had just turned in my seat to find a better position when I felt Lincoln's hand on my thigh. I opened my eyes to find him staring at me, with a smile on his face. "What?" I said with a lazy smile.

"I thought you said you were sleepy," Lincoln replied.

"I am," I lied.

"Liar," he chuckled. "You've turned from side to side six times in the past five minutes. Whenever you toss and turn like that, you're not sleepy. You're only trying to make yourself go to sleep."

I hated the fact that he knew me so damn well. I rolled my eyes at him and huffed. "You just had to bust me out. Ass," I chided.

He laughed heartily. "Come on, Ma. Don't be like that. I swear, you are putting one hundred on something that is only ten."

"You can laugh and joke and hee-hee to the fucking ha-ha, but these are your parents. They don't have to like me. I'd love to see how you act when you meet my parents," I said, irritated at his behavior.

His face dropped, but he regrouped when he noticed how honestly uncomfortable I was. Rather than be upset, he pulled me toward him. "Aw, I'm sorry, baby. I know it means a lot to you. I'm only trying to keep your spirits light. My parents are going to love you every bit as much as I love you," he assured me, then kissed my forehead.

"What if they—"

Wait . . . Did he just say what I thought he said? Okay, I knew I just revealed how close we were. Sure enough, I loved Lincoln, and I felt that he loved me too, but we'd never come out and confirmed it to the other. Yes, that was right. Lincoln and I had never told each other that we loved each other. I sat up and looked at him.

"Did you just say that you loved me?" I asked him.

He smiled, rubbed my chin with his thumb, and nodded, staring directly into my eyes. "Yes, I did, and just in case you need confirmation, Charice Taylor, I love you."

My heart literally skipped a beat. Butterflies fluttered in my stomach, and I swore I heard that sappy love song music that played in the background in movies, when couples united. Placing my hand over my heart, I sang out, "Aw, baby," and then I hugged him around the neck. "I love you too, and I so love being your lady."

"See, this is what my parents will see. They just want to make sure this is real, and not only is it real, but it's also right. So you don't have to worry about a thing." He pulled me closer, and I leaned against his chest. "Just sit back, relax, and enjoy the flight. Everything will be okay," he assured me as he stroked my hair.

I wasn't completely convinced that he was right, but being in his arms soothed me, and I drifted off to sleep.

***

"Lincoln!" Mrs. Harper screamed, running toward him, as soon as we entered the foyer. "My baby's home!" she declared when she reached him, and then she hugged him tightly.

"Hey, Mama!" he said excitedly, lifting her off her feet. "I've missed you."

She stood back and looked at him. "I've missed you too. Doesn't look like you've missed any meals, though."

He smiled. "Well, they say when you're happy, you're healthy."

"And I suppose that happiness you're referring to is due to the young lady standing next to you," she mused, looking at me.

Lincoln pulled me to him by my waist. "Yes, it is. It most definitely is." Just then his dad, his brother, and his brother's wife walked into the foyer and gathered around. Lincoln cleared his throat. "Everyone, this is the wonderful woman I've been raving about. Charice Taylor. Charice, this is my mama, Eleanora Harper, my dad, Leonard Harper, my big brother, Leonard Harper Jr., who we call Leo, and his lovely wife slash my adorable sister-in-law, Krista."

I hugged everyone. "It's a pleasure to meet all of you. I've heard so much about each of you."

"It wasn't too bad, I hope. Linc tends to exaggerate," Leo joked.

I laughed. "No, it wasn't bad at all."

"Well, I can honestly say all we hear are good things about you," Krista said sweetly to me.

"Yep, I don't care what they say about you," Leo said, pointing to his parents. My eyes nearly popped out of my head from fear. "I'm just playing!" he added with a laugh and hugged me with one arm.

I breathed a sigh of relief. "I was halfway out the door!" I laughed, as did everyone else.

Mrs. Harper looked at me and grabbed my hands. "Don't mind my son. He's a character. It is nice to finally meet you, Charice. I'm glad we have this opportunity to get to know each other. Besides, I have to learn more about the special lady who has stolen my Lincoln's heart. He's a good man and has grown up so much in recent years. I know that if he chose you, then he did so out of very sound judgment."

I nodded. "Yes, he did, and your Lincoln is also very special to me as well." Lincoln and I glanced at each other, and he kissed my cheek.

"Well, let's all go into the family room and stop making them stand here on their feet," his dad said to everyone.

We all moved to the family room. Lincoln and I sat on the sofa, beside Leo and Krista, while his dad sat in his La-Z-Boy and clicked on the TV, and his mom sat on the love seat by herself. For a few moments, we all made small talk among each other and then in individual groups. From my observations, Lincoln and Leo were extremely close. They kept joking with each other. Both of them loved their mom too. They showed her the utmost respect as she questioned Lincoln about his career and pressured Leo to give her some grandbabies. His father was very reserved and stuck to watching television. He may have been a man of few words, but he was extremely observant. In the meantime, I let loose and enjoyed talking to Krista. We conversed like old friends, and within a matter of minutes, I started to feel at home. Then his mom interrupted.

"Lincoln, baby, why don't you take your bags to the room that you and Charice will stay in? Leo, go and help Lincoln. And, Krista, please make sure the room is ready," his mom commanded.

They all stood.

"That's Mom's way of getting rid of us, so she can talk to you, Charice. Don't be scared," Leo said.

Lincoln hit him playfully. "Stop messing with my baby," he said, and everyone laughed. I looked up at him, and he leaned over and kissed my lips. "Don't be nervous," he whispered.

I usually wasn't one for public displays of affection, but that kiss spoke so many volumes, based on the reaction on everyone's faces. He must never have been so open with a woman before in front of his family. I guessed that made my standing a little better, but at the same time, I wondered if it meant I would get grilled that much more. Knowing that their son was so head over heels about me might conjure up caution signs in his parents' minds.

Once everyone was out of the room, Mrs. Harper addressed me. "Well, I wasn't trying to make you feel odd, sweetie, but I do feel it is necessary for us to speak with you."

His dad turned off the TV. "Eleanora, the girl just got in the door—"

"And now is as good a time as any," she said, cutting him off. "I mean, this is the best time. She has to spend an entire weekend here, so I want her to feel comfortable. We can get this awkwardness out of the way early. Don't you agree, Charice?"

I nodded. "Yes, ma'am." Honestly, I truly couldn't have agreed more. This way if I needed to find a Holiday Inn, I could do it now.

"You don't have to agree with my wife, Charice," Mr. Harper said as he shot a glare at her.

"No, really, it's okay. I understand. I'm much like that myself. I'd rather clear the air, instead of walking around on eggshells or with false pretenses. I want to enjoy myself this weekend, and I want you to be able to be comfortable around me so that you can enjoy your time with your son," I told them.

I amazed myself. It was times like this that showed me just how much I'd grown as a person. I had been so nervous on that plane, and even when I'd got to the house, that I had thought I wouldn't even be able to speak. But just now I had successfully agreed with his mom without making it appear as if I'd kissed her ass, which I would not do regardless of how much I loved Lincoln.

His mom cracked a genuine smile, and his dad winked at me. "Okay, well, since it doesn't bother you, let the grilling begin!" he joked and sat back.

Mrs. Harper fanned him off. "You see where Leo gets it from!"

I grinned. "Linc has a cynical sense of humor too."

"Yes, he does," Mrs. Harper replied. "Look, sweetie, I just want to say that I've never seen

Lincoln so open. He's like a new man around you. He's usually very reserved, but in the short time that you all have been here, he's been so vibrant and alive. You must be doing something right, because I have never seen him so . . . happy. That's all I want. I want my son to be happy."

"I do too. Lincoln makes me happy, and I'm glad that I make him feel the same way. He is very special to me, and I pray that we will continue to grow in our relationship," I revealed.

His mom smiled. "Good," she said. "But you know I have to ask about this whole thing with Ryan. I'm sure Lincoln has told you about my concerns, but I will tell you myself. As I said, I want to see my son happy, both emotionally and physically, not hurt. Ryan is like a son to me too, and I can't help but feel bad about what you two are doing to him. I'm happy that Lincoln is happy, but at the same time I'm worried about the professional and personal relationship between Ryan and him," she stated matter-of-factly. She exhaled, as if she really didn't want to say what came out of her mouth next, but she did anyway.

"I also must say that I am concerned about your feelings toward Ryan. You're the mother of his children, and it's no secret to us that you were head over heels in love with him. Not to mention how your children will feel about this," she added, furrowing her eyebrows.

Mr. Harper looked at me. "I agree with my wife, Charice. I believe you're a good woman, and I trust that what Lincoln has found in you is truly what he wants and needs. However, many men have suffered gravely behind the love of a woman. Two best friends vying for the same woman never turns out well," he said. Mrs. Harper nodded in agreement.

No matter how I had tried to prepare myself for this conversation, nothing could have prepared me for this moment. I took a brief moment to collect my thoughts, then leaned forward, looked them both directly in the eyes, and exhaled deeply. "Mr. and Mrs. Harper, I have sons too, so as a mother, I sincerely understand and appreciate your concerns. I would never want any hurt or harm to come to Lincoln in any form or fashion. I won't lie to you or cut any corners here. I share your concerns, and I can't tell you what Ryan's reaction will be once he finds out. If I knew that, I would try to alleviate it now. Unfortunately, that is something that Lincoln and I will have to face and deal with together when the time comes.

"However, what I can assure you of is that I love and care for Lincoln just as much as he loves and cares for me. He is a great, loving, caring, gentle, respectful, and loyal man, whom I would never take advantage of, and I am not willing to give up our relationship to spare anybody's feelings. I care about Ryan, but that is because he is the father of my children. Our relationship chapter was written and closed before Linc and I began dating, so that is something that you can rest easy about. As for the rest, I'm there with Lincoln for whatever comes our way, as this was our decision, and this is our relationship. As long as he is willing to fight for it, I'm going to be right there beside him with my boxing gloves on, because being with him is where I truly want to be." I said all this to them with so much conviction that I surprised even myself.

I'd been nervous, but when it had come down to defending my relationship with Lincoln, I had proven to everyone, including myself, that I was not going to be moved. I wanted that man, and nobody was going to stop me from being Lincoln Harper's lady. Nobody. With that, I sat back and waited for the next set of questions. I knew I was ready for whatever they had to throw at me. When Mr. and Mrs. Harper looked at each other, smiled, and nodded, I knew that I'd won them over. Mrs. Harper stood and walked over to me.

"So, do I need to find a Holiday Inn?" I asked jokingly.

"Only if you and Lincoln need a bit of privacy," she responded as she hugged me. "I can honestly say that I see why my son is so happy."

"And why he'd give Ryan his ass to kiss over you!" his dad chimed in, and I felt my cheeks redden with embarrassment. "I guess I'm playing referee between those two, because I don't foresee my son giving up on you."

"Well, don't you worry, Mr. and Mrs. Harper. I've got Lincoln's back!" I joked.

"Oh, I believe that," his mom said and laughed. Then she grabbed my hands. "I appreciate your honesty, and I trust that you really do care for my son. You all have my blessing."

She did not understand what those words meant to me. I'd been so worried about his parents' acceptance of me. They had had so many reasons not to give me a chance, but they had remained open, and I had won them over. The mere fact that they had given me an opportunity without judgment was already enough.

Tears came to my eyes. Lincoln's mother wiped them away, then hugged me. "Thank you so much, Mrs. Harper. Thank you."

"You're welcome, love, and stop calling me Mrs. Harper. Eleanora or Mama will do just fine."

His dad hugged me next. "Just call me Pop," he said.

Mrs. Harper left the family room, walked to the staircase, and looked up the stairs. "You all can come down now."

Soon, Lincoln, Leo, and Krista ran down the stairs and entered the family room, with questioning looks on their faces.

Lincoln walked toward me. "So, are we staying?" he asked a bit nervously.

His mom linked arms with me. "Oh, you're not taking my baby away. We have so much to get to know about each other, and I want to see pictures of the triplets," she gushed, smiling at me.

Lincoln walked up and kissed us both on the cheek.

"Come on, Krista," his mom called out. "You, Charice, and I are going to the sunroom." And off we went.

Lincoln began to follow us, and we stopped.

"Babe, go chill with Leo and Pop. Mama, Krista, and I are going to do our girl thang," I said, smiling at the ladies.

The men laughed at the shocked look on Lincoln's face. "Mama, you've never let anyone call you Mama besides Krista," Lincoln noted.

"That's because you've never brought anyone here worthy of that privilege," she said. That set everyone off in a fit of laughter. "Now, go on, like Charice said, and do your man thang. We'll catch up with you three later."

"So tell me about your first date with Linc," Krista said excitedly to me as we walked away, laughing and giggling in our own little world.

I felt on top of the world. Ryan was finally supporting his children, I had the man of my dreams, and his parents approved of us. I had to admit, Lincoln was right. I needed to know that his family stood behind us, because I felt this moment solidified our relationship. I felt confident that this was just what we needed to make our relationship strong, because now we had nothing to hold us back. For the first time since I'd been with Lincoln, the thought of being called Mrs. Lincoln Harper crossed my mind, and it didn't sound bad at all.

Trinity

Pooch had stayed out of my way for the past month. He'd really put in a lot of time into streamlining his crew since those last fools had tried him. He had to make sure his people stayed close to him so no one else would be able to infiltrate like that again. He had worked day and night to check, recheck, and double-check every nigga and every nigga's move, along with every brick, sack, and dime that came and went through his organization.

His next point of pain was that he had to replenish his supply. He had to meet his connect sooner because of the hit. While he was able to recover the money, he had no idea where his three bricks were. For all he knew, they had smoked it up or had sold it themselves. He was pissed because now he had to spend more money on extra product and still make shit right on the lost product. He had money, so it didn't hurt him. It just pissed him the hell off. Pooch hated to spend money on things he felt were unnecessary, and I would put this incident in that category.

In the meantime, I continued with school, and Terrence continued to help me with the kids. Terrence supported me in a major way, and we were closer than ever. We could talk about any and everything, and we often did. Regardless of what the subject was, whether I talked about my classes or, hell, even the weather, Terrence listened and hung on my every word, as if I were President Obama. His attentiveness was so genuine and sincere. In fact, everything about Terrence was genuine and sincere. It felt good to be listened to and adored.

What I respected the most about him was that despite his feelings for me, he didn't play any bitch-ass moves, like trying to pull me from Pooch, even though he had the opportunity. I wondered if he ever would. What man paid for day care for a child that ain't his so you could go to school? Exactly. At first, I had thought it was a ploy to get me away from Pooch, but it had soon become clear that Terrence wanted only to help me. He felt that he owed it to me from when he got locked up, and he wanted the mother of his children to be successful so that I could be a role model for our children.

Ain't that a bitch? A man who wanted nothing but what was best for the woman. Do you see why my heart was doing somersaults? But somersaults or not, I was with Pooch, and I always remembered that shit.

At any rate, I was so excited because I had found out that I had passed all my midterms and had even got As. I was on cloud nine as I went to pick up Princess from Terrence's sister Tomika's house. I wished I was able to share my good news with Pooch, but unfortunately, there were just some things in life that would never change. So, I figured I'd pick up my baby and have my own mini celebration.

"So, what did you make on your tests?" Terrence asked as he walked into his sister, Tomika's living room while I packed up Princess's diaper bag.

I jumped. "You scared the shit out of me. You didn't tell me you were going to be here."

"I wanted to surprise you. I came because I wanted to see how you did on your tests," he said, walking up to Tomika, Princess, and me.

When I turned to face him, I damn near choked. I didn't know what it was, but for some reason, I swore he looked extra fine. He had on a short-sleeved, button-down, collared shirt, a white T-shirt underneath, some dark denim jeans, and some fresh chukkas. His shoul-der-length dreads were fresh and hanging loose. "Look at you, looking all fresh, dressed like a million bucks," I sang.

"I'm always fresh dressed, li'l mama. You know how I do it."

"Yeah, she knows how you do it," Tomika joked, pushing me and laughing. I blushed. "He's been waiting over here for the past half hour for you to come. I'ma give y'all some space." And with that, she kissed Princess, gave me a hug, then took the money from Terrence and dashed up the stairs.

"Your sister is so cool. I appreciate the help from both of you. I don't know how I'm ever going to repay you guys."

"Well, my sister is getting paid for her services, and as for me, the only payment I need is to see you get that degree," Terrence said.

A smile graced my face, and I blushed again. Words couldn't explain how grateful I was for him. "You are too much, Dreads. I swear."

He shrugged. "I'm just that kind of man. But are you going to keep me in suspense all day?"

The same smile I had on my face broadened now, and then I revealed my semester grades. "Your girl made all As!" I shouted, doing the snake from side to side as my little victory dance.

"Aah! That's what's up. Give me some!" Terrence said, then gave me a high five and did the wop as I continued my dance.

"We are some lame fools!" I laughed at our wacky dance moves.

"Yeah, we are," he said and chuckled lightly. "Listen, if you have a minute, I bought some Chinese food from P.F. Chang's. It's in Tomika's fridge. I was going to save it for dinner, but this is a good occasion to have a little victory lunch."

I checked the time. I knew Pooch wouldn't be home for another three hours. "That's cool. You are always celebrating my little successes. You don't have to."

"I know that, Trinity. I do it because I want to and because you deserve it. All these little successes lead up to the ultimate goal, so every one of them needs to be celebrated. I just want to keep you encouraged and motivated," he said seriously.

"Thanks. It really does mean a lot to me."

Terrence took Princess upstairs to Tomika, then came back and heated up the food. We sat down on the family-room floor, on pillows on one side of the coffee table, with our P.F. Chang's and sodas to celebrate my As.

"Let me make a toast," Terrence said. We both held up our Sprite cans. "To one of the smartest, most talented, and loving women I've ever known. I am proud that you are the mother of my children. May you have continued success."

I toasted with him and pushed my hair out of my face. "Aw, Dreads. That's so sweet. You are so amazing. Thank you so much."

He shrugged. "I try," he said, and then we dove into our food.

For over thirty minutes, we sat there and laughed and joked while we ate. I have no idea what all the bullshit was that we discussed, but as I said, I could talk about things that had nothing to do with anything and still have fun with Terrence.

"Shit. I'm full," I said, rubbing my stomach. "I put a hurting on that food."

Terrence laughed. "That's 'cause you don't eat right. Pooch have you eatin' them bourgeois-ass five-star meals every night." He caught my eye. "Pardon me, but could you pass the Grey Poupon?" Terrence joked in his "white boy" voice. "As if that fool could tell the difference between a cube steak and a filet mignon."

I couldn't help but laugh. Terrence was a fool. "You know you wrong for that!"

"No, you know I'm right."

"Whatever." I giggled. "That's why you have a little bit of noodle in your chin hair," I pointed out.

He took his napkin and wiped but missed it. "Did I get it?"

Shaking my head, I rolled my eyes at him. "No, sloppy self," I said, getting up on my knees and taking the napkin from him. He always managed to get food on his face somewhere, and he never could wipe it off himself. "Let me get it. You still don't know how to feed yourself."

"Fine then. Get it. You know how I do. Ain't nothing changed," he said as I wiped his face.

Exhaling, I thought to myself that he'd always been a good man. "No, you've never changed," I admitted.

"And I'm never going to." His eyes were fixed on mine. "At least not for the worse. Always and only for the better." He licked his luscious ass lips.

"What's better than number one?" I asked, biting my bottom lip.

"Having the number one woman," he replied.

My knees buckled, my heart rate increased, and I swore somebody had put the heat on hell. I felt flushed, and my insides instantly started trembling. What the hell kind of effect did Terrence have on me? I felt like I was going to lose it on his ass, literally.

"I think I better get Princess and head on," I said, beginning to stand. Before I could get up off my knees, Terrence pulled me back down to him.

Now, as I sat between his legs, he wrapped his arms around my waist and interlocked his fingers behind my back to hold me in place. I was more nervous than a whore in church, while he seemed cool as a damn cucumber.

"You don't have to run from me. I'm not going to force myself on you, Trinity. I'm a patient man. I'll wait for you."

I fanned myself. "Um, you shouldn't wait on me, because . . . ," I began, and the next thing I knew, Terrence pulled my chin down, leaving inches between our lips. I closed my eyes in anticipation of his inviting kiss and delectable lips, but I felt nothing. When I opened my eyes, he looked at me.

"Wh-what?" I asked.

He chuckled. "As I said, I'm a patient man. For a woman who is so secure in her relationship, you sure didn't put up much of a fight."

"I . . . um . . . I . . . ," I stammered.

"I understand." He winked at me. "I'm patient, and I'm patiently waiting," he said, letting me go.

"Waiting for what?" I asked, rapidly gathering my things.

When I turned around, Terrence was standing in front of me. "One day, I'll tell you what I'm waiting on. You're not ready to hear that right now."

"I have to go. This was nice, and I appreciate everything that you do." I sighed.

"But?" he said.

"But I have to go."

He curled his mouth into that sexy-ass half smile, which drove me insane. "Do you want me to get Princess?"

"Yes, please," I said with exasperation. He left to go upstairs and was back within moments.

"All right, Princess. You're such a sweet little girl, like your mom." He kissed her forehead and handed her to me. "Be easy, li'l mama," he said as I grabbed her baby bag and headed out the door.

"You too," I responded without looking back.

I hurried to my car, arranged Princess in the backseat, then climbed behind the wheel, started up the car, and sped off, all the while refusing to think about what had just happened between Terrence and me. I was going to have to find someone else to keep Princess. I couldn't continue to go around Terrence like that. He stirred up too many emotions and feelings that I thought had long since died. I didn't know how long I could keep up pretenses like that, and I didn't know how long I could keep pretending that I didn't want him.

Moment of truth. I wanted him so bad. So bad. He was on my mind like the 7-Eleven stores. In other words, he had me wide open 24-7. My thoughts, my dreams, and my desires were filled with memories of my past life with Terrence and the possibility of a future with him. I was Pooch's woman, though. That was what I kept telling myself. That was what I wanted to believe, that I still wanted to be with Pooch.

I slammed on the brakes in a fit of anger when I got to a light. I was pissed with myself for letting shit get so out of hand. My emotions and my sexual desires ran rampant, and I was confused as hell as to how he was able to infiltrate my heart. Even the simplest things had me confused, like our near kiss. I should be mad that he had even pretended like he was going to kiss me, but no, I was mad because he actually hadn't kissed me. I had wanted that kiss so bad, so bad. I was going to have to think of a game plan to stay away from Terrence unless the occasion involved our kids.

Once I was home, I put Princess down for a nap and was determined to focus on finding a new day-care provider before I ended up in some shit for real. As soon as I sat down on the living-room sofa to rack my brains about a new sitter, Pooch came inside the house with Big Cal.

I looked up in surprise. "Hey, babe. What are you doing home so early?"

He bent down and kissed my lips. "I finally have a chance to meet up with Tot, so I have to make a move. I came home to gather some shit. I'll be gone for a couple of days."

"Dang. On the weekend?" I asked with a pout.

Looking at Big Cal, Pooch smiled and pointed at me. "See how my baby be missin' her daddy and shit? That's how you do it, Big Cal. She be missin' my quality time," he said, and Big Cal chuckled.

"You know the weekend is our time," I whined.

Yes, I was pissed for purely selfish reasons. I needed to be with Pooch this weekend to clear out all this emotional shit with Terrence. I figured if I could spend time with Pooch, it would tame these fucked-up feelings for Terrence that had surfaced. And it didn't help that Pooch had been MIA lately. He'd been so fucking busy with realigning his business that we hadn't had sex in, like, three weeks. Yes, two things Pooch loved more than sex were power and money. He wasn't fit for shit unless the first two were together. He'd been leaving at sunup and been gone until sundown most days recently, and he'd been consumed with knowing every fucking move anyone made. His cell phone had been blowing up with calls and text messages from his crew anytime he'd been at home, which had made intimacy a no-go. But right now, I needed him . . . really needed him. The intimacy would remind me that he loved me and that this relationship was what I wanted.

"I'll make it up to you. That's my word, babe," Pooch said, then bent down and kissed me. "But you know I gotta get this situation squared with Tot."

"I know," I said, not bothering to hide my disappointment.

Pooch pulled me up to him gently. He held me about the waist as he pleaded his case in an attempt to soothe my irritation. "Come on now." He lifted my chin so that we were eye to eye. "You know this is what I gotta do. I have to continue this lifestyle for you. I'll spend time with you when I get back." When I rolled my eyes from disappointment, he kissed my cheek. "Shit. I'll buy you something," he offered, grasping for straws as to how to make me happy. "What do you want? I saw you looking at them new Range Rovers. You want one of them?"

Just then my cell phone rang. Normally, I wouldn't answer, but my irritation caused me to pull back from Pooch's embrace, turn, and pick up my cell from the sofa. "Hello?"

"Hey, cuz! What's up?" Charice said.

"Ain't nothing, Charice. I'm talking with Pooch right now."

"Well, I ain't gonna hold you up. I was wondering what you're doing tonight. It's Friday. I just got paid, and I am kid free the whole weekend. I wanted to do a ladies' night. It's been a long time since me, you, Lucinda, and LaMeka hung out. LaMeka's sister is gonna watch her kids, so she's in. Do you think you and Lucinda could go out? I was thinking of dinner and then going to the Compound."

"Um, I'm sure Lucinda could. Ms. Ana is keeping Nadia this weekend. I'll have to check on my end," I answered.

"Cool. Just hit me back. I'm gonna call Lucinda."

"A'ight," I said and hung up.

Pooch pointed at me, with a smile plastered on his face. No doubt grateful for this unforeseen blessing. "That's what you need. You need to get out and have a ladies' night. Call my sister to keep Princess. I'll break her off and make sure she straight, so I know she will do it. Then see if that nigga Terrence will get his two."

"This is Terrence's off weekend. I'm not going to burden him like that. I'll check if my mom or his sister can keep the kids," I said.

He shrugged. "Whatever. You need to go out and have some fun." He pulled a gwop of money from his pocket. "Here you go. Go buy something fly as hell, and this is to keep your pockets laced," he said, handing me two wads.

My lips were pursed because I knew he was using this moment to be able to slide his ass right out the door. Although I preferred to be holed up in the house with him, I'd accept his money as a consolation gift. I wasn't crazy, now. "All right. Thanks, baby." I kissed him.

He held me tight, kissed me longer and deeper. "Damn. It's been a minute, huh?"

"Uh-huh," I said, getting caught up in the moment.

Pooch looked over his shoulder at Big Cal, who was burning a hole in the floor with his eyes, trying not to look at Pooch and me. Pooch turned to face me and looked at the clock. "Damn. I wish I had some time to knock this shit out of the box. Plus, I have to be careful around that nigga. He might try to watch and shit, and I ain't wit' that fuckin' voyeurism shit. I don't need none of these niggas knowing what you working with."

"All right, Pooch. Besides, I like it better when your mind ain't preoccupied. So when you gettin' back?"

"Sunday evening, around six."

"A'ight," I said, pulling away from him.

"Keep that shit wet," he whispered, smacking me on the ass.

Pooch left the room to gather his stuff, and I got everything set up. Pooch's sister was gonna watch Princess, and Terrence's sister was gonna watch Terry and Brittany. I called Charice back to confirm that I'd be there, and she told me that Lucinda was going. I knew Lucinda was going through a rough time trying to take care of Nadia with no help from Raul's stankin' ass, so I wanted to look out for my best friend for life by hooking her up with a new, fresh-to-death outfit. If anybody deserved it, it was her. That girl stayed on the grind for herself and her baby. I was excited, because it had been a long time since we'd done some shit like this. Between all our personal trials and men troubles, we needed this shit. Now I was actually glad Pooch would be gone this weekend. I wanted him here only to calm down my heart and pussy desires for Terrence. Truth be told, Pooch had been another stressor as of late his damn self. A girls' night out was just what the doctor had ordered. A bitch was due for a few drinks and a bit of parlaying.

"A'ight, babe. I'm 'bout to head out," Pooch said when he walked back into the living room. "You get everything set up?"

"Yeah, your sister is keeping Princess, and Terrence's sister is keeping Brit and Terry," I told him.

He nodded. "Cool. That's what's up," he said, handing me three hundred dollars. "When you drop off Princess, give that to my sister."

"What about Tomika?" I asked.

To be honest, I didn't give a damn if he paid Tomika. I just wanted to see where his heart was at. Tomika didn't mind keeping her niece and nephew. She loved them, and she loved me, but Pooch wasn't aware that Terrence was footing a bill for his daughter. See, what I knew and understood was that regardless of the fact that Princess was Pooch's child, Terrence did for her because his love for me allowed him to see past the fact that she wasn't his daughter. I knew Pooch wasn't Brittany's and Terry's father, but didn't he love me enough to see that as long as he was with me, their well-being was also his responsibility? Of course, my kids knew Pooch wasn't their daddy, but they did respect him as a father figure in their life, so did he not see them as a part of his life?

"*Shit*! Get the fuck outta here with that, babe," Pooch said, waving me off. "Miss me with that shit. That's *your* baby daddy's sister. Tell that nigga to lace his sister's pockets."

"Come on. He's not asking his sister to watch the kids. I am."

"Then ask his ass to watch his own kids. This sister shit was your idea. I told you to ask him to begin with. That way if he couldn't, he'd probably ask his sister, and then that shit would be on him. But you always trying to look out for that nigga's time and feelings and shit," Pooch said with irritation. In essence, he was right, but he was being an ass because she was Terrence's sister.

"A'ight," I said, relenting. I didn't need him hyped up on no Terrence bullshit today.

"I just gave you a stack. If you want to pay his sister, take it out of that. I already got unnecessary shit to deal with," Pooch said, fussing some more. I told you. I knew he felt like this buyout was a waste of his money.

He must've missed it when I tried to dead the conversation the first time, I thought. Instead of being pissed that he had continued to rant, I placed my hands on his shoulders and said, "A'ight, baby. Be safe. I love you." I kissed him.

When I saw his shoulders deflate, I knew the subject had been dropped. Thank God. Ain't nobody had time for Pooch and all that noise. Damn. Here, I wanted to spend time with him so I could put these pent-up emotions for Terrence to rest, and all he could do was bitch and moan because I had asked for money to pay someone to watch the kids. The more I tried to show him that being in this relationship was what I wanted, the more he had to remind me why I had reconnected with Terrence in the first place. *Grouchy and ungrateful-ass nigga.* And he wondered why Dreads was so fucking appealing to bitches. He did shit that appealed to bitches, like spend fucking time and paying for other men's kids, that was why. *Dummy. Lawd! Help me.* I want to try with him because I did love him, but I swear, I was on the verge of losing my shit with Pooch.

He sighed. "I love you too. Remember that shit." He turned to Big Cal. "Let's go, nigga."

"A'ight. Bye, Trinity," Big Cal said.

"Be easy, Big Cal," I said.

They walked out of the house and then left in a rented Escalade.

You know what? Fuck it. All I ever heard out of his mouth was criticism, fussing, and questions. Why would I want to give his ass the honor of my time? The peace of alone time was exactly what I needed. It was the perfect reward after so much hard work in school. Also, it would give me the time to figure out how to deal with things with Terrence and to dig deep on what

I wanted out of my relationship with Pooch. I loved him, but I'd grown weary of these antics. Was this lifestyle enough to continue to put up with the attitude and disrespect? And I hadn't forgotten the bedroom incident, either.

It was a lot to think on, but tonight I wouldn't think about anything except parlaying with my girls. This girls' night was just what the doctor ordered. The more I thought about it, the more excited I got. Ladies' night, here I come!

Trinity

"What's up, ladies?" Lucinda and I hollered in unison when we met up with Charice and LaMeka outside the entrance to Ruth's Chris Steak House.

"Hey, divas!" Charice greeted excitedly, hugging us.

"My girls!" LaMeka said as she took her turn to hug us.

"I'm so glad we got to do this. And, Ms. Charice, that dress is fire! Have we been BCBGMAXAZRIA shopping?" I said, zooming in on her designer duds. "Shit, Ryan has stepped his game all the way up. He's got his baby mama straight as hell, I see."

"Oh, yes, ma'am," Charice confirmed with a confident twirl. "I know you know the real deal. Pooch keeps you laced and icy," she added.

"Shit, that's her *new* man, who she refuses to give up the info about," LaMeka blurted, rolling her eyes.

Lucinda and I looked at each other. "*New man*?" we chorused, in utter shock.

Lucinda threw her hands on her hips, with her head cocked to the side, in confusion. Her blunt ass asked the question that I was sure we all were thinking. "When the hell did you get off Ryan's dick long enough to find someone else?"

After stepping in front of Lucinda, LaMeka wagged her finger and then pointed back at Charice. "She ain't gon' tell you. She won't even tell *me*," LaMeka said, pointing to herself and rolling her eyes again. "All I know is brotha is paid, and he keeps her draped, dripped, and dazzled. This heifer is flying everywhere, and the way that phone has been ringing, it's for real."

Sucking her teeth, Charice scoffed at LaMeka and pushed her back to the side. "Ain't you got nerve?" she muttered to LaMeka, who simply shrugged it off. Charice held her hand up, as if she was under oath. "Ladies, I promise you that when my new beau and I are ready to reveal our relationship, you all will be the first to know, besides my kids and parents."

Wow. Honey had come up. Admittedly, Charice was the most educated of all of us. If Ryan hadn't abandoned her and left her with three children to raise solo dolo, there was no doubt in anybody's mind that she'd be owning her own dance company or some shit right now. Charice had three children and had still earned a degree before all our asses, and she had a decent job. However, Mr. Man had elevated not only her clothes and shoes but also her damn mind and vernacular. Hella impressed was I. *Damn. High fives to this bitch.*

"Did y'all hear that shit?" I said, smiling. "He must be a real bourgeois brotha. She talkin' 'bout her new *beau.* Who the hell in the hood calls they man a damn beau? This nigga money must be hella long!"

Charice giggled. "Like I said, when he and I are ready to reveal our relationship, you all will be among the first to know."

We all looked at each other. Then we shouted things at her as she laughed.

"Is he married?"

"Is he gay?"

"He's white, right?"

"Y'all are too funny, but in due time you all will know," Charice said. "Now, can we go in here, before we lose our reservation?"

Reluctantly, we dropped the subject, seeing that she was not going to reveal a thing to us, and shuffled inside the restaurant. Once inside, I reveled in the fact that we were all grown up and looked hella good. Smiling as I reminisced,

I realized we were a far cry from the skinny teenagers who rocked the ponytails and jeans, ate at McDonald's, and hung out at the teen clubs. We'd become some fly-ass, sexy divas.

We really enjoyed ourselves as we ate, caught up, and had a true ladies' night. Our flirtatious waiter even hooked us up with a free bottle of wine. Not that we needed it after all those Caribbean Pearls, but that move clinched him an excellent hundred-dollar tip.

Afterward, we headed over to the Compound and got in free and enjoyed VIP treatment because of Charice, or rather because of her new, well-known title, Ryan Westmore's baby mama. The place was jam-packed tonight, but we didn't have to worry about crowding as we made our way to our lounge sofa in the back and sat down to talk and listen to the music. After a while, I was ready to get my drink on.

"How about a bottle of Cîroc?" I asked.

"I'm in," the ladies all said in unison.

"When the waitress comes by, I'll order," Charice volunteered.

I stood up. "Cool. I'll be right back. I'm going to head over to the ladies' room." On my way, I bumped into the waitress. "Excuse me. When you get a moment, our table would like to order a bottle of Cîroc, please," I told her, and she nodded, then rushed over to the table.

"What do you know about Cîroc?" I heard a man behind me ask.

I turned to see who was addressing me. "Say what?" I asked, throwing my long, wavy jet-black hair over my shoulder. Terrence and two of his homeboys were standing there. This shit brought me back to when I first officially met Terrence in the club when I was fifteen. He looked as fly now as he had back then, and I was just as giddy to see him now as I'd been back then. He looked fine in his Polo ensemble and his Polo chukkas. I smiled at him, and we embraced.

"What are you doing in here, bugging me?" I joked.

"I was just hanging out with the fellas. Tomika told me you were having a ladies' night out. That's good that Pooch let you come out and live a little," Terrence said.

"Oh, whatever." I fanned him off and turned to speak to his two friends. "What's up, Skeet and Rome?"

They hugged me.

"Ain't nothing. What's up, Miss Trinity?" Skeet said.

"Just chillin' out with my girls," I replied.

"Long time no see. We miss you around the block," Rome said.

"Well, I'm sorry you niggas miss a sista. A sista misses y'all niggas too." Skeet, Rome, and I shared a laugh, and when I looked up at Terrence, he eyed me closely as he stuck the toothpick he'd been holding in his mouth.

Rolling the toothpick around in his mouth, Terrence sucked his teeth and then rubbed his hands together. "So what the hell Pooch have going on that he is letting you hang out without the entire dope-boy clique being around?" he asked.

This nigga was slick with the snide remarks. Crossing my arms, I leaned on one foot, my hip poking out to the side, attitude on high. "You know, this whole *thing* between Pooch and you is so aggravating at times, but on the real, Pooch is out of town on some business. And before you make another smart-ass comment, he knows I'm out with the ladies. In fact, he thinks it's a great idea," I said, rolling my neck and eyes at Terrence.

"But I bet he doesn't know that you're killing that dress," he complimented slickly, then sipped on his Henny.

Blushing, I couldn't help but notice the fact that he still noticed me. But I played it off. "This old thing?"

"Ha! Why you playing like it ain't brand new? Even when we were together, you always bought a new outfit when you went out," Terrence said and laughed. "But on the real, you look hella good," he added, the effects of the brown liquor showing in his eyes.

I laughed nervously. He was right about the outfit and the "looking good" part, but on that note, I had to slide out. "You look good yourself. I better go. You fellas be easy." I turned to walk away.

"Yo, Trin!" Terrence yelled after me.

I stopped and turned to face him.

"Save me a dance."

I laughed and winked at him before continuing on to the restroom.

"You were gone forever," Lucinda said when I got back to the table. She was pouring the concoction for everyone.

"I was just—"

"We saw you over there talking to Dreads. You two seemed mighty close," Charice said before taking a sip of her drink.

Sitting back, I picked up my glass and took a sip. "He's my children's daddy. We gon' always be close."

The three of them looked at me and laughed.

"Honey, well, you 'bout one in a damn million of sistas who is close to their baby daddy. Hell, I'm technically still in a relationship with mine, and we ain't nowhere near as close as you and Terrence, so please miss me with that shit," LaMeka said.

Charice and Lucinda agreed.

"Ryan is cool now, but our kids are five years old. You and Dreads have always been cool," Charice chimed in.

"And, hell, look at me. Raul ain't never been a daddy. You were damn sure blessed," Lucinda added.

Fuck was this? "Gang up on Trinity" night? Besides, I had chosen to hang with my girls to get my mind off Terrence, not to focus on how great he was. Nothing about this conversation helped with these crazy up-and-down emotions I had been experiencing over Terrence lately, either. It damn sure didn't help Pooch's case, either. So I needed them to change the damn station.

"Okay. I get the point, but can we just enjoy each other? That is what we came for, right?" I asked, getting aggravated.

They nodded, and we continued to tear up the Cîroc. I was good and tipsy when the DJ began playing throwback songs. The first was very appropriate for our situation—"Tipsy," by J-Kwon. We all got up and hit the dance floor on that one. I guessed it was the "get drunk" song hour, because the next one was "Wasted," by Gucci Mane and featuring Plies, and the rest of the songs struck the same theme. We danced to a few more songs when the DJ switched it up a bit and played this old joint called "Headboard," by Hurricane Chris and featuring Mario. OMG! If that shit was not fire, I didn't know what was! It had everyone in there singing the lyrics and dancing.

"We be in the bed girl . . . getting all wild . . . fucking like it's going out of style. And we be like, yeah . . . yeah . . . getting all loud . . . fucking like we tryin'a have a child . . . Got you up against the . . . headboard . . . Got your body screaming like, oh, oh, ooh . . . Baby grab the headboard . . . make it go . . . make it go . . . oh, oh, ooh," I sang as we wound on the dance floor.

Suddenly, I felt somebody behind me. I knew it was Dreads. I was so fucking tipsy, though, that I didn't give a damn, and apparently, neither did he, as he was grinding up on me, and I threw it back to him.

"I'll make your head hit the headboard till it squeak. I'll put it on you, have you thinking 'bout me for a week," Dreads sang, rapping along with the song in my ear.

I turned to face him. "You think so, huh?" I said as he pulled me by my waist and began to grind up on me.

"I know so. I've already done it plenty of times before," he whispered in my ear. I giggled.

I felt a tap on my shoulder. It was Lucinda. "Be cool, hon. You don't know who knows Pooch up in here," she whispered to me. I looked back to see my girls and Terrence's boys staring at us in utter shock and disbelief.

I pulled back from Terrence. "Dreads, I better get back over to where my girls at."

"Running again?"

"You know I can't," I told him. I stepped back, walked away abruptly, and rejoined my girls in the lounge area.

"Girl, the hell is wrong with you, wilding out with Terrence like that?" LaMeka asked me as I sat down.

I pointed at the bottle as I eased back in the seat. "It was just this damn liquor and shit," I lied.

"Well, we're going to get out of here and hit another club. You down?" Charice said.

The turnup had gotten a bit too real for me. Although I wanted to hang with my girls, if I wilded out any more, Pooch was bound to catch wind of it, and ain't nobody had time to play Twenty Questions with him. I was good on that.

"Nah. I think I better get back home," I said as we all stood up to leave.

Lucinda decided to hang with Meka and Charice, so I said good-bye to all three of them before they all headed to Charice's SUV. I headed toward my Mercedes. As I turned the corner, I ran smack into Dreads.

"My bad. My boys and I were just leaving," he said.

"Me too."

"Ain't that your girls heading out over there?"

I looked back. "Yeah. I'm a little tipsy, so I'm calling it a night."

"Yeah, I am too. Skeet was gonna drop me off and head to a strip club. I can't feel giving my money to a broad who ain't doing nothing but showing me what she got. Hell, I know what the hell a woman has."

"It's not about that," I said, laughing at him. "It's about the illusion of wanting something you can't have."

"I don't need a strip club for that," he said with a seductive look in his eyes.

I bit my lip nervously. "Well, good night, Dreads."

"Still running, huh?" he called out as I began to walk away. "What are you scared of?"

I sighed and turned back, then got up in his face. "I ain't scared of nothing."

"Bullshit," he challenged.

"Well, we both should be scared of Pooch," I said matter-of-factly.

He laughed almost mockingly. "Since when have I ever been scared of Pooch?" He exhaled slowly as a serious look crossed his face. "Look. We both should be, but neither one of us is, so you tell me, li'l mama, what are you really afraid of?"

Damn, he knew me so well. I shook my leg nervously and looked down, but he lifted my chin so that my eyes met his. "Stop please," I begged him.

"You don't ever have to be shy or ashamed around me. You've always kept it one hundred with me, and me with you. So keep it one hundred right now," he said, pressing.

Looking into his eyes, I admitted, "I'm scared of . . . Shit! I can't believe this. I'm scared of what I might do if I keep being around you."

"Me too," he murmured.

Nervously, I walked slowly past him. I couldn't believe that I'd finally spoken my feelings aloud and to him. Something about knowing that my feelings were out in the atmosphere made it all seem real, like I couldn't turn back the hands of time and could just move forward. I didn't know what took over me, but I stopped in my tracks, and without bothering to look back, I addressed him. "So you coming or what?"

Without any hesitation, Terrence walked with me to my Mercedes and got in on the passenger side. He texted his boy and told him to go ahead without him, and I called Lucinda and asked her to cover for me in case Pooch checked for me and to tell the others that if anyone asked, I was with her. We rode around for a few minutes in silence before Terrence suggested we head to a hotel for some alone time. That was a good thing, because there was no way my car could be seen at his apartment. And there was no way I would ever risk having him in the house I shared with Pooch.

I half expected him to jump all over me the moment we were out of the club parking lot, but I think Terrence recognized my nervousness. He didn't say much to me as I drove. Rather he showed affection. Not lust. Affection. Slowly, his fingers glided through my wavy hair. Jesus. His touch damn near drove me insane. Since I couldn't close my eyes and savor the moment, I simply pulled my bottom lip between my teeth and suckled on it. His strong fingers found my delicate neck and softly kneaded the tension as

I drove. Though desire dripped off him like running water, he never allowed it to ooze over onto me. He behaved like a champion, full of grace and patience. But, hell, I didn't need him to seduce me. I was already seduced, and my own desire was evident by the moans that escaped my lips.

When I finally arrived in Suwanee, which was far enough away to avoid anyone with direct links to us, I pulled into the parking lot of the nearest hotel, a Marriott, and Terrence hopped out and rented a suite. After parking, we walked to the suite in complete silence. I think we were afraid that if we said something, we'd lose the nerve to go through with this.

Once inside the suite, I went into the bedroom and sat on the bed, feeling nervous anticipation. When Terrence entered the bedroom, desire replaced the nervous energy that coursed through me. Leaning back on my elbows, I took in all six feet of his sexy ass. With a flirtatious smirk, he licked his teeth and then made his way over to me and pulled me up into a deep kiss.

"You are so fucking beautiful," he whispered between kisses. "Being back in your arms again is so incredible. I'm so glad you are giving us this moment."

His joy was evident on his face. There was almost a new level of appreciation for the time lost between us. Thinking of his earlier comment at his sister's house, I wrapped my arms around his neck and asked the question that had been plaguing my mind for weeks. "So what were you waiting on?" I asked as he gazed down at me with inquisitive eyes. "You said earlier that you couldn't tell me, because I wasn't ready. So can you tell me now?" I asked as he kissed my neck.

He pulled up and traced my lips with his thumb. "You," he answered, then bit his lip. "I've been waiting for you to realize that you want and need me just as much as I want and need you."

Any leftover ice I had built around my heart completely melted at his words. I was supposed to purge him from my system, and now I was trapped in the rapture of his love again. My heart thundered at the connection. It felt as if our heartbeats were aligned like the moon and the stars, separate but together.

"Aw, Dreads." I kissed him. "I wish it was that simple. But we both know it ain't."

"Whether this is temporary or permanent, I'm always there for you, and I won't pressure you," he assured. "I love you too much."

Those were the golden words. He had said them aloud. He still loved me, and so help me

God, I loved him too. The way my feelings swelled in my chest, it made me wonder if I'd ever stopped loving him. *Fuck Pooch.* I was where I wanted to be, with my sexy, rugged, dreadlocked, and fine as hell baby daddy. With that, I lifted my dress above my head. He led me over to a chair, sat, and pulled me toward him, his hands about my waist. As I wrapped my fingers in his long dreads, he kissed my stomach and made love to my belly button with his tongue. In ecstasy, I let my head fall back as he slowly guided his tongue upward. He worked his hands up and removed my bra and devoured each breast one by one. This was what I meant. It wasn't just "Assume the position" with Terrence. He took his time and made every moment, every kiss, every touch, every sensation, and every pump count. When he put his thing down, he put it down with emphasis and left his blueprint. Tonight I wanted him to write his name all up inside my kitty cat, and, boy, it purred for his love tonight.

He stood up and slowly undid each button of his shirt and pants before he removed them. His erection begged to be freed from its boxer-brief prison, but he held it at bay. He knelt down before me, took my thong in his teeth, and pulled it down. Once the thong got around my rotund ass, it fell to the floor, and I kicked it aside. He then sat me down on the bed and removed my shoes.

"I almost wanted to leave those on, but I want to taste all of you, li'l mama," he said in a husky voice.

I had no idea what he meant until he lifted my right foot and began to lick my toes. Yes! Licked my toes. And not just a lick, but he suckled each one. Ecstasy took over again as my eyes rolled back as he kissed and licked from side to side, up to my legs and thighs, and then spread my legs, zoomed in on his destination. He blew and licked, which sent electrical shock waves from the top of my head to the tips of my toes. Suckling on my bud, he savored it as if it was a juicy, flavorful slice of fruit. My Terrence's head game was so on point!

"Dreads!" I moaned, gripping his dreadlocks and pushing his head farther downward. I flowed like a river and knew a climax was close.

He moved his tongue gingerly yet fluidly over my bud and inside my sugar walls. I wrapped my legs around him, holding on for dear life, as my back arched against my will, and then I exploded with the force of a geyser on his tongue. He slowly licked all my juices as I panted and struggled to regain my composure.

Dreads looked up at me and wiped the tears
from my eyes. "I know, baby. You haven't been
truly pleasured in a long time. This is what it
feels like when a man loves a woman. This is
what making love feels like. Let me love you," he
said seductively.

If I could've found my voice, I would've told
him to please love me all night long. Damn, I
forgot how good it felt to be with Terrence. Even
still, I didn't remember it ever being this good.
Before I could process it, he flipped me onto my
stomach and massaged my neck and shoulders.
Sensually, he massaged my ass and then slowly
trailed kisses down my back to his new destination. I didn't want to believe that I could get off
on getting my salad tossed, but damn it, that was
exactly what Terrence did. He had no fear of any
part of my body and loved every inch of it.

Once he'd had his fill, I rolled onto my back
and motioned for him to come to me, then patted the bed so that he would lie next to me. Once
he had lain down next to me, I turned onto my
side and gently removed his briefs. His muscle
sprang forward like a sword being unsheathed. I
gently massaged it and watched Terrence's eyes
begin to roll back. He would soon find out that
Pooch's stripper-girl routines that I had enacted
were no joking matter. I asked him to get on
top of me as I lay on my back. While Terrence

hovered over me, I lifted his sack with my nose and inhaled his scent. The sensation made him yelp in delight, so I did it again and then again. I could feel his body tense, so I placed his sack in my mouth and suckled softly.

"Oh Gawd! Damn it!" Dreads yelled out. "Baby! Damn, this shit feels so fucking good."

Happiness spread through me at the fact that I could please Dreads. I smiled as I slid back up and positioned myself on my knees and slurped his candy stick. Bobbing my head up and down, I sucked and licked as if he was an ice cream cone on a hot summer day. He grabbed my head in order to stop me.

"No," I said to him.

"Please . . . please stop. I want to save this for you," he pleaded, trying desperately to restrain himself.

Regrettably, I stopped, and he instructed me to lie back. As I spread my legs, I noticed he was extra long and extra hard. "Damn, Daddy. You've been saving it for me? Or did you grow?"

He chuckled. "No, you just forgot what Dreads is working with. It's okay, though, baby, because I'm about to give you a refresher course you won't ever forget."

Gasp. Dreads entered me, and it reminded me of the first time we made love. The connection was nothing short of amazing. It felt like the finale of a fireworks show on the Fourth of July. He took his time and glided in and out of me with so much skill it was as if he'd never stopped being my lover. He made sure he touched every spot and corner and worked the middle as it'd never been worked before. With the unfamiliar sensations growing in my G-spot, I felt virginal again. As pure, raw emotion and climactic urges rose and fell in my body, I looked up at my Dreads and saw that his only focus was on me. He pleased me by giving me everything that I needed and wanted. That alone could've brought me to a climax, but I didn't want to release yet. I wanted to enjoy this moment. I wanted it to last so that even long after it was finished, I could reminisce about it as if it'd just happened a moment ago. As I clutched his sweat-drenched back for dear life, our strokes found a rhythm that was all our own. It was so good to me that I put my hands in the back of his locks and started twirling them around my fingers.

Terrence looked down at me. "Go ahead and come for me, li'l mama. I feel it. You done gave me the signal."

My eyes rolled in the back of my head. Every time I came with Terrence, I always twirled his locks with my fingers. It was funny that after all these years, subconsciously, I still did that. Unable to suppress my mounting sensations, my back arched and my head snapped back, and then ripples of electric charges surged through my body, sending me into mini convulsions. My legs trembled as I desperately held on to Terrence.

"Oh, my Gawd! Dreads . . . my Dreads! Oh, Terrence!" I screamed as my body finally released and I found my voice.

A sexy smile a mile wide spread across Terrence's face as he took pride in fulfilling my sexual desires. That was when he went into action. He pumped and glided as his own climax began to take hold of him. I added to his sensations as I threw everything I had back up to him.

"Oh, fuck, li'l mama! Damn, you got some skills, baby," he said, both in shock and euphoria. I was happy to please him. Within a few minutes, he gripped the bed and tried to rise up, but I locked my legs around his waist. Leaning in close, he held on to me so damn tight. "Oh shit . . . li'l mama. Fuck! I'm 'bout to explode," he panted, and his eyes told me that it'd been a long time since he'd climaxed with such complete satisfaction. "Ooh, Trinity . . . damn! I love you so goddamn much!" he screamed as he released.

Shit. His climax sent me over the top again for my damn self. "Oh, baby. Yes, Terrence! I love you too!" I shouted as I came.

He pulsated inside of me as he emptied all of himself into me and etched his name in my pussy in permanent ink. After our breathing returned to normal and we came down from our euphoric high, Dreads slid over next to me and we faced each other. I couldn't hide it now. I couldn't fight it. I was in love with Terrence, and I wanted him. I palmed his cheek with my hand. He smiled at me and pulled me close to him.

"You are amazing. Do you know that?" he said.

"Dreads," I said coyly.

"Baby, I love you," he told me, reassuring me.

"Aw, Dreads. I love you too," I said, and then we kissed each other. My head fell against his chest, and we just lay there, engrossed in each other.

I had almost drifted off as he stroked my hair when he spoke again. "Baby, you've acquired some mad skills," he said softly. "Damn. You were so good."

I giggled. "I'm glad you like them," I whispered.

What could I say? *Pooch has taught me well*? I thought. *Oh . . . my . . . God! Pooch!* My smile quickly faded, and I sat straight up.

"Oh, God, Pooch," I said, panic-stricken, as I scrambled out of the bed to grab my cell phone. I'd turned my phone off so that I wouldn't be distracted. Just as I'd suspected, I had seven missed calls and three voice mails. "Oh shit!"

"Baby. Fuck Pooch! I don't care about him!"

"Dreads, please!" I pleaded in frustration as I examined my phone and saw that five of the missed calls were from Pooch and two were from Lucinda.

"Trinity," Terrence called out with exasperation as he sat at the foot of the bed.

I put my hand up to signal him to give me a moment. The clock on the bedside table read 3:25 a.m. Pooch had called me since about 1:25 a.m. I dialed my voice mail and put it on speakerphone. The first message had been left by Pooch at 1:27 a.m.

"Hey, babe. I was just checking on you. Hit me back. Love you."

The second voice mail came through at 2:45 a.m., and it was from Lucinda. "Girl, I don't know where you're at or who you're with—although I have a pretty good damn idea—but you better call Pooch. He's called Charice and LaMeka once and me . . . three times. The first time I answered 'cause we were still in the club, and I told him that you and I were just hanging out and that you were in the restroom, but I haven't answered since. Charice and LaMeka told me they told him that you and I were hanging together, and they didn't know where we went. I didn't answer this last time, because I didn't know what to tell him. It's two forty-seven now. Call me."

The last voice mail came in at 3:15 a.m. and was from Pooch. "Yo, Trin, I don't know what the fuck kind of game you and your girl Lucinda is playing wit' me, but I'm tellin' you this shit ain't cool. She told me you were in the restroom. That was an hour and thirty muthafuckin' minutes ago, and now she ain't answering. And what the fuck is up wit' your cell going straight to fuckin' voice mail? You better not be fuckin' wit' my emotions. Call me as soon as you get this fuckin' message!" he said angrily.

I turned and looked at Terrence. "Pooch is going to flip out!"

"No he ain't!" he barked. Swiping his hands down his face, he huffed. "Fuck him. Move in with me."

Unbelief was plastered across my face. "Are you insane? Do you hear yourself right now?" I asked, pacing the floor. "Yeah right. Pooch will not hesitate to kill us both!"

"Didn't you just say that you loved me?"

I rolled my eyes. "Yes, I did, but I can't leave like that. I just need time."

Terrence stood. Confusion and anger were written all over his face. "What the fuck is wrong with you, Trinity? I love you. I want to be with you. Five minutes ago you were fucking the shit out of me and professing your love, and now you're going back to Pooch? What the hell is that about?" he said angrily.

"Survival! Mine and yours, especially yours," I snapped. "You said you wouldn't pressure me."

He looked away with an attitude, but I stepped up to him and turned his face back to me to try to get him to understand my position.

"Look, I just have to do this my way."

For a few moments, he stared at me. His internal struggle was obvious. Finally, he exhaled and hugged me. "Okay, you're right. I hate how he treats you, but I'm going to let you do this your way. In the meantime, I'm going to help you out. If it makes you feel better, do this . . . Call Lucinda and ask her the latest news on Pooch."

Thank God he didn't fight me on that. It was not that I didn't want to be with him. I just knew that leaving Pooch required a level of finesse. Lifesaving finesse. My concern was more for him than for myself, but if I told Terrence that, he'd brush it off and push the issue. He may not have been afraid of Pooch, but I was afraid, more so for him than for myself. Bottom line, I would not allow Pooch to touch Terrence. Period. If that meant I had to dance with the devil a little while longer, then that was what I would have to do.

Desperate to implement some type of plan, I did exactly what Terrence had said. I quickly dialed Lucinda's number. "Hey, girl," I said when she picked up.

Lucinda laid into me as soon as she heard my voice. "Where the fuck are you? Pooch has called me two more times since I left you that voice mail!"

"I'm in Suwanee with Terrence—"

"I knew it!" she yelled, cutting me off.

"Did you talk to him since the first call?" I asked, getting straight to the point.

"No. I was too fucking scared for you to answer the phone."

"Ask her if he called her cell phone only," Terrence instructed.

"Did he call only your cell phone?" I asked her.

"Yeah. That's it. I'm at the house, in the dark, praying none of his boys come by, thinking I'm home, to try to see if you're here," she said as I put her on speakerphone.

"Good. Keep doing that," Terrence said. "Listen. Don't answer your phone if he calls you.

But if he does ask you in the future or if any of his boys drop by, tell him you all drove up to Athens to go clubbing."

"All right, Terrence." She took a deep breath. "*Mira, chica*. When are you coming home?" Lucinda asked.

"I'm on my way now," I told her.

Terrence motioned for me to hand him the phone, and I did, before sitting on the bed to await our next move. "Listen to me, senorita, this is your story. You all went clubbing in Athens after you left Charice and Meka at the Compound. You forgot to give Trinity Pooch's message, and after that, you passed out in the car on the ride back. Trinity couldn't get to your phone to answer it since she was driving. Trinity's phone went to voice mail because she forgot to charge it and didn't think anything of it, since you had yours. You got home around four fifteen, and that's when you remembered to tell Trinity about Pooch's call. You got it?"

"Clubbing in Athens, forgot to give her the message, passed out in the car, Trinity's phone was dead, got home at four fifteen, and then gave her the message. I got it," Lucinda said. "Thanks, Dreads."

"No problem. Be easy, senorita," he told her before handing the phone back to me.

"So what do I do now?" I asked him after I hung up from the call.

"Wash up and get dressed quickly. Time is of the essence."

I moved at light speed. By 3:40 a.m., we were in my car, and I was driving like mad, crazy to get out of Suwanee.

"So what are we going to do?" I asked about thirty minutes later, as I tapped on the steering wheel nervously.

Terrence laughed. "By the time you call Pooch, you will be dropping me off at my boy's house, which is only two minutes from Lucinda's house."

"Who? Skeet?"

"Yes. I called him while you were in the bathroom, and he's gonna be up waiting on me. I did that so that if Pooch does have his boys on the troll, they will think you just left Lucinda's, and the time frame would match up."

The way this man's brain worked had always been mesmerizing. "You are slick. I hope you never did me like this when we were together."

He laughed. "Never, baby. I learned this skill from working the streets. Besides how much I care for you, I would never do anything to hurt you. Only help you."

I blushed. "I know you do care. I know," I said, rubbing his thigh. "But on the real, with how well you are at ducking and dodging, how the fuck did you get caught up?"

Dreads huffed and looked out the passenger-side window. "I used to wonder the same thing."

Just then my phone rang. "Damn! I forgot to turn it off. It's Pooch!" I said frantically, though we were five minutes from Skeet's house. I picked up the phone.

"Don't answer that."

I gave him a desperate look. Not answering could spell more trouble for me.

"I know, but if you answer now, Pooch will be real slick and will throw you off your game. Call him from Lucinda's house," Terrence advised, and I put the phone down.

I pulled up at Skeet's house, and Terrence jumped out of the car quickly. As promised, Skeet had waited on him. I called Lucinda and drove to her house the back way. Once inside her house, I called Pooch.

"Where the fuck have you been?" he yelled so loud I had to hold the phone away from my ear.

"I was with Lucinda in Athens. Why?"

"She didn't tell you I called?"

"She just told me now, like, as you were calling me. She was so fucking drunk that she passed out in the car, and I had to help her get in the house. That's why I just missed your call."

Lucinda played along in the background. "I'm so shorry, Pooch. I shraight up forgot, yo," she said, slurring. "All the single ladies," she sang and gave me the evil eye.

"Damn! She drunk as fuck," Pooch said, apparently buying Lucinda's act. "Well, what the fuck happened to your phone?" he asked, switching gears in a flash.

"It went dead, baby. I didn't even think about charging it until we got back into the Atlanta city limits, since Lucinda had her cell in case of emergencies," I lied.

"Well, didn't you hear her fuckin' phone ringing on the ride home?" he asked, anger once again consuming him.

"Yes, Pooch, but she was asleep and I was driving. I couldn't get to the phone, and I was trying to focus on getting home. Damn! Where is the fire?" I shot back, feigning irritation.

"Ain't no damn fire unless I need to stomp one out of your ass," he said with an attitude. "I'm just tryin' figure out what the fuck was going on, since I called you hours ago to check on you, with no answer."

"I'm headed back home, and I'm good," I reassured him with a slight attitude of my own.

"Why the fuck was you clubbing in Athens, of all places, anyway? And what club did you go to?" Pooch quizzed me.

"I don't know. Just a change of scenery. We haven't been club hopping in a while, and we just wanted to get away and see what was happening. We just went to 40 Watt and some other little hole-in-the-wall. Nothing was jumping, so Lucinda got drunk, and then we came on back," I informed him, silently thanking God that Terrence had remembered to tell me the name of some club in Athens during the drive back.

Pooch paused for a second, then sighed. "A'ight. So you on your way home?"

"Yes. I'm walking out of Lucinda's house now," I said, waving at her. She shook her head at me and motioned for me to call her.

"A'ight then. Call me when you get home and let me know you cool. I mean that shit. If my phone ain't ringing in the next twenty minutes, I'm sending my peeps looking for your ass, and then I'm on the fuckin' road, locked and loaded. Do you hear me?" Pooch warned me.

"Yes, I hear you," I said as I got inside my car. "Would you stop being so paranoid and handle your business?"

"Shit! I've been up all night, huntin' yo' ass. My business is gon' get handled, but now I'm sleepy as fuck, when I should've been resting. Fuckin' wit' yo' ass," Pooch complained.

"Aw, baby. I'm sorry I had you worried. I'm cool, and everything is good. I promise."

Pooch huffed. "A'ight, babe. I hear you."

"I'm going to call you as soon as I get in the house. I promise. I love you, Pooch," I sang into the phone, content that he believed my lies.

"I love you too, Trinity. Remember that shit."

"I do, babe," I said in a sappy voice into the phone.

"You better," he warned and hung up.

When I got home exactly fifteen minutes later, I immediately called Pooch. I wasn't crazy. As I talked to Pooch, I made sure there were no remnants of Terrence in my car and sprayed my perfume inside it. Once he was content enough to let me off the phone, I showered and threw my clothes in the washer. Then I sent Lucinda a text message letting her know I was cool and deleted all her messages off my phone. Just as my head hit my pillow after five in the morning, my cell rang.

"Hello?" I answered sleepily.

"Just checking on you," Terrence said. "Were you asleep?"

"Just laid my head down," I responded.

"My bad. I take it Pooch bought the story."

"Yep."

"Good. I knew he would. Well, you have a good night, baby."

I yawned and stretched. "You too."

"I love you," he said nervously.

"And I love you too. That hasn't changed."

He chuckled. I could sense the relief in his voice. "We'll talk."

"Most def. Good night," I said and hung up the phone to go to sleep, but not before I deleted his call out of my cell.

As I drifted off, my mind began to reminisce about the awesome night I'd had with Dreads, and I felt myself smiling. I loved Dreads, and I wanted him so bad. I knew I had to figure out a way to get back to him, but real talk, a part of me still felt obligated to Pooch. He'd been there for me when I couldn't depend on anybody else, and I'd just betrayed him in the worst way. Did it mean I still wanted to be in the relationship? Absolutely not. I wanted Terrence. If I was truthful with myself, it'd always been Terrence for me, and it always would be. I'd choose him a hundred times over. But like Terrence said, if I was nothing else, I was loyal, and that was the part that made me feel bad for the exit I would soon make from this relationship with Pooch. If only I knew exactly how to do that . . . safely.

Ugh! It bothered me that I didn't know what or how I was going to do anything. The only thing I knew for sure was that even though I had love for Pooch, in my heart, I was in love with Terrence and I longed to be with him.

With thoughts of Terrence on my mind, I didn't even hear my cell phone ringing with another call from Pooch.

Charice

Dressed in a long yellow tube dress, with a matching yellow flower in my hair, I held my flip-flops in my hand as I walked along the beach. The beach was pure white sand, not hot, just warm, and it stretched for miles, farther than the eye could see. The ocean tide was low, and as I walked along, the warm water cascaded back and forth over my feet, tickling my toes, and carried each footprint back out to a sea that was so blue and pristine, it looked mystical. I couldn't help but stare at the water as the sun beamed brightly over it. It was as if God Himself smiled down on the beauty of it. The climate was just right, sunny and warm, with bursts of cool, refreshing winds. It was as if Heaven had adorned the day itself and blessed us earthlings with a little piece of paradise.

As I walked along, I enjoyed the serenity of the moment and basked in the beauty of the day. Suddenly, I felt two strong arms around my waist, and the person attached to those arms offered the sweetest, most succulent kiss to the nape of my neck. I turned my head slightly to see who'd blessed me with this delectable treat, and I saw Lincoln in a tank top and linen shorts. I offered him a small peck on the lips as we lovingly giggled at each other. Our love was as natural and pure as this little slice of Heaven. I lovingly leaned against him, and we swayed back and forth to the rhythm of the waves that crashed on the shore.

As I leaned back, wrapped in his embraced, I grasped his huge python arms and slid my fingertips down his bulging muscles, making sure to trace the tattoo of a heart that showed the date that we began dating on a banner that wrapped around it. On the banner, written in Swahili, was the saying "The day I gave my heart away." Engulfed in the essence of romance, we kissed passionately on the beach. Once our desires consumed us, he carried me back to our cabana, which opened up to a private oceanfront view, laid me on the huge circular bed situated in the center of the bedroom, and made slow, sweet love to me for hours.

I smiled as my eyes fluttered and finally opened. I sat up, stretched, and looked around as I realized I'd had the sweetest dream. Do you want to know what's better than having that dream? To wake up and realize it wasn't a dream at all. It was my reality. I was in Paradise Island, on a four-day, three-night vacation with my man, and we were only on day one.

As I swung my legs to the side of the bed, I picked up my flower off the nightstand, placed it back in my tangled hair, and wrapped myself in a sheet from the bed. When I stood up, I spotted Lincoln out on the terrace. His focus was trained on the ocean as the sun prepared to set on the horizon, to rest and prepare for another day. I walked out, sat in the chair next to him, and placed my feet in his lap.

"This is beautiful. You should've woken me up so I could come to see this with you." I sighed, sitting back in the chair.

His gaze fell on me as he toyed with my feet. "You beat me to it. I got so lost in the peacefulness of the moment that I forgot that I was going to come and wake you. But I am so glad you're here now."

Giddiness spread through me, and a blush crossed my face. He reached for my hand and pulled me into his lap. I leaned against him as we watched the sunset together. As I rubbed my hand across his bare chest, feeling his every muscle, his body felt a little tense, and I wondered what was wrong with him.

"What's on your mind?" I asked.

"Just thinking, baby."

"Thinking about what?"

"Us."

"What about us?"

"Just thinking," he responded softly.

"Is that a bad thought or a good thought?" I asked, probing, as I eyed him intently.

His jawline tightened as he kept his focus on the skyline. "Stop looking for trouble, Ma. We're good."

He was right. I was looking for trouble, that is. See, a couple of weeks ago, I'd had to deal with one of the pressures of being his woman. He had had to make a couple of appearances and attend a benefit dinner, and women had fawned over him left and right. I had been there, in the background, but still had witnessed everything front and center. He hadn't done anything wrong. It had been the relentlessness of the women that had me on edge. Who wanted to sit back and watch women hug and grab on their man and attempt to give him phone numbers? Shameless heifers. By the night's end, I'd been so mad I could have spit fire.

Afterward, I had questioned him, and a huge argument had ensued. I had claimed that his lifestyle was too much for me, and he had claimed I allowed my past with Ryan to interfere with us. I had been prepared to storm out, because I didn't think I could handle the pressure, but Lincoln had told me point blank that if I left, he wouldn't chase me. He'd said that he needed a woman who could be confident in who she was as his woman, and that if he didn't give me a reason to walk away, then obviously I was walking away because I wanted to. He'd professed that if that was the case, he wouldn't force me to stay. I loved Lincoln, so of course, I had stayed and we'd made up, but it just seemed that since then, there had been a tense feeling between us. That was the reason we had decided to take this trip. Everything had been going well up until this moment, when I began looking for trouble again.

"I'm sorry. I just want us both to enjoy this trip," I told him.

"And I am," he said reassuringly. "I just want you to relax and know that I'm here with you."

"And I know that," I admitted. "I do."

He smiled and kissed me. "I love you."

"I love you too."

We both stood up, and Lincoln looked down at me with lustful eyes as he slowly removed the sheet from around me. "Let's make love right here."

Nudging him forward for a kiss, I whispered, "Whatever you want, Mr. Harper."

What a damn rush. The knowledge that we were in seclusion allowed us to set loose our inhibitions. I rode him in every position. We let it all out, every moan and whimper, as we unleashed our love on each other. Our lovemaking took us to the rail of the balcony, and as I leaned over it and received all Lincoln had to offer, I noticed in the distance a couple of the retreat's employees look up at us and smile, with surprised looks on their faces. There wasn't another cabana for miles, and no guests had access to our ocean view, but the employees did. Oh, well, they got an eyeful tonight. I didn't bother to ask Lincoln if he saw them or not, but I didn't give a damn who saw me at this point. He laid down some oil-line pipes, and I wasn't about to stop getting it for no damn body.

The two men who looked on stopped two of the women employees who appeared ready to leave with them. I smiled devilishly as I looked at them. Then Lincoln flipped me around and leaned my back against the rail. He hoisted my legs around his waist to hit it from the front. His stroke game was so fierce, it caused my head to tilt back from pleasure. My breasts bounced ferociously up and down as he unleashed fury on me.

"Oh damn, baby!" I moaned loudly.

"We have company," he whispered seductively.

"I know," I replied. "So what?"

He laughed, and I leaned forward to kiss him as he carried me to the sliding-glass door. My back hit the door with a light thud, but we never broke our stride. The freakiness of it turned us on in a major way. As my back slid up and down the glass while he pumped, the small group of employees cheered. We laughed and kicked it into overdrive. Soon we were both at our breaking point, and as we hit our climax, our moans reached a high crescendo together before we collapsed to the floor. The employees let out thunderous applause, and we looked up from the floor, then waved and laughed with them.

"Good night!" they yelled in unison, then turned to walk away.

"It already was!" we yelled back.

They continued to laugh as they walked away, leaving us to enjoy the solitude once again. Once we collected ourselves, we sat back against the sliding glass and watched as the moon shone brightly in the sky.

"I wonder if this is what Heaven is like," I said softly.

"Ma, I don't need to wonder, because I have Heaven on Earth, right here," he said, then kissed me on the shoulder.

"Aw, baby." I snuggled closer to him. I wanted to stay like that forever, but I had worked up quite the appetite during that session. "So are we going to eat or stay in and hibernate all night?"

"This is your time. We'll do whatever you want," he said.

"Well, I say, 'Feed your woman.' I need my strength," I joked.

He helped me up, and we walked inside the cabana together. "Well, let me feed you, then, because you most definitely need your strength."

We showered together and then quickly got dressed. We decided to go to one of the restaurants in the main building of the resort. It was a luau-style dinner, and I had a frozen daiquiri with the famous umbrella stuck in the glass. Dinner and the fireworks show that accompanied it were simply amazing. As we sat there, sipping our drinks and watching the show, a few guys and some employees came up to us and got autographs from Lincoln. Of course, this got the ladies' attention, and soon a few female onlookers made their way over to our table.

"Excuse me. Are you a ballplayer?" one silicone beauty asked.

Lincoln looked up at her. "Yes, I'm an athlete," he said, subtly correcting her. When it came to his career, Lincoln took it seriously and hated when anyone referred to him as a "ballplayer," as if his livelihood was a mere joke.

"Let me guess. Football, right?" her friend said as they giggled flirtatiously.

"You would be correct," Lincoln responded, unfazed by their flagrant flirting.

"Ha! I knew it! I could tell. You have the build of a football player, wide, lean, and firm," the friend said. She laughed and pinched his bicep. I had to giggle at that.

"Can I help you, ladies?" Lincoln leaned back.

They looked at me. "Do you mind if we sit here?" the first girl asked.

"Of course not. Pull up a chair," I lied.

Lincoln looked at me as if I was half crazy, and the ladies both slid chairs around him, then gushed and fawned over him. They even asked him to sign their fake boobs. He refused but signed napkins instead. They went on and on about visiting Dallas, and how they'd love to have front-row seats to see his games. The whole time I watched the show as Lincoln pretended to stay engrossed in the conversation.

"Ladies, it's been real, but I'm here with my girlfriend, and I would like to get back to enjoying my evening with her," Lincoln said to them after a good twenty minutes.

They looked at each other and then at me. "You're his girlfriend?" the first girl half stated and half questioned.

I nodded. "Yes, I am."

The second girl laughed. "Some girlfriend you are. I thought you were his sister or something. There's no way I'd let a man this fine sit in the presence of two beautiful women and not say a word," she said in an attempt to jab me.

The nerve. Honestly, I didn't know whether I wanted to go off or laugh at these birds. Lincoln went to speak, but I put up my hand to intercept him. I had it covered.

"It doesn't bother me," I announced. I shrugged as I took the final sip of my drink before I placed down the empty glass. "I don't have to vie for his attention. He gives it to me willingly. Case in point, he asked you all to leave for me. I'm not worried about your intentions, because I know *his* intentions. So, whether it's two okay-looking young ladies or twenty bombshells that fawn over him, it doesn't bother me. I know that I am more than enough for him." I sat back and addressed Lincoln. "Honey, are you sure you're ready to dismiss your fans?"

The grin on his face as he winked at me spoke volumes. "Actually, I'm ready to go back to the room if you are. I can think of a million other things to do right about now," he said, rubbing my thigh seductively.

I looked over at the girls, who scoffed at us in disbelief. "Well, ladies, that's my cue. You all have a lovely evening. I know I will," I said slyly to them as Lincoln stood up. "Ready, baby?" I asked.

I stood, and Lincoln pulled my chair out so I could walk around the table. Then he wrapped his arm around my shoulders. "Yes, baby," he replied. "Good night, ladies. Enjoy the show," he said.

They smacked their teeth, rolled their eyes, and sank down in their seats.

We walked off, and he kissed my cheek. "I just fell in love with you all over again."

"I'm just an amazing woman like that?" I giggled.

"That you are, Ma. That you are."

Once we got to the room, I headed to the bathroom to change, but Lincoln stopped me. 'Let's go for a walk along the beach," he said.

"So we're going to pull an all-nighter on our first night?" I replied.

"It's so beautiful that I wanted to soak it up one last time before we hit the bed. Don't make me beg," he whined, giving me those puppy dog eyes.

I sighed as I put my hair in a ponytail and slipped my flip flops back on. "Oh, come on you, big baby," I said, grabbing his hand and heading out to the beach.

Lincoln walked behind me with his arms around my waist. The ocean breeze made the beach cool during the night, but Lincoln's embrace warmed me to the core. It was every bit as beautiful at night as it was during the day. The full moon shone brightly in the sky and cast a beautiful glow over the ocean, which gave it the appearance of a shiny black diamond. The waves crashed gently against the rocks. The swishing noise was so gentle, you could rock yourself to sleep. This was truly serenity at its finest hour. If there was ever any question in anyone's mind about whether there was a God, then this beautiful sight before me would tell them yes. Only God, in his omnipotence, could make a sight this breathtaking. As we walked along and the breeze whipped through my hair, I couldn't decide if the beach and the seascape were prettier at night or during the day. We walked in silence for at least five minutes, until Lincoln spoke.

"Isn't it beautiful?" he asked as we walked along the shore.

"Yes. I'm glad we took this trip."

"I'm glad you are enjoying yourself, because I am definitely enjoying you," he said. "And I'm also glad that you did what you did at dinner tonight." He hugged me closer. "I was so proud of you. The way you handled that with such class and confidence turned me on."

"I just wanted you to know that I am confident in us, but there are times when I get weak too, Lincoln. I'm human. I know what I have in you, so don't you think it scares me to know that thousands of other women want it too? I mean, they want you for the looks and the materialistic things alone, but if they really knew you as a man, I'd have to fight every day, literally. So I'm sorry if sometimes I get upset, but I promise not to run away if you promise me I'll never have a reason to run," I confided in him.

He stopped in his tracks, then turned me to face him and held my face in his hands. "Baby, I promise you'll never have a reason to run away from me. Never. I'll never do anything to hurt you. That's my word. I want to be in this relationship just as much as you do. You are my world, my heart, and my joy. Hell, I talked shit that night. I know it. But believe me, it was only to get you to stay. If you had left, I would've chased you, and if I hadn't, I would've died." He paused for a moment. "Think about it. If you're my Eve, cut from my rib, how can I live without you?" he asked, staring into my eyes.

I kissed him deeply. "Aw, baby, I love you."

"Mmm. I love you too."

After laying my head on his chest, I yawned as I listened to the sound of his heartbeat and the waves. They seemed to be in sync with each other, playing a melody back and forth.

"Getting sleepy?" he asked.

I chuckled. "Of course. You wore my ass out."

"I'm going to wear that ass out again before the night is over too," he said with a laugh.

"I doubt that," I countered, turning my back so that it pressed against his chest again and gazing at the moon. "Nothing could keep me up too much longer."

"Not even this?" he asked. In front of my eyes was a sparkling diamond engagement ring.

I gasped and covered my mouth. "Lincoln," I whispered softly. Within seconds, he was in front of me and down on one knee.

"I was trying to find the perfect moment to do this. You see, this trip is more than just a getaway. It's an engagement trip for us," he said, looking up at me as tears of joy flooded my eyes.

He went on. "Baby, I don't think there is anything else I can say or do to show you how much I love you and want to be with you other than to show you that my commitment is permanent. Love is strange. It strikes at the oddest times in the most unexpected places. But once you have it, you hold on to it, and you cherish it for life. That's what I want to do for you, baby. I want to love you for a lifetime. I want to love the triplets for a lifetime. I want to love our future babies for a lifetime. I want to be married to you for a lifetime. Will you accept this ring as my commitment to you? Charice, will you marry me?"

Nodding my head rapidly, I cried, "Yes! Yes! Yes!"

He slipped the ring on my finger, stood up, and kissed me passionately. "I love you, Ma."

"Baby!" I screamed, admiring my rock of a ring. "I love you too, Pa!" I brought his face to mine, and we kissed, and our kiss was filled with passion. We held each other.

"Oh my God! I'm getting married!" I screamed after a moment, jumping up and down in his arms.

He grinned down at me. "Yes, you are. So can we go and celebrate?" he inquired with a wink.

I slipped off my flip flops and held them in my hand. "No fair. You *knew* I was going to be up all night."

He shrugged and laughed. "Yeah, I kinda did."

I turned to walk toward the cabana. "By the time I get there, I'm going to be naked and waiting," I threw over my shoulder as I raced back.

"And I'm going to be right behind you," he called out. He caught up to me with ease, then took his shirt off as I slipped off my sweater.

He picked me up and carried me, as if he was carrying me over the threshold.

"Getting your practice in?" I asked.

"Yep, without a doubt, Mrs. Harper. Without a doubt," he confirmed and carried me into the cabana.

Oh, yes, tonight would most definitely be an all-nighter. After so much turmoil with Ryan, I finally had a real man who loved me just as much as I loved him. I was so very happy that I, Ms. Charice Taylor, was about to become Mrs. Charice Harper!

Now we just had to break the news to Ryan.

Lucinda

As soon as I got off work, I swore I was going to rip Raul a brand new asshole. This shit with this *puto* had only gotten worse, and I was beyond livid with him. He paid his child support like he was supposed to, but along with it came a lot of unnecessary drama on account of his ass. Recently, he had popped up three different times at the day care when I was dropping off Nadia. The first time, he had complained that I needed all his money because I created unnecessary expenses, like before-school and after-school care when I could leave Nadia at Shanaya's house instead. Had he lost his fucking mind? Did he really think I was going to drop my child off with that *culo de basura perra*, who couldn't stand the ground I walked on, and trust her with my child?

The second time he had popped up was because his visitation with Nadia was canceled because his mom was sick. Like clockwork, on

Monday morning he had shown up and had straight up clowned at the day care. Now, I probably wouldn't even trip if I knew he was the type of father who truly cared about his daughter, but I knew better. He clowned because he knew he had no choice but to pay that child support, so the only way he could get back at me was to aggravate the shit out of me.

Now, when he had appeared at the day care today, while I was saying good-bye to Nadia, I had sworn this would be his last time, because it was the third time he'd made me late for work in the past two weeks with his antics. He had talked about how it was hard for him to pay that much support for Nadia, because he had to take care of Raulina and Doodlebug too. Now, if you wanted to make a woman mad as hell, you'd let her baby daddy tell her that he felt he was doing "too much" for one child and had to do for the others, especially when she knew he didn't really do shit for any of his kids. Raulina's and Doodlebug's welfare was between him and the bitches he had lain down with, not between him and me. If he had to get two or three fucking jobs to support all his kids, that was his problem and not mine. My responsibility was to Nadia and my job, which was why I now sat in my supervisor's office, getting my ass ripped because of my abysmal schedule adherence.

"Lucinda, you are usually our most punctual person. I'm not sure what exactly is going on with you lately, but I can't overlook these tardies," Mr. Sharper said to me.

I sighed, rubbing my forehead. "I understand, and I'm sorry."

"I'm glad you are, but twenty minutes late today, Lucinda? Come on. What's going on?" he said.

I sat up straight and gripped my hands together to suppress the anger that had welled up inside me. "I took my daughter's father to court for child support, and he's been making my life hell. He's popped up at the day care and picked fights with me just to aggravate me. I'm sorry," I said, explaining as best I could without breaking down or going off.

He exhaled and sat back. "I like you, Lucinda. I see that you try so hard, and I truly admire that. You know I really don't want to reprimand you, because we both know you're the best in this damn department." He stood and removed his suit jacket before sitting on the desk in front of me. "Do you need time off to be able to handle this situation?" he asked, and I could tell that he was genuinely concerned. "I'm hard pressed right now, but I will grant it for you."

I shook my head. "Even if that were to help, I can't afford the time off." I looked up at him with tears in my eyes. "I'm sorry, Mr. Sharper. I just have a lot that I'm dealing with, and I apologize for being late. I promise it won't ever happen again," I told him as slow tears streamed down my face.

He handed me a tissue and shook his head. "I'm sorry, Lucinda. I'm sorry that you are going through so much," he said as I cried. He patted my back. "It's okay. Let it out," he said, and I did.

I would have never let my emotions show like that, but I had been so overwhelmed lately, and I had no one that I could really turn to or talk to, and so my distress came out the only way it could . . . through my tears. Mr. Sharper was a gentleman, though. He patiently allowed me to get it out of my system.

"Thanks for that. I really needed it," I told him as I dried my face and threw the tissue in the wastebasket.

"You're welcome," he said and handed me a sheet.

"What is this?" I asked, confused. It wasn't a write-up form.

"That is your 'time off' request form," he told me.

I shook my head. "I know that, but it's blank."

"It's the form that I mistakenly misplaced when I gave you the approval to come in thirty minutes late today," he said. "Remember . . . you put in your request last week and I approved it? Don't you remember that?"

I smiled and took out a pen to fill out the form. "Oh yes. I thought that you had given this to HR already." I quickly completed the form and handed it back to him.

"No, I hadn't. I put it in my file cabinet by accident," he said as he looked back at his desk calendar to choose a date during the previous week and then signed the form. "I'll make sure that you get a copy and that I get this over to HR right away. I apologize for the mix-up, Lucinda."

"It's no problem. I appreciate you looking into that for me," I said, standing up.

"It's no problem at all." And with that, he walked me to the door.

The first half of my workday was a breeze. I was so relieved about the break Mr. Sharper had cut me that I zipped through the majority of my work by lunchtime. A couple of my nosy coworkers were sorely upset to find out that my tardiness was actually an "approved" request. Ann and Katherine, two of my coworkers who, like me, had been there awhile, were more than happy to see those hating heifers with their mouths wide open. Those heifers claimed I was the "pet" because of my awards, or whatever reason they chose to cook up. People killed me. It was not worth all that for a twelve-dollar-an-hour job, so I couldn't help but smile when I saw the looks on their faces. They really would've flipped if they knew the real deal, but I would never tell that, because Mr. Sharper was a good dude who tried to help this *chica* out, and I couldn't be mad at that.

Due to my strained finances, I usually didn't indulge in eating out, but by lunchtime, I felt so much better that I decided to step outside the box and go with Ann and Katherine to Sweet Georgia's Juke Joint for lunch. No lie. I had a really good time as we ate and chatted it up, and it felt good to get my mind off my problems. That was, until I saw Raul near the entrance to my building when we returned to work.

My heart skipped a beat as my steps slowed behind the ladies. It felt as if all the air had been sucked out of the atmosphere. My legs felt like jelly, and it was as if he and I had tunnel vision and saw only each other. I wanted desperately to believe that this visit was nothing to worry about, but the flutter in the pit of my stomach and the tension that crept up the back of my neck told me otherwise. Raul's steps were fluid as he quickly met me halfway. The look in his eyes was one of sheer determination and pure devilment. He was up to no fucking good.

"*This* is the fucking reason why you need all this damn money!" he yelled as he got near me. "Eating out and shit!" he hollered, knocking my doggy bag out of my hands.

"What the hell is wrong with you?" I yelled and pushed him back a notch. "I'm adding that to my bill, you *bastardo*."

"I'm going to sue you for custody of Nadia," he sneered. "You worthless bitch."

"I wish you muthafucking might!" I yelled, getting up in his face. "If you don't get the hell away from me, I'm going to fuck you up!" I snarled.

"Lucinda, are you all right?" Katherine asked, approaching us, with Ann at her side.

"Do we need to call someone?" Ann asked, looking at Raul as if he had better chill the hell out.

Raul looked back at them. "Y'all bitches need to mind your fucking business."

"No, you need to mind *your* fucking business and get away from this business. This is my job, Raul. What the hell is wrong with you?" I shouted.

"Oh, I know he didn't go there!" Ann said, with her head cocked to the side. "Lucinda, you better get him."

"I'm getting security," Katherine said, then turned and walked away.

Raul turned quickly, as if he was going to run after Katherine. I jumped in front of him.

"Get away from here!" I yelled, pushing him, and he pushed me back.

"Get your hands off me!" he thundered.

"Get the hell on!" I screamed back as we engaged in a shoving match.

"Stop grabbing her!" Ann yelled at him as Robin, another manager, and her assistant ran from one direction and Katherine and a security guard from the other.

"Stop it now!" the security guard yelled as he pulled us apart.

"What the hell is going on here?" Robin asked sternly.

"He's trespassing!" I shouted, pointing at Raul.

"And he threatened us!" Katherine added.

"Just calm down, and let's go discuss this," the security guard said.

Once the guard was able to de-escalate the situation, he ushered Raul and me to the back of the security office. I had to issue statements and sign forms, like I was being booked. Even though the police arrived and Raul was arrested for trespassing, my attorney would definitely hear about this foolishness the first moment I could speak to him. I was so embarrassed, and of course, the gossip about our fight made it back to the office before I could. Not that I was fit to do any work, but I wasn't able to get any done, because Ann and Katherine fussed to me about Raul, and the rest of the heifers—who knew we weren't cool like that—asked questions just to be nosy. Hell, I hadn't been at my desk a good hour when Mr. Sharper called my desk phone and asked me to meet him in his office to discuss what had happened. Needing the break, I slowly got up and headed to his office.

"You wanted to see me?" I asked, standing timidly at his open door.

He sighed. "Yes. Please come in." He motioned for me to enter. When I did, he said, Shut the door, please."

Standing in front of his desk, I began, "I know what you're—"

"Lucinda, please have a seat," he said, stopping me.

"If you will just allow me to explain."

"I will. Just please sit down." His tone was polite, which gave me a bit of comfort, so I pulled the chair back to sit down. "Please continue," he said as soon as I was seated.

I went into the entire story, from when I saw Raul at the entrance to the building up to the point when the police hauled him off. "And that's the story. I'm so sorry this happened, but I assure you, it won't again. I'm going to see my attorney first thing in the morning," I said matter-of-factly.

Heaving a sigh, he sat back, with his fingertips to his lips. At first, I thought he was in deep contemplation, but the more I focused on him, the more I realized he looked unsure and sympathetic but mostly troubled, in turmoil even.

"What is it?" I asked him.

He closed his eyes, and I saw his jaw twitch. "I should have followed my first mind. I knew I should've just given you the rest of the day off today, but you insisted that you couldn't afford it."

I leaned forward, with my hands on his desk. I was afraid now. Something wasn't right. "Mr. Sharper, *what* is it?" I asked more forcefully and deliberately.

"Lucinda." He paused, and when he looked at me, I knew it wasn't good. It wasn't good at all. "Lucinda, I have to ... I must ... I have to let you go," he stammered.

"Wh-what?" I asked, the word barely audible. I knew he hadn't said what I thought he had, and even if he had, surely he had to mean for the rest of the day. "What do you mean, 'let me go'?"

"There is no easy way to say this. I really don't want to, but I have to terminate your employment." He let out an exasperated sigh.

I put my hands up and pleaded with him as hot tears instantly flowed from my eyes. "But why? I didn't do anything wrong! It's not my fault he showed up here. You can't be serious!" I exclaimed as my chest heaved up and down. Mr. Sharper stood up and walked around to comfort me. I shrugged away from him. "No! Don't touch me! Give me my job back. That's all I need. You know I have a daughter, Mr. Sharper. How could you do this to me now?"

"It's not me that's doing this."

I jumped up, in a fit of rage, my eyes nearly bugging out and my hands trembling. "I'll go to upper management on your ass! I won't be had like this," I seethed, getting up in his face. 'I'm always the first here and on time! I'm the best at this job! I don't call in! I don't make frivolous time-off requests! And you do *me* like this? What happened to looking out for me?" I demanded, pointing my finger.

"Please calm down!" he said sternly yet calmly, grabbing my hands and gently putting them down at my sides. "It's not me, Lucinda. It's not me," he repeated.

"Well, who?" I demanded, with my arms folded.

Mr. Sharper rubbed his temples and shook his head.

My attitude was on go, and I wouldn't leave without my answer. I deserved that damn much. Rolling my neck, I jutted my head out and knew my eyes had to be bugged damn near out of my sockets. "Who?" I repeated.

"Robin," he blurted before he knew it. The look on his face told me that he'd let that tidbit slip, because of his frustration. I assumed that since he'd already let the cat out of the bag, he would explain further. He did. "Robin went to upper management about the incident and got them all riled up. They demanded that I release you. My hands are tied. I'm so sorry."

That news knocked the wind out of me, and I fell down into the chair. "I don't believe this. That bitch!" I grumbled, thinking of a hundred ways to get at Robin.

He sat beside me in the other chair. "Listen, I don't want to do this. I went to bat for you and even told them I was aware of the issues you'd been having, but it didn't do any good. They want you gone. I agree that Robin is wrong, but you mustn't retaliate, because I was able to get the company to arrange a few things for you.

You can work until the end of your shift today, so it won't be so obvious, and I was able to finagle a two-month severance pay package out of HR for you."

"Two months," I whispered.

"If you file for unemployment, just give them my direct number, and I won't deny the claim, so you'll have those benefits until you can find something else," he explained.

He said some other stuff, but I didn't hear him. It was as if time had stopped and I was stuck in a paradox. I felt the panic rise in my chest. What the fuck was I going to do? I had rent, day care, bills and . . . my daughter. Oh, God. How was I going to afford to take care of Nadia? Susie Q didn't pay a fraction of what I needed. Now, I had only two fucking months, in the middle of a recession, to figure some shit out. And I had no college education. Four years I had been with this bullshit company, and I get a "Thank you but fuck you" out the door. Yet the workers who called in constantly, were late constantly, and had substandard performance were able to look forward to coming to a nice twelve-dollar-an-hour job.

"Why are they doing this to me?" I asked, looking at Mr. Sharper. My voice cracked, as it was so full of emotion.

His expression was so sympathetic and sorrowful. "They say having you here is a security risk to the rest of us. I really don't know what else to say besides I'm sorry," he told me.

I stood, rubbing the back of my neck. "Well, I guess there is nothing else to say."

Following suit, he stood as well. "Ms. Rojas, you have my sincerest apology again. I know none of this is any consolation right now. I'll be sure that your checks are mailed to your house," he said in an attempt to comfort me. He swiped a business card from his desk and handed it to me. "And, like I said, if you need anything, please don't hesitate."

I took his card and turned it around in my hand. "I better go."

"You can stay for the rest of the—"

"No. I can grab my picture and purse and go. I can't sit here like this. I have to go and try to find . . . a job," I said in disbelief.

"I'm so sorry," he said again, sympathetically.

"It's not your fault. You only did what you were told."

"It doesn't make it right or make me any less of an ass," he said.

His words caught me off guard. It was the first time I realized how truly earnest he was about his regret about this situation. Although I was pissed, his kindness gave me a brief moment of comfort and pity for the position he was in.

"You can't put your livelihood at risk for me. This is my problem, and I'll deal with it like everything else. Don't stress for me," I offered, putting up a huge-ass front yet thankful for his genuine concern.

A look of surprise crossed his face, and he folded his arms across his chest. "I truly admire you," he told me.

I didn't respond. Politely, I simply nodded my head, turned, left his office, gathered my picture of Nadia and my purse, then walked out. I didn't want to leave my friends on stuck, so I called Ann's extension once I got to my car, and told her what had happened. She and Katherine wished me well and told me that they'd miss me, and we exchanged telephone numbers so that we could keep in touch. Once I got in my car, I drove to a nearby office building parking lot and parked, let my seat back, and cried my eyes out. My soul felt as if it had been ripped out of my body. How much pain could a twenty-one-year-old woman take? Sometimes I wished I would just die, because Heaven had to be better than this place. I was convinced that Earth was a nickname for Hell, since that was all I had ever experienced on it.

I thought about my situation and what the hell I could do. I was a twenty-one-year-old woman with a high school diploma and no college education, and I had a child, a mountain of bills, and no job. I couldn't sit around and wait on unemployment and severance pay. I had to make shit happen now. After picking up my cell, I made a call I never thought I'd make in a million years.

"Please pick up," I said aloud.

"Talk to me. Who dis?" Pooch answered.

"Pooch, this is Lucinda."

"Hey, what's up, Mama?" he greeted. "Ain't nothing going on with Trinity, right?" he asked almost as soon as he said hello.

"No. I assume she's fine. This is actually a personal call between you and me. I don't want anyone to know about this," I told him. "Not even Trinity."

"Hold up," he said. It sounded like he was walking. "I had to get away from my crowd. So what's up? What's this all about?"

"Um, do you still own that club downtown?"

"Club Moet?"

"Yeah."

"Yeah, I do. What the hell you asking about that for?"

"How much do your waitresses make?"

"Banana money. Minimum, plus tips. Lu, what's the deal?"

I sighed. "Um, I really don't need my business on the streets, Pooch," I said after taking a deep breath. "Raul got me fired today."

"Oh fuck! Damn! That's some foul shit, Mama! You need me to handle up on that nigga?"

If Raul's ass wasn't in jail, I'd probably take Pooch up on his offer, I thought. "Nah, he ain't even worth it. That *hijo de puta* is in jail right now anyway. Meanwhile, I'm jobless, and I need a gig until something breaks through," I said, getting to the point.

"You know how to mix drinks?" he asked. "They make twenty an hour, plus tips. You know the club is open only six hours, five days a week. They make decent."

"Can you teach me?"

"Shit, Lu, I ain't got time for that. The fuckin' patrons be complaining and shit if they liquor ain't right and shit, so if you don't know how to mix it up already, I can't afford to put you on the bar. If you want to waitress and learn from there, then I could put you on after that."

"I can't fucking be a waitress for the minimum. I was struggling to survive on what I was making at the insurance company."

"Unless you know about rims and auto mechanics, there really ain't shit I can help you wit', 'cause I know you ain't down for the other stuff," he said matter-of-factly.

"You would know correct too," I confirmed, knowing he was talking about slinging dope.

"I understand, everybody ain't built." He blew out air. "Sorry. I ain't got nothing else. If I come across something, I'll hit you up and shit," he offered.

This news broke me down. There was no one else I could reach out to for a quick lick. Applications took time. And that was something I did not have. Fear struck me and I panicked about what I would do to take care of my kid. There was no way I could burden my mom with two additional mouths, and my bridge with Emilio had already been burned. Not that he'd extend the olive branch anyway. Desperate times called for desperate measures, and I was more than desperate. I was destitute.

"Wait, Pooch," I called out before he hung up. I couldn't believe I was about to ask this. But Nadia's picture on my key chain stared back at me, and for her, I'd do the unthinkable. "Um, do you, um, do you need any . . . you know . . . dancers at Moet?" I asked timidly, hiding my eyes as I even asked the question.

"I mean, we always auditioning. If you got talent, we'll put you on. Of course, you know they make good."

"Can I audition?"

Pooch paused for a moment and then slowly said, "You do realize by *dance*, I mean strip. Moet is a strip club, Lu."

"I know that. I'm desperate."

"Damn," he grumbled before continuing. "Well, if you're serious, meet me and my manager, Greg, down there at eight tonight. We'll audition you on the stage. You gon' have to strip. Thong and sexy heels only. No tops, not even a bra. You got to show us some true skill. Something we can claim as your specialty."

Wait. I knew I would do anything for Nadia, but that pushed the limits. He couldn't possibly mean I would have to strip in front of him. *Nope.* "Pooch, I ain't auditioning in front of you! You're my best friend's man!"

"Your choice, Lu. You called me. Greg and I make that decision together. Trust me, it's only business. If you feel like you can't do it, then don't be there. But I'm trying to lace your pockets, Mama."

He was serious. *Wow.* I'd hit a true crossroads. I sat there for a moment in contemplation. "I don't have to get down with y'all to get on, do I?

'Cause I'm not betraying Trinity like that. Hell, I'm not even sure I want to betray her by the audition."

"Hell naw. I'm a businessman, Lu. Too many of these skank-ass bitches get down with these grimy ass niggas. I ain't bringing my babe back shit, and I'm scared shitless of that fuckin' package."

"A loyal thug."

"You know how I am about Trin any fuckin' way. So, look, all I'm saying is you got an audition, so show up and you could have a job. Don't show up, and that's your choice too, but then don't call me again, because money I have to blow, but time I don't," Pooch said seriously.

"I hear you," I said, still undecided.

"So I'm going to say, 'See you at eight o'clock.' Whether you do or don't is up to you, but you've been put on notice. Remember that shit."

"Yeah, I know. Thanks."

"It's all love," he said and then hung up.

There were some lines that I felt that a person shouldn't cross. Auditioning for a stripper gig in front of my homegirl's dude surely was at the top of that list. The struggle stared me down like a hound, but my spirit felt disturbed about Pooch's offer. Still, I entertained the idea for no other reason besides my kid. Maybe it was better to wait it out.

Holding my head in my hands, I sat there for a few minutes, then called information to get the unemployment office's number and made an appointment to go down there about my unemployment. At least that was taken care of. It was a start.

After I hung up, I noticed a message on my cell phone. I retrieved it and was reminded about my overdue light bill. Disconnection was set for next week if I didn't have their money. When it rained, it fucking poured. I shook my head at the message and my predicament. Anger consumed me. *Fuck it. Fuck Raul. Fuck National Cross. Fuck school. Fuck my entire life.* Wrong or not, I had to do what I had to do. I couldn't allow Nadia to go without because of my fucked up life. Rolling my eyes at my phone, I deleted the message and cranked up my car.

I headed downtown to go shoe shopping for some sexy heels. I had an appointment to keep tonight, at eight.

LaMeka

All Tony did these days was snort and drink. That nigga had dropped, like, thirty pounds and still thought his shit didn't stink. None of his old crew— those that had any morals and standards—even fucked with him anymore, because he always stole and lied. His parents had even tried an intervention, but that shit had been a bust. Everybody except him was the damn problem, and especially me, because I didn't have his back. Needless to say, that night I spent the night with Charice, because I knew an ass whupping was certain. By the time I got back the following day, he was so fucking high, all he wanted to do was fuck me any which way possible. Speaking of, the smartest move I had made in that regard was to invest in female condoms and get tested immediately after he and Kwanzie raped me. If that muthafucka had brought me back something, I would kill his ass on sight. That was a fucking promise. But he hadn't. Thank God for small favors or, rather, big favors.

To add to my concerns, I had to deal with my sister. I loved her like one of my own kids, but dealing with a seventeen-year-old wore on my nerves. We had begun butting heads, but it was only because I refused to let her get caught up with some shiftless Negro and end up like me. Uh-huh. Not finna happen. The last couple of weeks, she'd acted out terribly, and I was about to put a leash so tight around her damn neck that she wouldn't be able to spit without me knowing what the hell she was doing.

I just didn't understand her. Didn't she see the shit our mama and I had gone through? Didn't she want better? I had got trapped only because I got pregnant. Otherwise, my life with Tony would be a different story. I constantly thought about what my life would've been like if I hadn't got pregnant in high school and if Tony had fulfilled his dreams. He'd be an Olympian now, and I'd be an RN. Yeah, the good life. Instead, I lived off the system, stayed in city housing, and drove a car that a local drug dealer had bought for me, in addition to putting up with my abusive drug addict of a man and being solely responsible for the care of my autistic child. That was my life. That was my reality. People had killed themselves for less stressful things, and that was why I wanted better for Misha and myself.

The combination of everything had set me on a mission, because Lord knows I couldn't take this shit between Tony and me no fucking more. I was tired of being a prisoner in my own home. I had children to look out for, and I couldn't do that if I was constantly stressed the hell out or beaten the fuck up. In the meantime, I did exactly what I needed to do: I saved up money between my job and Tony Jr.'s checks to get the hell away from Tony. My goal was to save at least a couple grand and then get the hell on.

In the meantime, I found solace in the church and in confiding in the pastor. The Word of God was a powerful thing. I felt that my soul was cleansed with each visit to church, and I knew God wanted better for me, and He had helped me see that I needed better for myself. My life wasn't to be spent suffering because of my and Tony's mistakes. I was supposed to learn to live life despite them, so that was what I aimed to do. That was why I was saving up to move and pursuing an education. I had bought the GED book, and nowadays I studied so I could get my GED. And then I wanted to go to college to get my LPN and R.N. licenses.

With all that I'd planned, I felt guilty and sad, because despite all Tony's misgivings, he really needed help, and I felt like I was leaving him when he probably needed me the most. I felt sad because Tony was the only man I'd loved for the past eight years. It didn't matter what all he'd put me through. It all came down to my love for him, and I loved him with all my heart. I was down for him, and I was willing to ride or die for him, but I just wasn't prepared to die *because of him*. At some point, I had to draw a line in the sand. At some point, I had to say, "Never again. No more will I deal with this abuse, this drug use, or this lifestyle." Sure, I loved him, but I just couldn't be a fool in love anymore, and I prayed for the strength to, as Pooch would say, remember that shit.

After finding out Bible study was canceled this particular day, I was bummed out the entire drive back home. Perhaps, I could use the free time to play with my sons and talk to Misha. I prayed Tony wasn't there. I liked when he went on binges and stayed gone for two or three days. It was sad that I had a man and didn't want him around as much as he didn't want to be around. But now I was just happy for the brief peace of mind.

When I walked in the house, I found the boys alone in the living room.

"Hey, babies," I said and kissed LaMichael and Tony Jr. on the forehead as they sat in the playpen together. "Where's your auntie?" I asked them as I sat my Bible and my purse down on the sofa.

I went into the hallway and knocked on the hall bathroom door, but Misha wasn't in there. That was strange. I knew she'd never put Tony Jr. in the playpen unless she had to use the bathroom. I figured she must've gone to my bathroom, since I heard the stereo as I opened my bedroom door.

"Hey, Misha, I—" My words lodged in my throat. I just knew . . . I mean . . . I just knew . . . my baby sister was not in the bed with my baby daddy . . . *fucking*!

Instantly, my mind replayed the day I had caught Kwanzie and Tony in my bed. Every time I left the house, I came back to a bitch in my bed. But this time, this muthafucking time, the low-down dirty bitch was my . . . sister. *My sister?* I couldn't believe this shit. And here I had felt sorry for this nigga and shit, but it definitely wasn't going down like the last time. Hell to the muthafucking no.

"What the fuck is going on here?" I screamed, looking around the room.

There was cocaine lined up on a mirror that lay flat on the dresser, with two rolled-up dollar bills. A couple of bottles of beer were on the dresser too, and Tony was straight gettin' Misha raw from behind. Tony and Misha looked like deer caught in headlights. He stopped mid pump, removed his wet, dripping dick from her, and hurriedly pulled up his pants. As he did, she scrambled across the bed to get her jeans.

"Baby, baby, baby!" Tony slurred, staggering toward me. "She wanted to get some of this dick. I had to oblige her, you know. She so loose. Come on and hit this shit with us," he said, licking coke off his fingertip.

"Misha!" I cried as tears threatened to spill over. "What are you doing? How could you do this to me?"

She staggered toward me, drunk and high. "I'm sorry, Meka." She giggled. "We were just kickin' it, and he asked me to try the coke. But I swear, this is the first time we fucked. You don't want him no way." She giggled again.

I reached back to the depths of hell and slapped the shit out of her, which sent her flying to the floor. "I bring you in my fucking house, bust my ass to make a way for you, and this is how you repay me? This is what you do? You fucking little bitch! I should've left your trifling, good-for-nothing ass at Mama's house!" I shouted.

Tony walked so close to me that the stench of alcohol emanating from him nearly knocked me out. "Don't trip, Meka. Come on. We can make this shit a family affair. Me, you, and your sister. Ooh-wee, that shit will be so tight. Just get down with the prog—"

I was so fucking pissed that I reached back to the depths of hell again and slapped the shit out of him, cutting him off mid-sentence.

"You fucking bitch!" he screamed and back-handed me. I felt my head snap to the side as I flew into the dresser. "Who the fuck do you think you are?" he questioned in a rage and charged toward me.

Misha jumped in front of him. "No, Tony, no! That's my sister. Please don't!" she shrieked, but he smacked the shit out of her, and she fell to the floor again.

He turned to charge at me again, but I was ready for his ass this time. I slid the dresser drawer open and retrieved the gun I had hidden the last time he beat me. Enough was fucking enough. Just as he got close, I turned around with the gun and aimed it directly at his head. That stopped him dead in his tracks.

"Come on, muthafucka! Do it! Hit me! Try to, anyway, and I promise you, I will spread every last one of your evil-ass thoughts across this floor!" I shrieked.

"You don't know what you doing with that thing!"

"Oh, yes I do! Point and shoot. That's all I need to know."

"Fucking bitch!" he yelled.

"Get your child-molesting bitch ass out of my house! And don't come back!" I hollered.

Instead of leaving, as a normal person would, he threw caution to the wind and lunged toward me because of his coke-induced high. I tried to shoot, but the safety was on, so I took the butt of the gun and bashed him across the face just before he was able to hit me. The force knocked him backward, and he collapsed on the floor, with blood running from his mouth and nose.

"Goddamn bitch!" he screeched, holding his face in his hands. "Ah shit!" he yelled from the shock of seeing his blood.

I grabbed Misha by the arm. "Let's get the fuck out of here," I said, hoping to escape before he got himself together.

She staggered with me into the living room. I grabbed Tony Jr., and she grabbed LaMichael. Thankfully, LaMichael's baby bag was by the door, so I snatched it and my purse, and we ran out the door. By the time I'd put Tony Jr. in the car, Tony was running out of the house. I jumped in the driver's side, slammed my door, and locked all the doors just as Tony was about to snatch my door open.

"Open this fucking door!" he yelled, enticing a few neighbors to gather and gawk at the scene.

"Leave me alone, Tony!" I yelled, tears of fear streaming down my face. "Please."

He hit the glass with his fist, and the force of the impact caused Misha and me to jump. "Open up, before I break the muthafucka!" he hollered.

"Find the car keys!" I yelled at Misha as I frantically searched for them.

She shook so bad that when she retrieved the keys from my purse, she dropped them on the floorboard. She bent down, picked them up, and handed them to me. I put the key in the ignition just as Tony busted my driver's-side window. Shards of glass flew onto the curb, on my hair, and all over my face and hands, leaving bloody gashes. As blood started running down my face, he reached in the car, grabbed my throat, and choked me as I turned the ignition. Tony applied more pressure to my windpipe as I stared into the angry, bloodshot eyes of the man I used to know. I swear to God, I saw my life flash before my eyes, and I prayed that God would see me through. Misha and the kids cried as Misha tried to pry his hands off my throat.

"Somebody help me, please!" Misha screamed.

A couple of guys from the neighborhood ran over and tackled Tony to the ground just before I was about to lose consciousness. Gagging and coughing, I held my throat as I heard Jena, my neighbor, and Misha frantically yelling for me to drive away. Still coughing, I grabbed the steering wheel with one hand, threw the gear-shift into drive, and hauled ass. I drove around aimlessly for an hour to gather my thoughts. My adrenaline was pumping, and my nerves were so bad, I still shook. The boys had fallen asleep, and Misha sat on the other side of the car, in tears.

"I'm so sorry, Meka," she cried, looking over at me. "I knew better. It just seemed all right at the time. I'm so sorry for everything."

I ignored her. My thoughts were going a mile a minute, and my emotions were running rampant.

"Meka, say something, please," she begged.

I looked over at her and rolled my eyes.

"Please say you forgive me."

"You fucked Joe, didn't you? Admit it," I said, staring at the road.

She nodded slowly. "Yes," she said quietly.

I hit the steering wheel. "I should've fucking known it! I can't believe that all this time Mama and Joe were right! You ain't nothing but a scandalous trick!"

"The way Mama kicked me out . . . I guess she got what she deserved," she said sadly.

"So why did you do it to me? I sure as hell didn't deserve it!"

She shrugged. "I don't know. It's just so much . . . ," she said, her voice drifting off. "Please say you forgive me," she begged. "I'll die if you don't."

As I pulled up to Mama's house, I addressed her. "I forgive you because regardless of the fact that you may be seventeen years old, you're a baby in the mind, and you don't know shit."

"What are we doing here?" she asked.

"You are going back to Mom's. I can't deal with you," I said angrily.

"No, Meka, please," she pleaded.

"Get out of my car," I said sternly, looking at her.

"LaMeka—"

I looked straight ahead as she slowly opened the door and slid out.

"I'm sorry, Meka. I don't know how to make it right—"

"Go home, finish school, and grow the fuck up," I interrupted and then drove away. I didn't even have the heart to make sure she made it in the house first.

I drove until I pulled up to a twenty-four-hour shelter for abused women and children. The pastor had told me about it. Now that the adrenaline rush from the incident and my sister had worn off, I felt weak from the loss of blood. I got out of the car somehow and staggered to the door of the shelter, which was half open. My pastor was standing in the foyer, engrossed in a conversation with some lady.

"Pastor Gaines," I said weakly and stumbled inside.

"Oh, God, LaMeka!" he yelled. My legs finally gave out, and Pastor Gaines caught me just before I hit the floor.

"My babies are in the car. I'm too weak. I need a place—"

And suddenly everything went black.

Stay tuned for . . .

***Never Again, No More 2:
Getting Back to Me***